A SCANNER DARKLY

A SCANNER DARKLY

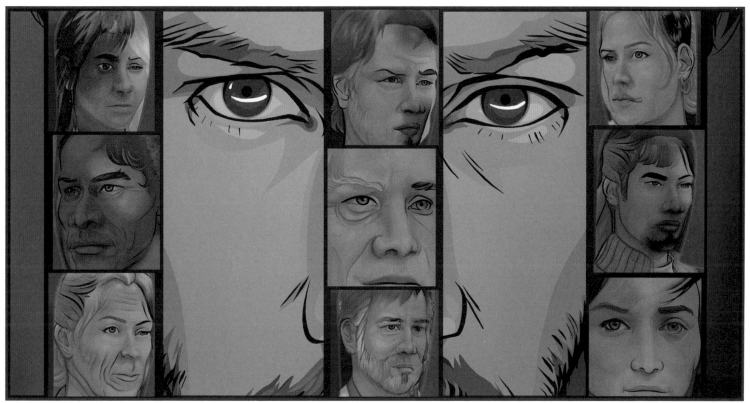

Philip K. Dick
Pantheon Books, New York

This is a work of fiction. Names, characters, places, and incidents either are the product of the author's imagination or are used fictitiously. Any resemblance to actual persons, living or dead, events, or locales is entirely coincidental.

 Published in the United Kingdom by Pantheon Books, a division of Random House, Inc., New York, and in Canada by Random House of Canada Limited, Toronto.

Pantheon Books and colophon are registered trademarks of Random House, Inc.

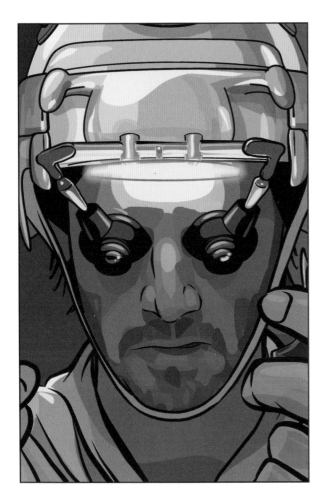

Library of Congress Cataloging-in-Publication Data
Dick, Philip K.
A Scanner Darkly / Philip K. Dick.
p. cm.
Graphic novel based on the movie, A scanner darkly.
ISBN 0-375-42402-4
I. Scanner Darkly (Motion picture). II. Title.
PN6727.D53S33 2006 741.5´973—dc22 2005051842

www.pantheonbooks.com

Book design by Laura Dumm and Gary Dumm
Additional Text by Harvey Pekar
Special Thanks to Fouad Fallah, Betty Kim and Aaron Yarbrough.
Printed in the United Kingdom
First Edition
9 8 7 6 5 4 3 2 1

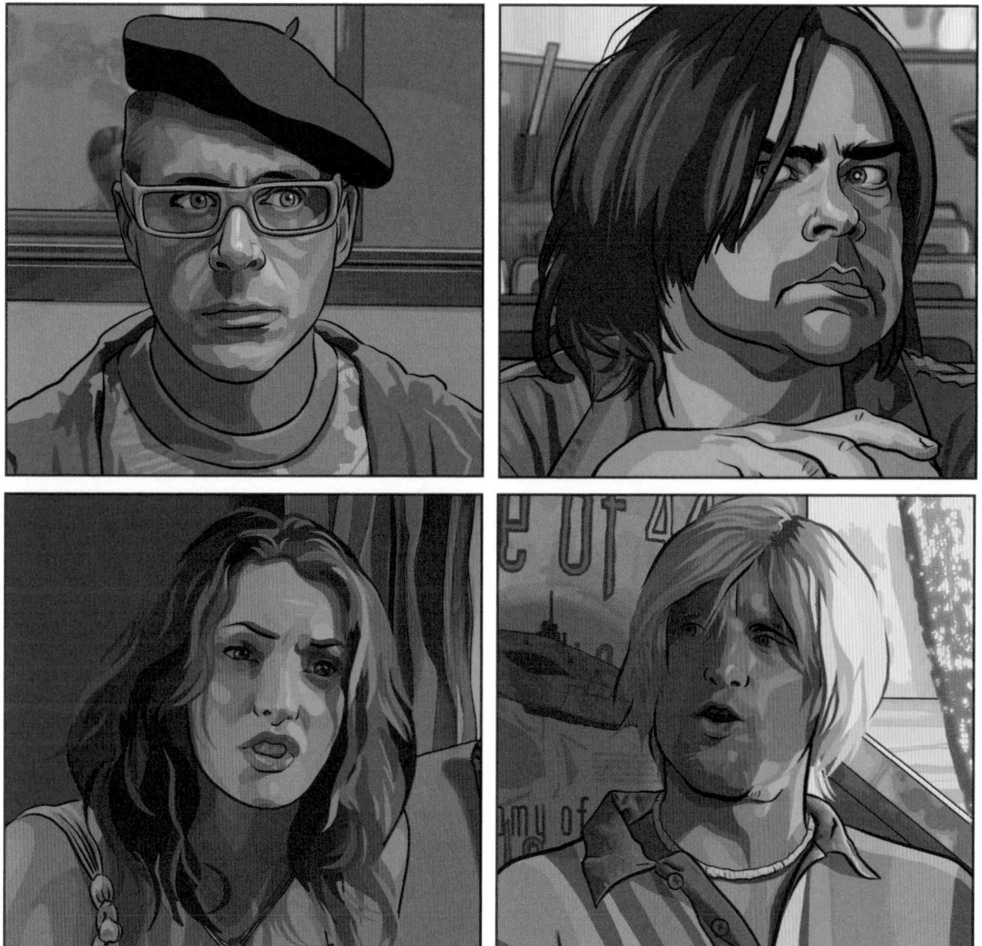

WHAT DOES A SCANNER SEE? INTO THE HEAD, DOWN INTO THE HEART? DOES IT SEE INTO ME? INTO US? CLEARLY OR DARKLY? I HOPE IT SEES CLEARLY, BECAUSE I CAN'T ANY LONGER SEE INTO MYSELF. I SEE ONLY MURK. I HOPE, FOR EVERYONE'S SAKE, THE SCANNERS DO BETTER. BECAUSE IF THE SCANNER SEES ONLY DARKLY, THE WAY I DO, THEN I'M CURSED AND CURSED AGAIN AND WILL ONLY WIND UP DEAD THIS WAY, KNOWING VERY LITTLE AND GETTING THAT LITTLE FRAGMENT WRONG TOO.

— PHILIP K. DICK

A SCANNER DARKLY

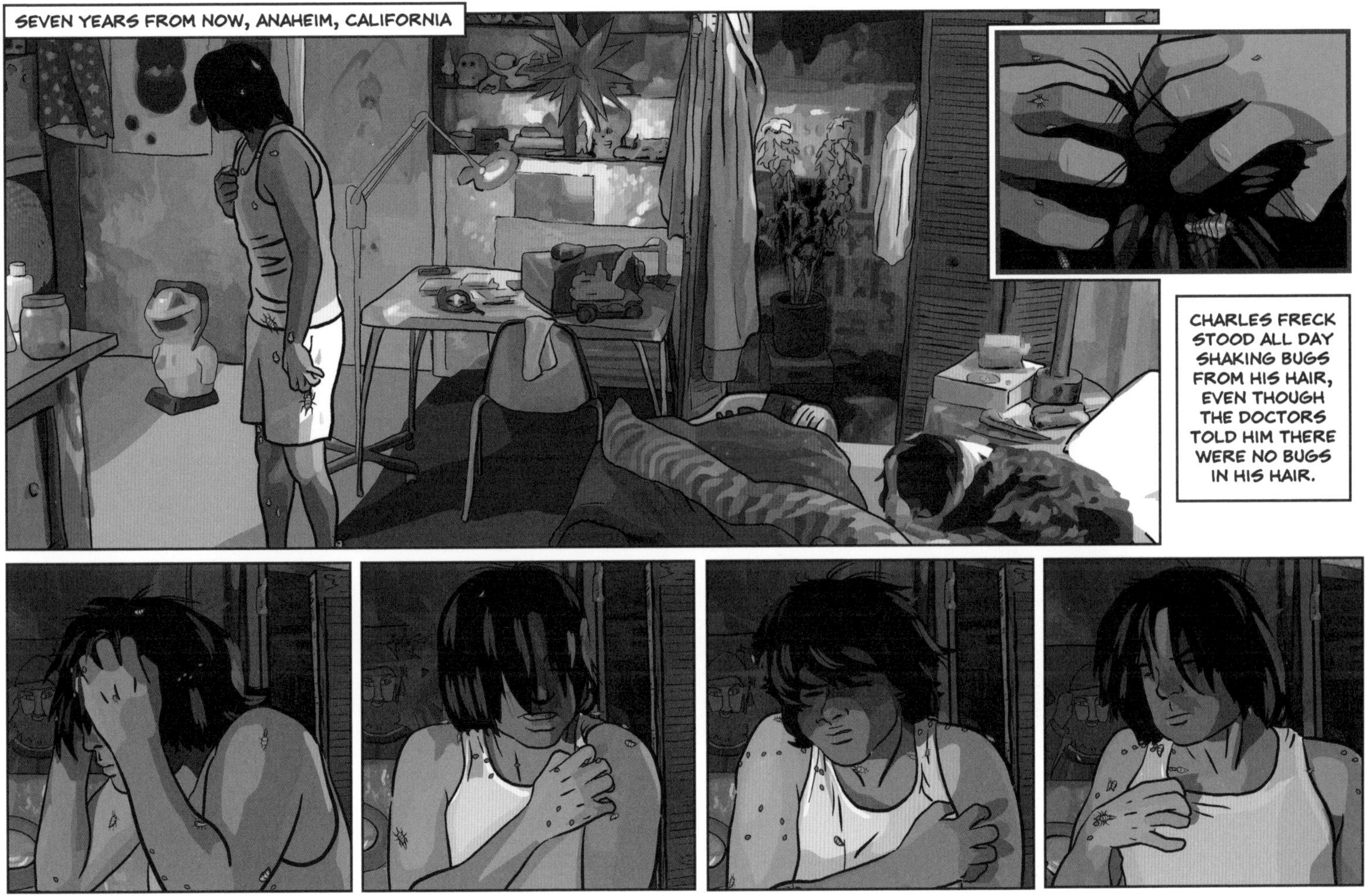
SEVEN YEARS FROM NOW, ANAHEIM, CALIFORNIA
CHARLES FRECK STOOD ALL DAY SHAKING BUGS FROM HIS HAIR, EVEN THOUGH THE DOCTORS TOLD HIM THERE WERE NO BUGS IN HIS HAIR.

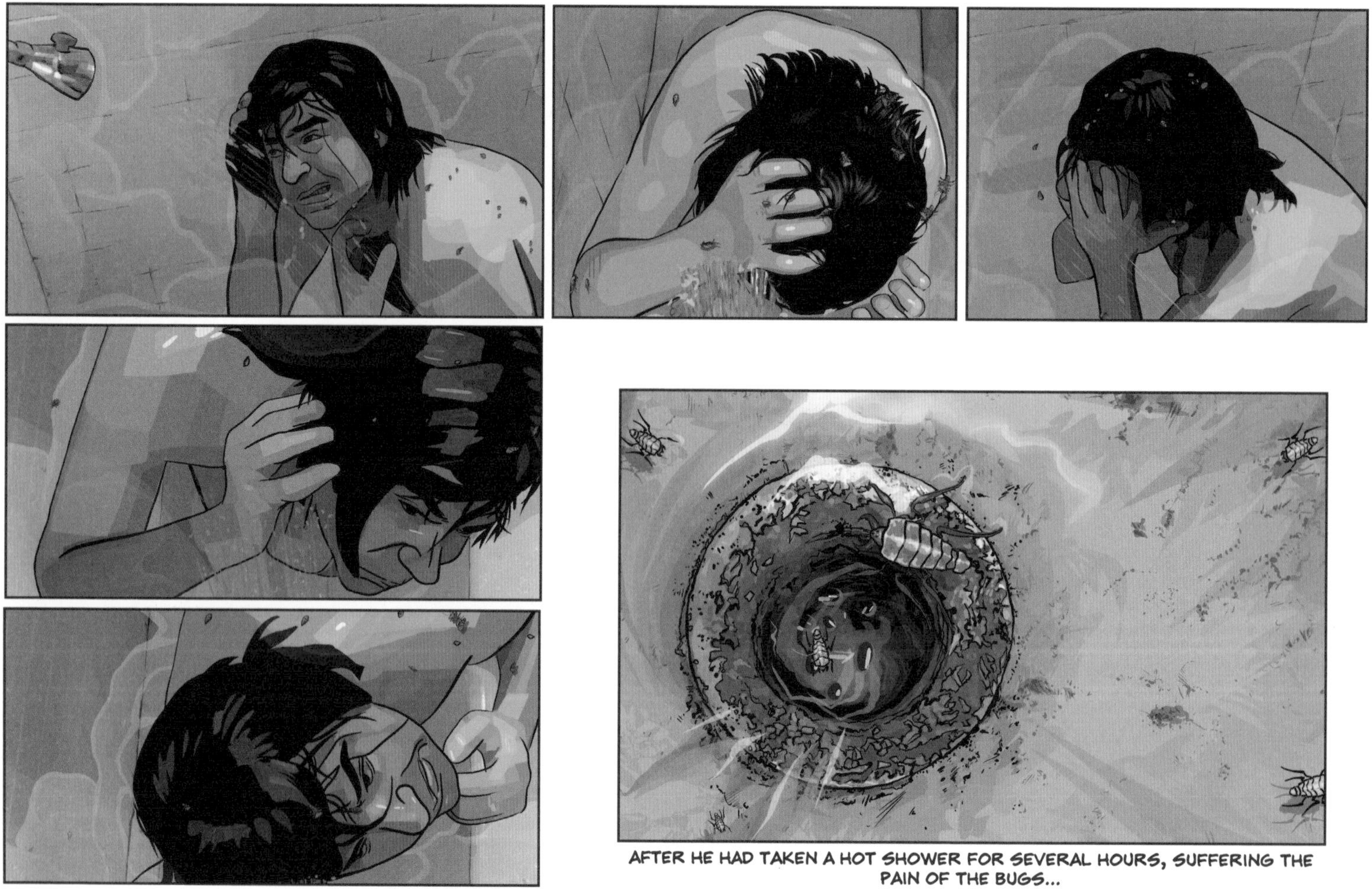
AFTER HE HAD TAKEN A HOT SHOWER FOR SEVERAL HOURS, SUFFERING THE PAIN OF THE BUGS...

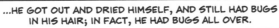

...HE GOT OUT AND DRIED HIMSELF, AND STILL HAD BUGS IN HIS HAIR; IN FACT, HE HAD BUGS ALL OVER.

EEP!

REMEMBERING A CAN OF INSECT SPRAY, HE FIRST SPRAYED THE HOUSE. THEN HIMSELF.

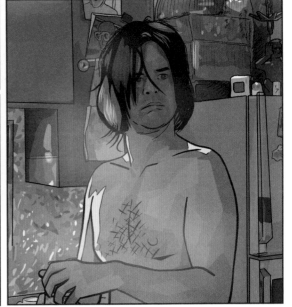

HIS DOG GAZES CALMLY AT HIM...

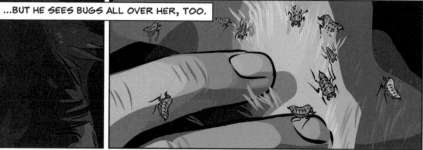

...BUT HE SEES BUGS ALL OVER HER, TOO.

SO IT'S BACK INTO THE SHOWER...

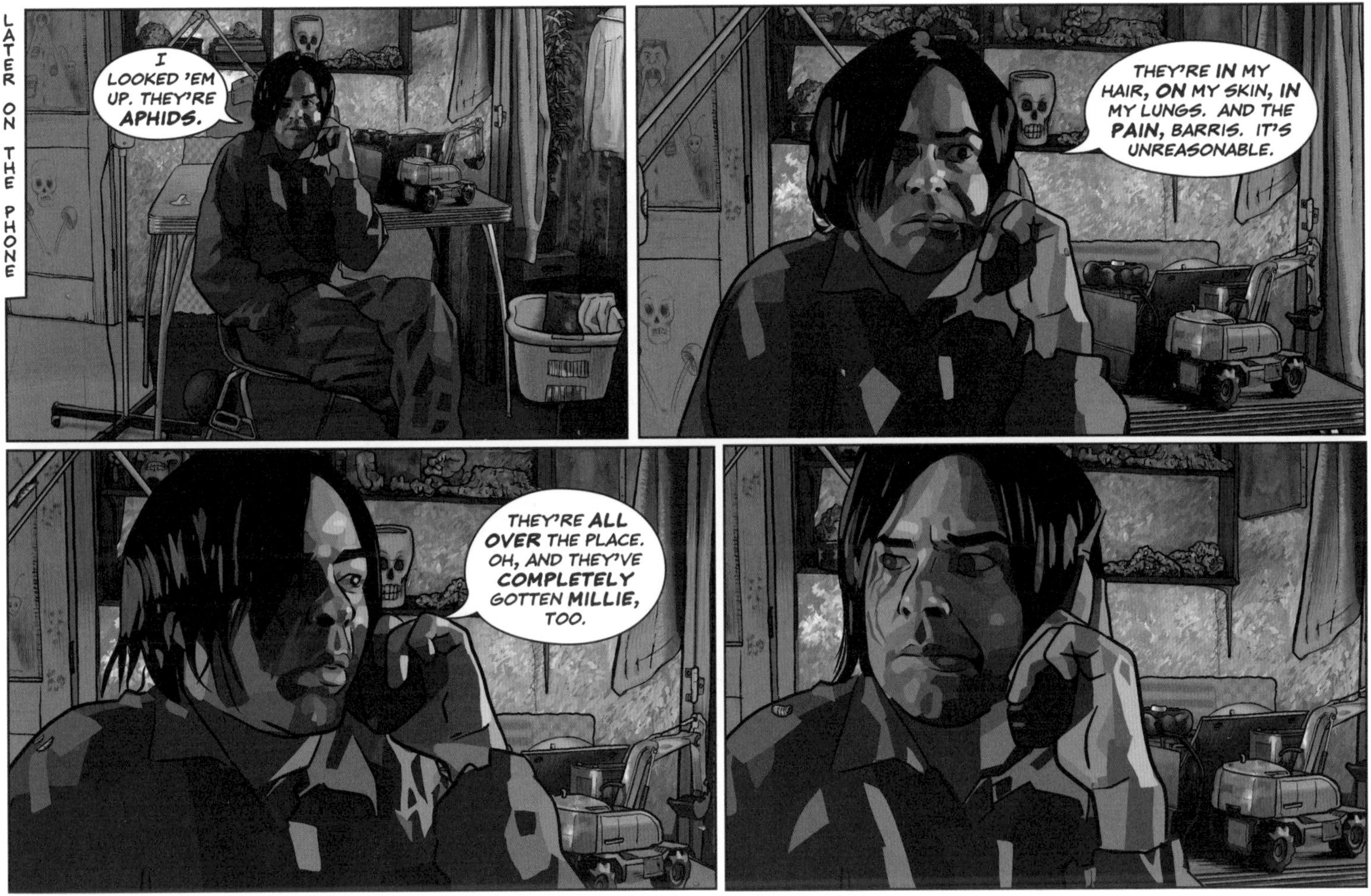

LATER ON THE PHONE
I LOOKED 'EM UP. THEY'RE APHIDS.
THEY'RE IN MY HAIR, ON MY SKIN, IN MY LUNGS. AND THE PAIN, BARRIS. IT'S UNREASONABLE.
THEY'RE ALL OVER THE PLACE. OH, AND THEY'VE COMPLETELY GOTTEN MILLIE, TOO.

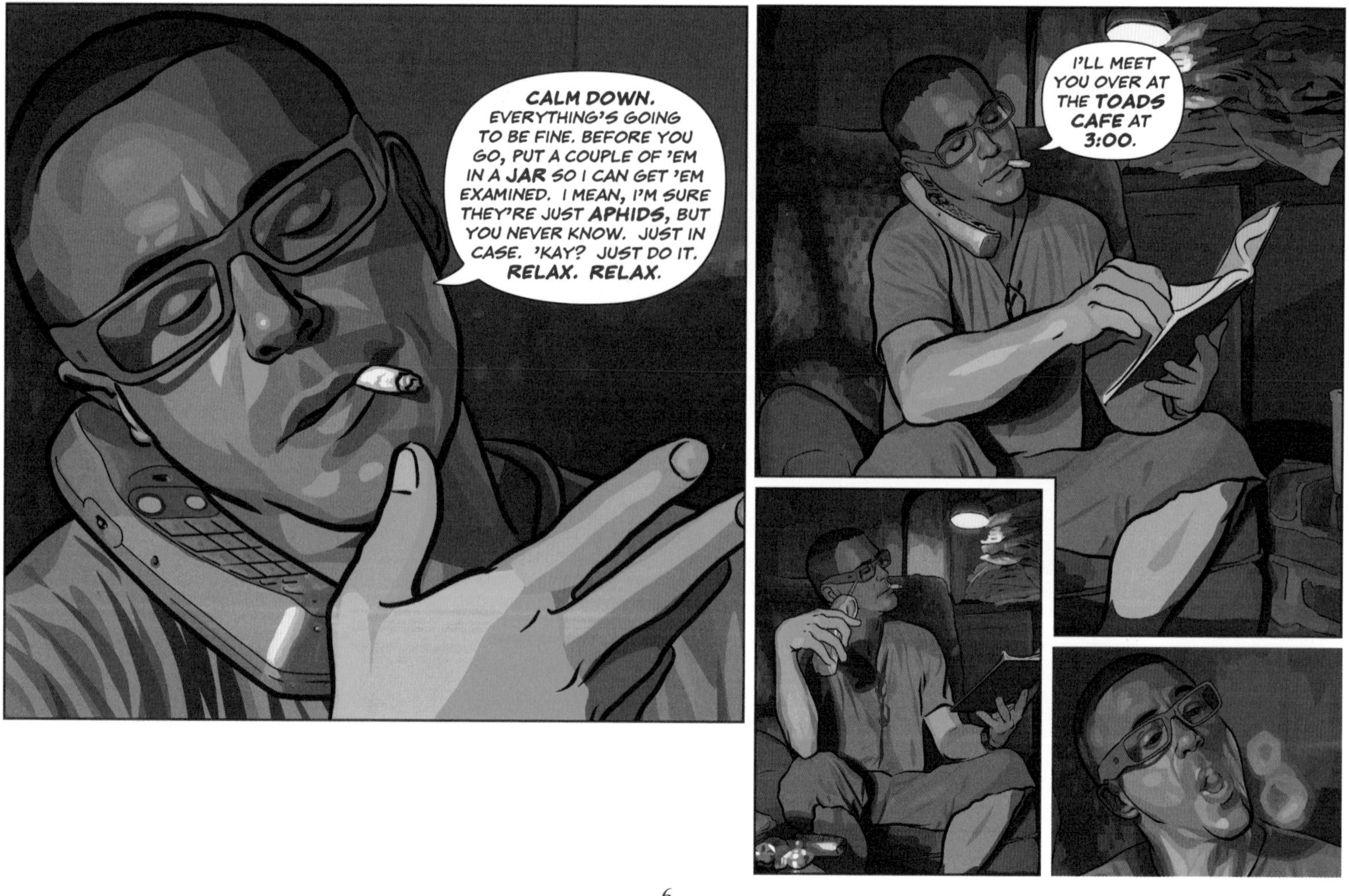
CALM DOWN. EVERYTHING'S GOING TO BE FINE. BEFORE YOU GO, PUT A COUPLE OF 'EM IN A JAR SO I CAN GET 'EM EXAMINED. I MEAN, I'M SURE THEY'RE JUST APHIDS, BUT YOU NEVER KNOW. JUST IN CASE. 'KAY? JUST DO IT. RELAX. RELAX.
I'LL MEET YOU OVER AT THE TOADS CAFE AT 3:00.

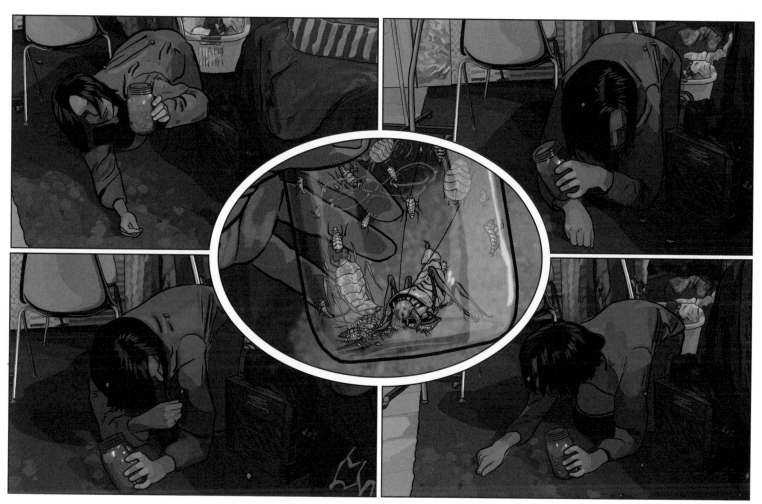

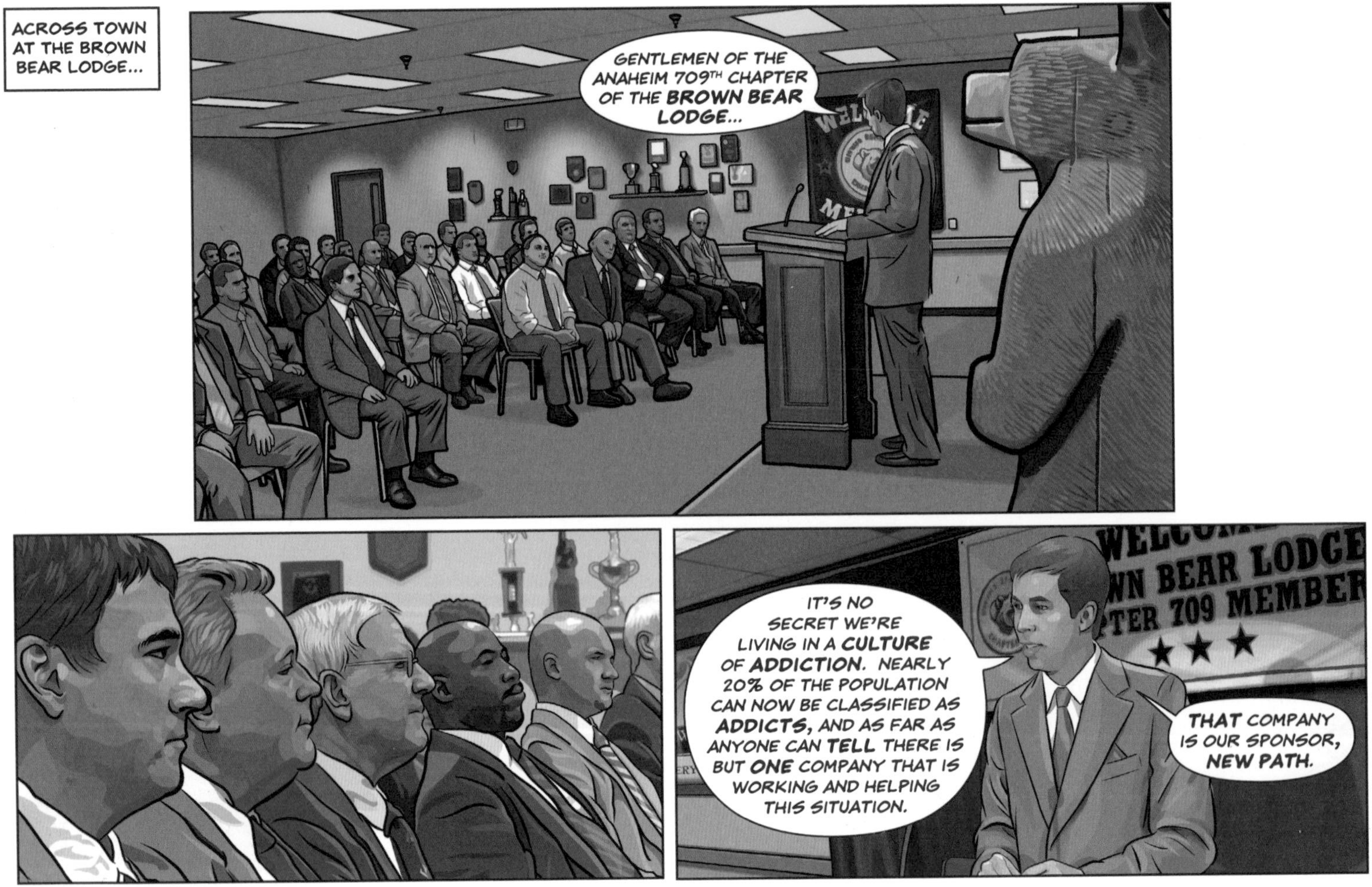
ACROSS TOWN AT THE BROWN BEAR LODGE...
GENTLEMEN OF THE ANAHEIM 709TH CHAPTER OF THE BROWN BEAR LODGE...
IT'S NO SECRET WE'RE LIVING IN A CULTURE OF ADDICTION. NEARLY 20% OF THE POPULATION CAN NOW BE CLASSIFIED AS ADDICTS, AND AS FAR AS ANYONE CAN TELL THERE IS BUT ONE COMPANY THAT IS WORKING AND HELPING THIS SITUATION.
THAT COMPANY IS OUR SPONSOR, NEW PATH.

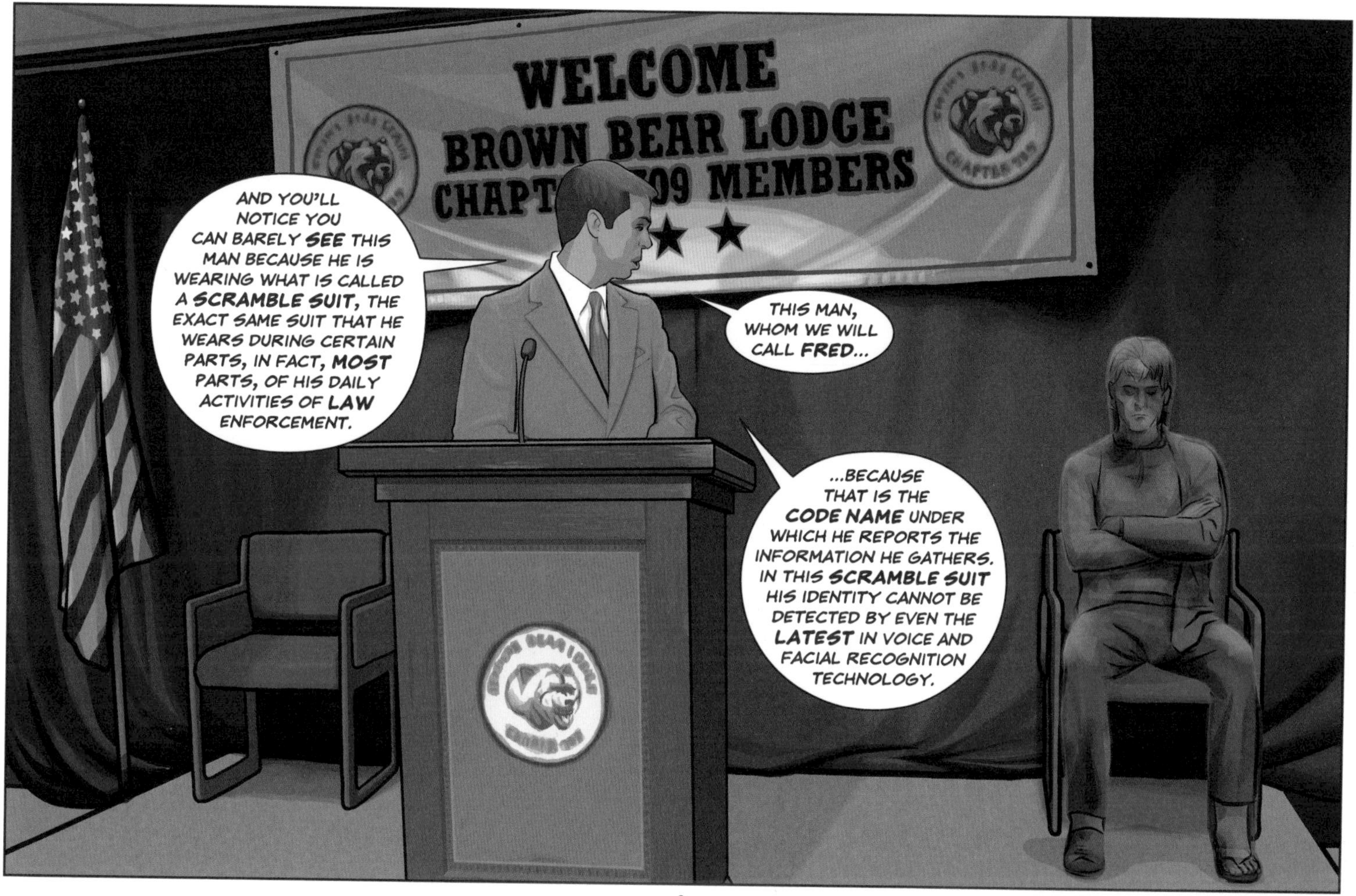
WELCOME
BROWN BEAR LODGE
CHAPT 709 MEMBERS
AND YOU'LL NOTICE YOU CAN BARELY SEE THIS MAN BECAUSE HE IS WEARING WHAT IS CALLED A SCRAMBLE SUIT, THE EXACT SAME SUIT THAT HE WEARS DURING CERTAIN PARTS, IN FACT, MOST PARTS, OF HIS DAILY ACTIVITIES OF LAW ENFORCEMENT.
THIS MAN, WHOM WE WILL CALL FRED...
...BECAUSE THAT IS THE CODE NAME UNDER WHICH HE REPORTS THE INFORMATION HE GATHERS. IN THIS SCRAMBLE SUIT HIS IDENTITY CANNOT BE DETECTED BY EVEN THE LATEST IN VOICE AND FACIAL RECOGNITION TECHNOLOGY.

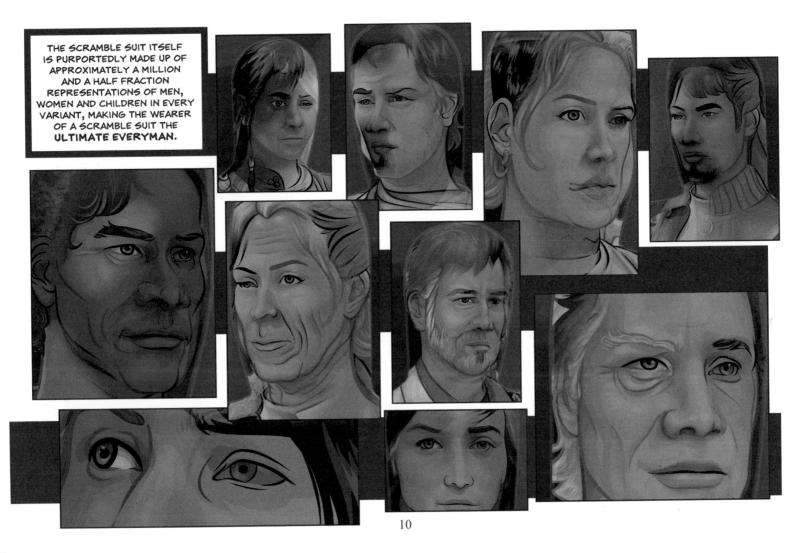

THE SCRAMBLE SUIT ITSELF IS PURPORTEDLY MADE UP OF APPROXIMATELY A MILLION AND A HALF FRACTION REPRESENTATIONS OF MEN, WOMEN AND CHILDREN IN EVERY VARIANT, MAKING THE WEARER OF A SCRAMBLE SUIT THE **ULTIMATE EVERYMAN.**

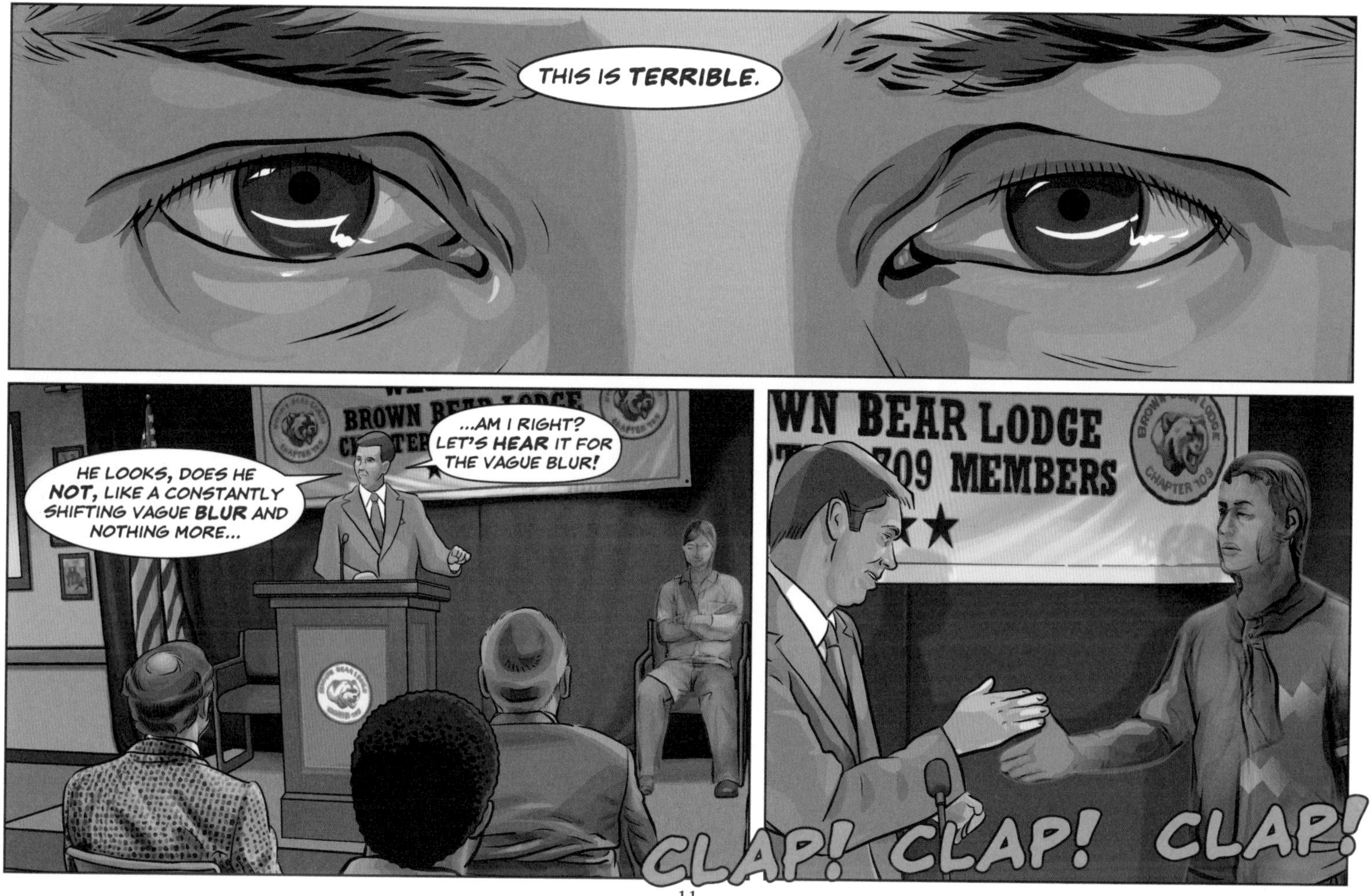
THIS IS TERRIBLE.
HE LOOKS, DOES HE NOT, LIKE A CONSTANTLY SHIFTING VAGUE BLUR AND NOTHING MORE...
...AM I RIGHT? LET'S HEAR IT FOR THE VAGUE BLUR!
BROWN BEAR LODGE
CLAP! CLAP! CLAP!

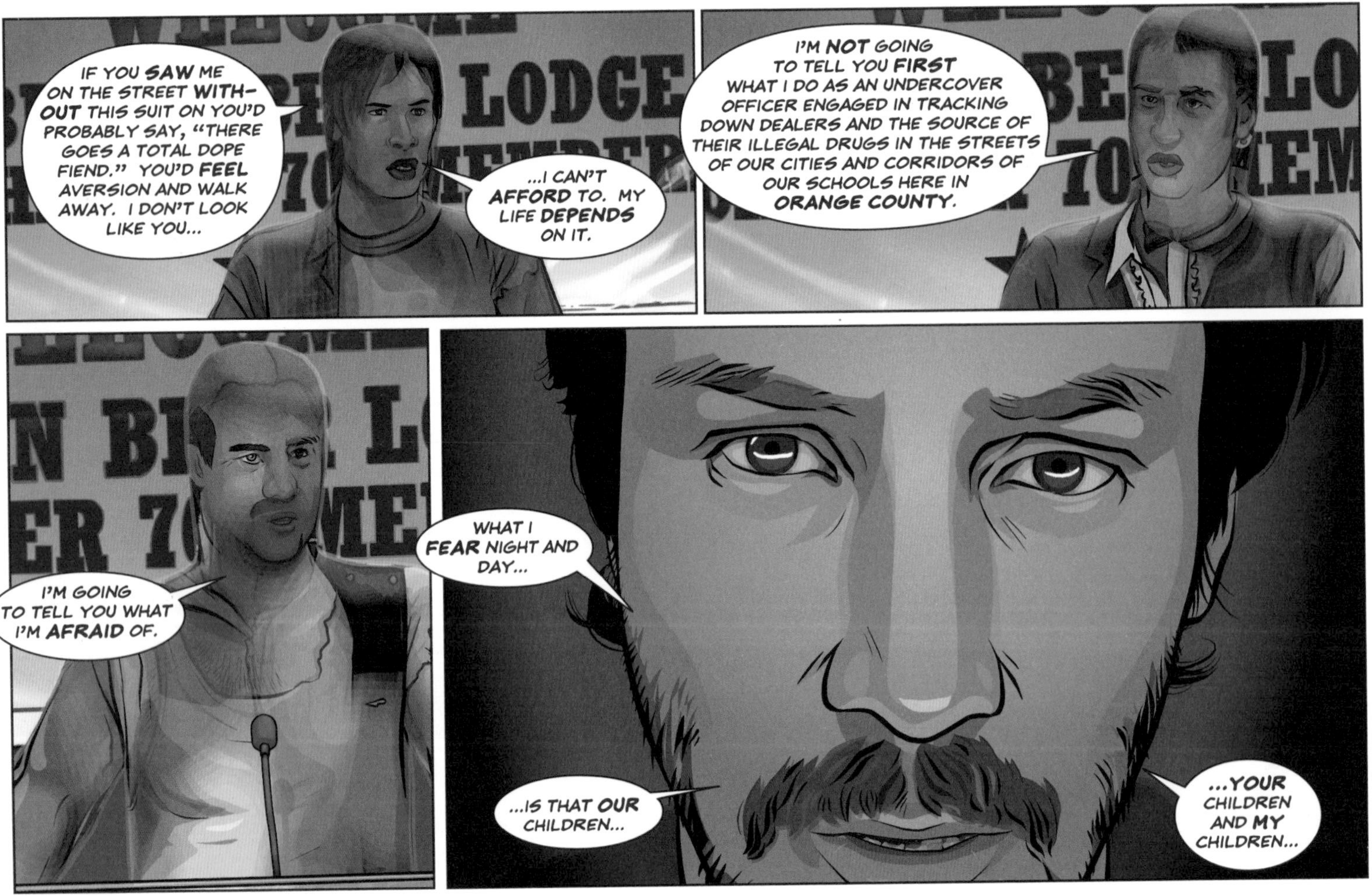
LODGE
IF YOU SAW ME ON THE STREET WITH-OUT THIS SUIT ON YOU'D PROBABLY SAY, "THERE GOES A TOTAL DOPE FIEND." YOU'D FEEL AVERSION AND WALK AWAY. I DON'T LOOK LIKE YOU...
...I CAN'T AFFORD TO. MY LIFE DEPENDS ON IT.
I'M NOT GOING TO TELL YOU FIRST WHAT I DO AS AN UNDERCOVER OFFICER ENGAGED IN TRACKING DOWN DEALERS AND THE SOURCE OF THEIR ILLEGAL DRUGS IN THE STREETS OF OUR CITIES AND CORRIDORS OF OUR SCHOOLS HERE IN ORANGE COUNTY.
I'M GOING TO TELL YOU WHAT I'M AFRAID OF.
WHAT I FEAR NIGHT AND DAY...
...IS THAT OUR CHILDREN...
...YOUR CHILDREN AND MY CHILDREN...

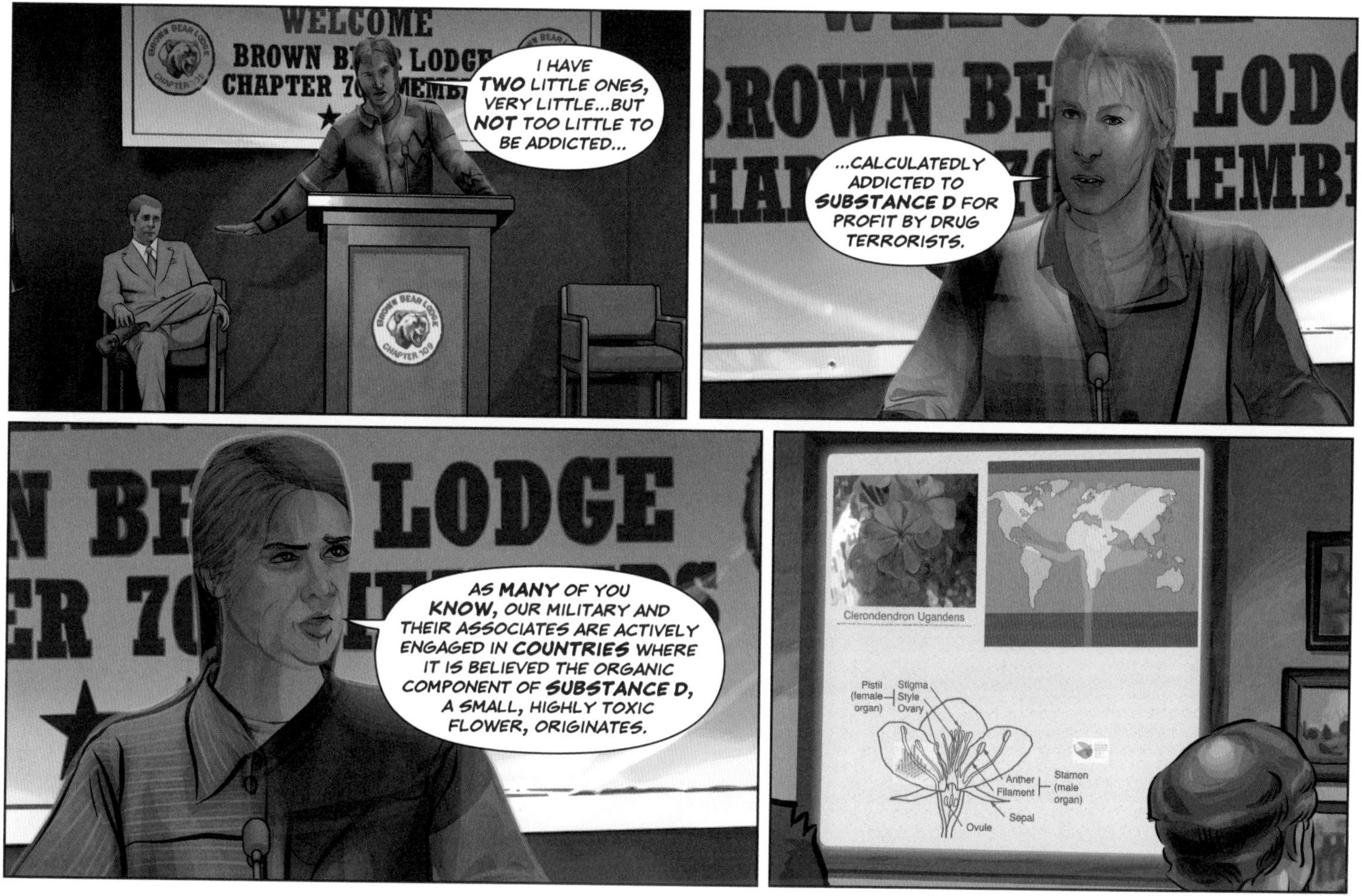
WELCOME
I HAVE TWO LITTLE ONES, VERY LITTLE...BUT NOT TOO LITTLE TO BE ADDICTED...
...CALCULATEDLY ADDICTED TO SUBSTANCE D FOR PROFIT BY DRUG TERRORISTS.
AS MANY OF YOU KNOW, OUR MILITARY AND THEIR ASSOCIATES ARE ACTIVELY ENGAGED IN COUNTRIES WHERE IT IS BELIEVED THE ORGANIC COMPONENT OF SUBSTANCE D, A SMALL, HIGHLY TOXIC FLOWER, ORIGINATES.
Clerondendron Ugandens
Pistil (female organ)
Stigma
Style
Ovary
Anther
Filament
Stamen (male organ)
Sepal
Ovule

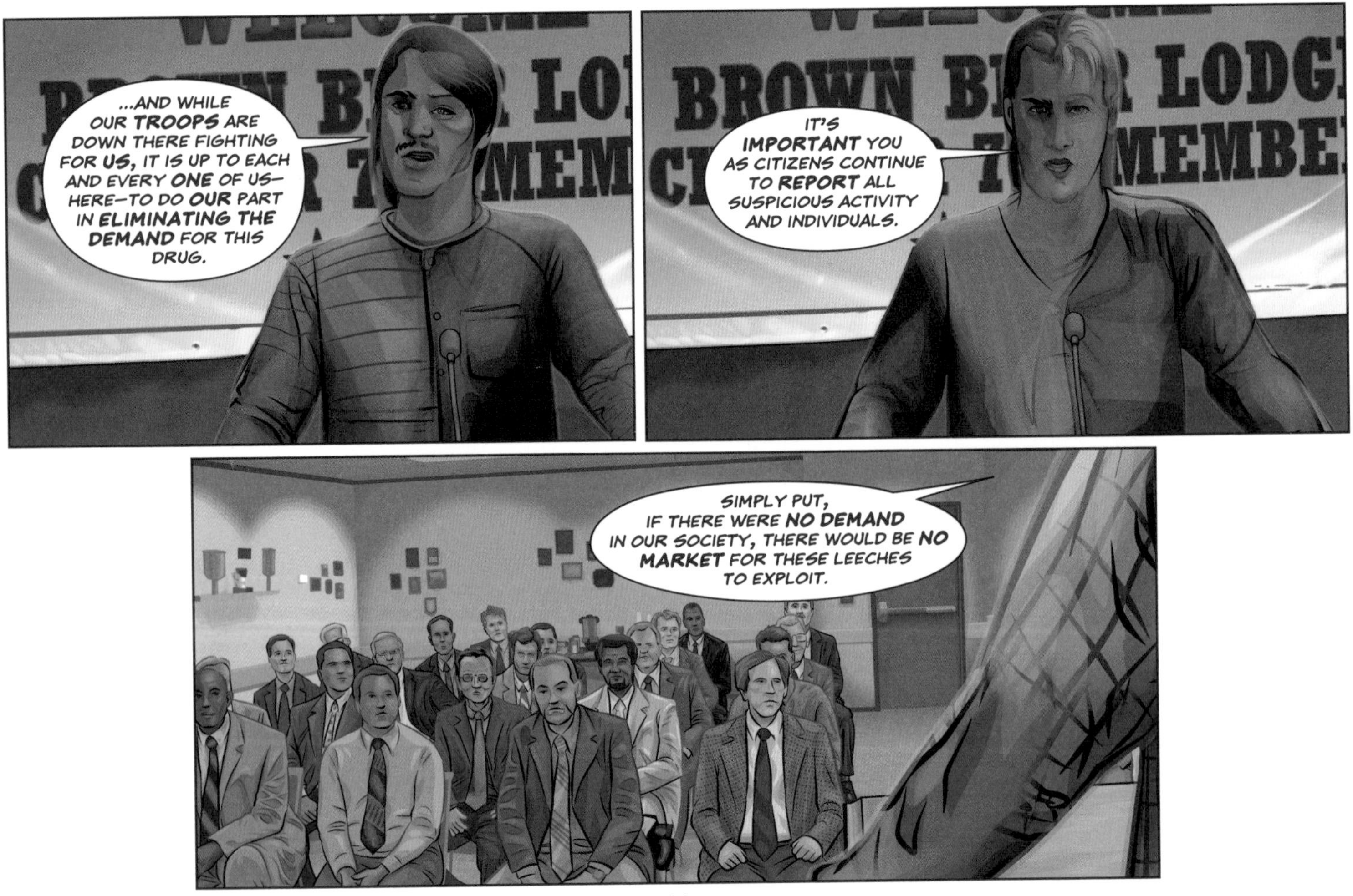
...AND WHILE OUR **TROOPS** ARE DOWN THERE FIGHTING FOR **US**, IT IS UP TO EACH AND EVERY **ONE** OF US—HERE—TO DO **OUR** PART IN **ELIMINATING THE DEMAND** FOR THIS DRUG.
IT'S **IMPORTANT** YOU AS CITIZENS CONTINUE TO **REPORT** ALL SUSPICIOUS ACTIVITY AND INDIVIDUALS.
SIMPLY PUT, IF THERE WERE **NO DEMAND** IN OUR SOCIETY, THERE WOULD BE **NO MARKET** FOR THESE LEECHES TO EXPLOIT.

EACH DAY THIS DISEASE TAKES ITS **TOLL** ON US AND **EACH** DAY THE FLOW OF PROFITS AND WHERE THEY GO...

WELL, IT **ISN'T** ABOUT THE PROFITS ANYHOW. IT'S... SOMETHING **ELSE.**

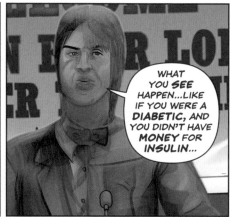

WHAT YOU **SEE** HAPPEN...LIKE IF YOU WERE A **DIABETIC,** AND YOU DIDN'T HAVE **MONEY** FOR INSULIN...

...WOULD YOU **STEAL** TO **GET** THE MONEY OR JUST **DIE?**

15

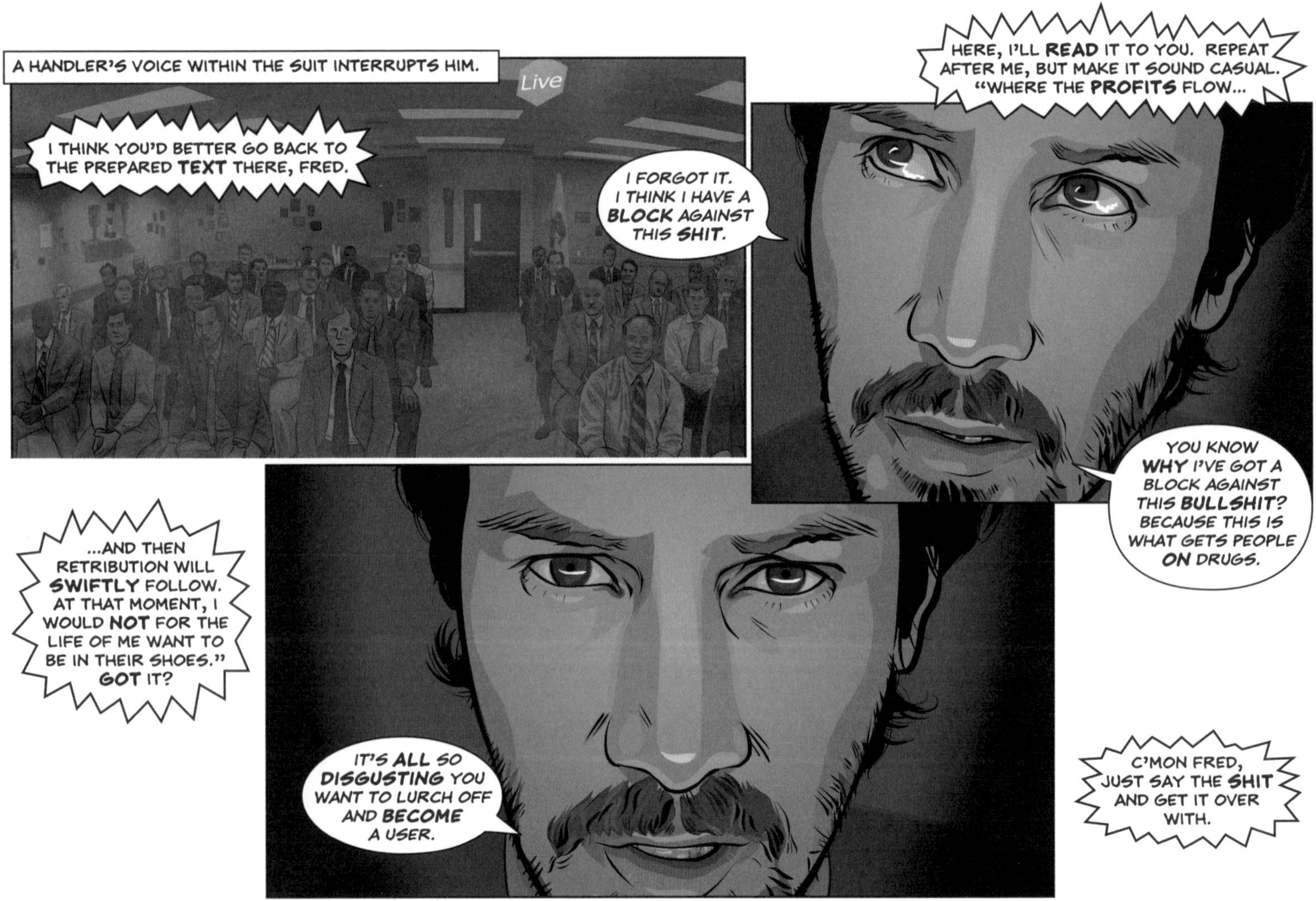
A HANDLER'S VOICE WITHIN THE SUIT INTERRUPTS HIM.
Live
I THINK YOU'D BETTER GO BACK TO THE PREPARED TEXT THERE, FRED.
I FORGOT IT. I THINK I HAVE A BLOCK AGAINST THIS SHIT.
HERE, I'LL READ IT TO YOU. REPEAT AFTER ME, BUT MAKE IT SOUND CASUAL. "WHERE THE PROFITS FLOW...
YOU KNOW WHY I'VE GOT A BLOCK AGAINST THIS BULLSHIT? BECAUSE THIS IS WHAT GETS PEOPLE ON DRUGS.
...AND THEN RETRIBUTION WILL SWIFTLY FOLLOW. AT THAT MOMENT, I WOULD NOT FOR THE LIFE OF ME WANT TO BE IN THEIR SHOES." GOT IT?
IT'S ALL SO DISGUSTING YOU WANT TO LURCH OFF AND BECOME A USER.
C'MON FRED, JUST SAY THE SHIT AND GET IT OVER WITH.

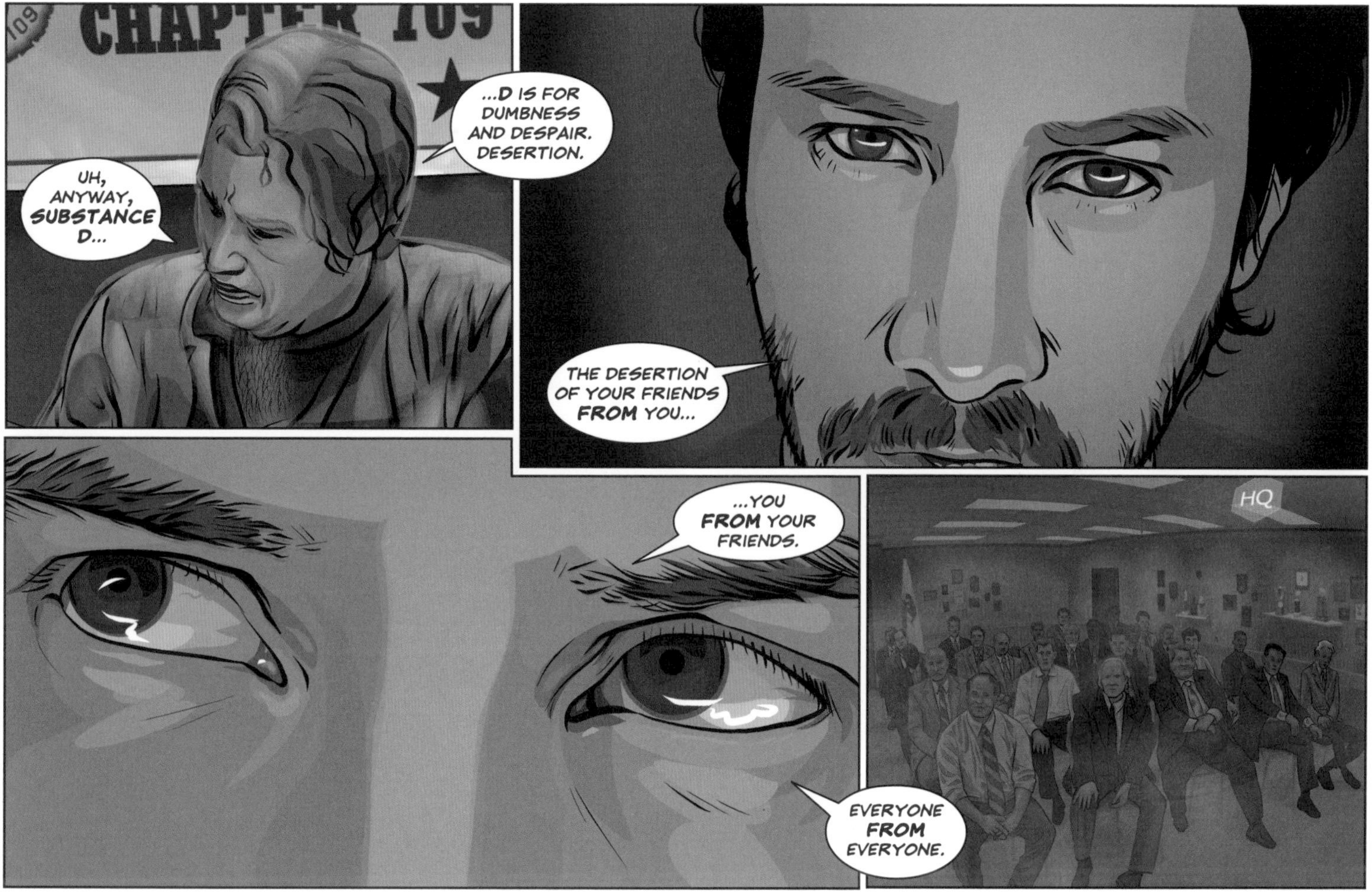
CHAPTER 109
UH, ANYWAY, SUBSTANCE D...
...D IS FOR DUMBNESS AND DESPAIR. DESERTION.
THE DESERTION OF YOUR FRIENDS FROM YOU...
...YOU FROM YOUR FRIENDS.
HQ
EVERYONE FROM EVERYONE.

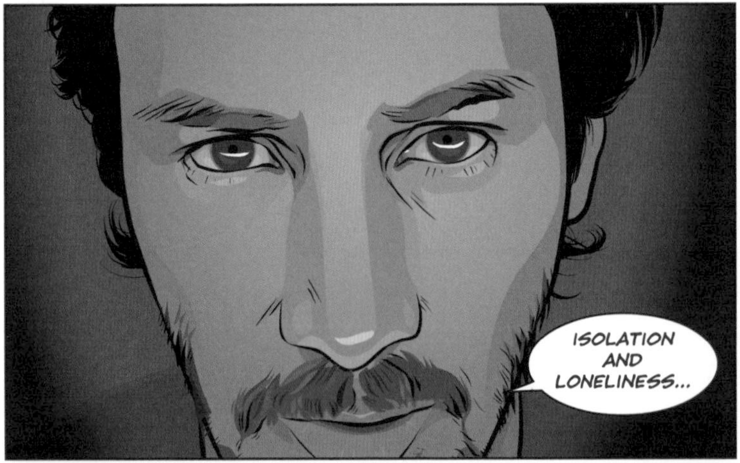
ISOLATION AND LONELINESS...

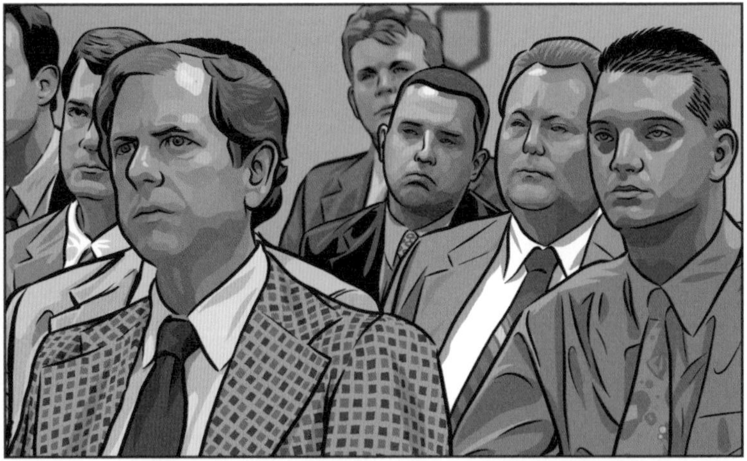

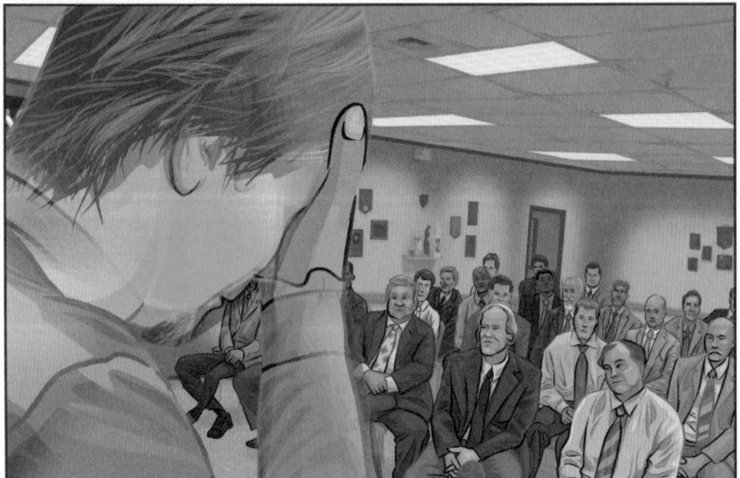

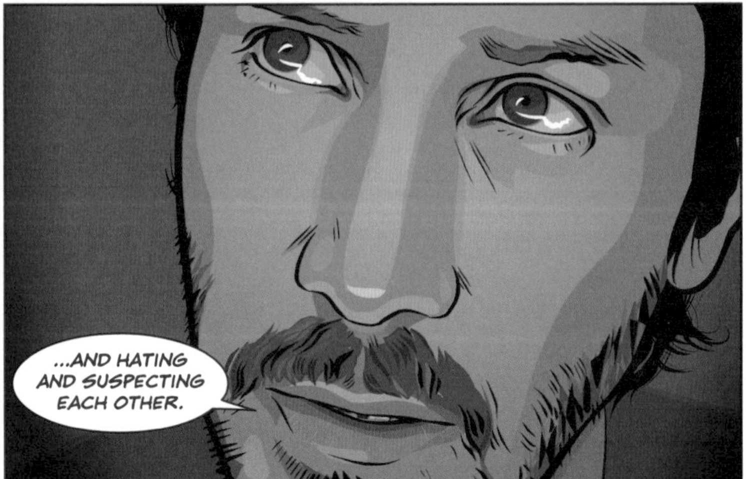
...AND HATING AND SUSPECTING EACH OTHER.

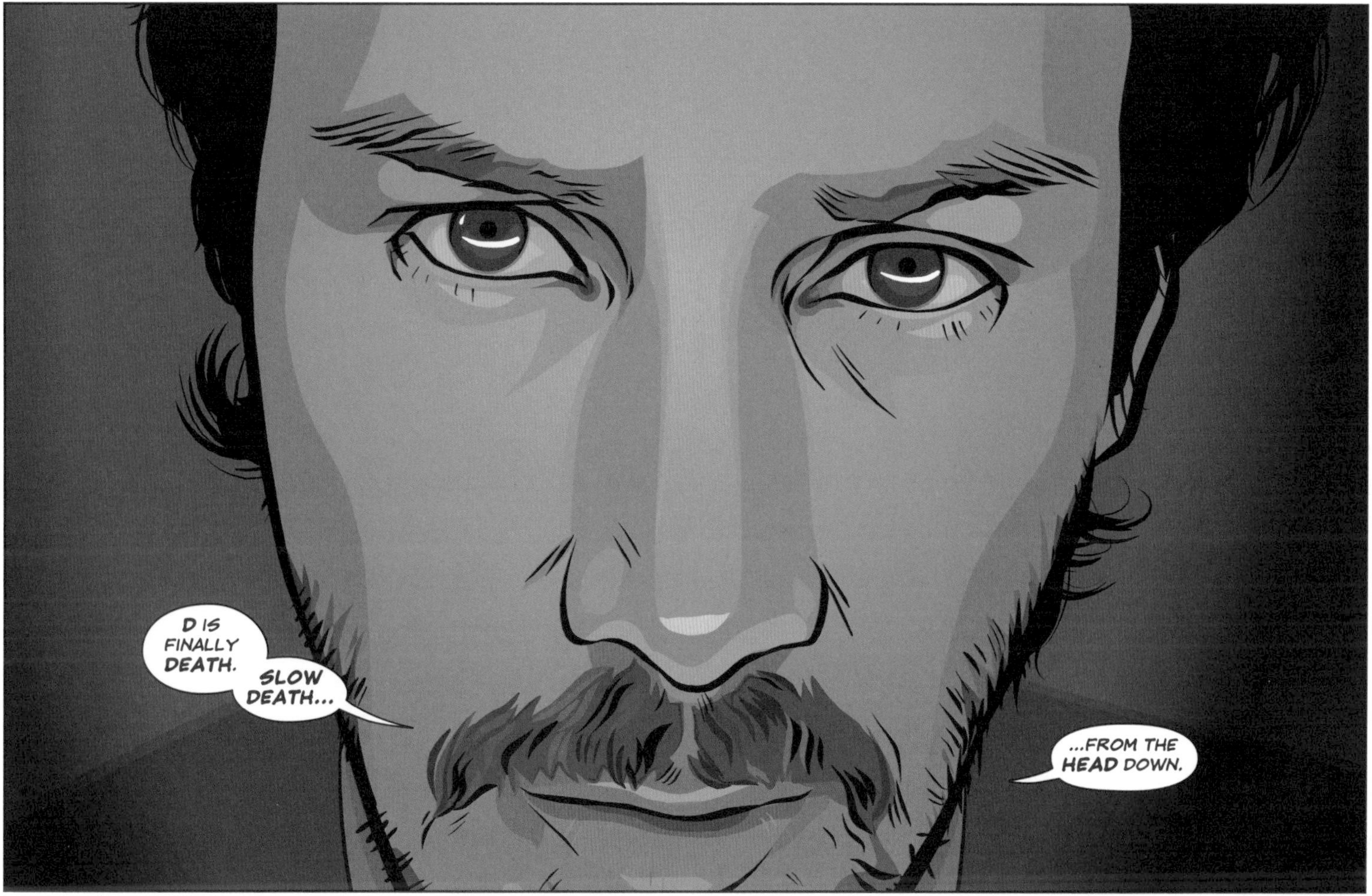
D IS FINALLY DEATH.
SLOW DEATH...
...FROM THE HEAD DOWN.

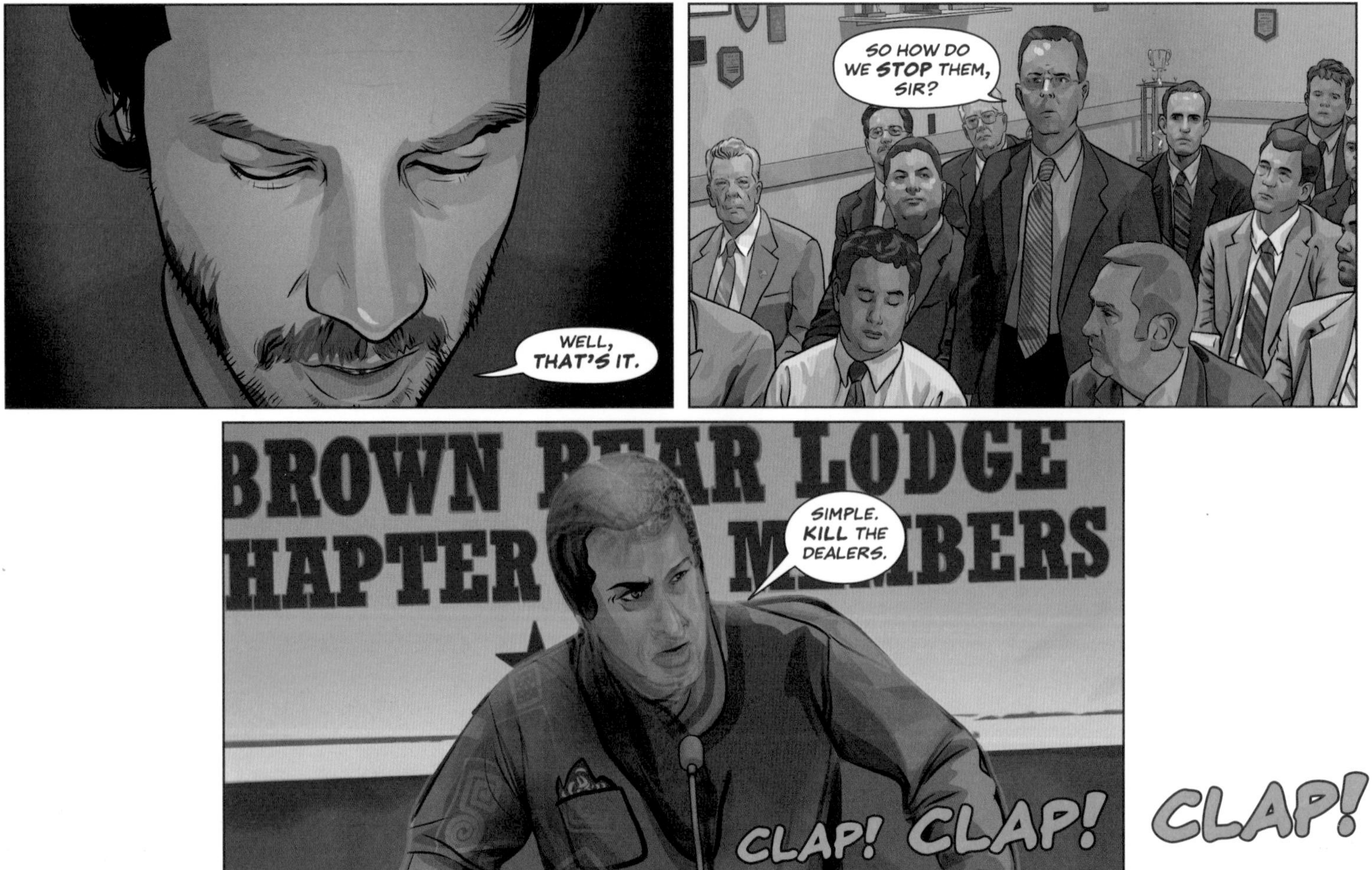
WELL, THAT'S IT.
SO HOW DO WE STOP THEM, SIR?
SIMPLE. KILL THE DEALERS.
CLAP! CLAP!
CLAP!

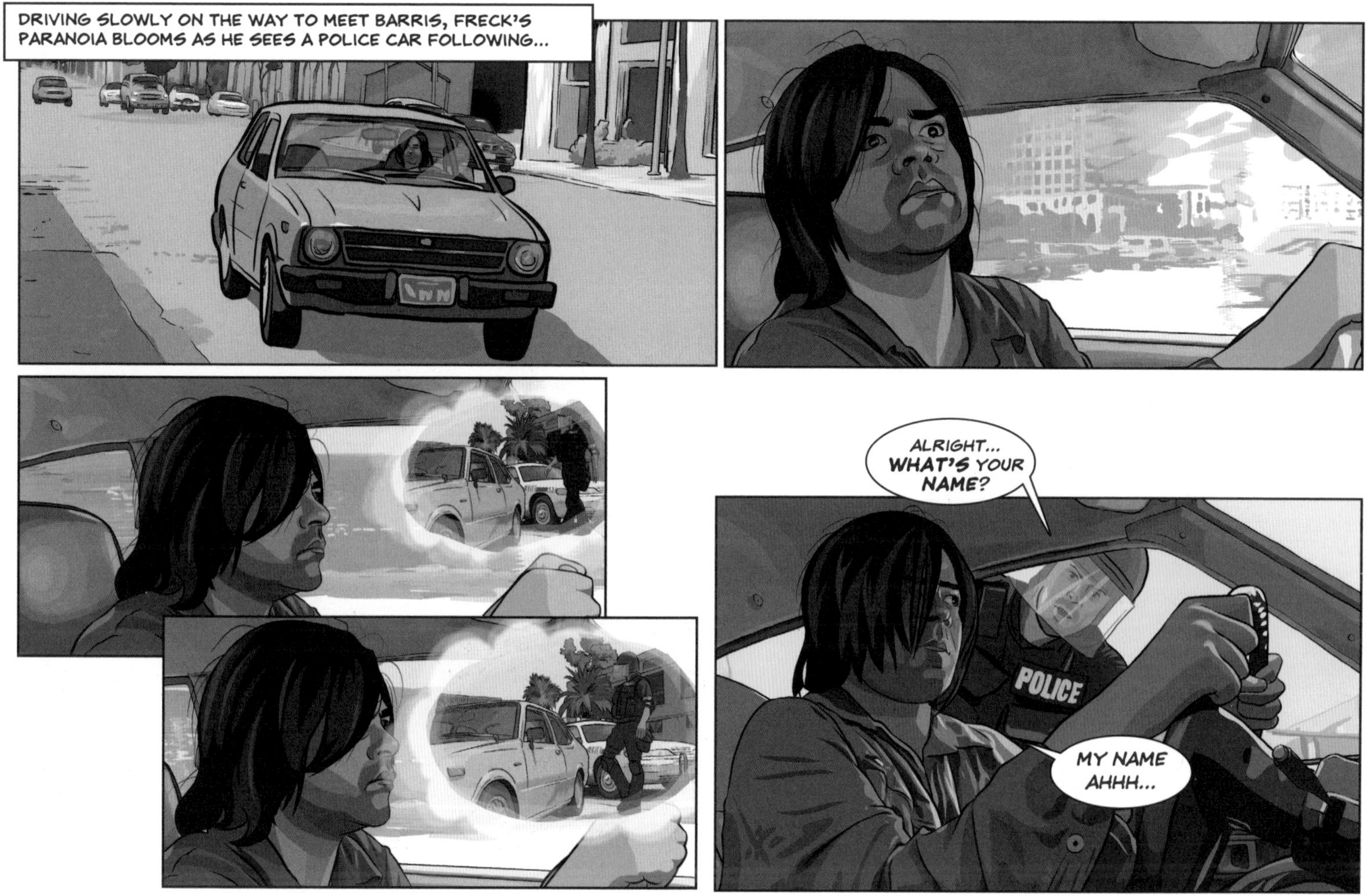
DRIVING SLOWLY ON THE WAY TO MEET BARRIS, FRECK'S PARANOIA BLOOMS AS HE SEES A POLICE CAR FOLLOWING...
ALRIGHT... WHAT'S YOUR NAME?
POLICE
MY NAME AHHH...

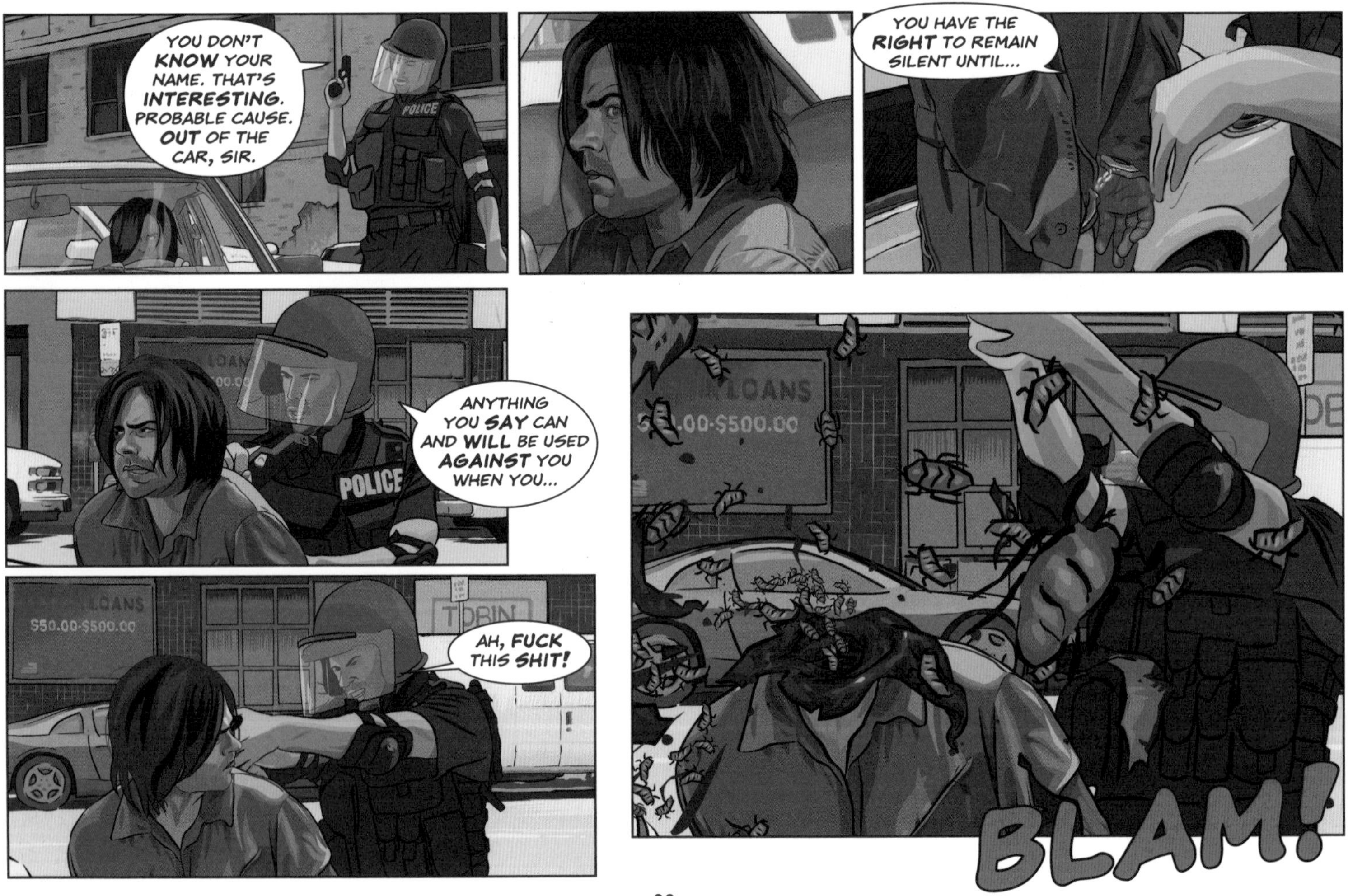
YOU DON'T KNOW YOUR NAME. THAT'S INTERESTING. PROBABLE CAUSE. OUT OF THE CAR, SIR.
POLICE
YOU HAVE THE RIGHT TO REMAIN SILENT UNTIL...
LOANS
$50.00-$500.00
POLICE
ANYTHING YOU SAY CAN AND WILL BE USED AGAINST YOU WHEN YOU...
LOANS
$50.00-$500.00
TOBIN
AH, FUCK THIS SHIT!
BLAM!

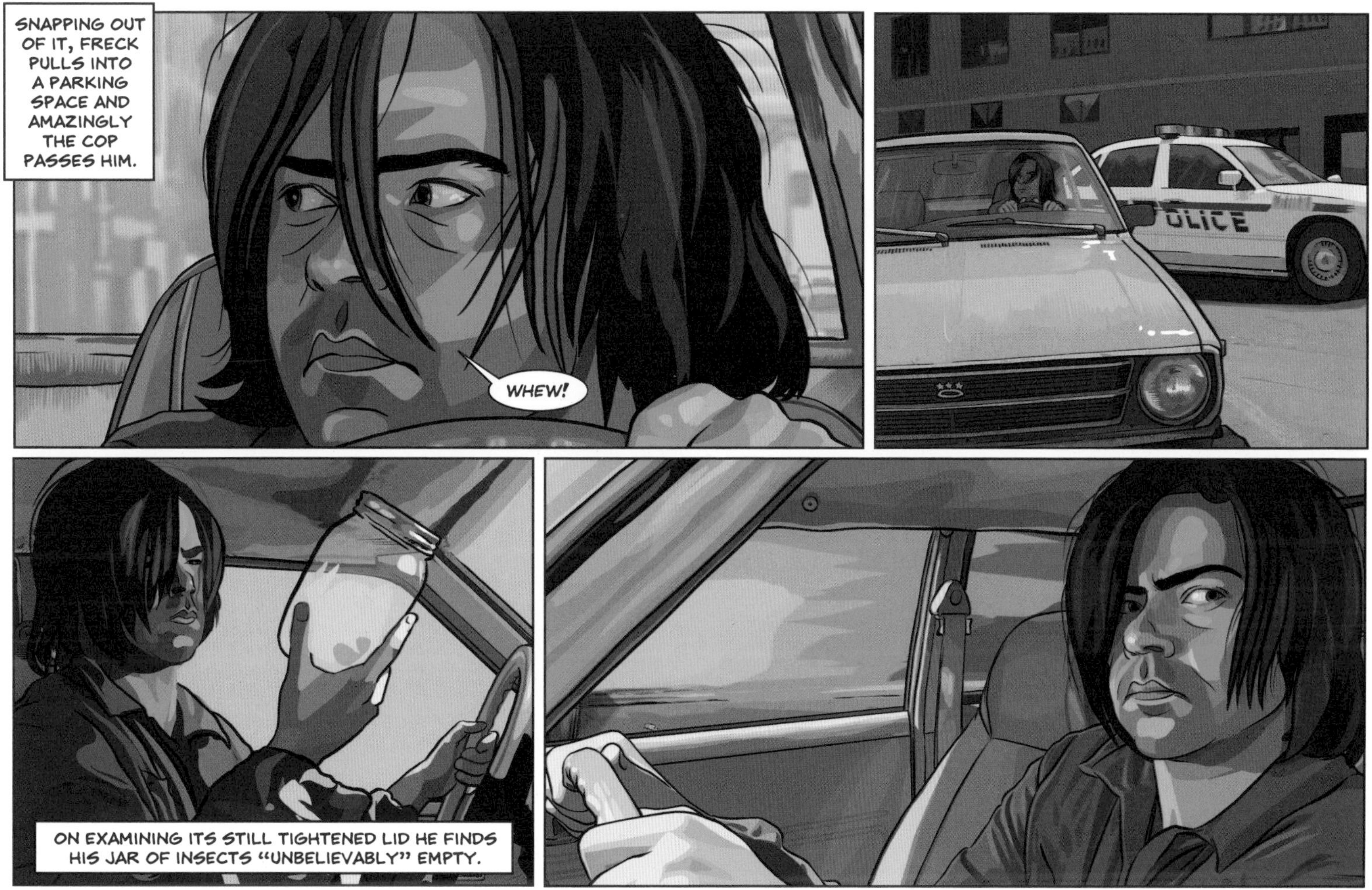
SNAPPING OUT OF IT, FRECK PULLS INTO A PARKING SPACE AND AMAZINGLY THE COP PASSES HIM.
WHEW!
ON EXAMINING ITS STILL TIGHTENED LID HE FINDS HIS JAR OF INSECTS "UNBELIEVABLY" EMPTY.

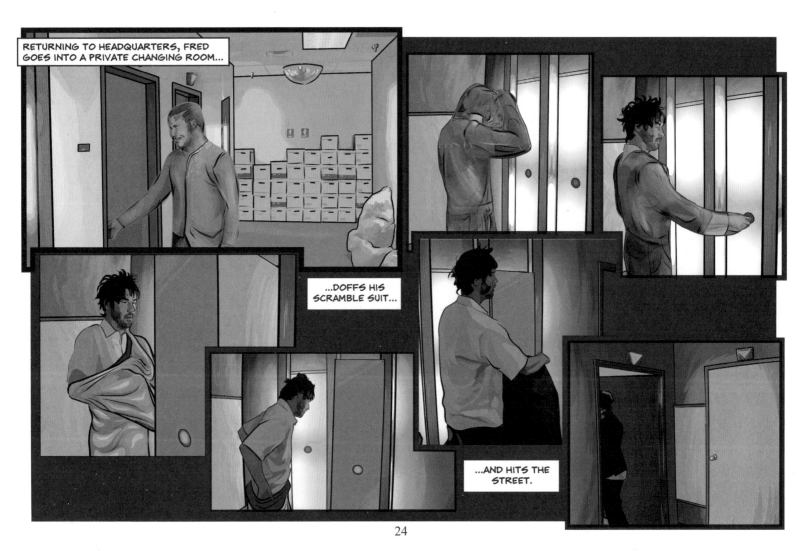

RETURNING TO HEADQUARTERS, FRED GOES INTO A PRIVATE CHANGING ROOM...

...DOFFS HIS SCRAMBLE SUIT...

...AND HITS THE STREET.

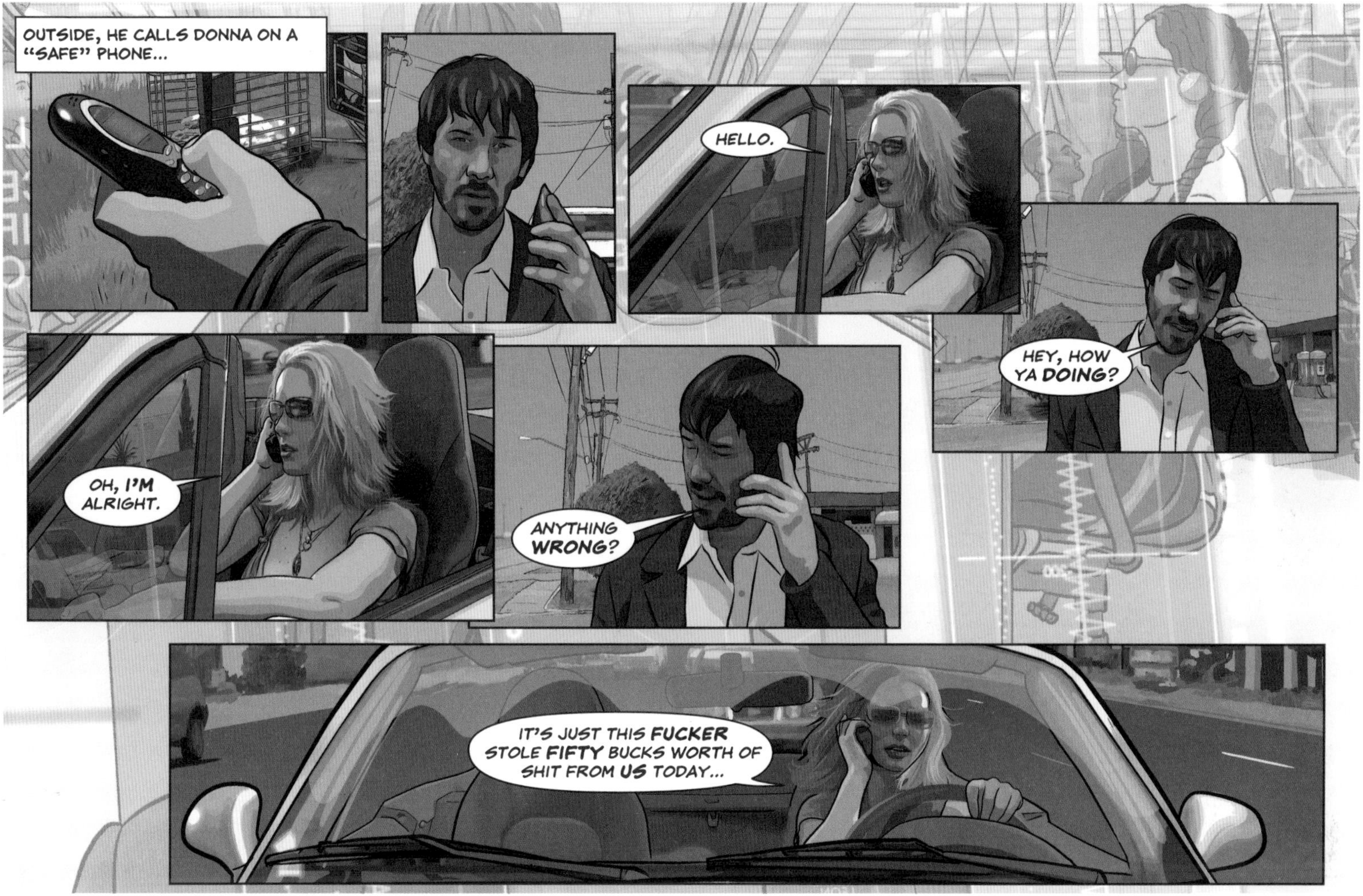
OUTSIDE, HE CALLS DONNA ON A "SAFE" PHONE...
HELLO.
HEY, HOW YA DOING?
OH, I'M ALRIGHT.
ANYTHING WRONG?
IT'S JUST THIS FUCKER STOLE FIFTY BUCKS WORTH OF SHIT FROM US TODAY...

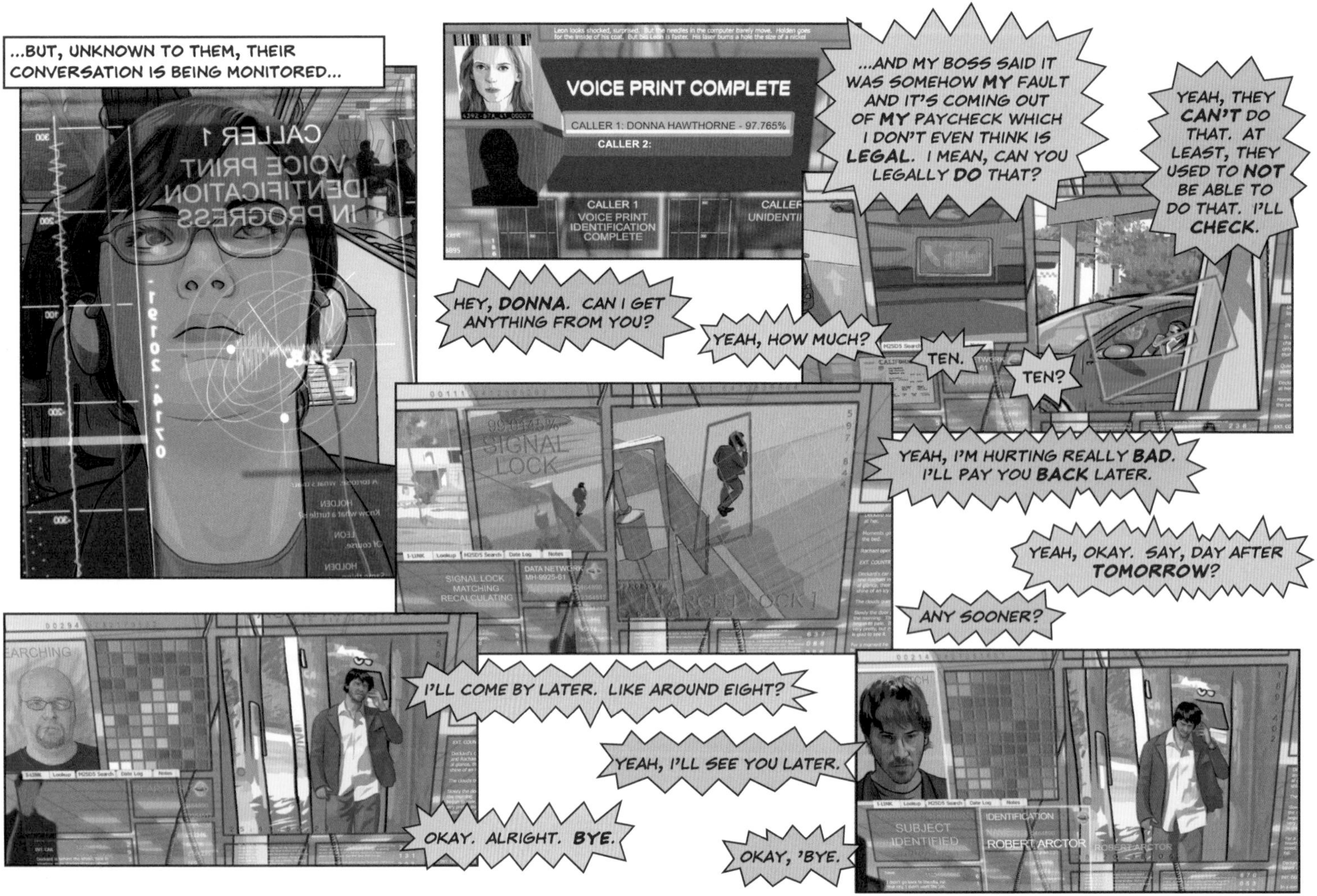

...BUT, UNKNOWN TO THEM, THEIR CONVERSATION IS BEING MONITORED...
CALLER 1 VOICE PRINT IDENTIFICATION IN PROGRESS
VOICE PRINT COMPLETE
CALLER 1: DONNA HAWTHORNE - 97.765%
CALLER 2:
CALLER 1 VOICE PRINT IDENTIFICATION COMPLETE
...AND MY BOSS SAID IT WAS SOMEHOW MY FAULT AND IT'S COMING OUT OF MY PAYCHECK WHICH I DON'T EVEN THINK IS LEGAL. I MEAN, CAN YOU LEGALLY DO THAT?
YEAH, THEY CAN'T DO THAT. AT LEAST, THEY USED TO NOT BE ABLE TO DO THAT. I'LL CHECK.
HEY, DONNA. CAN I GET ANYTHING FROM YOU?
YEAH, HOW MUCH?
TEN.
TEN?
SIGNAL LOCK
YEAH, I'M HURTING REALLY BAD. I'LL PAY YOU BACK LATER.
SIGNAL LOCK MATCHING RECALCULATING
YEAH, OKAY. SAY, DAY AFTER TOMORROW?
ANY SOONER?
I'LL COME BY LATER. LIKE AROUND EIGHT?
YEAH, I'LL SEE YOU LATER.
OKAY. ALRIGHT. BYE.
OKAY, 'BYE.
SUBJECT IDENTIFIED
IDENTIFICATION
ROBERT ARCTOR

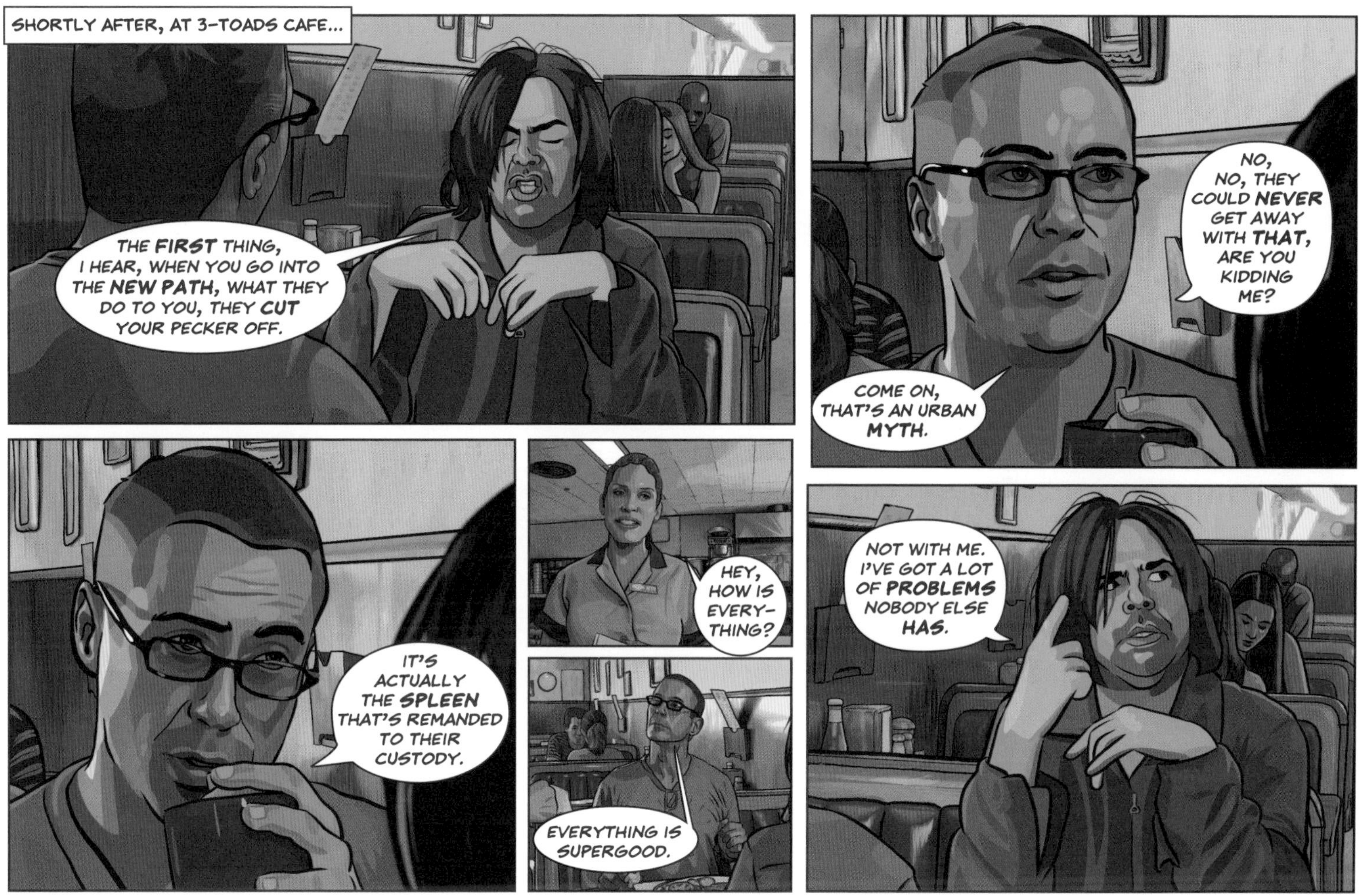
SHORTLY AFTER, AT 3-TOADS CAFE...
THE FIRST THING, I HEAR, WHEN YOU GO INTO THE NEW PATH, WHAT THEY DO TO YOU, THEY CUT YOUR PECKER OFF.
NO, NO, THEY COULD NEVER GET AWAY WITH THAT, ARE YOU KIDDING ME?
COME ON, THAT'S AN URBAN MYTH.
IT'S ACTUALLY THE SPLEEN THAT'S REMANDED TO THEIR CUSTODY.
HEY, HOW IS EVERY-THING?
EVERYTHING IS SUPERGOOD.
NOT WITH ME. I'VE GOT A LOT OF PROBLEMS NOBODY ELSE HAS.

IT'S NOT UNCOMMON. MORE PEOPLE THAN YOU THINK, AND MORE PEOPLE EACH DAY...

...THIS IS A WORLD GETTING PROGRESSIVELY WORSE, CAN WE NOT AGREE ON THAT?

WOULD YOU LIKE TO MAYBE ORDER SOME DESSERT?

WHAT'S ON THE DESSERT MENU?

WELL, WE HAVE FRESH STRAWBERRY PIE... AND...

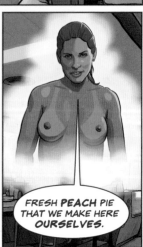

FRESH PEACH PIE THAT WE MAKE HERE OURSELVES.

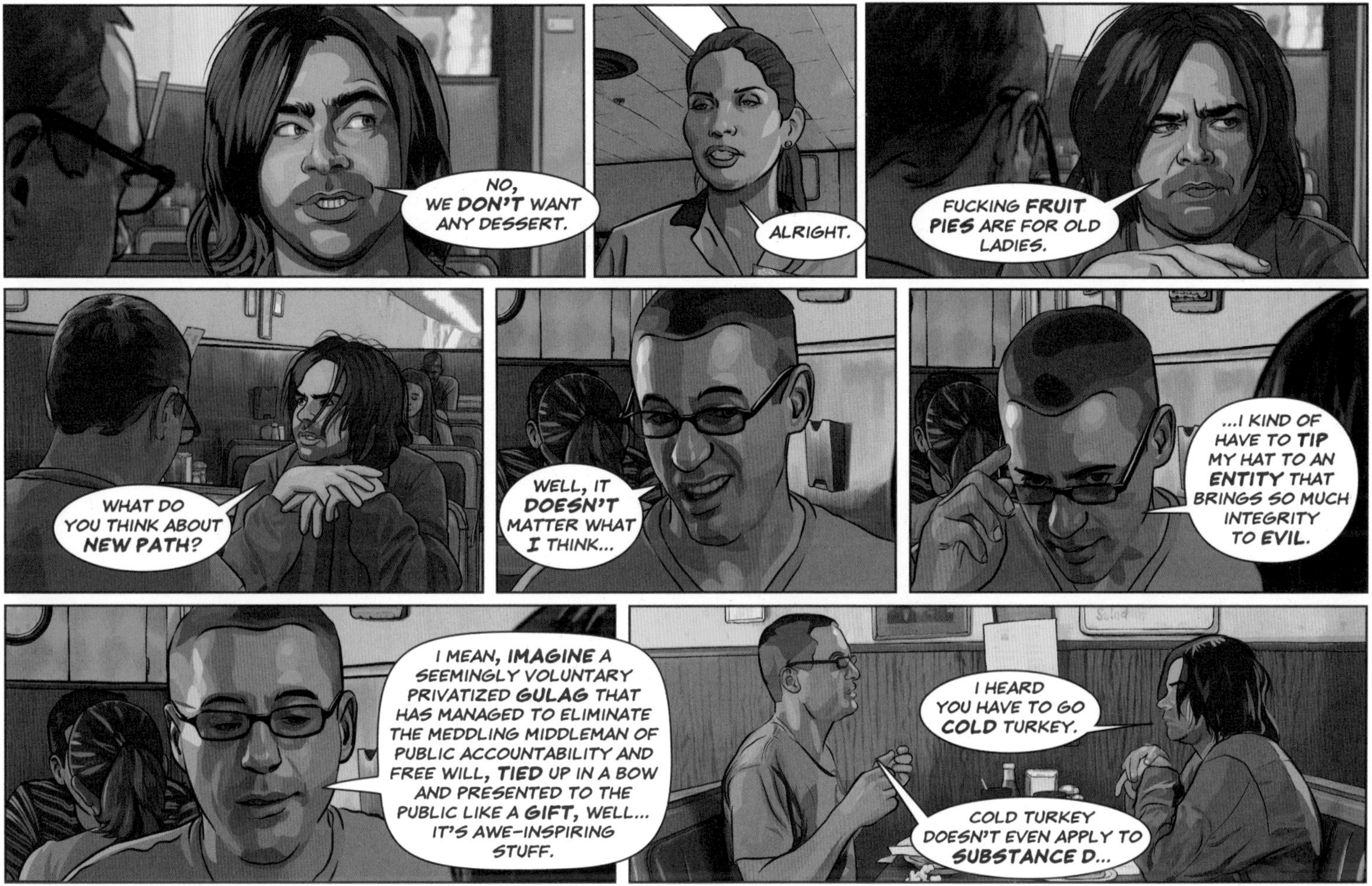
NO, WE DON'T WANT ANY DESSERT.
ALRIGHT.
FUCKING FRUIT PIES ARE FOR OLD LADIES.
WHAT DO YOU THINK ABOUT NEW PATH?
WELL, IT DOESN'T MATTER WHAT I THINK...
...I KIND OF HAVE TO TIP MY HAT TO AN ENTITY THAT BRINGS SO MUCH INTEGRITY TO EVIL.
I MEAN, IMAGINE A SEEMINGLY VOLUNTARY PRIVATIZED GULAG THAT HAS MANAGED TO ELIMINATE THE MEDDLING MIDDLEMAN OF PUBLIC ACCOUNTABILITY AND FREE WILL, TIED UP IN A BOW AND PRESENTED TO THE PUBLIC LIKE A GIFT, WELL... IT'S AWE-INSPIRING STUFF.
I HEARD YOU HAVE TO GO COLD TURKEY.
COLD TURKEY DOESN'T EVEN APPLY TO SUBSTANCE D...

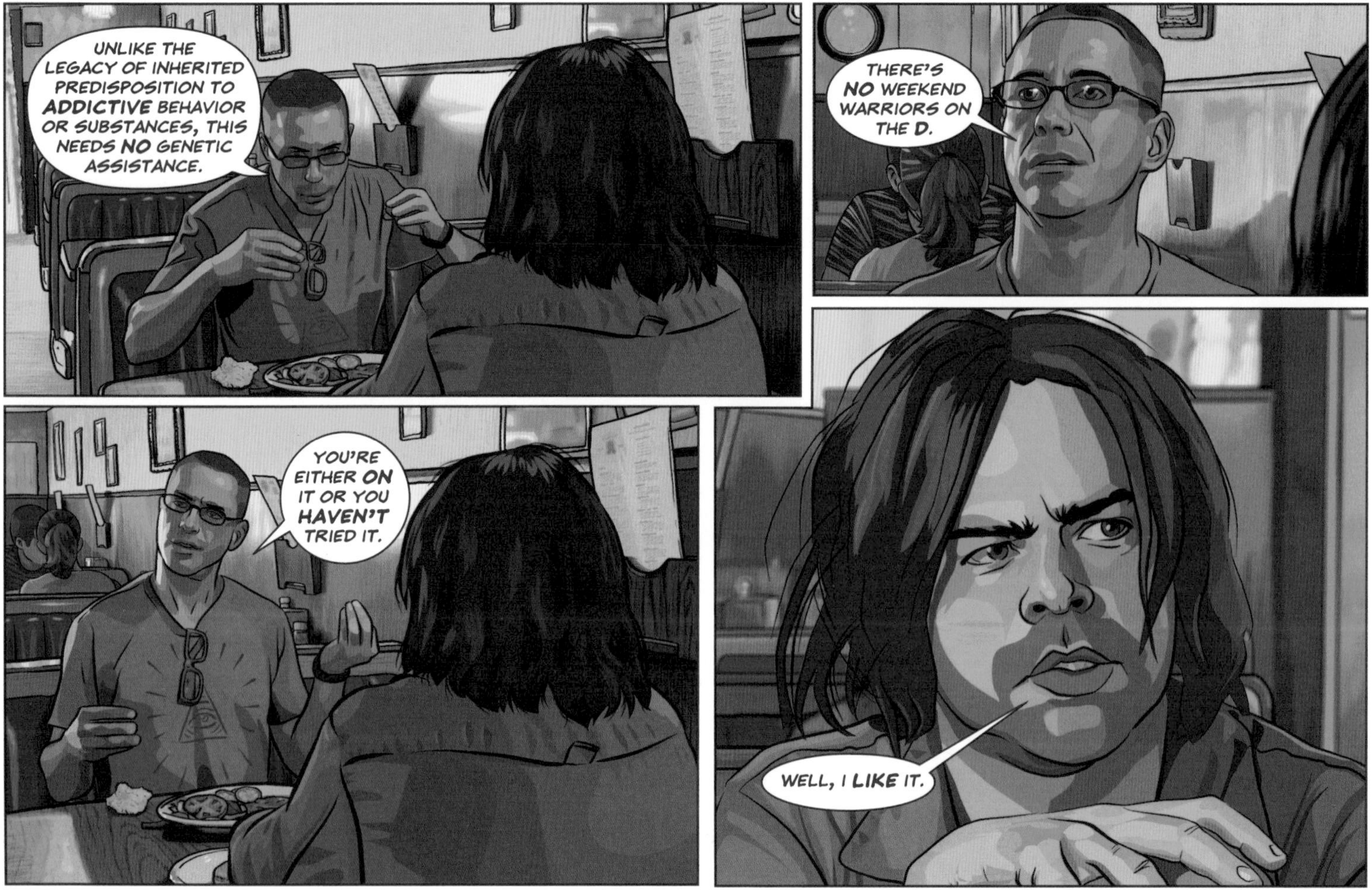
UNLIKE THE LEGACY OF INHERITED PREDISPOSITION TO ADDICTIVE BEHAVIOR OR SUBSTANCES, THIS NEEDS NO GENETIC ASSISTANCE.
THERE'S NO WEEKEND WARRIORS ON THE D.
YOU'RE EITHER ON IT OR YOU HAVEN'T TRIED IT.
WELL, I LIKE IT.

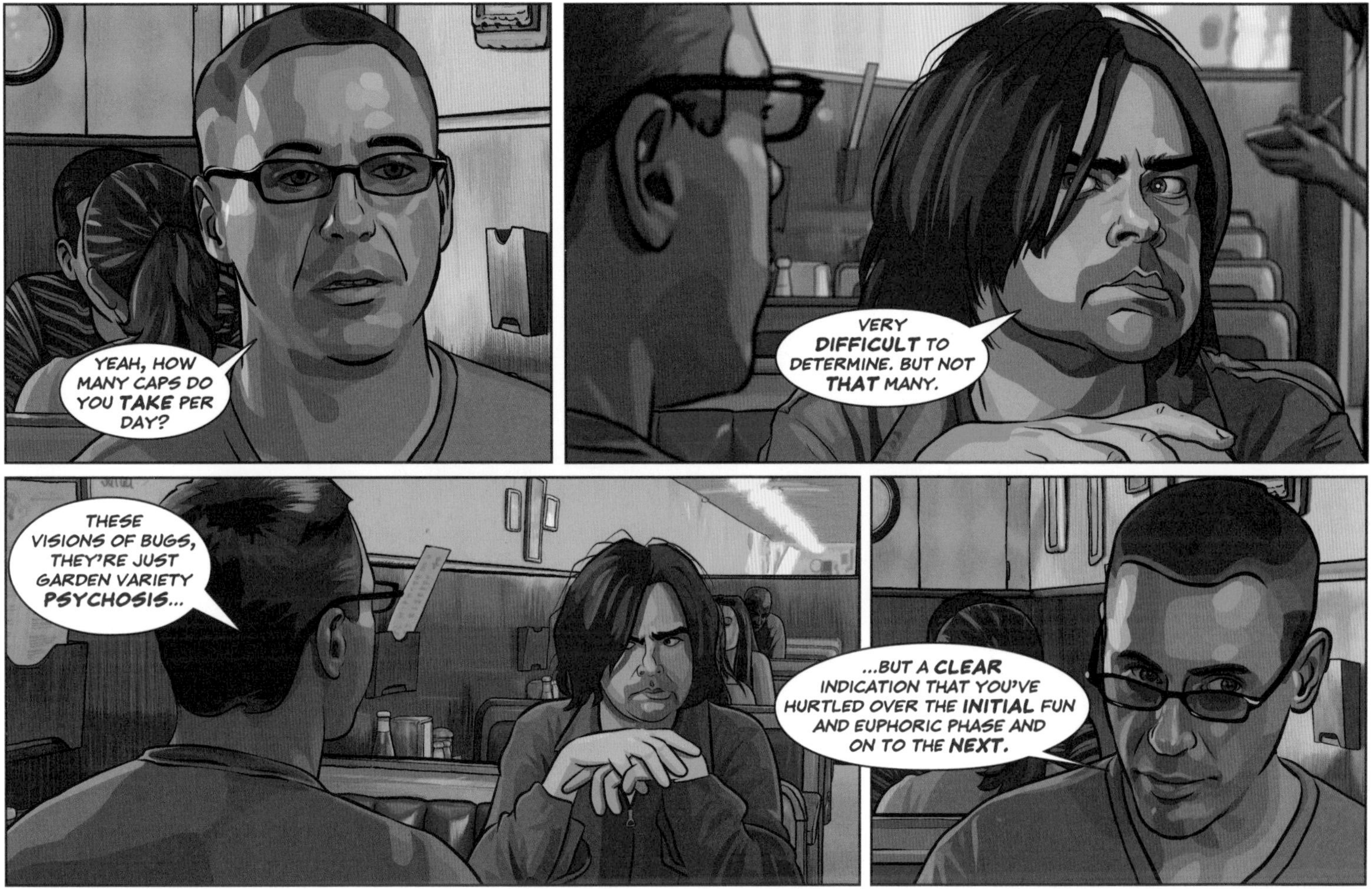
YEAH, HOW MANY CAPS DO YOU TAKE PER DAY?
VERY DIFFICULT TO DETERMINE. BUT NOT THAT MANY.
THESE VISIONS OF BUGS, THEY'RE JUST GARDEN VARIETY PSYCHOSIS...
...BUT A CLEAR INDICATION THAT YOU'VE HURTLED OVER THE INITIAL FUN AND EUPHORIC PHASE AND ON TO THE NEXT.

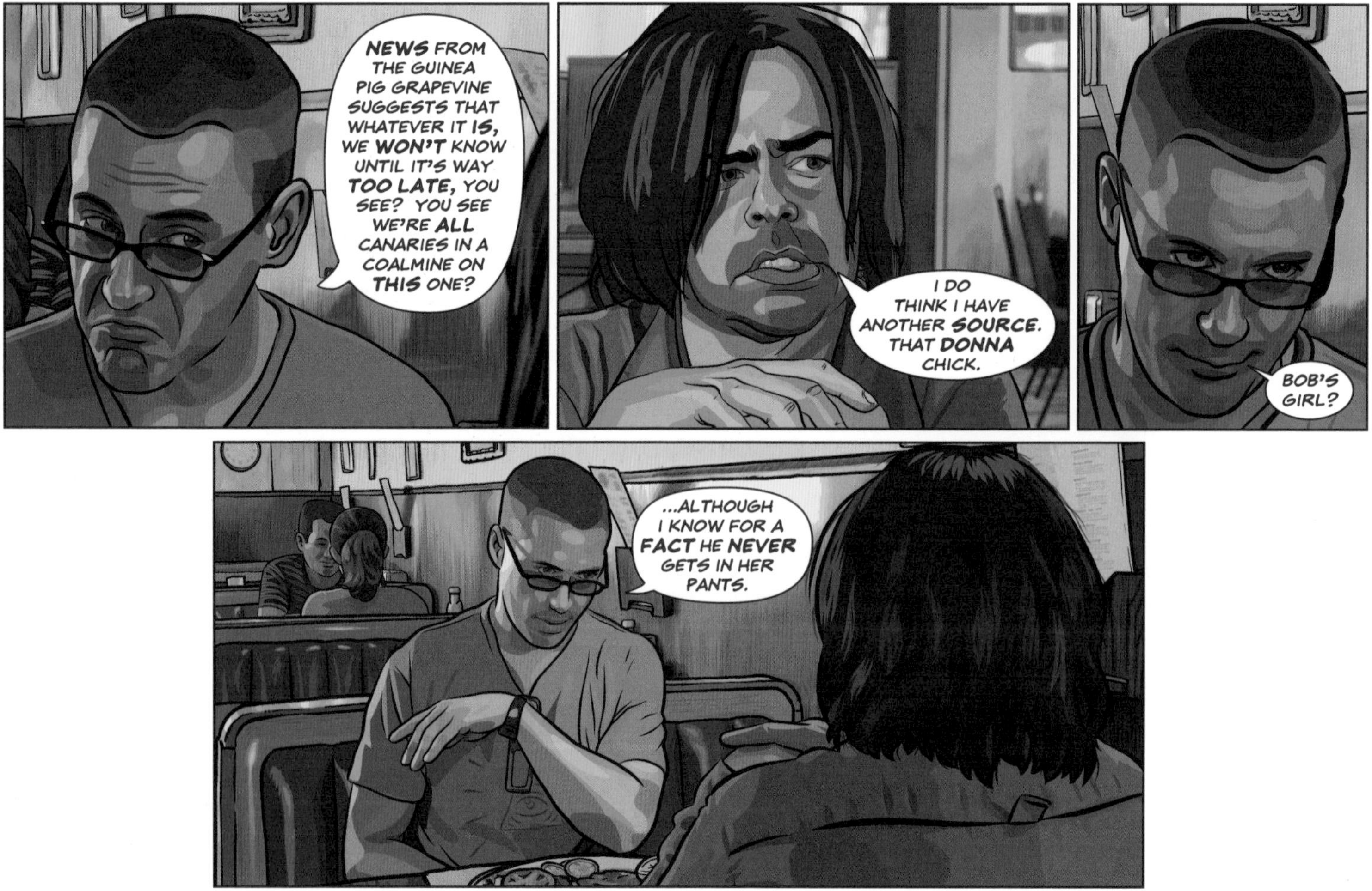
NEWS FROM THE GUINEA PIG GRAPEVINE SUGGESTS THAT WHATEVER IT IS, WE WON'T KNOW UNTIL IT'S WAY TOO LATE, YOU SEE? YOU SEE WE'RE ALL CANARIES IN A COALMINE ON THIS ONE?
I DO THINK I HAVE ANOTHER SOURCE. THAT DONNA CHICK.
BOB'S GIRL?
...ALTHOUGH I KNOW FOR A FACT HE NEVER GETS IN HER PANTS.

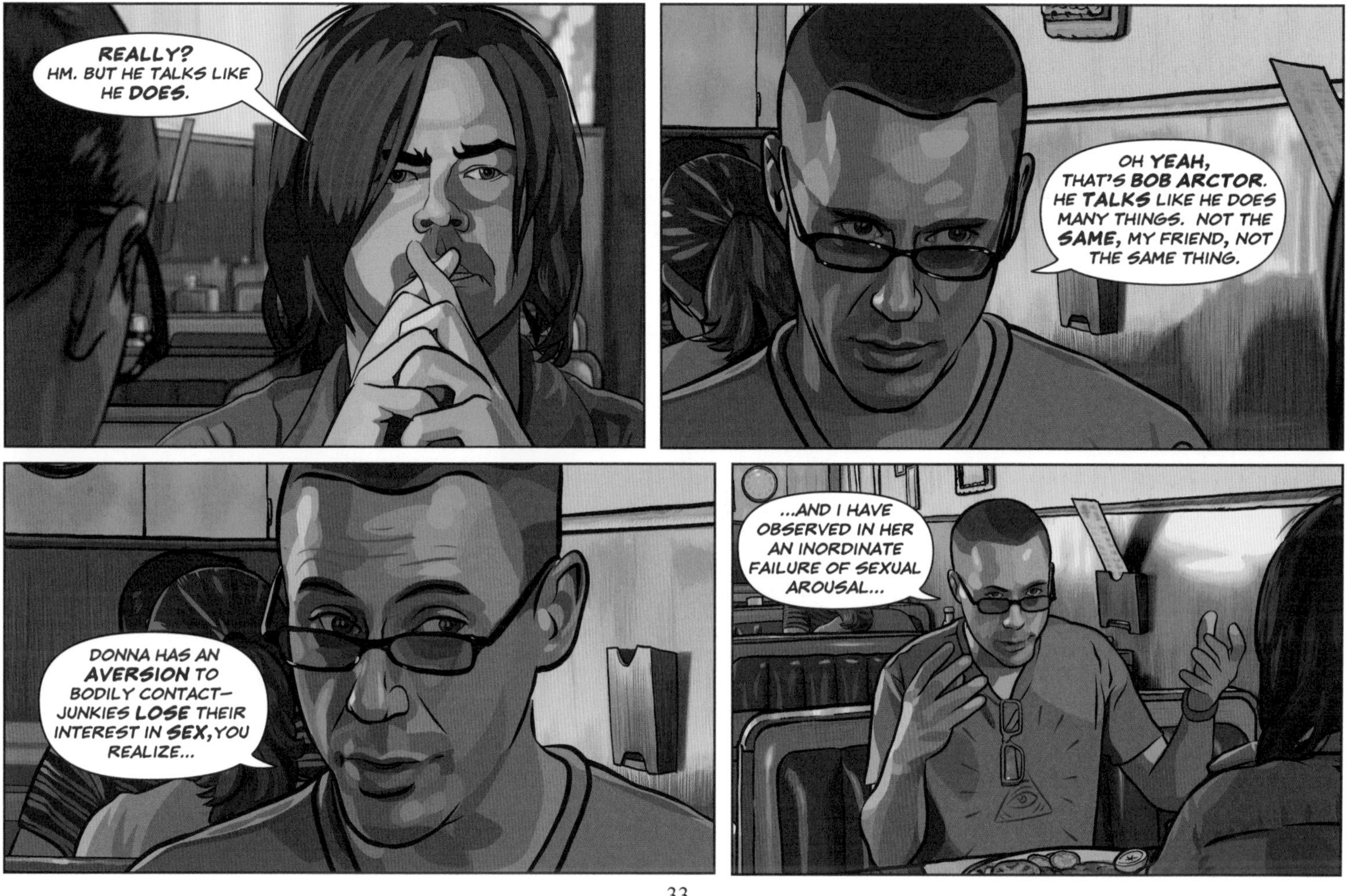
REALLY? HM. BUT HE TALKS LIKE HE DOES.
OH YEAH, THAT'S BOB ARCTOR. HE TALKS LIKE HE DOES MANY THINGS. NOT THE SAME, MY FRIEND, NOT THE SAME THING.
DONNA HAS AN AVERSION TO BODILY CONTACT– JUNKIES LOSE THEIR INTEREST IN SEX, YOU REALIZE...
...AND I HAVE OBSERVED IN HER AN INORDINATE FAILURE OF SEXUAL AROUSAL...

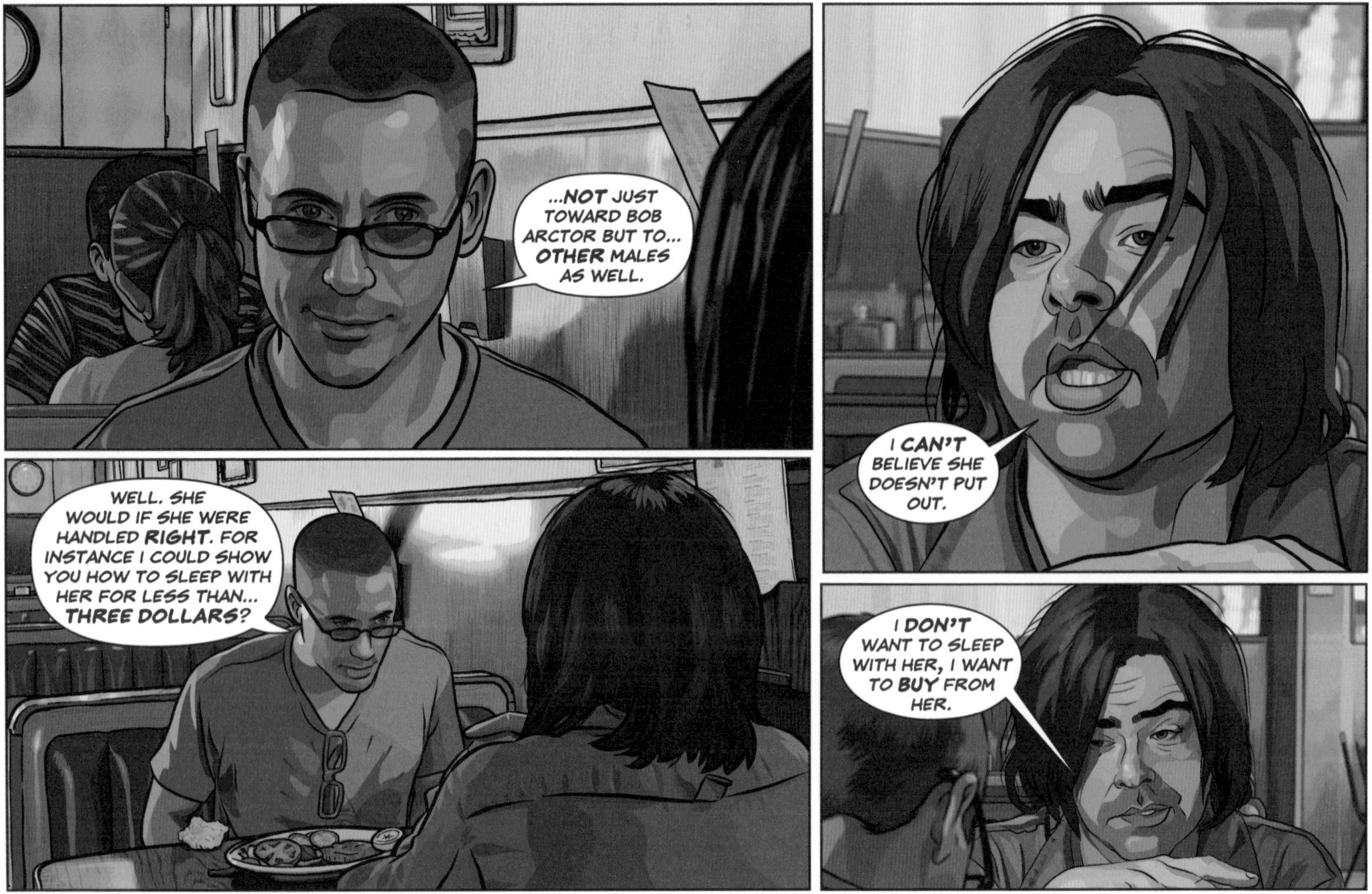
...NOT JUST TOWARD BOB ARCTOR BUT TO... OTHER MALES AS WELL.
I CAN'T BELIEVE SHE DOESN'T PUT OUT.
WELL. SHE WOULD IF SHE WERE HANDLED RIGHT. FOR INSTANCE I COULD SHOW YOU HOW TO SLEEP WITH HER FOR LESS THAN... THREE DOLLARS?
I DON'T WANT TO SLEEP WITH HER, I WANT TO BUY FROM HER.

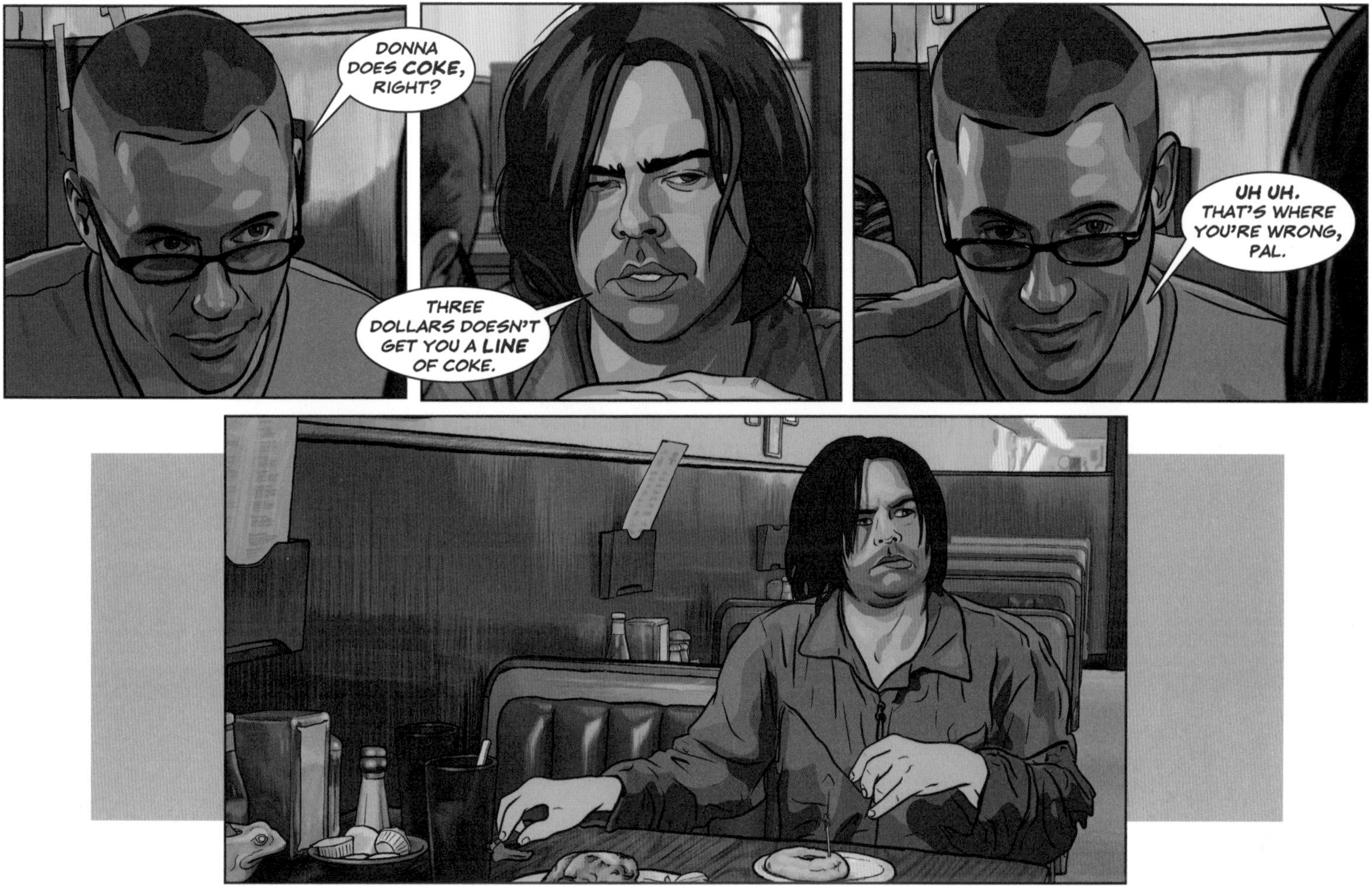
DONNA DOES COKE, RIGHT?
THREE DOLLARS DOESN'T GET YOU A LINE OF COKE.
UH UH. THAT'S WHERE YOU'RE WRONG, PAL.

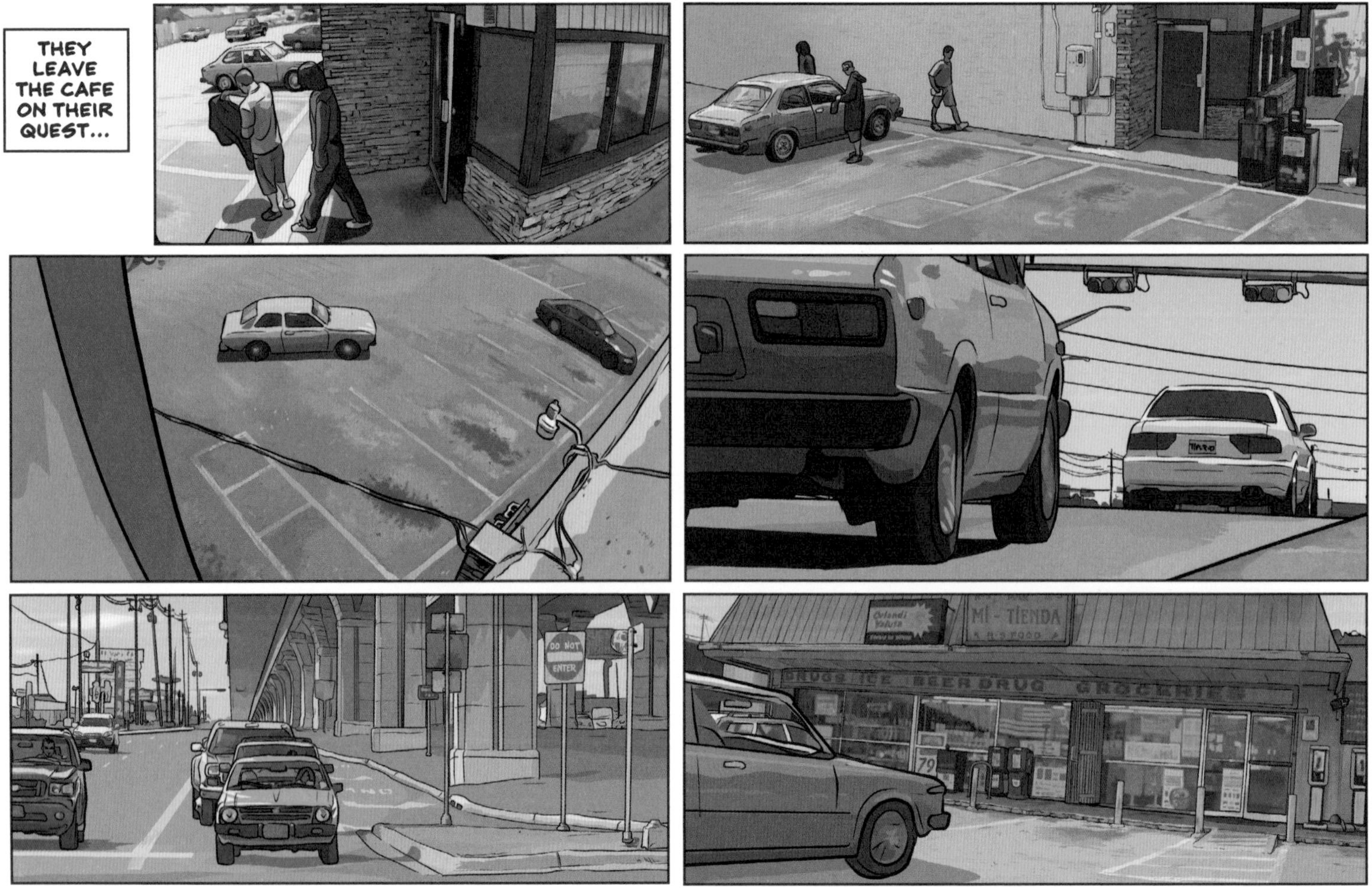
THEY LEAVE THE CAFE ON THEIR QUEST...
DO NOT ENTER
MI - TIENDA
DRUGS ICE BEER DRUG

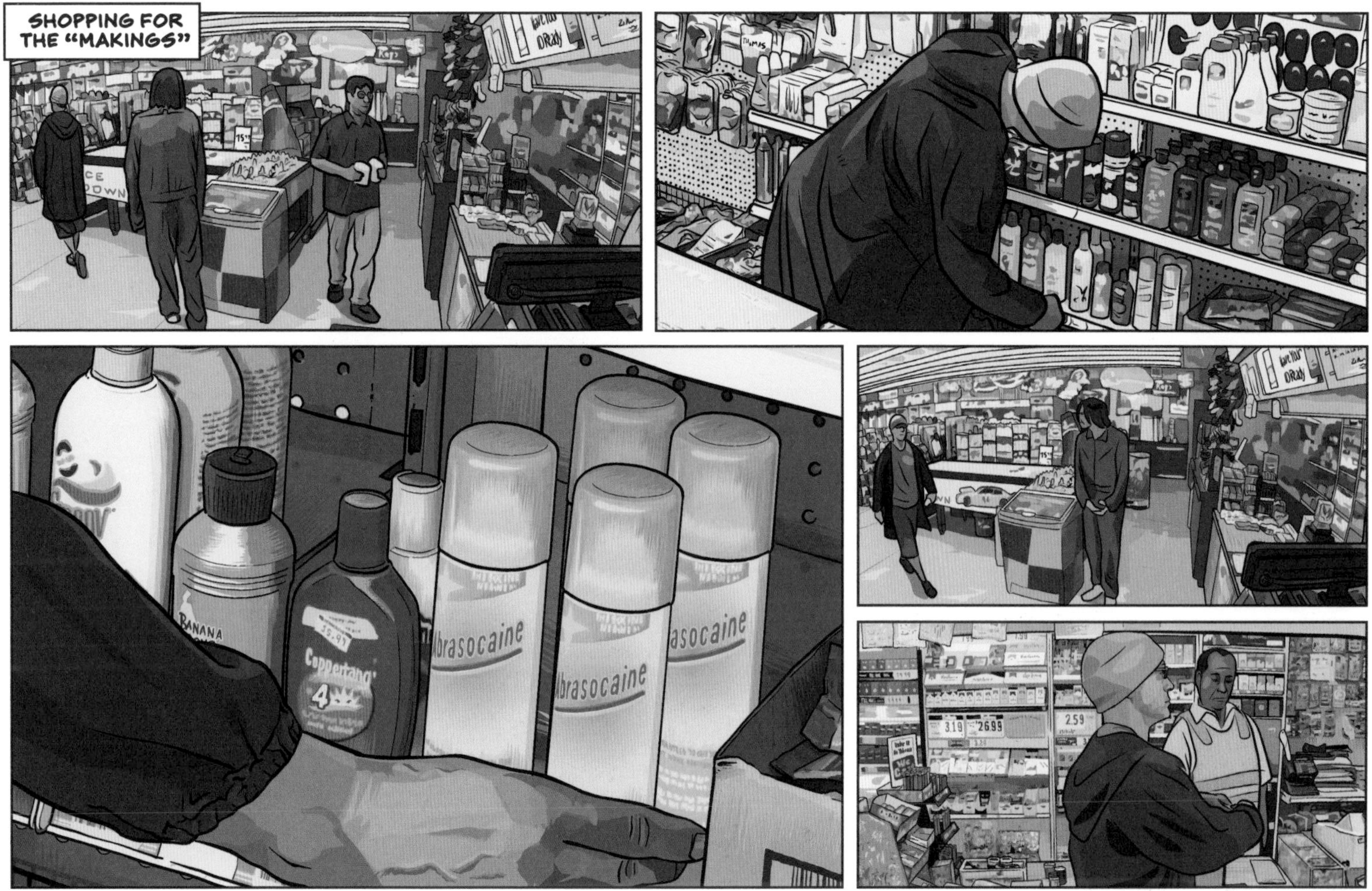
SHOPPING FOR THE "MAKINGS"
BANANA
Coppertang
4
Abrasocaine
3.19
26.99
2.59

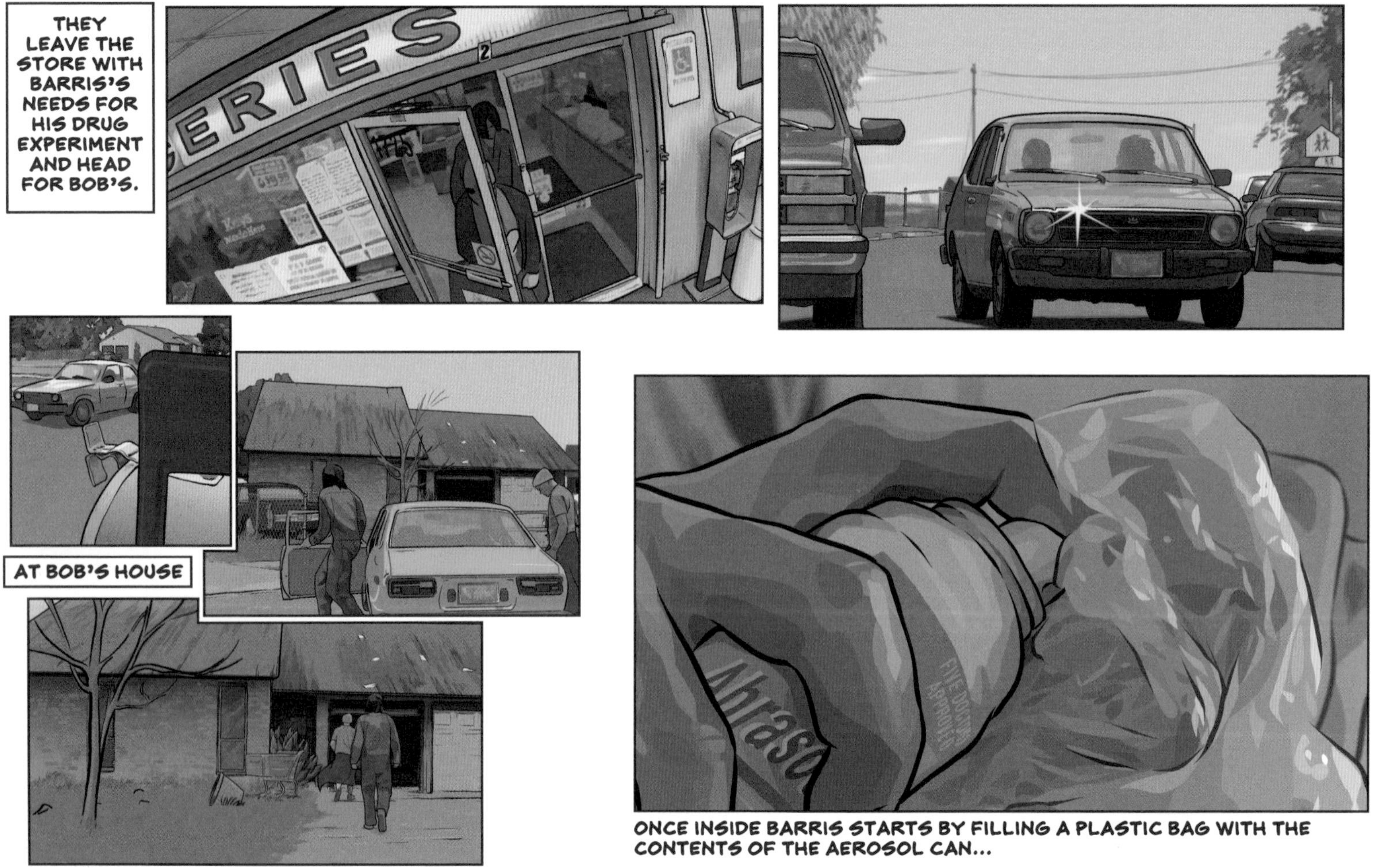
THEY LEAVE THE STORE WITH BARRIS'S NEEDS FOR HIS DRUG EXPERIMENT AND HEAD FOR BOB'S.
ERIES
AT BOB'S HOUSE
ONCE INSIDE BARRIS STARTS BY FILLING A PLASTIC BAG WITH THE CONTENTS OF THE AEROSOL CAN...

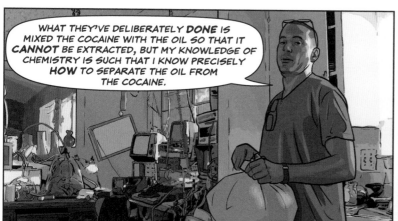

WHAT THEY'VE DELIBERATELY **DONE** IS MIXED THE COCAINE WITH THE OIL SO THAT IT **CANNOT** BE EXTRACTED, BUT MY KNOWLEDGE OF CHEMISTRY IS SUCH THAT I KNOW PRECISELY **HOW** TO SEPARATE THE OIL FROM THE COCAINE.

NOW, I WILL FREEZE IT TO **CAUSE** COCAINE CRYSTALS TO RISE TO THE TOP BECAUSE THEY ARE **LIGHTER** THAN THE OIL.

SHAKE! SHAKE!

THE TERMINAL **STEP**, OF COURSE, I KEEP TO MYSELF...

HOW LONG IS IT GOING TO BE IN THERE?

'BOUT HALF AN HOUR.

YOU KNOW, I'VE BEEN THINKING, BARRIS...

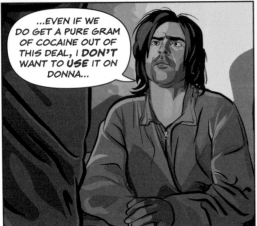

...EVEN IF WE DO GET A PURE GRAM OF COCAINE OUT OF THIS DEAL, I **DON'T** WANT TO **USE** IT ON DONNA...

BESIDES, WE'RE TALKING ABOUT **BOB'S** GIRL, HERE. AND THIS IS **HIS** HOUSE, HE'S MY FRIEND, HE **LETS** YOU AND LUCKMAN LIVE HERE.

THERE'S A **GREAT DEAL** ABOUT BOB ARCTOR YOU'RE **NOT** AWARE OF.

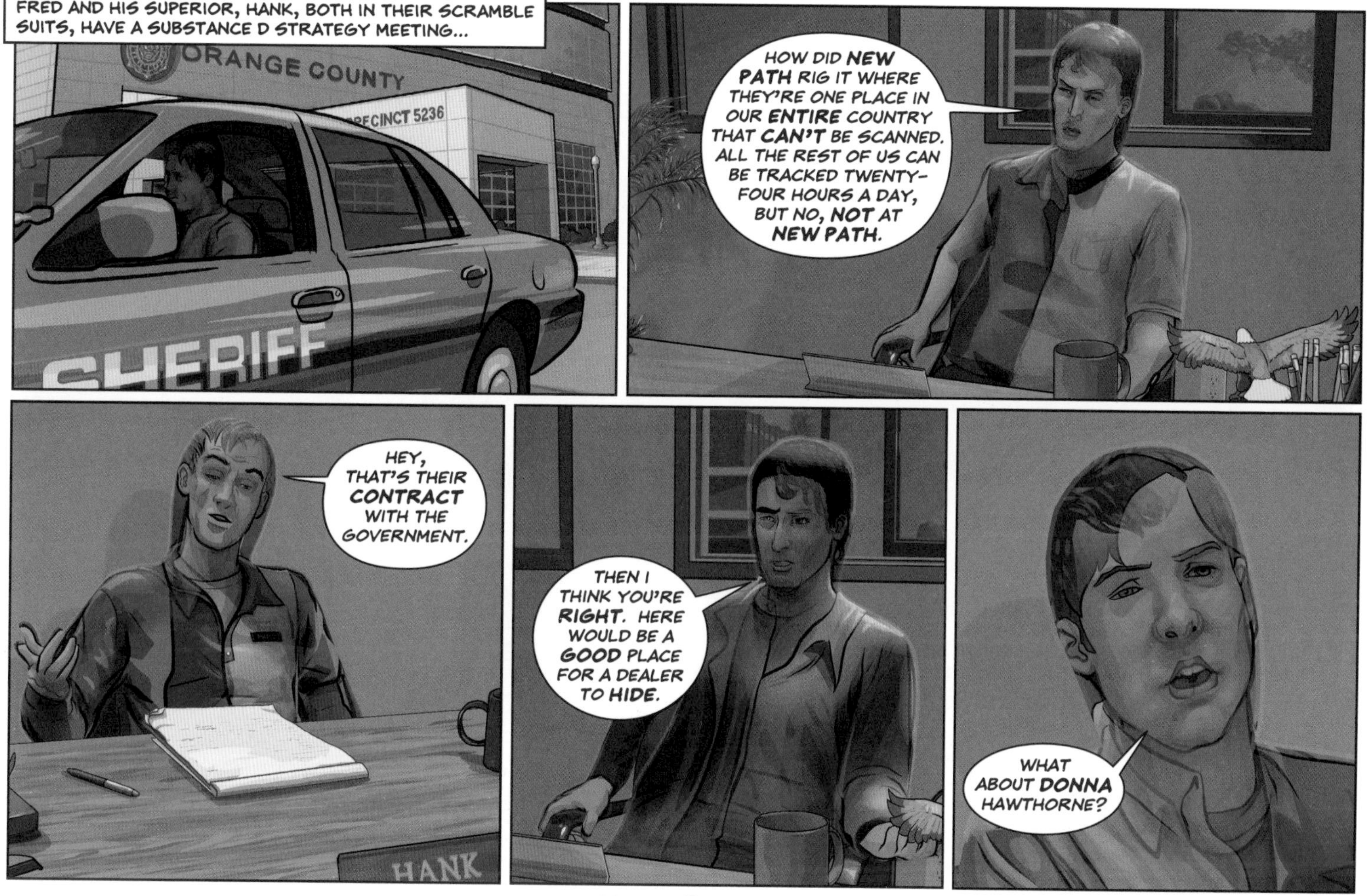
FRED AND HIS SUPERIOR, HANK, BOTH IN THEIR SCRAMBLE SUITS, HAVE A SUBSTANCE D STRATEGY MEETING...
ORANGE COUNTY
SHERIFF
HOW DID NEW PATH RIG IT WHERE THEY'RE ONE PLACE IN OUR ENTIRE COUNTRY THAT CAN'T BE SCANNED. ALL THE REST OF US CAN BE TRACKED TWENTY-FOUR HOURS A DAY, BUT NO, NOT AT NEW PATH.
HEY, THAT'S THEIR CONTRACT WITH THE GOVERNMENT.
HANK
THEN I THINK YOU'RE RIGHT. HERE WOULD BE A GOOD PLACE FOR A DEALER TO HIDE.
WHAT ABOUT DONNA HAWTHORNE?

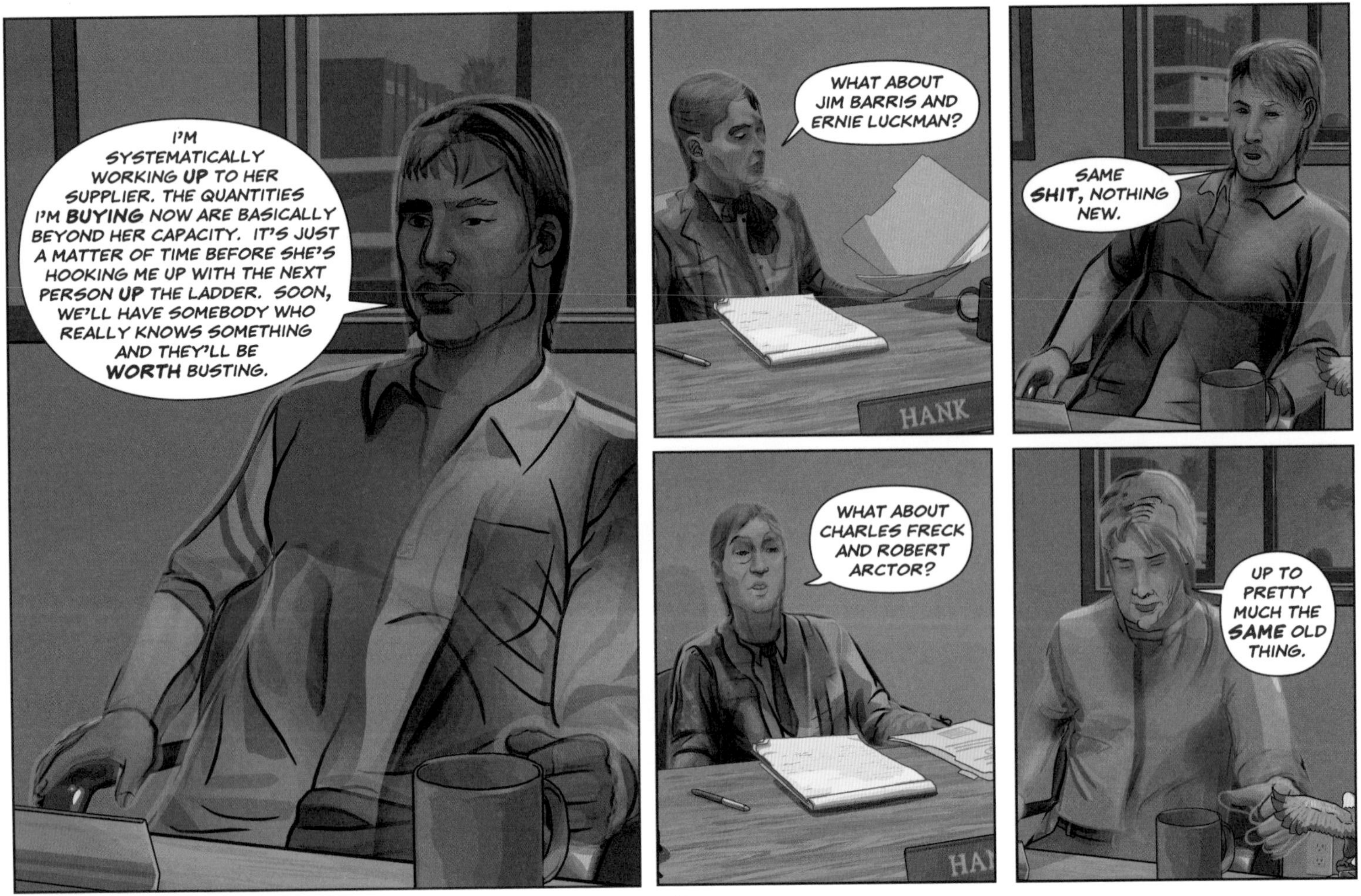
I'M SYSTEMATICALLY WORKING UP TO HER SUPPLIER. THE QUANTITIES I'M **BUYING** NOW ARE BASICALLY BEYOND HER CAPACITY. IT'S JUST A MATTER OF TIME BEFORE SHE'S HOOKING ME UP WITH THE NEXT PERSON **UP** THE LADDER. SOON, WE'LL HAVE SOMEBODY WHO REALLY KNOWS SOMETHING AND THEY'LL BE **WORTH** BUSTING.
WHAT ABOUT JIM BARRIS AND ERNIE LUCKMAN?
HANK
SAME **SHIT,** NOTHING NEW.
WHAT ABOUT CHARLES FRECK AND ROBERT ARCTOR?
UP TO PRETTY MUCH THE **SAME** OLD THING.

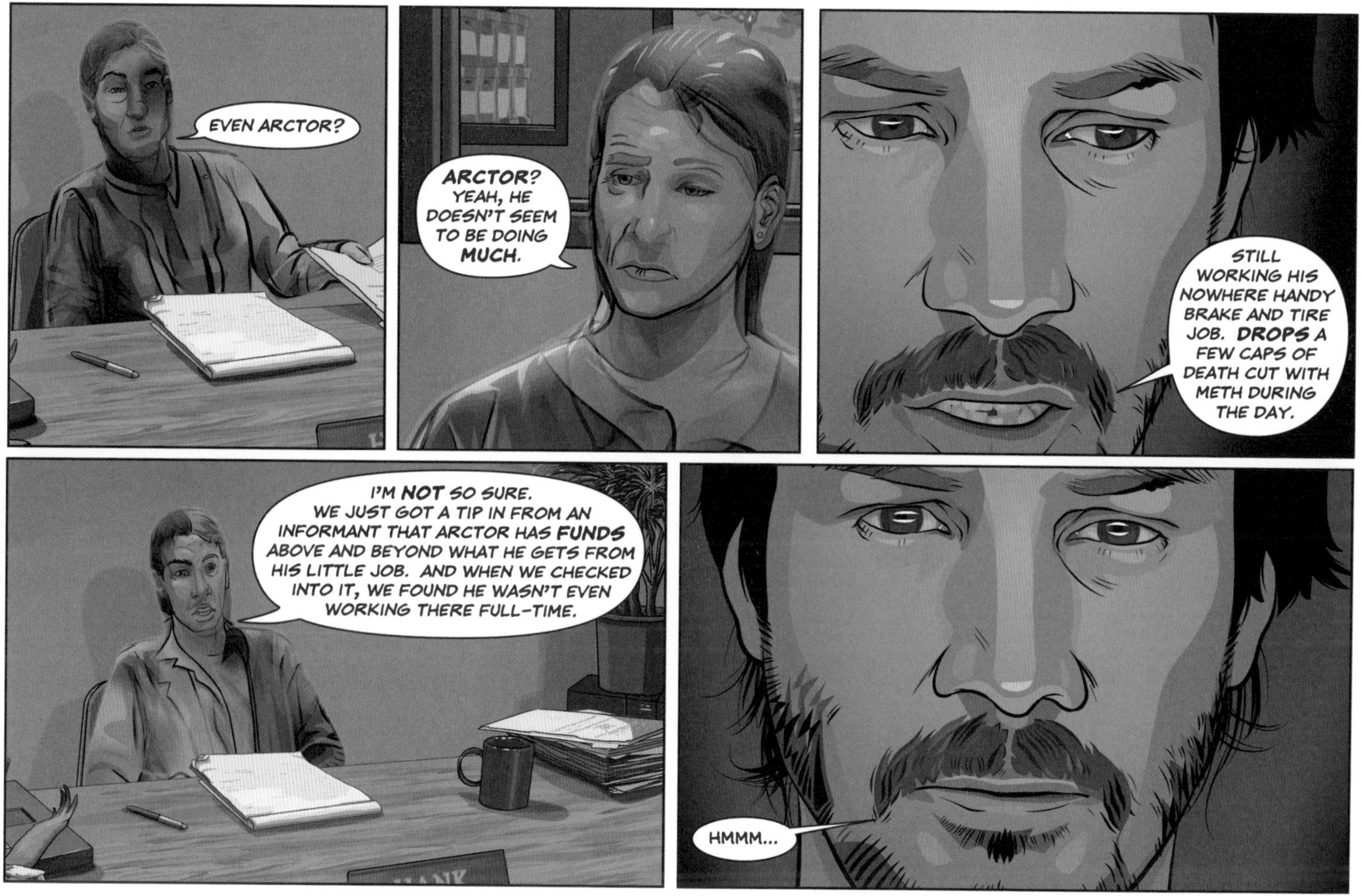
EVEN ARCTOR?
ARCTOR? YEAH, HE DOESN'T SEEM TO BE DOING MUCH.
STILL WORKING HIS NOWHERE HANDY BRAKE AND TIRE JOB. DROPS A FEW CAPS OF DEATH CUT WITH METH DURING THE DAY.
I'M NOT SO SURE. WE JUST GOT A TIP IN FROM AN INFORMANT THAT ARCTOR HAS FUNDS ABOVE AND BEYOND WHAT HE GETS FROM HIS LITTLE JOB. AND WHEN WE CHECKED INTO IT, WE FOUND HE WASN'T EVEN WORKING THERE FULL-TIME.
HMMM...

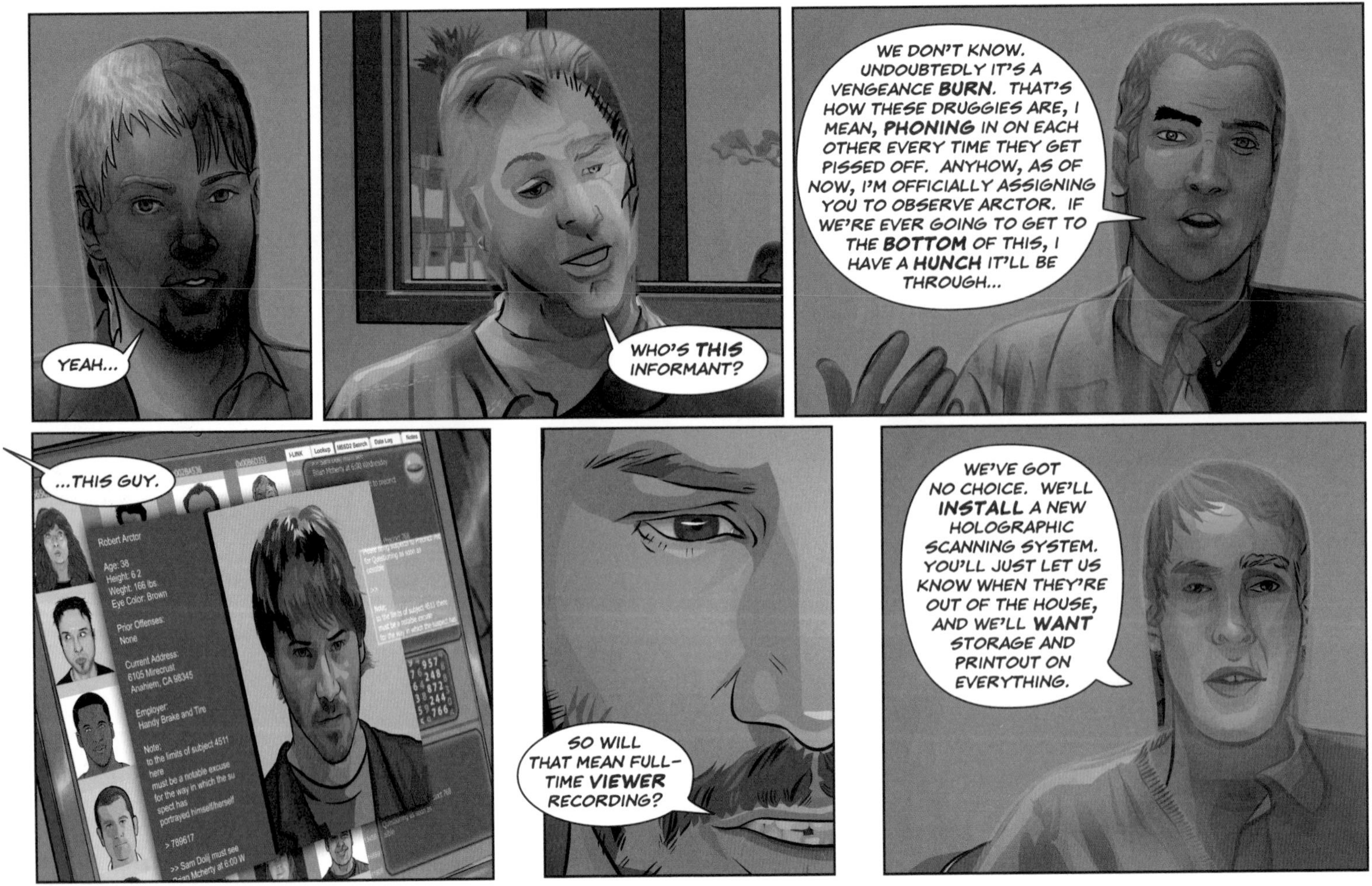
YEAH...
WHO'S **THIS** INFORMANT?
WE DON'T KNOW. UNDOUBTEDLY IT'S A VENGEANCE **BURN**. THAT'S HOW THESE DRUGGIES ARE, I MEAN, **PHONING** IN ON EACH OTHER EVERY TIME THEY GET PISSED OFF. ANYHOW, AS OF NOW, I'M OFFICIALLY ASSIGNING YOU TO OBSERVE ARCTOR. IF WE'RE EVER GOING TO GET TO THE **BOTTOM** OF THIS, I HAVE A **HUNCH** IT'LL BE THROUGH...
...THIS GUY.
Robert Arctor
Age: 38
Height: 6'2
Weight: 166 lbs.
Eye Color: Brown
Prior Offenses:
None
Current Address:
6105 Mirecrust
Anahiem, CA 98345
Employer:
Handy Brake and Tire
Note;
to the limits of subject 4511
here
must be a notable excuse
for the way in which the su
spect has
portrayed himself/herself
> 789617
>> Sam Dolij must see
SO WILL THAT MEAN FULL-TIME **VIEWER** RECORDING?
WE'VE GOT NO CHOICE. WE'LL **INSTALL** A NEW HOLOGRAPHIC SCANNING SYSTEM. YOU'LL JUST LET US KNOW WHEN THEY'RE OUT OF THE HOUSE, AND WE'LL **WANT** STORAGE AND PRINTOUT ON EVERYTHING.

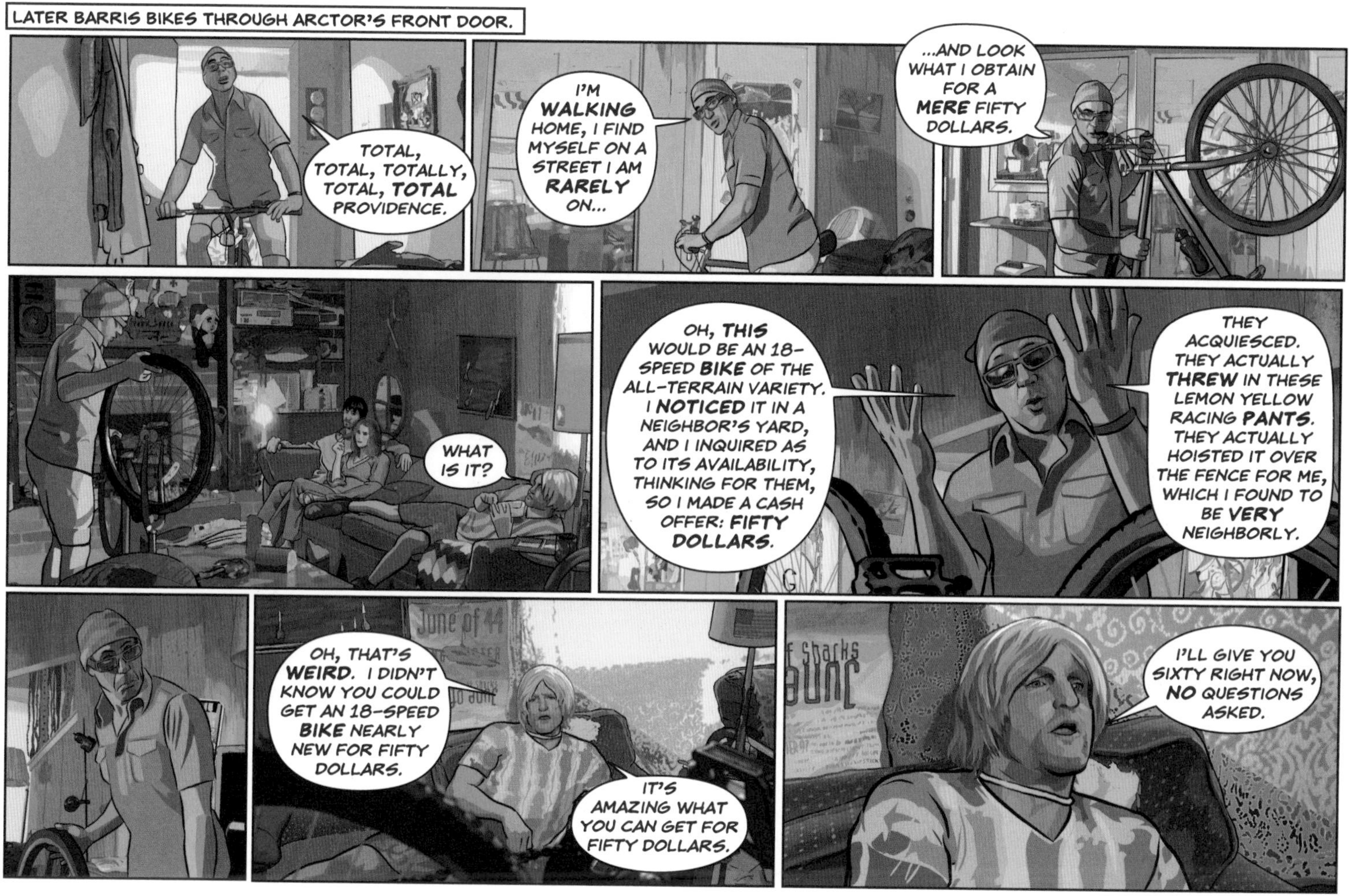
LATER BARRIS BIKES THROUGH ARCTOR'S FRONT DOOR.
TOTAL, TOTAL, TOTALLY, TOTAL, TOTAL PROVIDENCE.
I'M WALKING HOME, I FIND MYSELF ON A STREET I AM RARELY ON...
...AND LOOK WHAT I OBTAIN FOR A MERE FIFTY DOLLARS.
WHAT IS IT?
OH, THIS WOULD BE AN 18-SPEED BIKE OF THE ALL-TERRAIN VARIETY. I NOTICED IT IN A NEIGHBOR'S YARD, AND I INQUIRED AS TO ITS AVAILABILITY, THINKING FOR THEM, SO I MADE A CASH OFFER: FIFTY DOLLARS.
THEY ACQUIESCED. THEY ACTUALLY THREW IN THESE LEMON YELLOW RACING PANTS. THEY ACTUALLY HOISTED IT OVER THE FENCE FOR ME, WHICH I FOUND TO BE VERY NEIGHBORLY.
OH, THAT'S WEIRD. I DIDN'T KNOW YOU COULD GET AN 18-SPEED BIKE NEARLY NEW FOR FIFTY DOLLARS.
IT'S AMAZING WHAT YOU CAN GET FOR FIFTY DOLLARS.
I'LL GIVE YOU SIXTY RIGHT NOW, NO QUESTIONS ASKED.

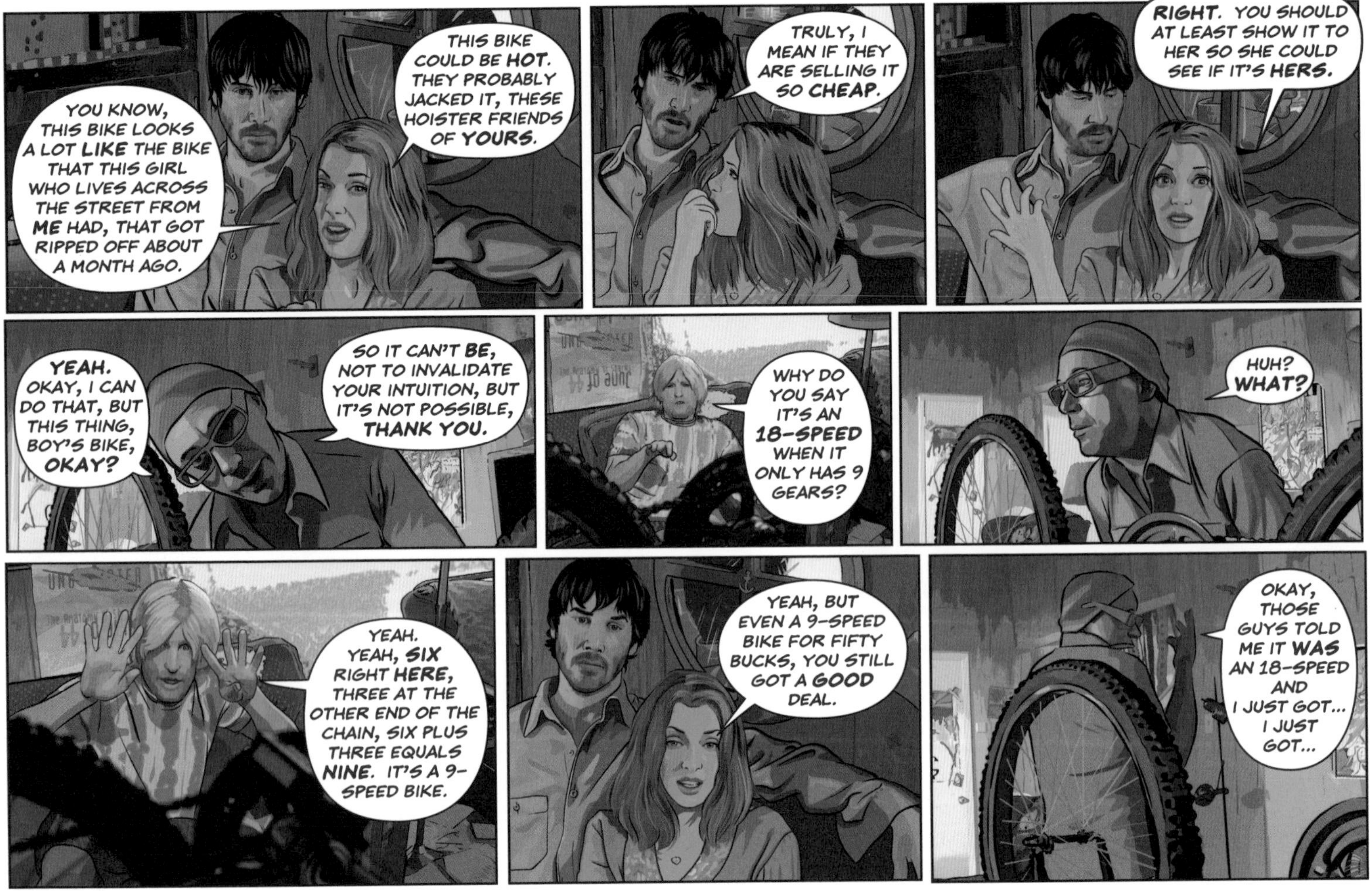
YOU KNOW, THIS BIKE LOOKS A LOT LIKE THE BIKE THAT THIS GIRL WHO LIVES ACROSS THE STREET FROM ME HAD, THAT GOT RIPPED OFF ABOUT A MONTH AGO.
THIS BIKE COULD BE HOT. THEY PROBABLY JACKED IT, THESE HOISTER FRIENDS OF YOURS.
TRULY, I MEAN IF THEY ARE SELLING IT SO CHEAP.
RIGHT. YOU SHOULD AT LEAST SHOW IT TO HER SO SHE COULD SEE IF IT'S HERS.
YEAH. OKAY, I CAN DO THAT, BUT THIS THING, BOY'S BIKE, OKAY?
SO IT CAN'T BE, NOT TO INVALIDATE YOUR INTUITION, BUT IT'S NOT POSSIBLE, THANK YOU.
WHY DO YOU SAY IT'S AN 18-SPEED WHEN IT ONLY HAS 9 GEARS?
HUH? WHAT?
YEAH. YEAH, SIX RIGHT HERE, THREE AT THE OTHER END OF THE CHAIN, SIX PLUS THREE EQUALS NINE. IT'S A 9-SPEED BIKE.
YEAH, BUT EVEN A 9-SPEED BIKE FOR FIFTY BUCKS, YOU STILL GOT A GOOD DEAL.
OKAY, THOSE GUYS TOLD ME IT WAS AN 18-SPEED AND I JUST GOT... I JUST GOT...

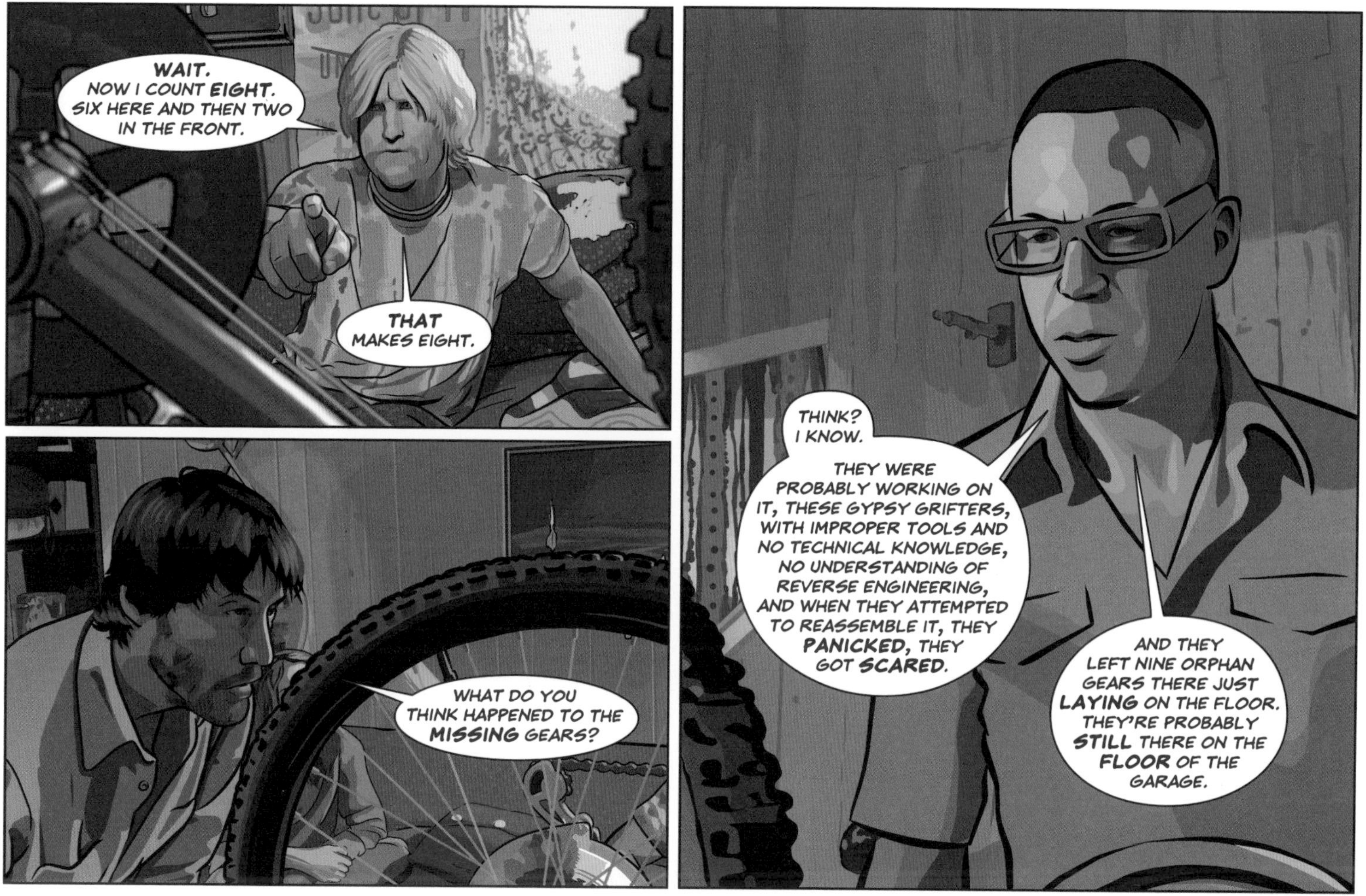
WAIT. NOW I COUNT EIGHT. SIX HERE AND THEN TWO IN THE FRONT.
THAT MAKES EIGHT.
WHAT DO YOU THINK HAPPENED TO THE MISSING GEARS?
THINK? I KNOW.
THEY WERE PROBABLY WORKING ON IT, THESE GYPSY GRIFTERS, WITH IMPROPER TOOLS AND NO TECHNICAL KNOWLEDGE, NO UNDERSTANDING OF REVERSE ENGINEERING, AND WHEN THEY ATTEMPTED TO REASSEMBLE IT, THEY PANICKED, THEY GOT SCARED.
AND THEY LEFT NINE ORPHAN GEARS THERE JUST LAYING ON THE FLOOR. THEY'RE PROBABLY STILL THERE ON THE FLOOR OF THE GARAGE.

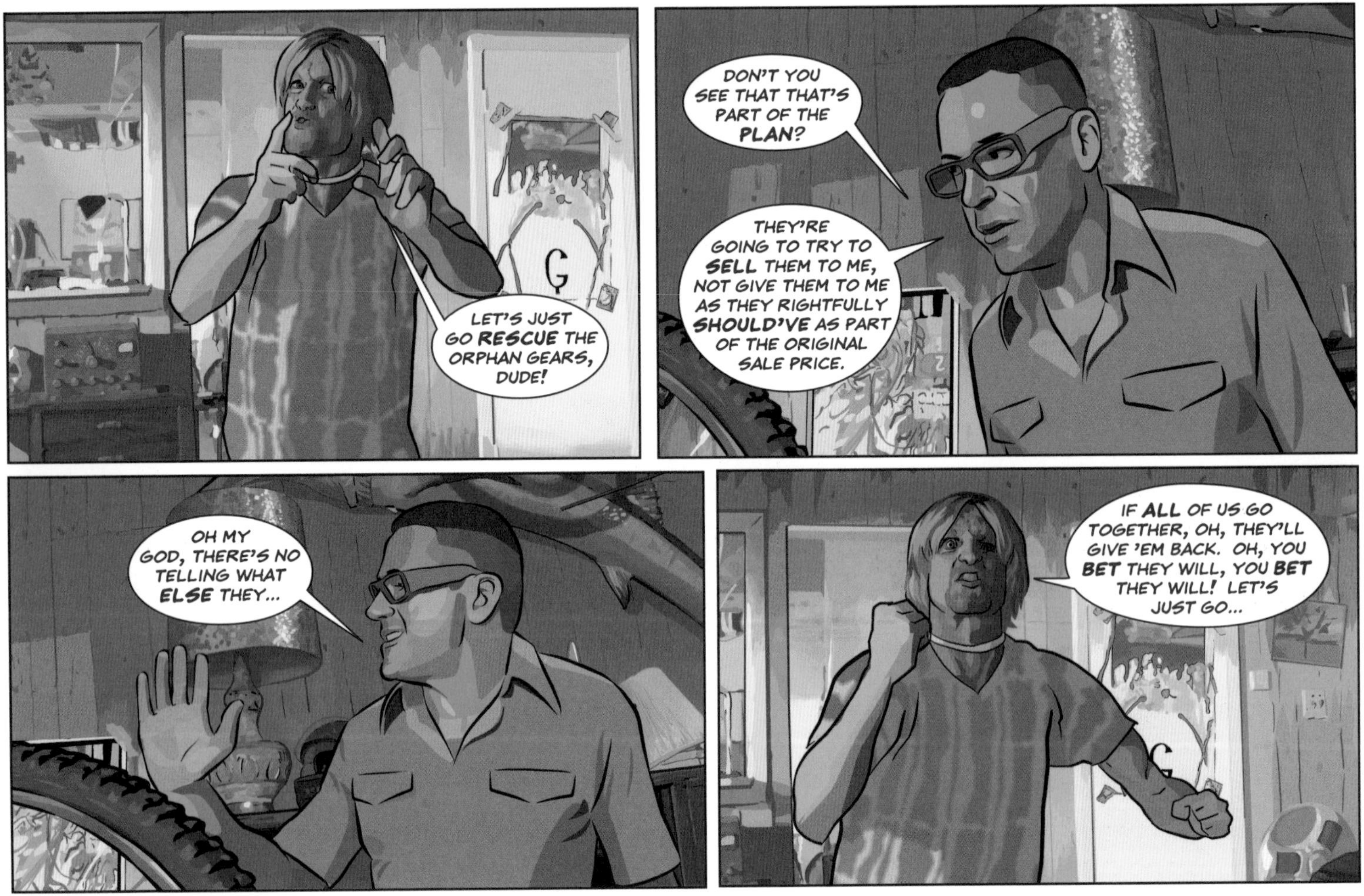
LET'S JUST GO RESCUE THE ORPHAN GEARS, DUDE!
DON'T YOU SEE THAT THAT'S PART OF THE PLAN?
THEY'RE GOING TO TRY TO SELL THEM TO ME, NOT GIVE THEM TO ME AS THEY RIGHTFULLY SHOULD'VE AS PART OF THE ORIGINAL SALE PRICE.
OH MY GOD, THERE'S NO TELLING WHAT ELSE THEY...
IF ALL OF US GO TOGETHER, OH, THEY'LL GIVE 'EM BACK. OH, YOU BET THEY WILL, YOU BET THEY WILL! LET'S JUST GO...

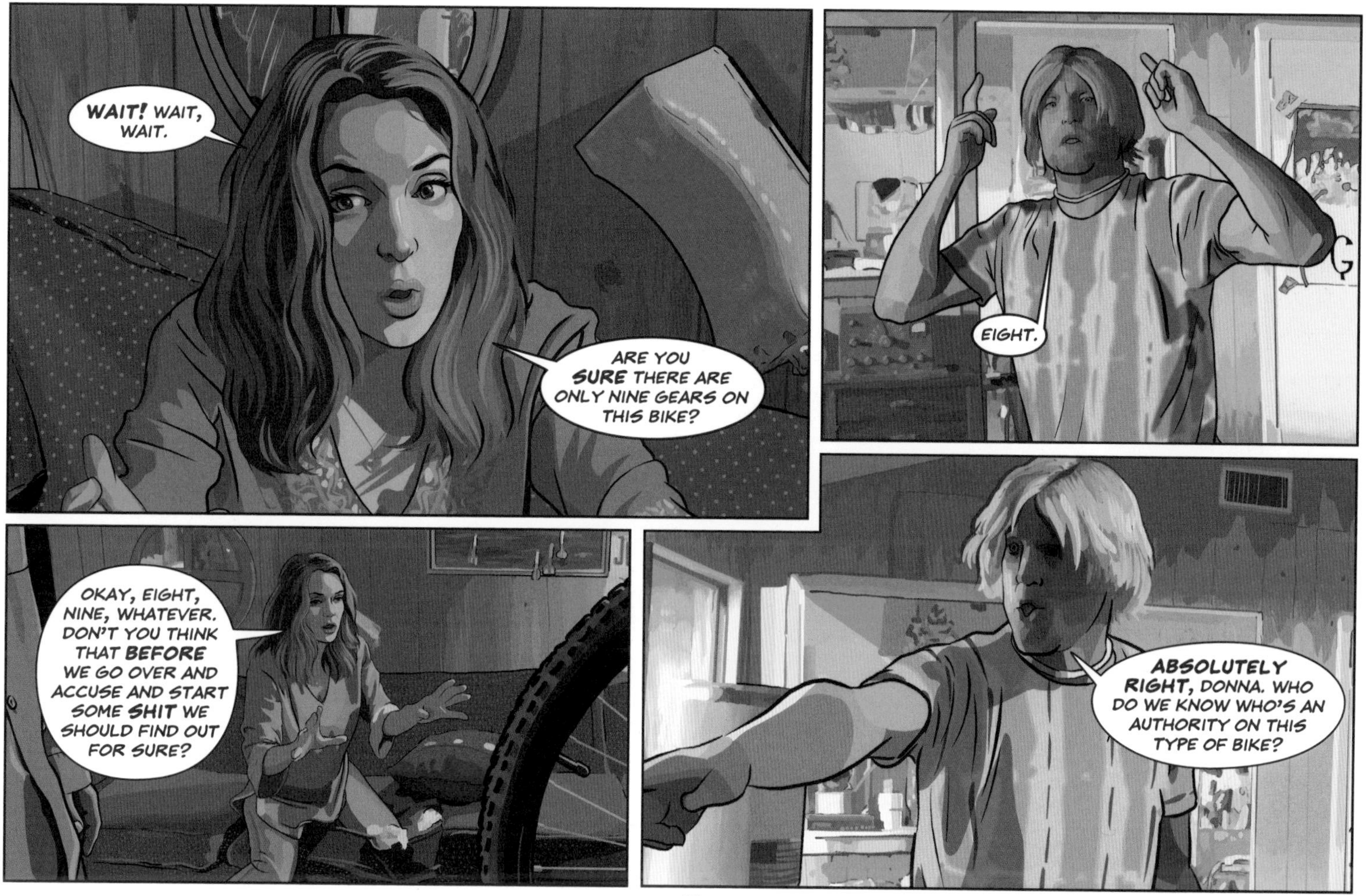
WAIT! WAIT, WAIT.
ARE YOU SURE THERE ARE ONLY NINE GEARS ON THIS BIKE?
EIGHT.
OKAY, EIGHT, NINE, WHATEVER. DON'T YOU THINK THAT BEFORE WE GO OVER AND ACCUSE AND START SOME SHIT WE SHOULD FIND OUT FOR SURE?
ABSOLUTELY RIGHT, DONNA. WHO DO WE KNOW WHO'S AN AUTHORITY ON THIS TYPE OF BIKE?

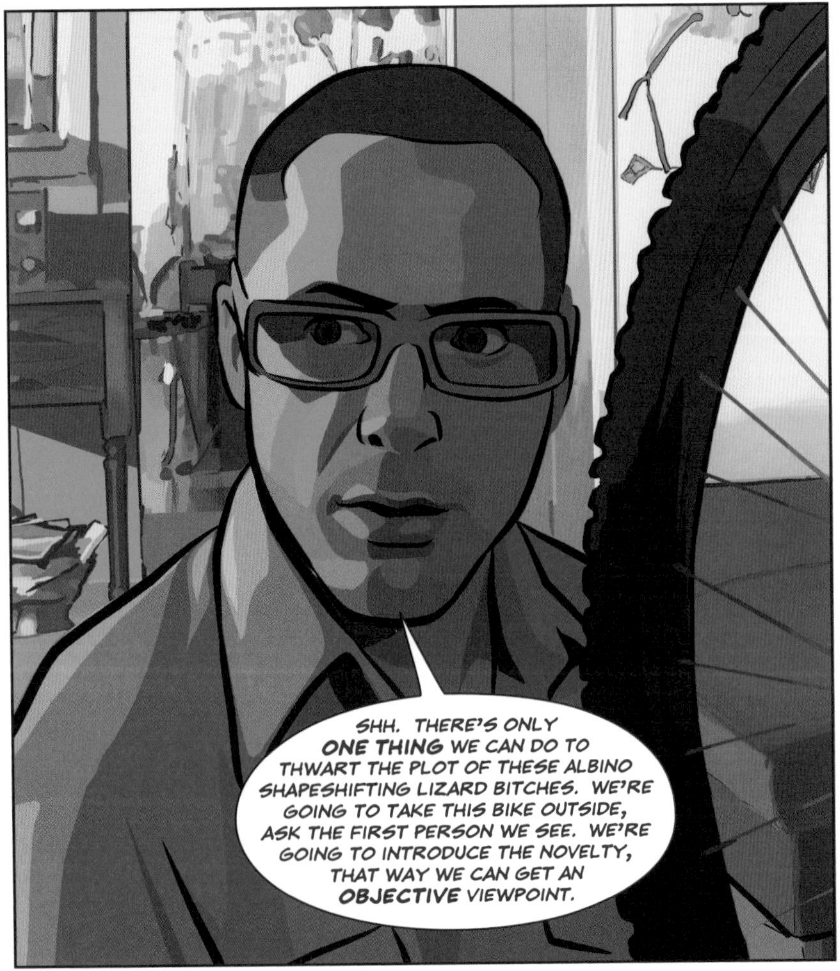
SHH. THERE'S ONLY ONE THING WE CAN DO TO THWART THE PLOT OF THESE ALBINO SHAPESHIFTING LIZARD BITCHES. WE'RE GOING TO TAKE THIS BIKE OUTSIDE, ASK THE FIRST PERSON WE SEE. WE'RE GOING TO INTRODUCE THE NOVELTY, THAT WAY WE CAN GET AN OBJECTIVE VIEWPOINT.

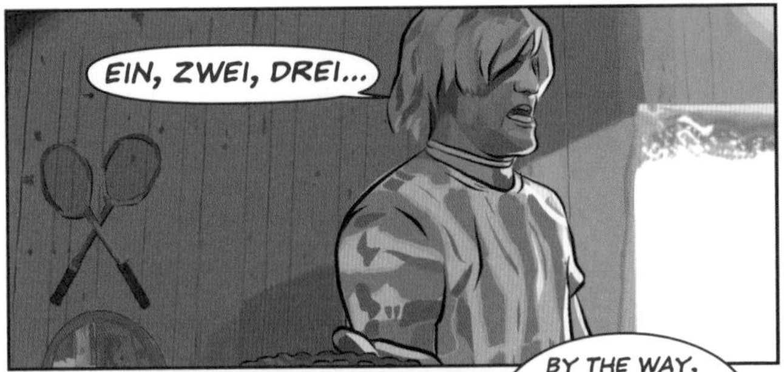
EIN, ZWEI, DREI...

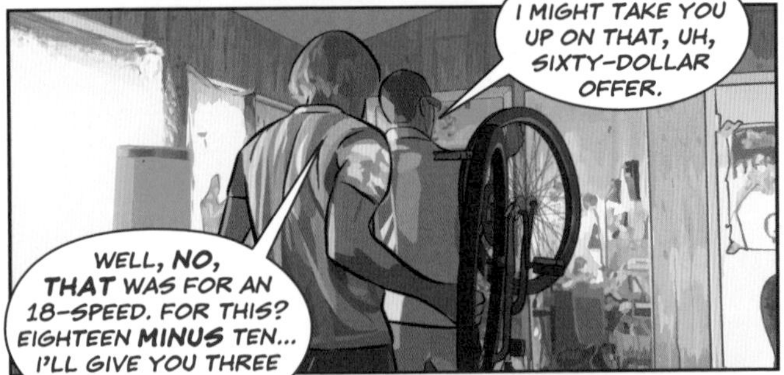
BY THE WAY, I MIGHT TAKE YOU UP ON THAT, UH, SIXTY-DOLLAR OFFER.
WELL, NO, THAT WAS FOR AN 18-SPEED. FOR THIS? EIGHTEEN MINUS TEN... I'LL GIVE YOU THREE SEVENTY-FIVE.

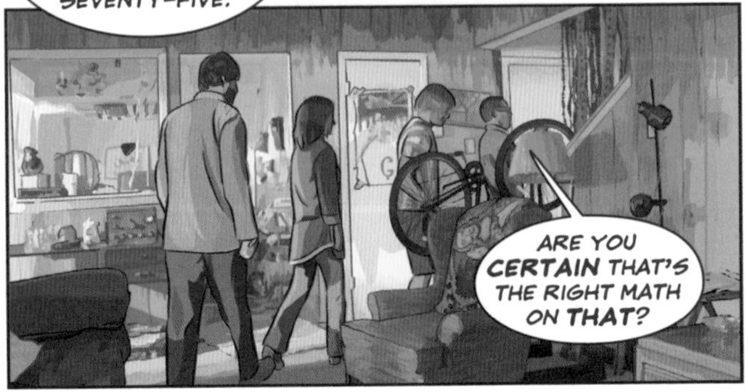
ARE YOU CERTAIN THAT'S THE RIGHT MATH ON THAT?

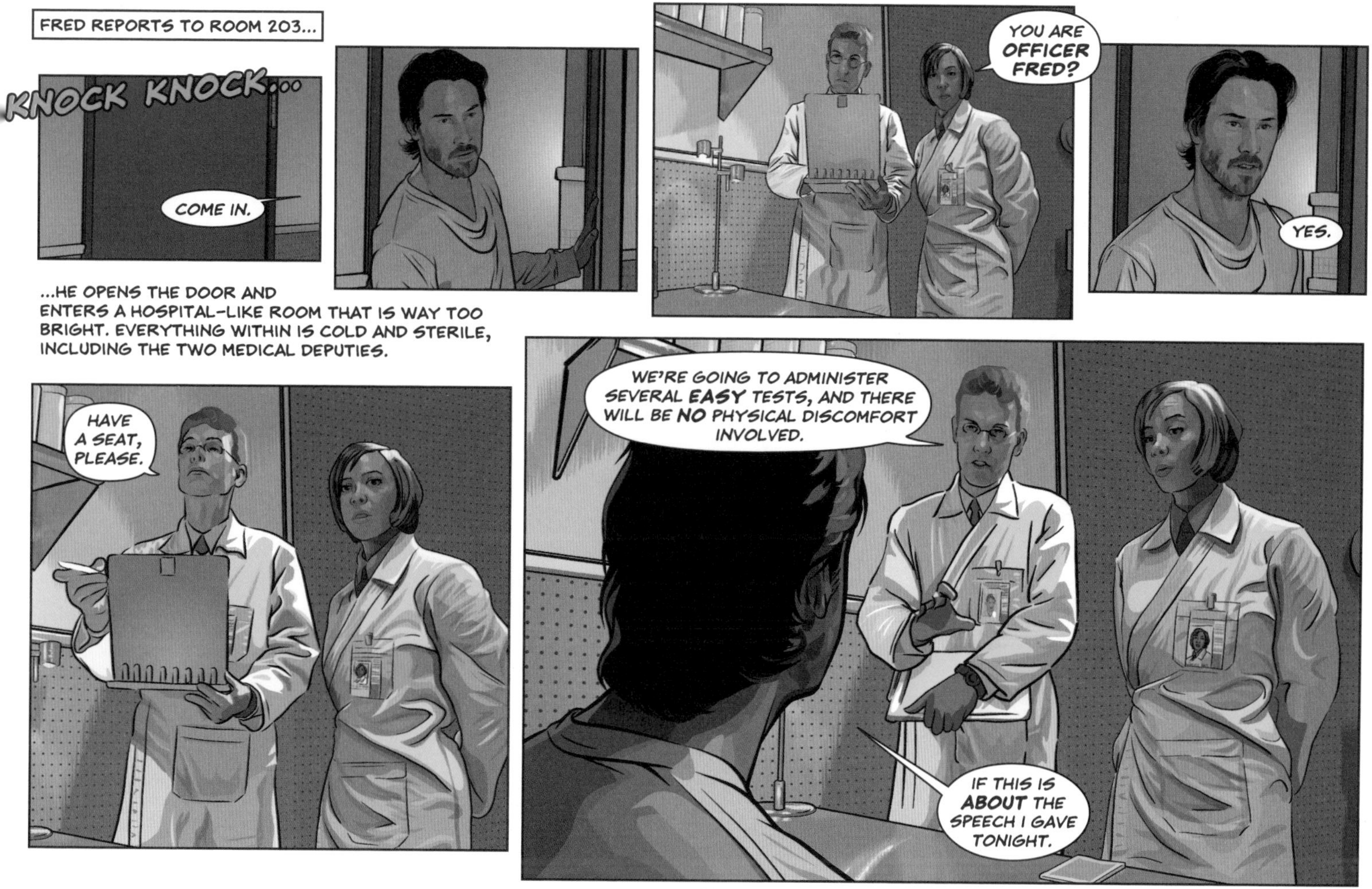
FRED REPORTS TO ROOM 203...
KNOCK KNOCK...
COME IN.
...HE OPENS THE DOOR AND ENTERS A HOSPITAL-LIKE ROOM THAT IS WAY TOO BRIGHT. EVERYTHING WITHIN IS COLD AND STERILE, INCLUDING THE TWO MEDICAL DEPUTIES.
YOU ARE OFFICER FRED?
YES.
HAVE A SEAT, PLEASE.
WE'RE GOING TO ADMINISTER SEVERAL EASY TESTS, AND THERE WILL BE NO PHYSICAL DISCOMFORT INVOLVED.
IF THIS IS ABOUT THE SPEECH I GAVE TONIGHT.

WHAT THIS IS **ABOUT** STEMS FROM A RECENT DEPARTMENTAL SURVEY SHOWING THAT SEVERAL UNDERCOVER AGENTS HAVE BEEN **ADMITTED** TO NEURAL APHASIC CLINICS DURING THE LAST MONTH.

YOU'RE **CONSCIOUS** OF THE HIGH FACTOR OF ADDICTIVENESS OF **SUBSTANCE D.**

OF COURSE I AM.

LET'S **START** WITH THE SET-GROUND TEST FIRST.

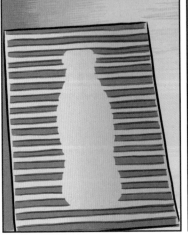

WITHIN THE **APPARENTLY** MEANINGLESS LINES IS AN OBJECT THAT WE WOULD **ALL** RECOGNIZE. YOU'RE TO TELL ME WHAT THAT OBJECT **IS** AND **POINT** TO IT IN THE TOTAL FIELD.

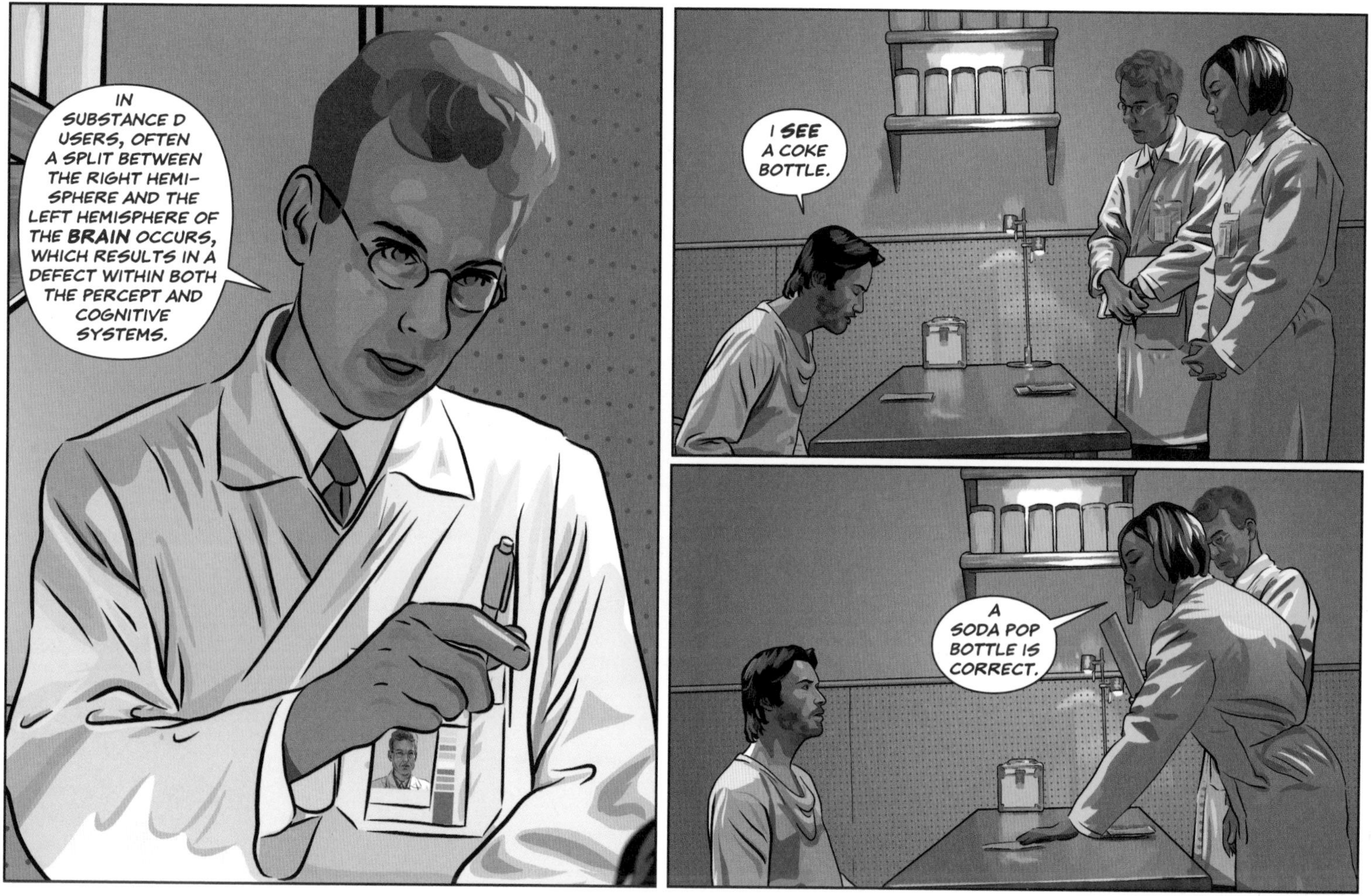
IN SUBSTANCE D USERS, OFTEN A SPLIT BETWEEN THE RIGHT HEMI- SPHERE AND THE LEFT HEMISPHERE OF THE **BRAIN** OCCURS, WHICH RESULTS IN A DEFECT WITHIN BOTH THE PERCEPT AND COGNITIVE SYSTEMS.
I **SEE** A COKE BOTTLE.
A SODA POP BOTTLE IS CORRECT.

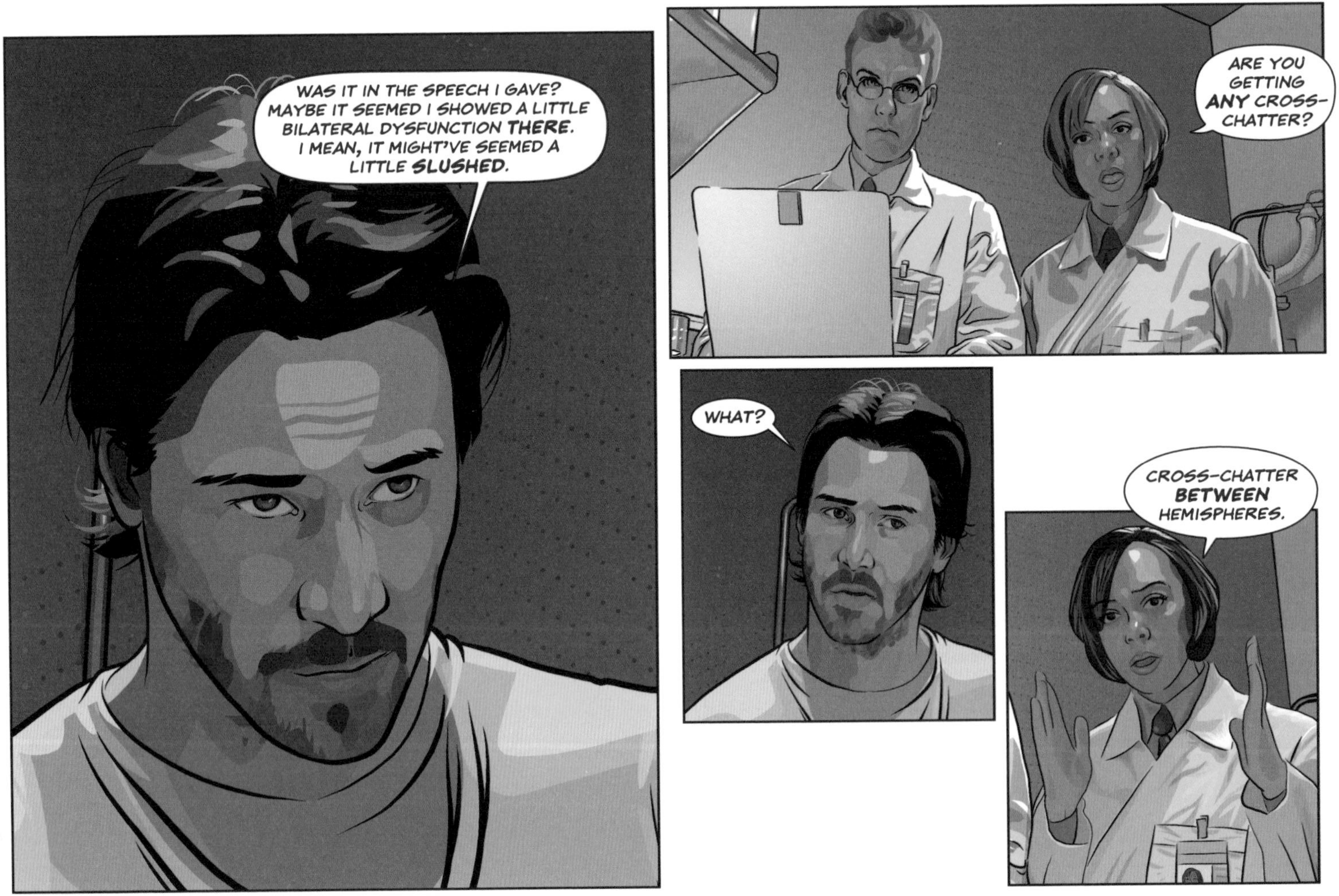
WAS IT IN THE SPEECH I GAVE? MAYBE IT SEEMED I SHOWED A LITTLE BILATERAL DYSFUNCTION THERE. I MEAN, IT MIGHT'VE SEEMED A LITTLE SLUSHED.
ARE YOU GETTING ANY CROSS-CHATTER?
WHAT?
CROSS-CHATTER BETWEEN HEMISPHERES.

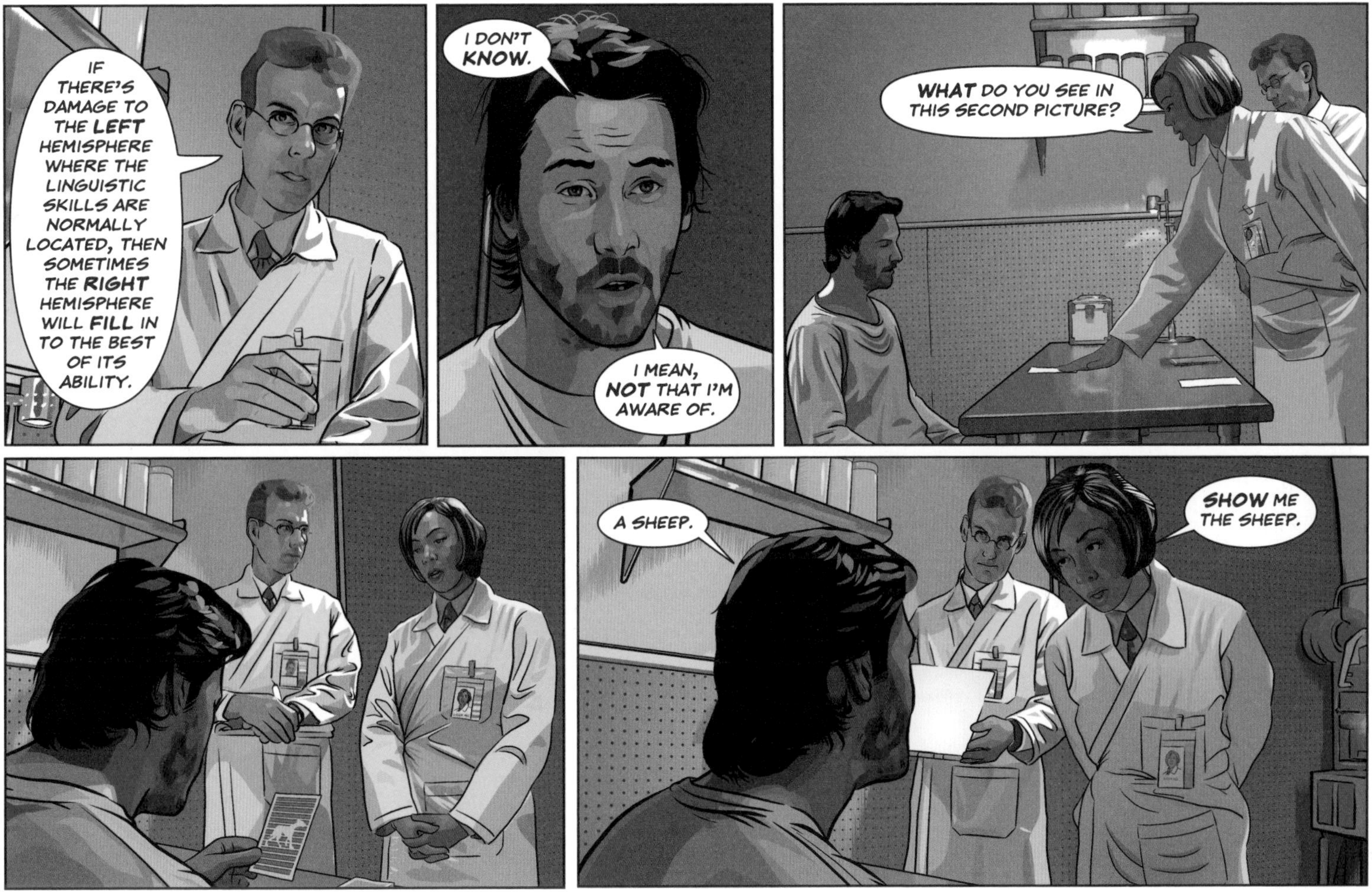

IF THERE'S DAMAGE TO THE LEFT HEMISPHERE WHERE THE LINGUISTIC SKILLS ARE NORMALLY LOCATED, THEN SOMETIMES THE RIGHT HEMISPHERE WILL FILL IN TO THE BEST OF ITS ABILITY.
I DON'T KNOW.
I MEAN, NOT THAT I'M AWARE OF.
WHAT DO YOU SEE IN THIS SECOND PICTURE?
A SHEEP.
SHOW ME THE SHEEP.

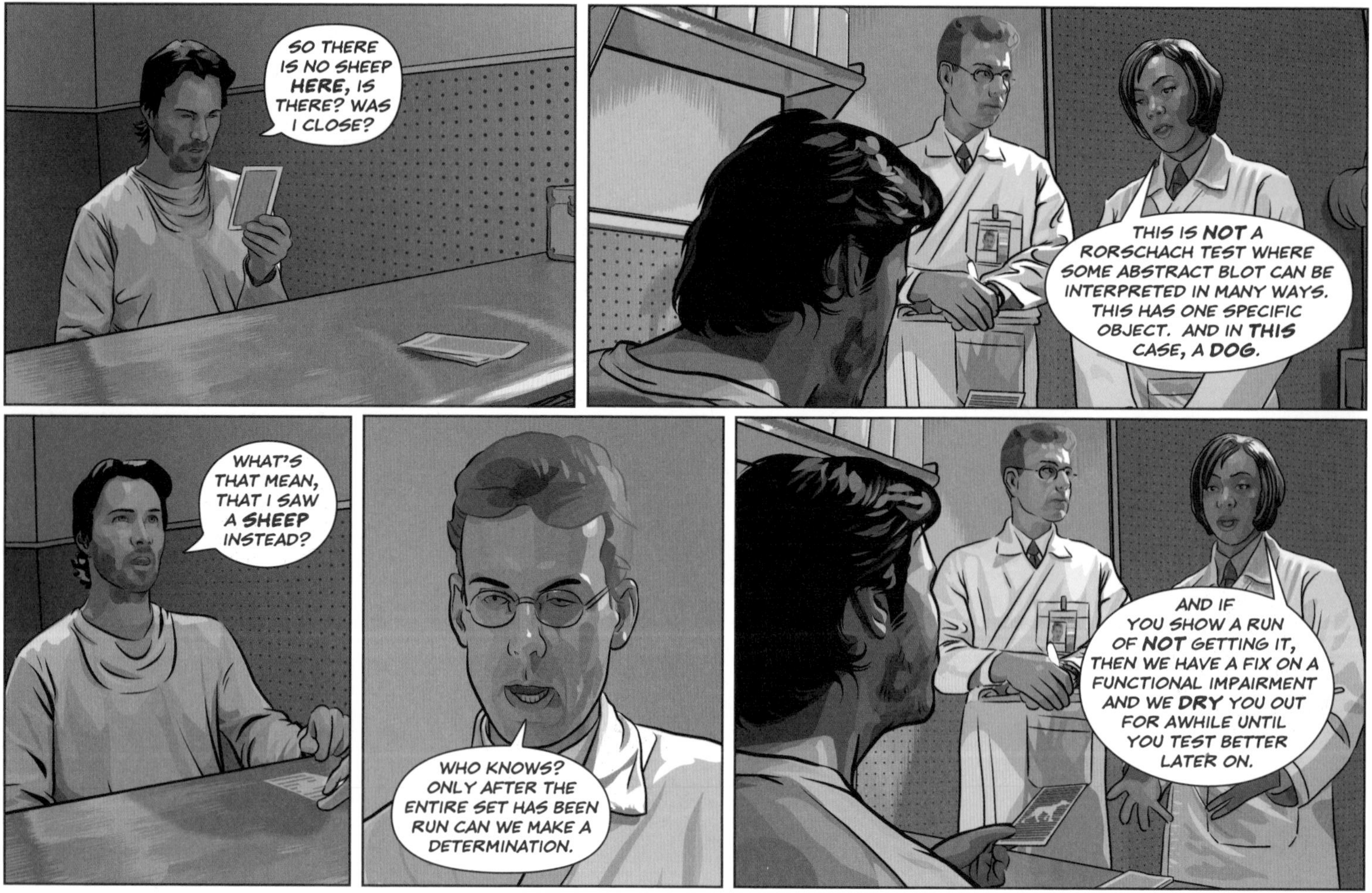
SO THERE IS NO SHEEP HERE, IS THERE? WAS I CLOSE?
THIS IS NOT A RORSCHACH TEST WHERE SOME ABSTRACT BLOT CAN BE INTERPRETED IN MANY WAYS. THIS HAS ONE SPECIFIC OBJECT. AND IN THIS CASE, A DOG.
WHAT'S THAT MEAN, THAT I SAW A SHEEP INSTEAD?
WHO KNOWS? ONLY AFTER THE ENTIRE SET HAS BEEN RUN CAN WE MAKE A DETERMINATION.
AND IF YOU SHOW A RUN OF NOT GETTING IT, THEN WE HAVE A FIX ON A FUNCTIONAL IMPAIRMENT AND WE DRY YOU OUT FOR AWHILE UNTIL YOU TEST BETTER LATER ON.

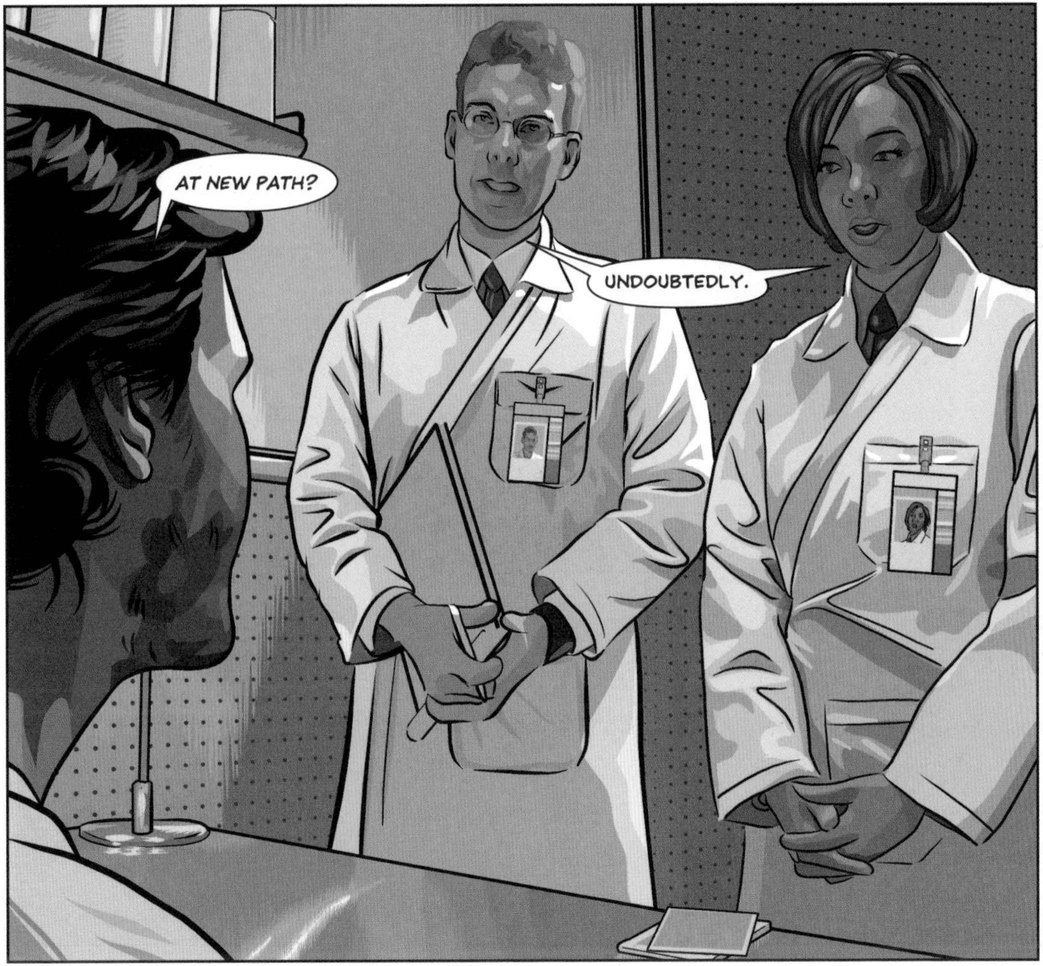
AT NEW PATH?
UNDOUBTEDLY.

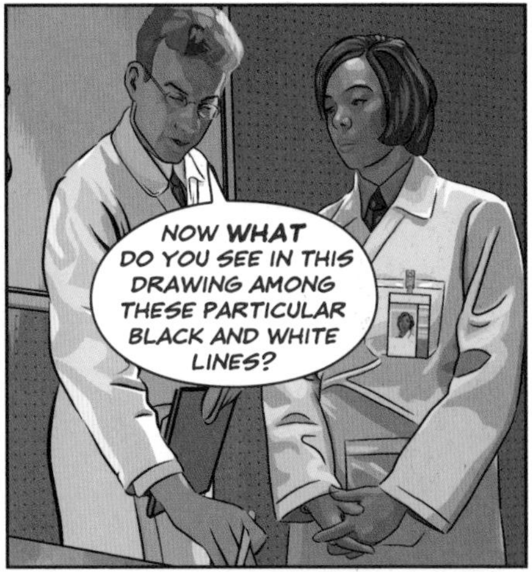
NOW **WHAT** DO YOU SEE IN THIS DRAWING AMONG THESE PARTICULAR BLACK AND WHITE LINES?

FRED'S IRRITATION THREATENS TO ERUPT AS HE GLARES AT A PICTURE OF A PYRAMID ON THE CARD...

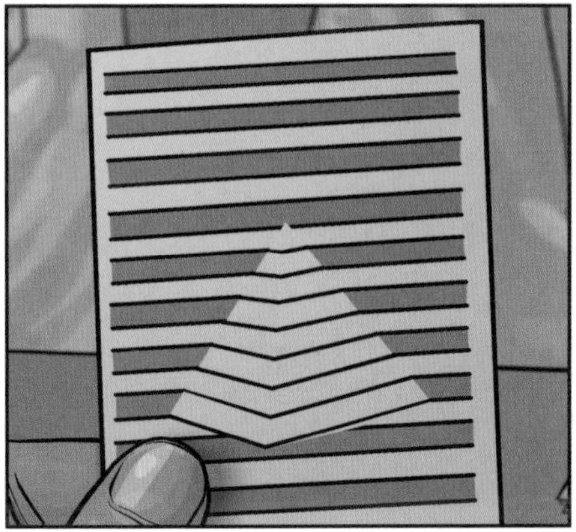

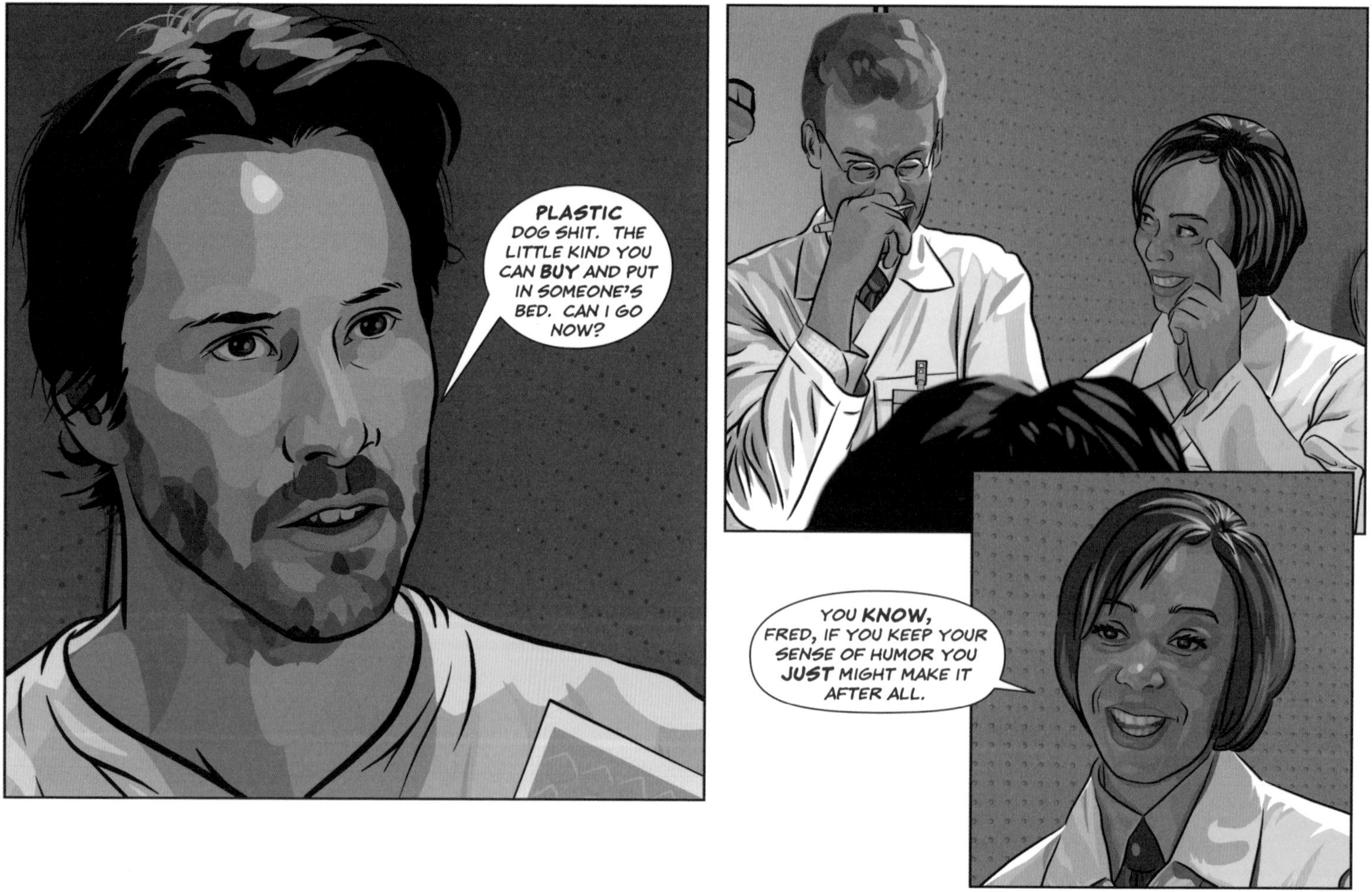
PLASTIC DOG SHIT. THE LITTLE KIND YOU CAN BUY AND PUT IN SOMEONE'S BED. CAN I GO NOW?
YOU KNOW, FRED, IF YOU KEEP YOUR SENSE OF HUMOR YOU JUST MIGHT MAKE IT AFTER ALL.

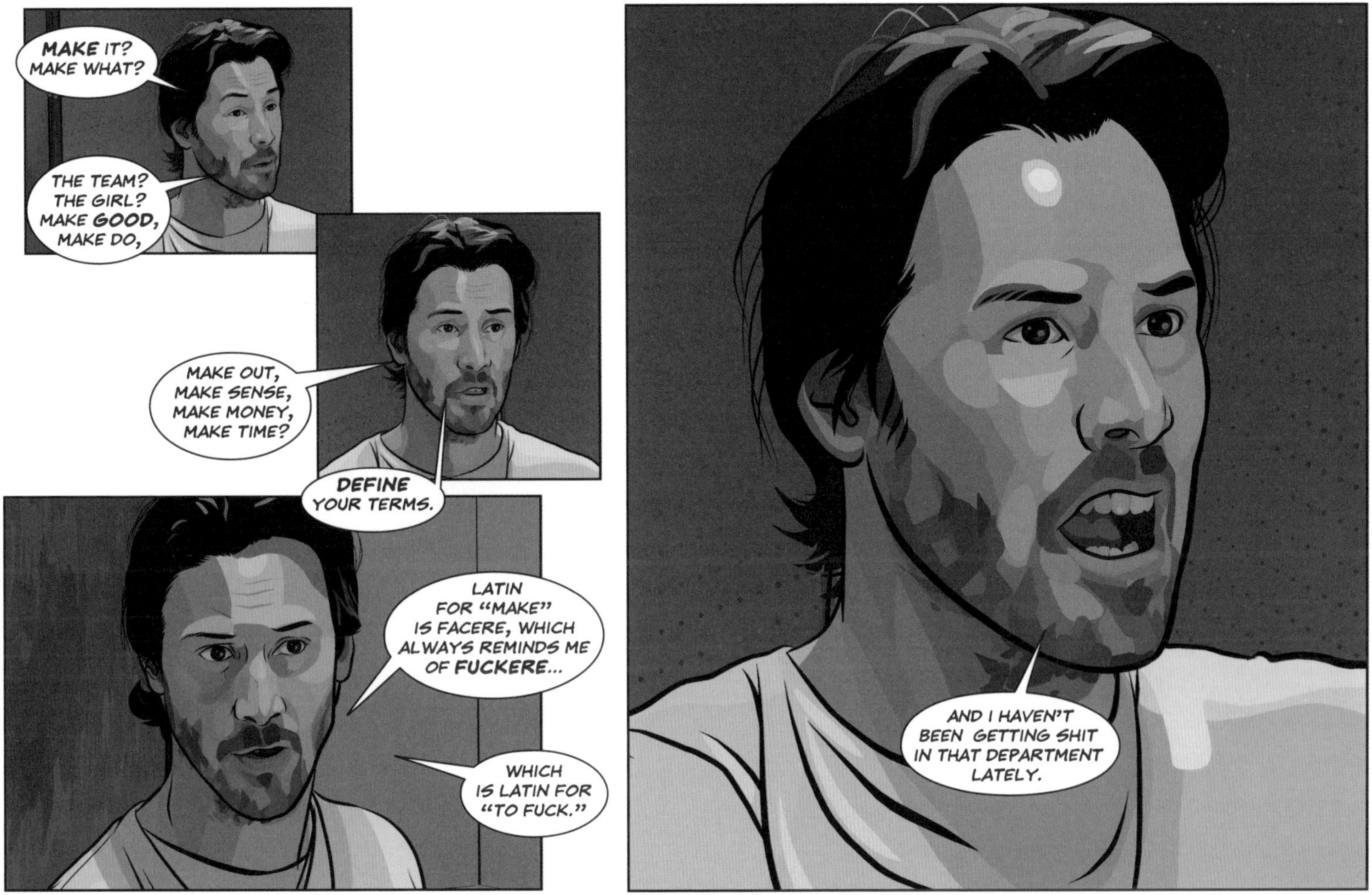
MAKE IT? MAKE WHAT?
THE TEAM? THE GIRL? MAKE GOOD, MAKE DO,
MAKE OUT, MAKE SENSE, MAKE MONEY, MAKE TIME?
DEFINE YOUR TERMS.
LATIN FOR "MAKE" IS FACERE, WHICH ALWAYS REMINDS ME OF FUCKERE...
WHICH IS LATIN FOR "TO FUCK."
AND I HAVEN'T BEEN GETTING SHIT IN THAT DEPARTMENT LATELY.

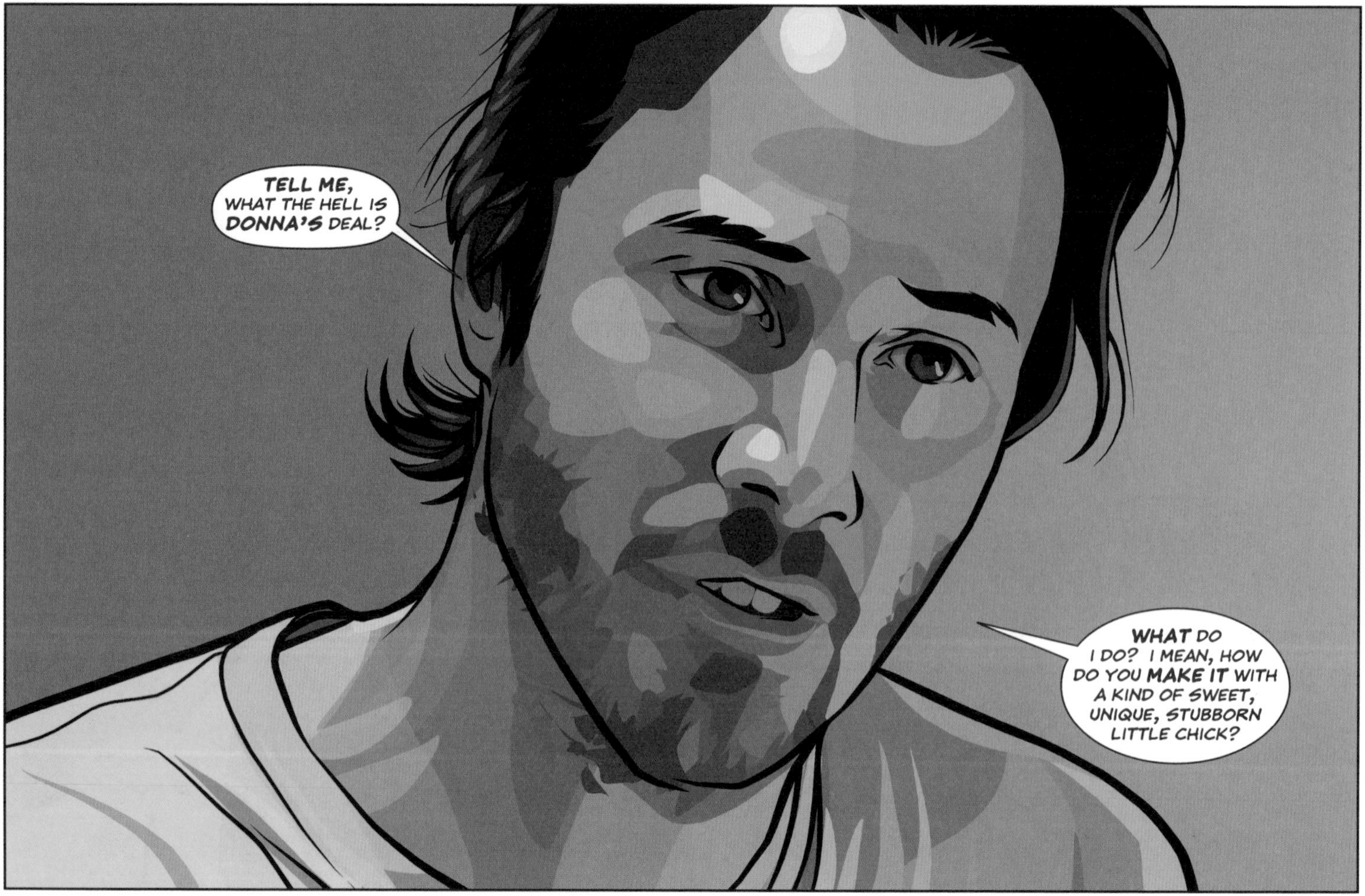
TELL ME, WHAT THE HELL IS DONNA'S DEAL?
WHAT DO I DO? I MEAN, HOW DO YOU MAKE IT WITH A KIND OF SWEET, UNIQUE, STUBBORN LITTLE CHICK?

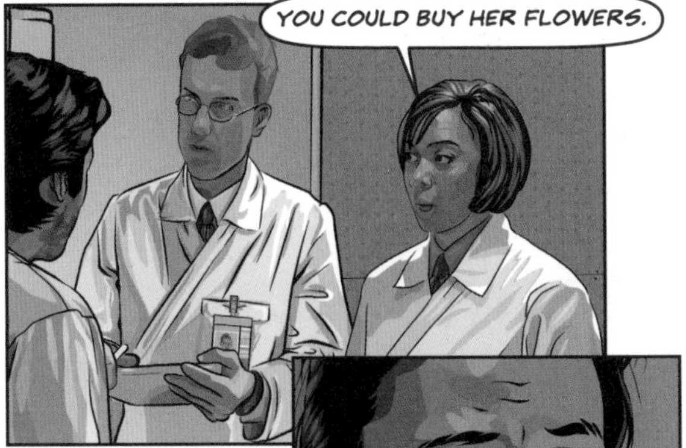
YOU COULD BUY HER FLOWERS.

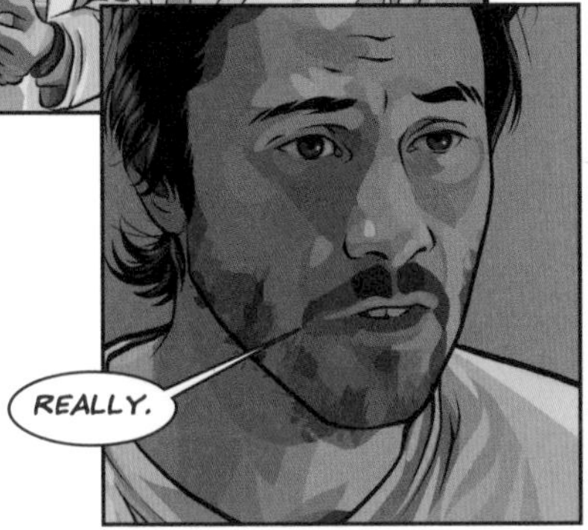
REALLY.

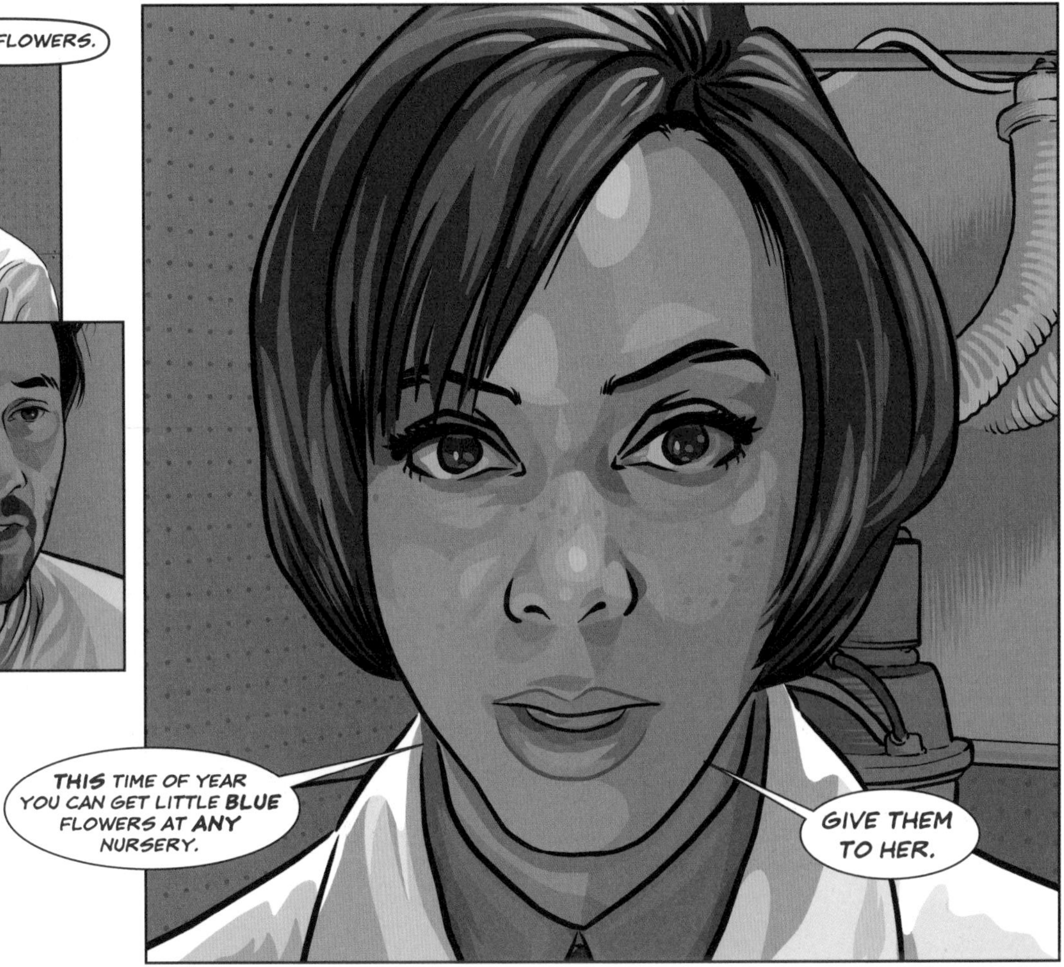
THIS TIME OF YEAR YOU CAN GET LITTLE BLUE FLOWERS AT ANY NURSERY.
GIVE THEM TO HER.

HANK'S OFFICE...

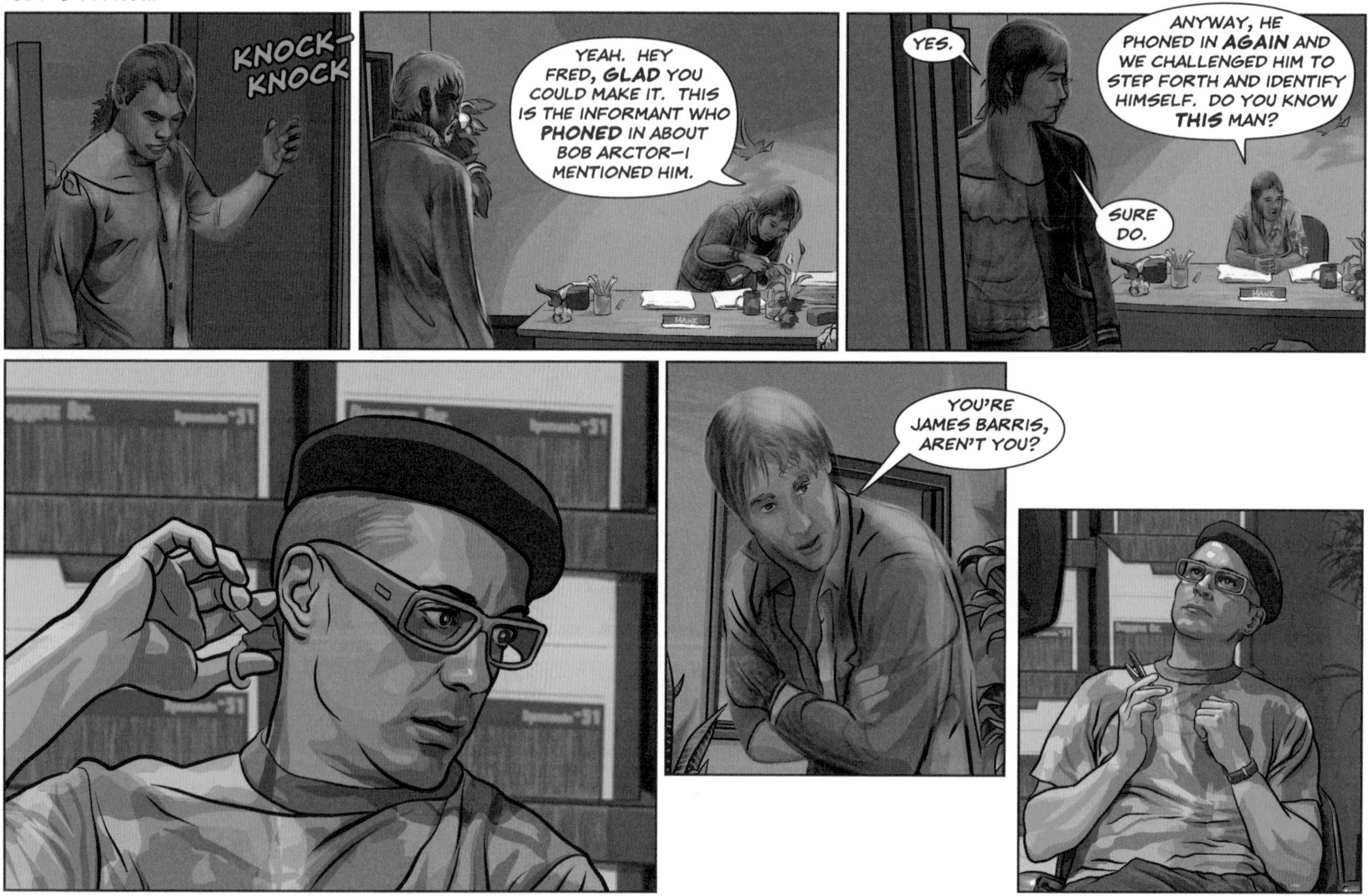

KNOCK-KNOCK
YEAH. HEY FRED, GLAD YOU COULD MAKE IT. THIS IS THE INFORMANT WHO PHONED IN ABOUT BOB ARCTOR—I MENTIONED HIM.
YES.
ANYWAY, HE PHONED IN AGAIN AND WE CHALLENGED HIM TO STEP FORTH AND IDENTIFY HIMSELF. DO YOU KNOW THIS MAN?
SURE DO.
YOU'RE JAMES BARRIS, AREN'T YOU?

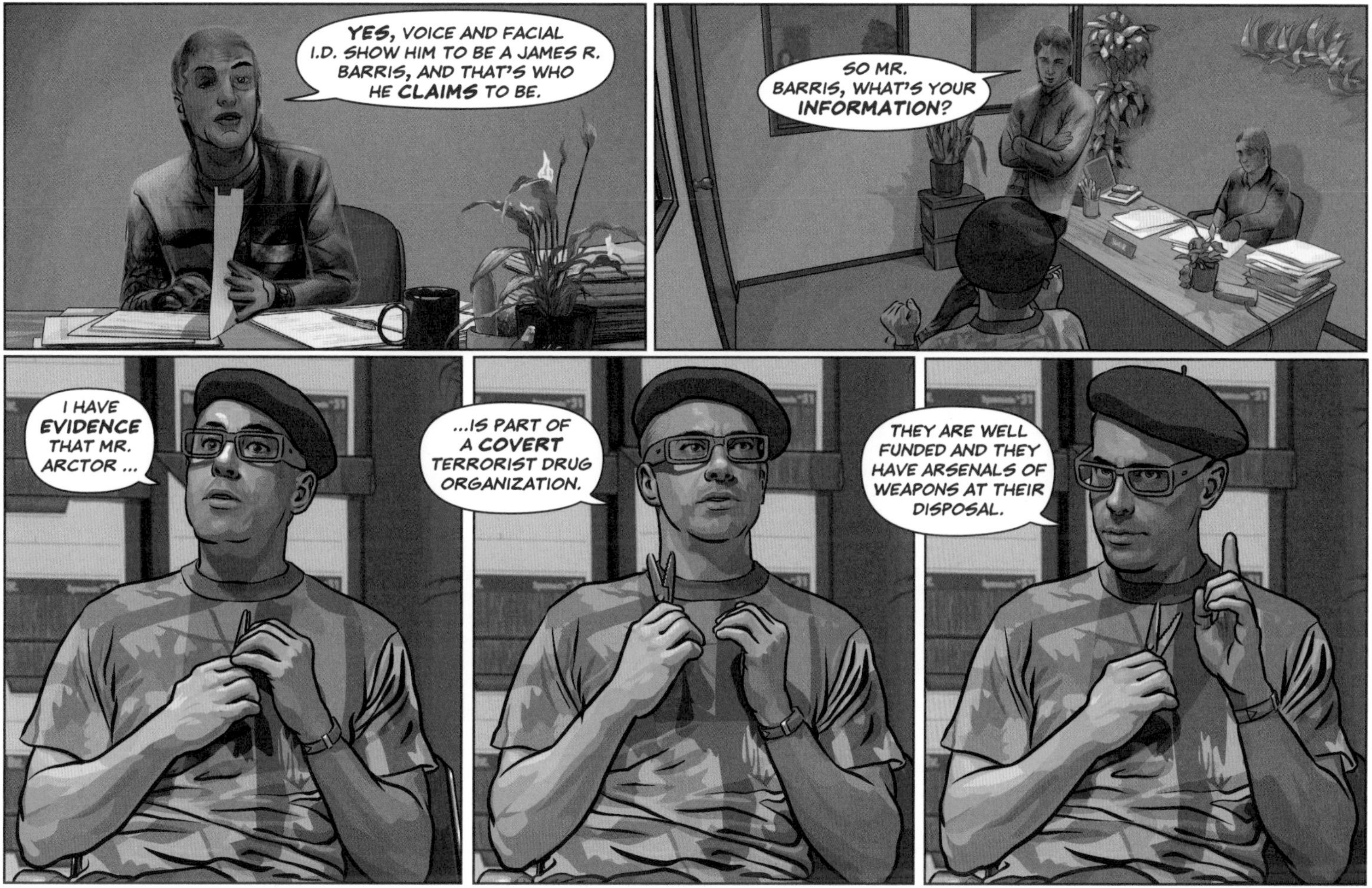
YES, VOICE AND FACIAL I.D. SHOW HIM TO BE A JAMES R. BARRIS, AND THAT'S WHO HE CLAIMS TO BE.
SO MR. BARRIS, WHAT'S YOUR INFORMATION?
I HAVE EVIDENCE THAT MR. ARCTOR ...
...IS PART OF A COVERT TERRORIST DRUG ORGANIZATION.
THEY ARE WELL FUNDED AND THEY HAVE ARSENALS OF WEAPONS AT THEIR DISPOSAL.

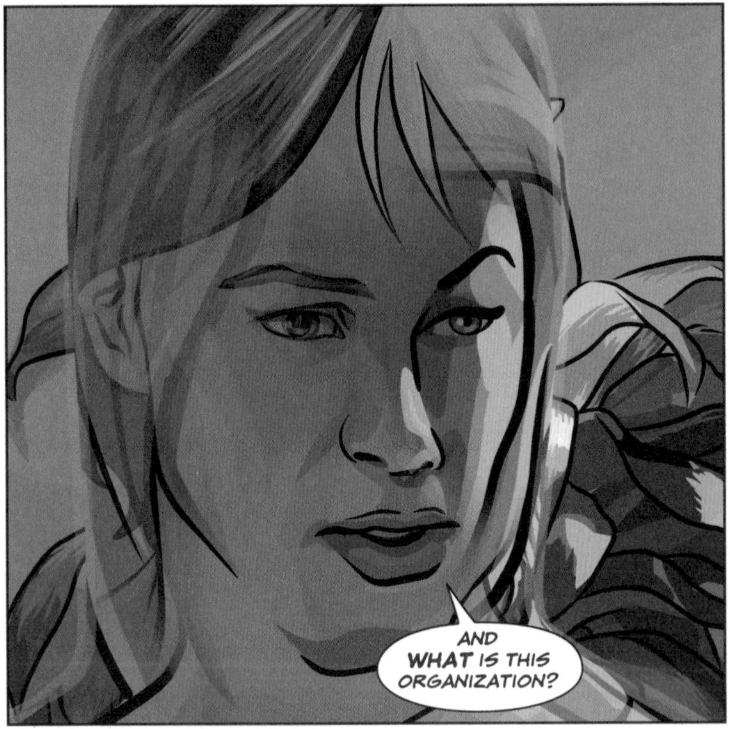
AND WHAT IS THIS ORGANIZATION?

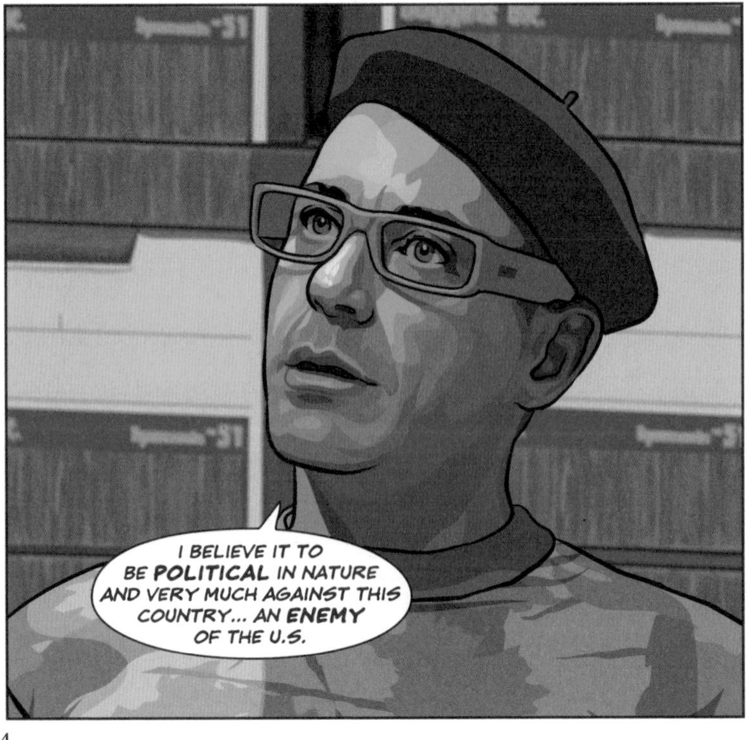
I BELIEVE IT TO BE POLITICAL IN NATURE AND VERY MUCH AGAINST THIS COUNTRY... AN ENEMY OF THE U.S.

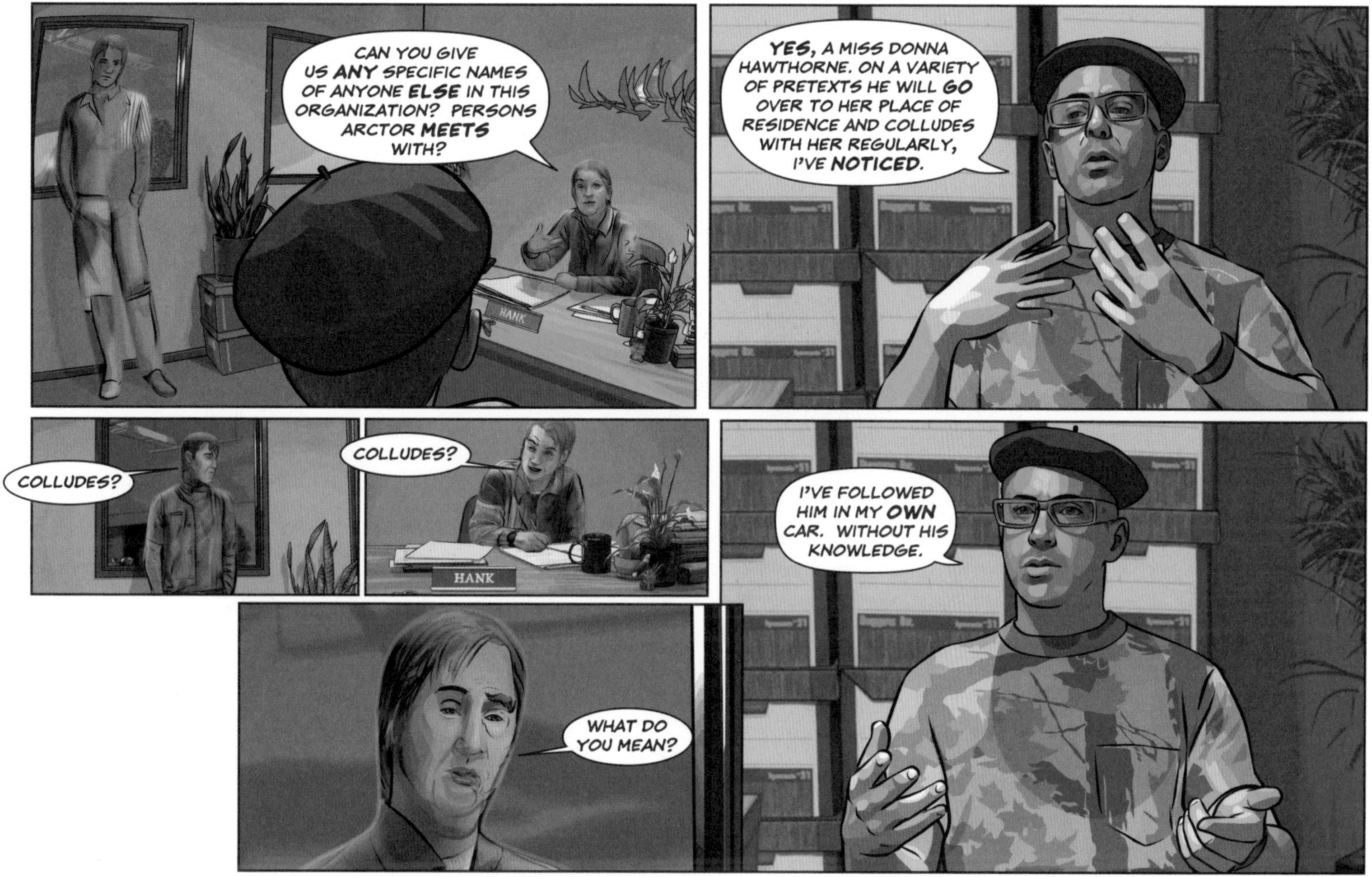
CAN YOU GIVE US ANY SPECIFIC NAMES OF ANYONE ELSE IN THIS ORGANIZATION? PERSONS ARCTOR MEETS WITH?
YES, A MISS DONNA HAWTHORNE. ON A VARIETY OF PRETEXTS HE WILL GO OVER TO HER PLACE OF RESIDENCE AND COLLUDES WITH HER REGULARLY, I'VE NOTICED.
COLLUDES?
COLLUDES?
HANK
WHAT DO YOU MEAN?
I'VE FOLLOWED HIM IN MY OWN CAR. WITHOUT HIS KNOWLEDGE.

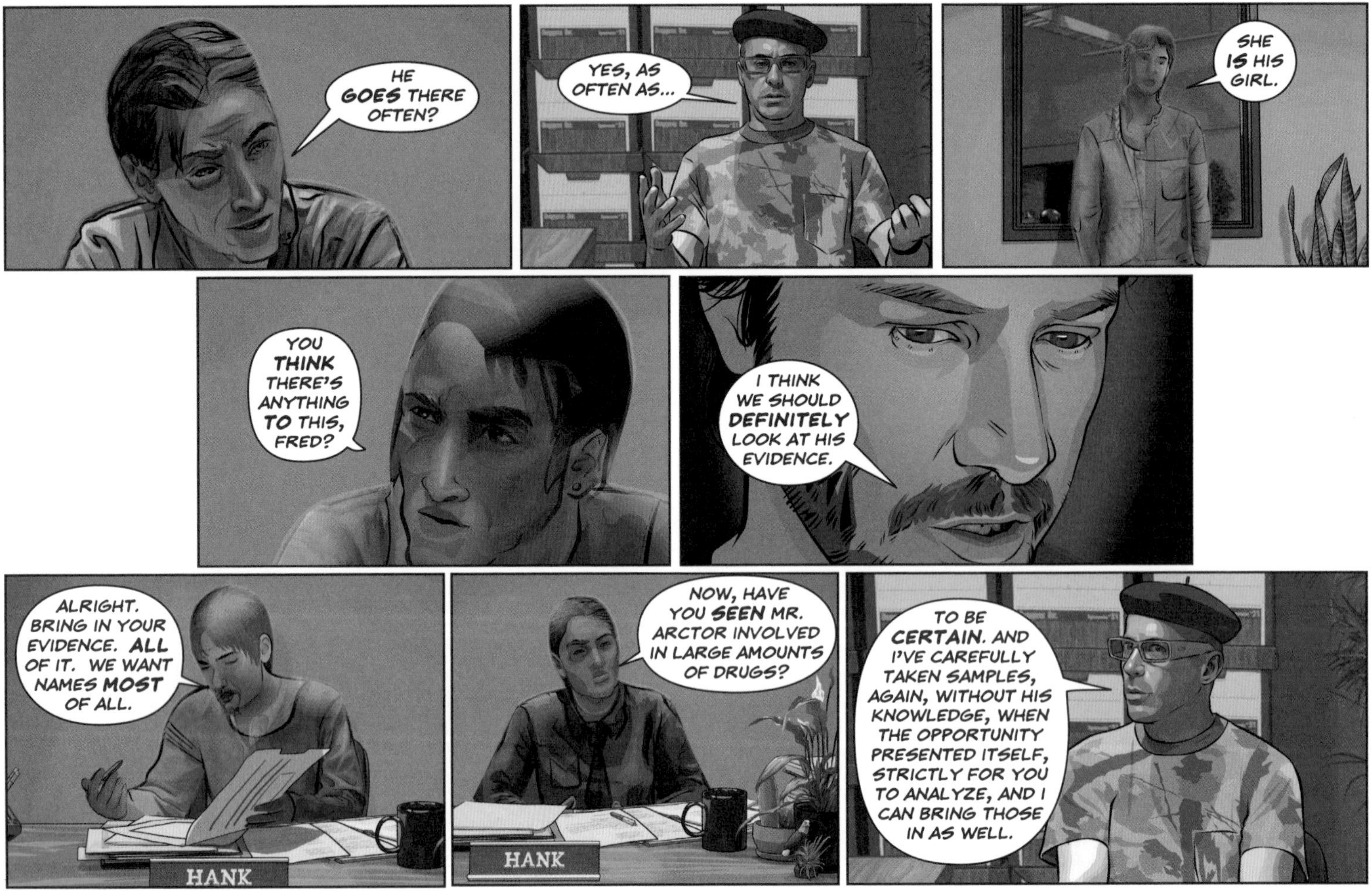
HE GOES THERE OFTEN?
YES, AS OFTEN AS...
SHE IS HIS GIRL.
YOU THINK THERE'S ANYTHING TO THIS, FRED?
I THINK WE SHOULD DEFINITELY LOOK AT HIS EVIDENCE.
ALRIGHT. BRING IN YOUR EVIDENCE. ALL OF IT. WE WANT NAMES MOST OF ALL.
HANK
NOW, HAVE YOU SEEN MR. ARCTOR INVOLVED IN LARGE AMOUNTS OF DRUGS?
HANK
TO BE CERTAIN. AND I'VE CAREFULLY TAKEN SAMPLES, AGAIN, WITHOUT HIS KNOWLEDGE, WHEN THE OPPORTUNITY PRESENTED ITSELF, STRICTLY FOR YOU TO ANALYZE, AND I CAN BRING THOSE IN AS WELL.

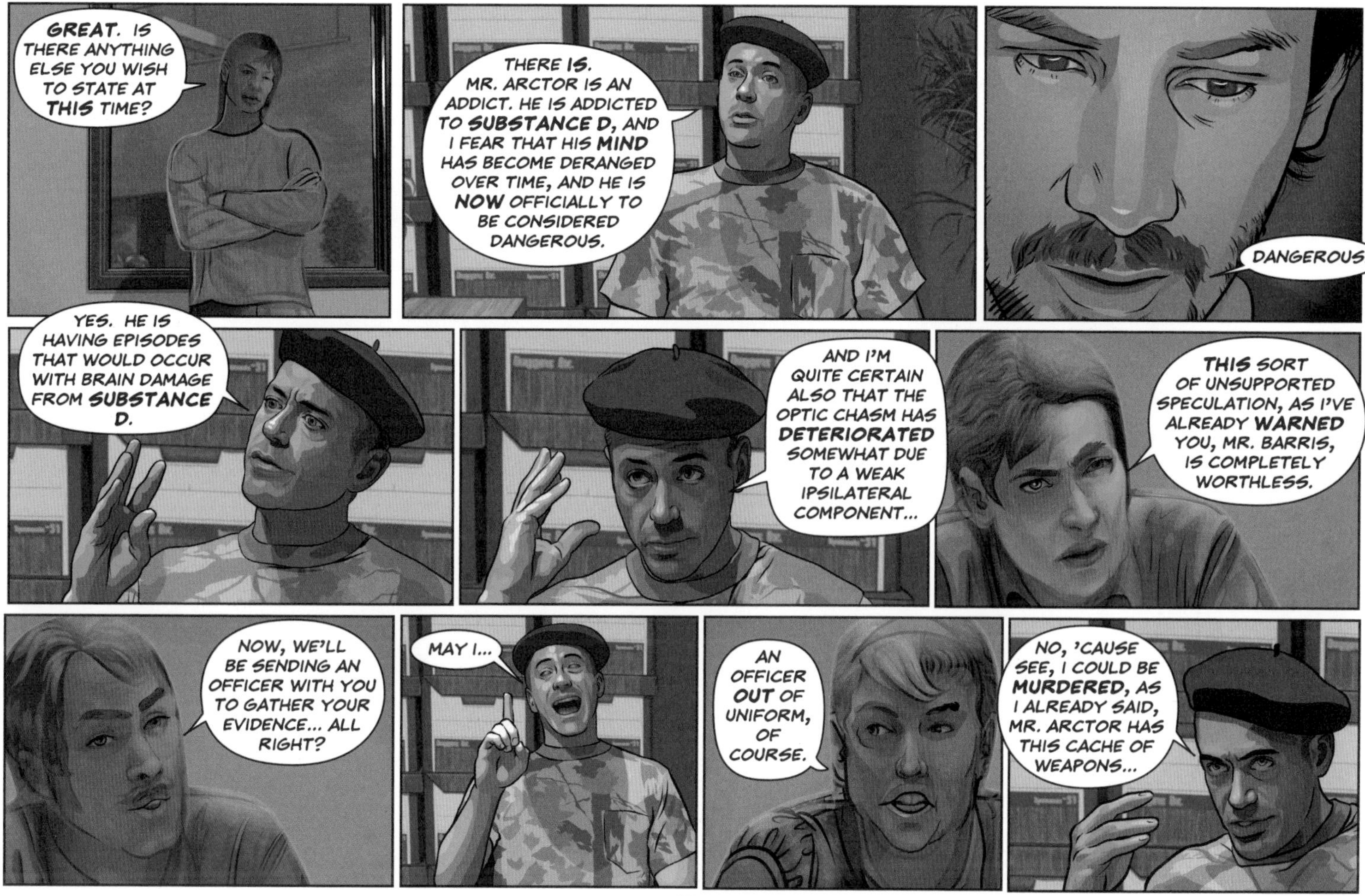
GREAT. IS THERE ANYTHING ELSE YOU WISH TO STATE AT THIS TIME?
THERE IS. MR. ARCTOR IS AN ADDICT. HE IS ADDICTED TO SUBSTANCE D, AND I FEAR THAT HIS MIND HAS BECOME DERANGED OVER TIME, AND HE IS NOW OFFICIALLY TO BE CONSIDERED DANGEROUS.
DANGEROUS.
YES. HE IS HAVING EPISODES THAT WOULD OCCUR WITH BRAIN DAMAGE FROM SUBSTANCE D.
AND I'M QUITE CERTAIN ALSO THAT THE OPTIC CHASM HAS DETERIORATED SOMEWHAT DUE TO A WEAK IPSILATERAL COMPONENT...
THIS SORT OF UNSUPPORTED SPECULATION, AS I'VE ALREADY WARNED YOU, MR. BARRIS, IS COMPLETELY WORTHLESS.
NOW, WE'LL BE SENDING AN OFFICER WITH YOU TO GATHER YOUR EVIDENCE... ALL RIGHT?
MAY I...
AN OFFICER OUT OF UNIFORM, OF COURSE.
NO, 'CAUSE SEE, I COULD BE MURDERED, AS I ALREADY SAID, MR. ARCTOR HAS THIS CACHE OF WEAPONS...

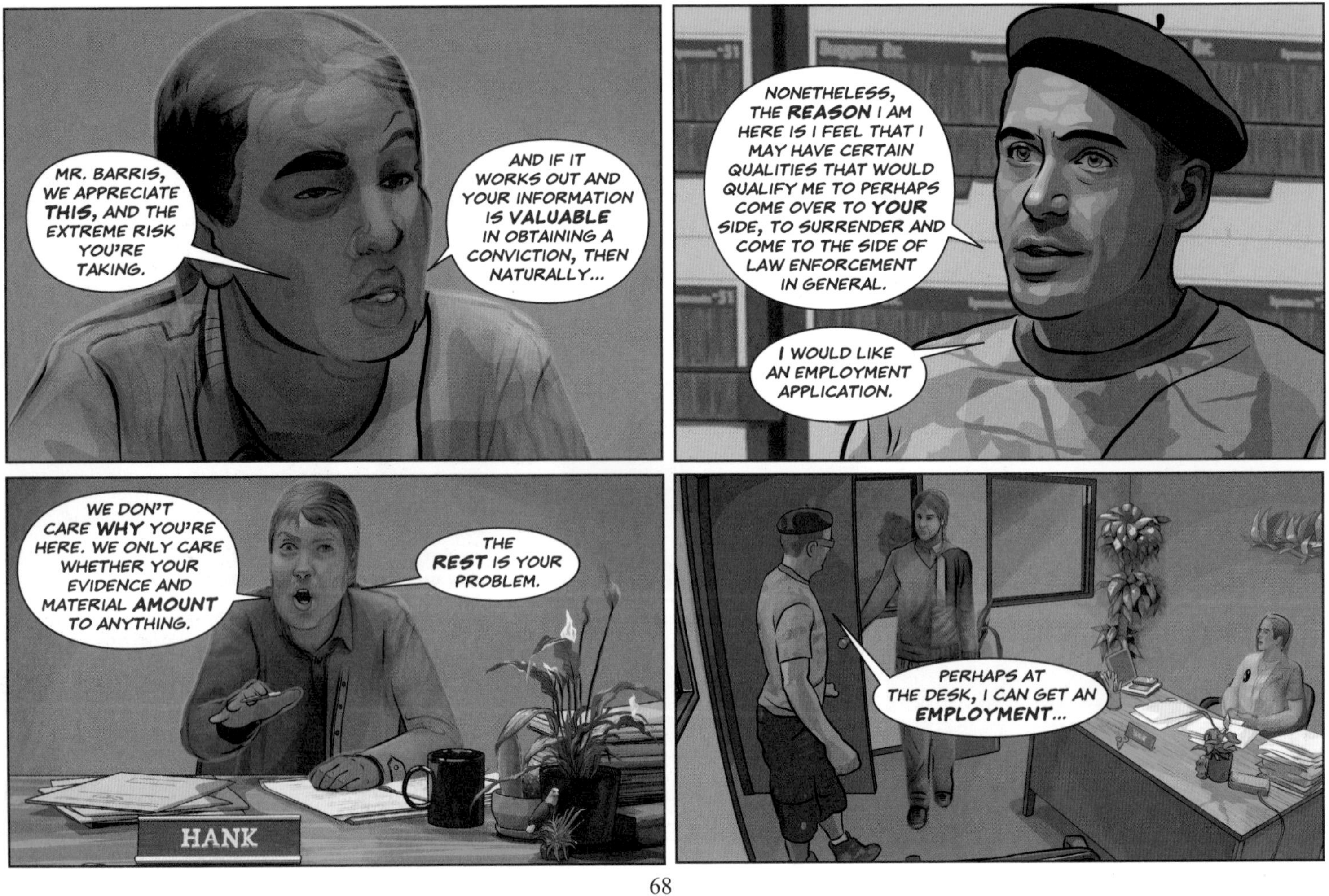
MR. BARRIS, WE APPRECIATE THIS, AND THE EXTREME RISK YOU'RE TAKING.
AND IF IT WORKS OUT AND YOUR INFORMATION IS VALUABLE IN OBTAINING A CONVICTION, THEN NATURALLY...
NONETHELESS, THE REASON I AM HERE IS I FEEL THAT I MAY HAVE CERTAIN QUALITIES THAT WOULD QUALIFY ME TO PERHAPS COME OVER TO YOUR SIDE, TO SURRENDER AND COME TO THE SIDE OF LAW ENFORCEMENT IN GENERAL.
I WOULD LIKE AN EMPLOYMENT APPLICATION.
WE DON'T CARE WHY YOU'RE HERE. WE ONLY CARE WHETHER YOUR EVIDENCE AND MATERIAL AMOUNT TO ANYTHING.
THE REST IS YOUR PROBLEM.
HANK
PERHAPS AT THE DESK, I CAN GET AN EMPLOYMENT...

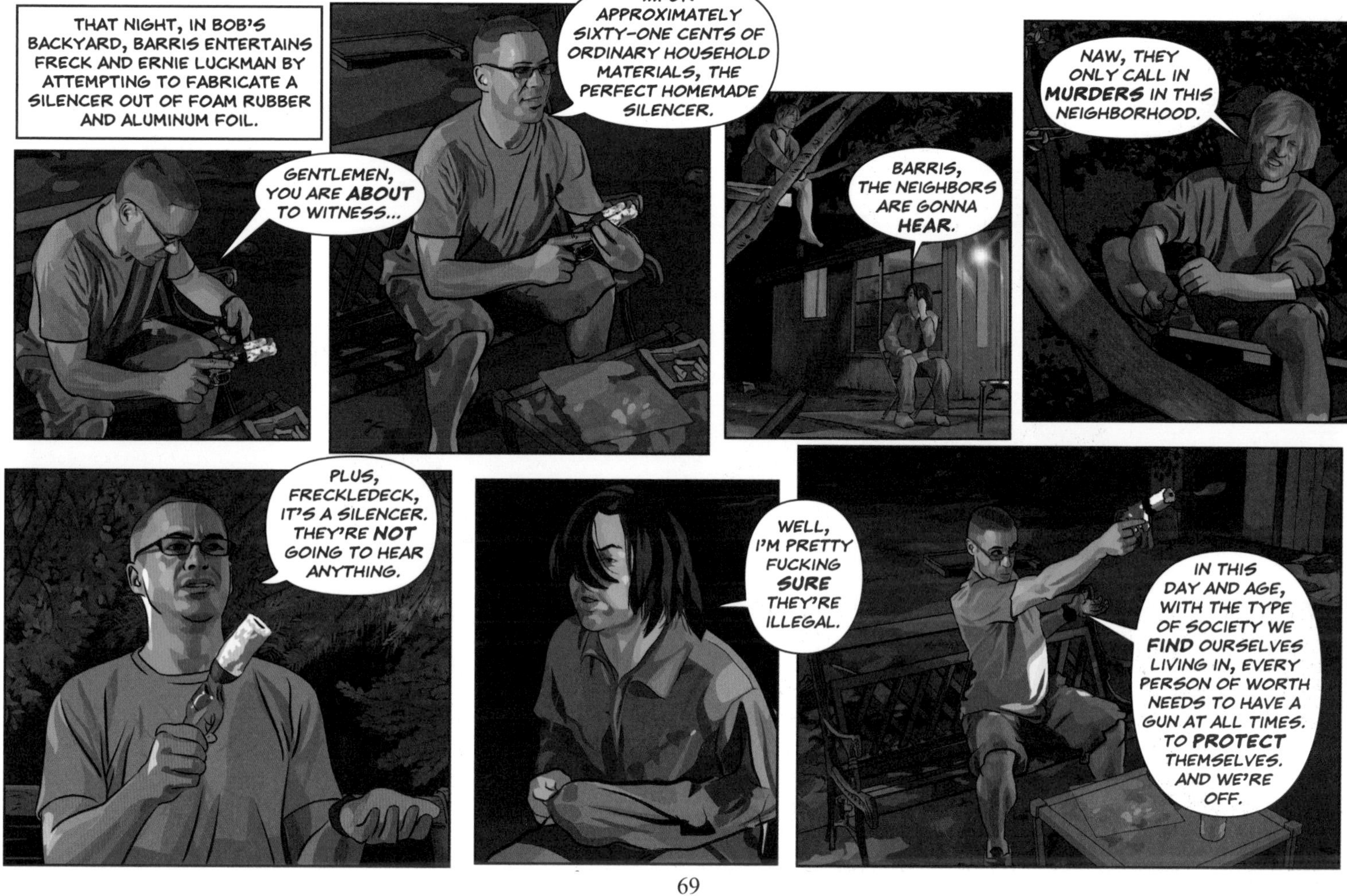
THAT NIGHT, IN BOB'S BACKYARD, BARRIS ENTERTAINS FRECK AND ERNIE LUCKMAN BY ATTEMPTING TO FABRICATE A SILENCER OUT OF FOAM RUBBER AND ALUMINUM FOIL.
GENTLEMEN, YOU ARE ABOUT TO WITNESS...
...FOR APPROXIMATELY SIXTY-ONE CENTS OF ORDINARY HOUSEHOLD MATERIALS, THE PERFECT HOMEMADE SILENCER.
BARRIS, THE NEIGHBORS ARE GONNA HEAR.
NAW, THEY ONLY CALL IN MURDERS IN THIS NEIGHBORHOOD.
PLUS, FRECKLEDECK, IT'S A SILENCER. THEY'RE NOT GOING TO HEAR ANYTHING.
WELL, I'M PRETTY FUCKING SURE THEY'RE ILLEGAL.
IN THIS DAY AND AGE, WITH THE TYPE OF SOCIETY WE FIND OURSELVES LIVING IN, EVERY PERSON OF WORTH NEEDS TO HAVE A GUN AT ALL TIMES. TO PROTECT THEMSELVES. AND WE'RE OFF.

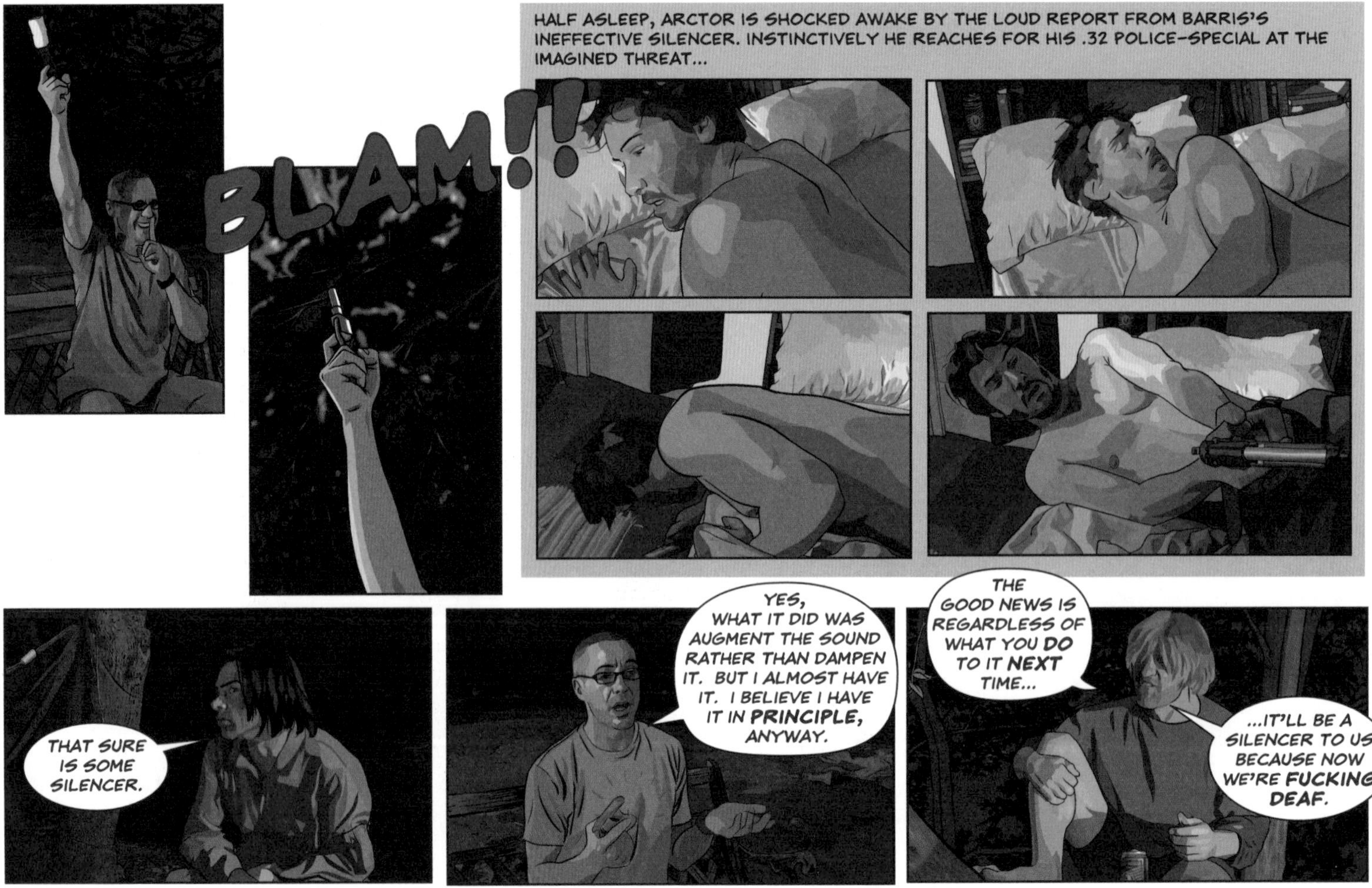

BLAM!!
HALF ASLEEP, ARCTOR IS SHOCKED AWAKE BY THE LOUD REPORT FROM BARRIS'S INEFFECTIVE SILENCER. INSTINCTIVELY HE REACHES FOR HIS .32 POLICE-SPECIAL AT THE IMAGINED THREAT...
THAT SURE IS SOME SILENCER.
YES, WHAT IT DID WAS AUGMENT THE SOUND RATHER THAN DAMPEN IT. BUT I ALMOST HAVE IT. I BELIEVE I HAVE IT IN PRINCIPLE, ANYWAY.
THE GOOD NEWS IS REGARDLESS OF WHAT YOU DO TO IT NEXT TIME...
...IT'LL BE A SILENCER TO US BECAUSE NOW WE'RE FUCKING DEAF.

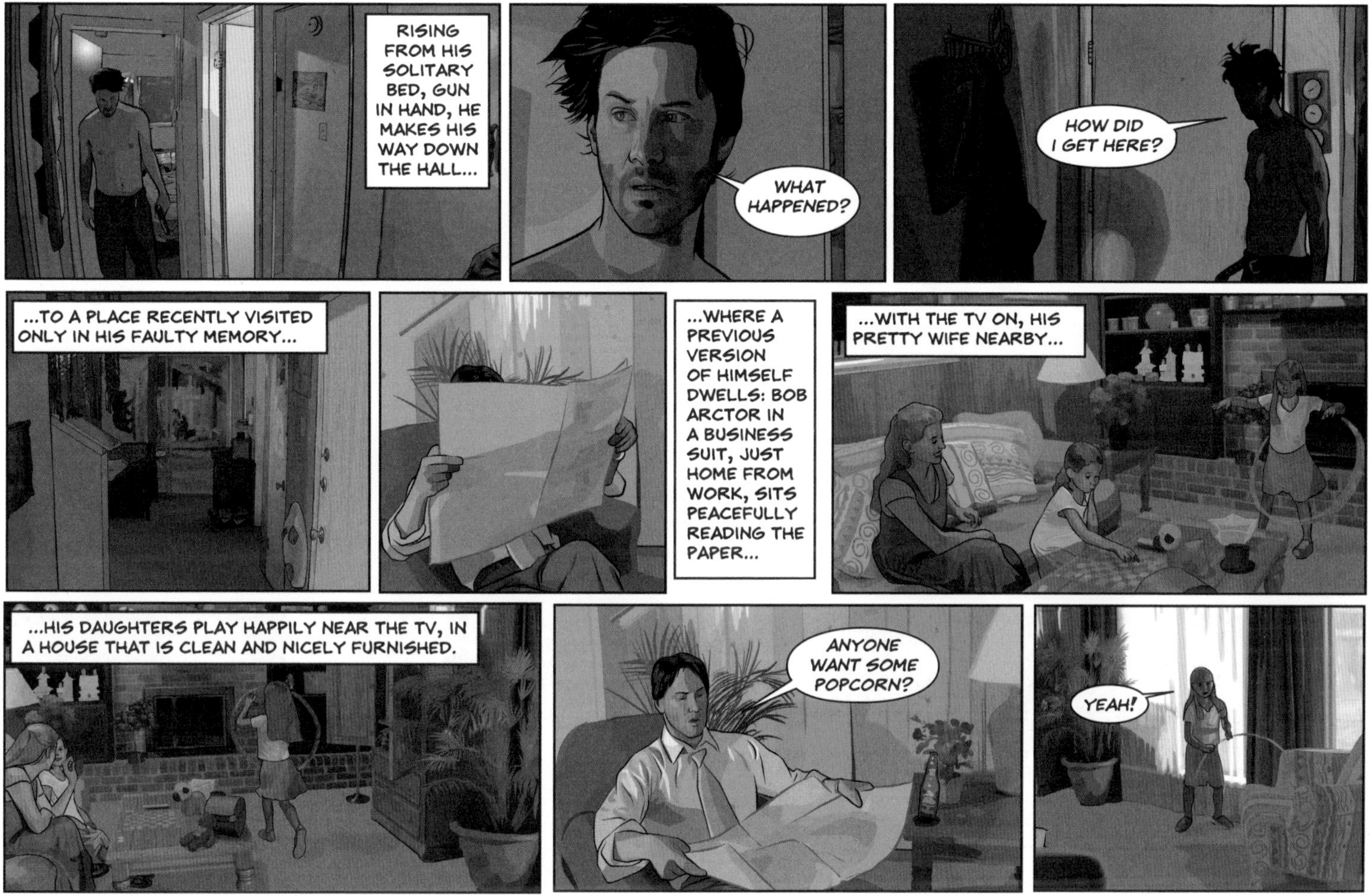
RISING FROM HIS SOLITARY BED, GUN IN HAND, HE MAKES HIS WAY DOWN THE HALL...
WHAT HAPPENED?
HOW DID I GET HERE?
...TO A PLACE RECENTLY VISITED ONLY IN HIS FAULTY MEMORY...
...WHERE A PREVIOUS VERSION OF HIMSELF DWELLS: BOB ARCTOR IN A BUSINESS SUIT, JUST HOME FROM WORK, SITS PEACEFULLY READING THE PAPER...
...WITH THE TV ON, HIS PRETTY WIFE NEARBY...
...HIS DAUGHTERS PLAY HAPPILY NEAR THE TV, IN A HOUSE THAT IS CLEAN AND NICELY FURNISHED.
ANYONE WANT SOME POPCORN?
YEAH!

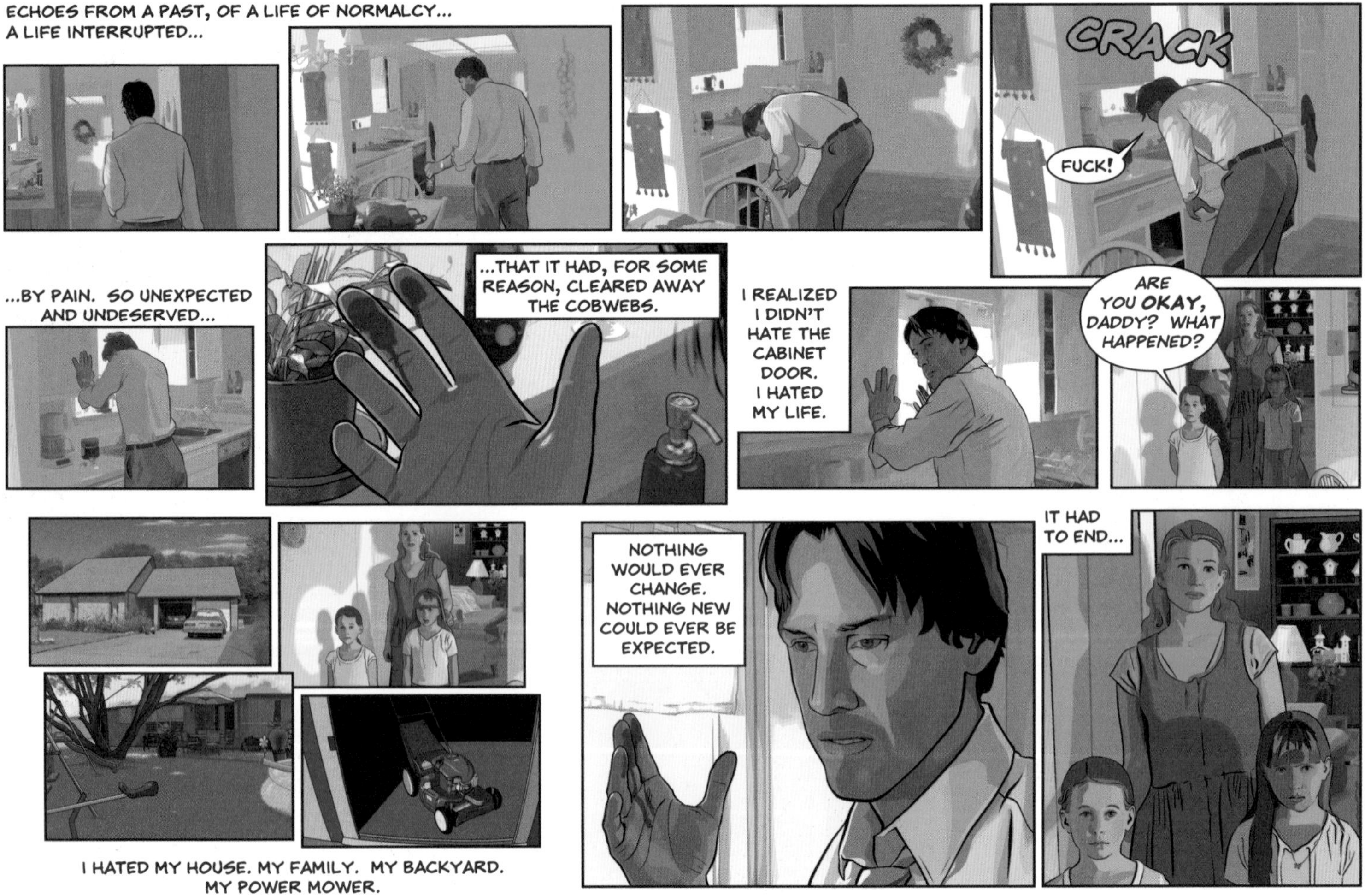
ECHOES FROM A PAST, OF A LIFE OF NORMALCY... A LIFE INTERRUPTED...
CRACK
FUCK!
...BY PAIN. SO UNEXPECTED AND UNDESERVED...
...THAT IT HAD, FOR SOME REASON, CLEARED AWAY THE COBWEBS.
I REALIZED I DIDN'T HATE THE CABINET DOOR. I HATED MY LIFE.
ARE YOU OKAY, DADDY? WHAT HAPPENED?
I HATED MY HOUSE. MY FAMILY. MY BACKYARD. MY POWER MOWER.
NOTHING WOULD EVER CHANGE. NOTHING NEW COULD EVER BE EXPECTED.
IT HAD TO END...

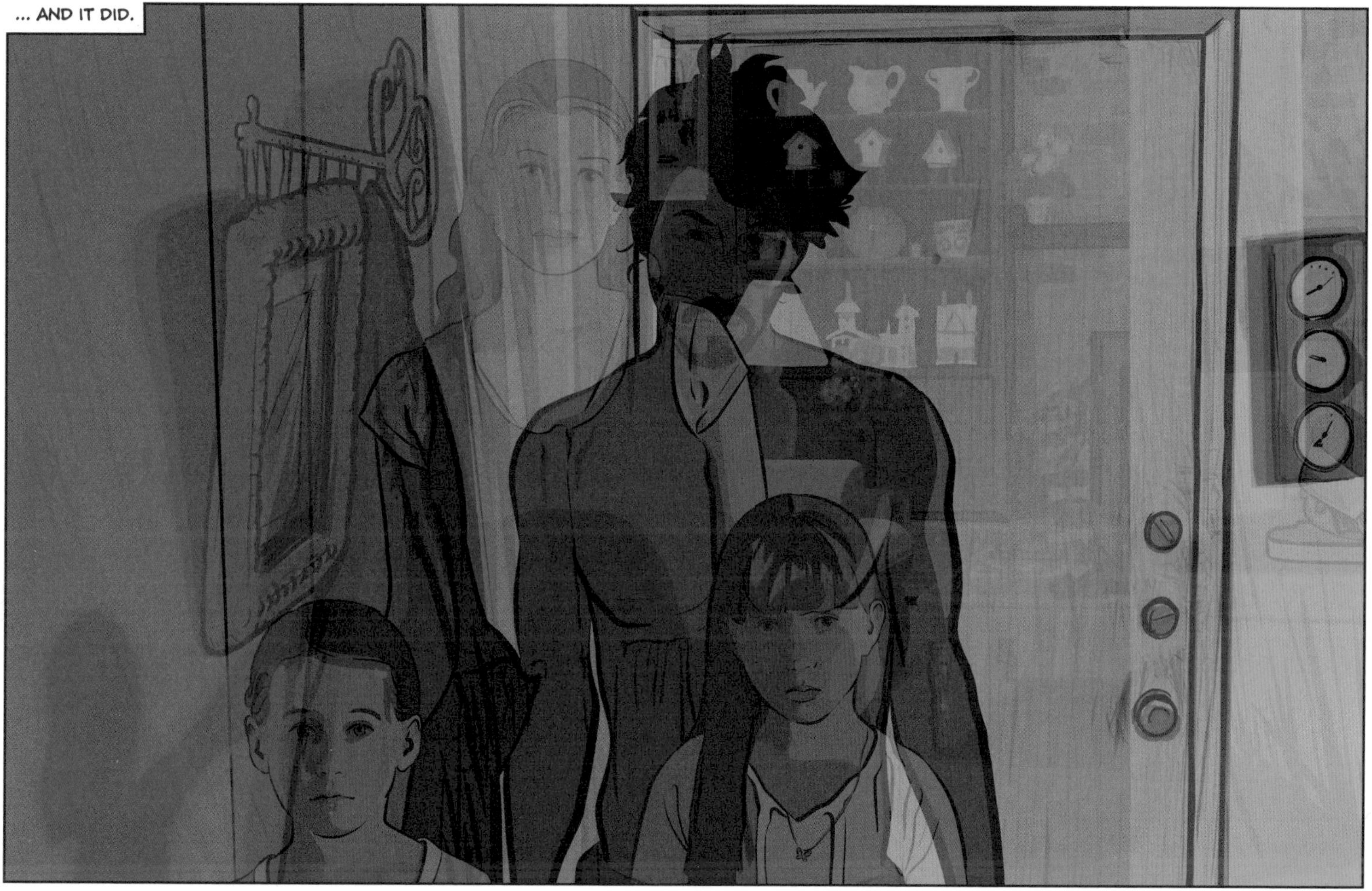
... AND IT DID.

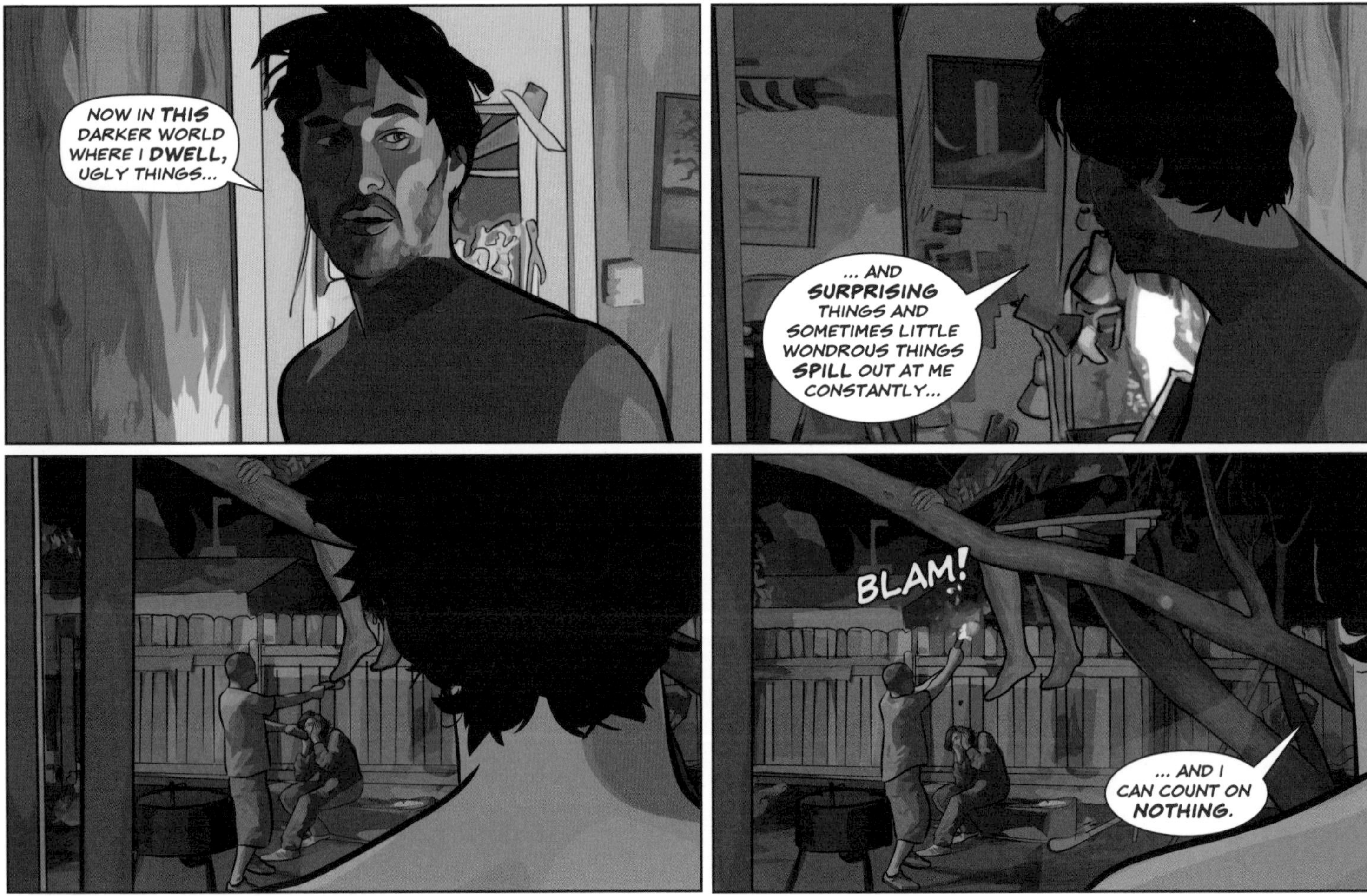
NOW IN THIS DARKER WORLD WHERE I DWELL, UGLY THINGS...
... AND SURPRISING THINGS AND SOMETIMES LITTLE WONDROUS THINGS SPILL OUT AT ME CONSTANTLY...
BLAM!
... AND I CAN COUNT ON NOTHING.

NEXT DAY ON THE FREEWAY TO SAN DIEGO, IMPATIENCE TURNS LAUGHTER INTO A NEAR-DEATH EXPERIENCE...

THANKS, SLOWPOKE.

GET AROUND HIM, WILL YA?

THERE WE GO.

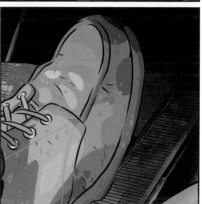

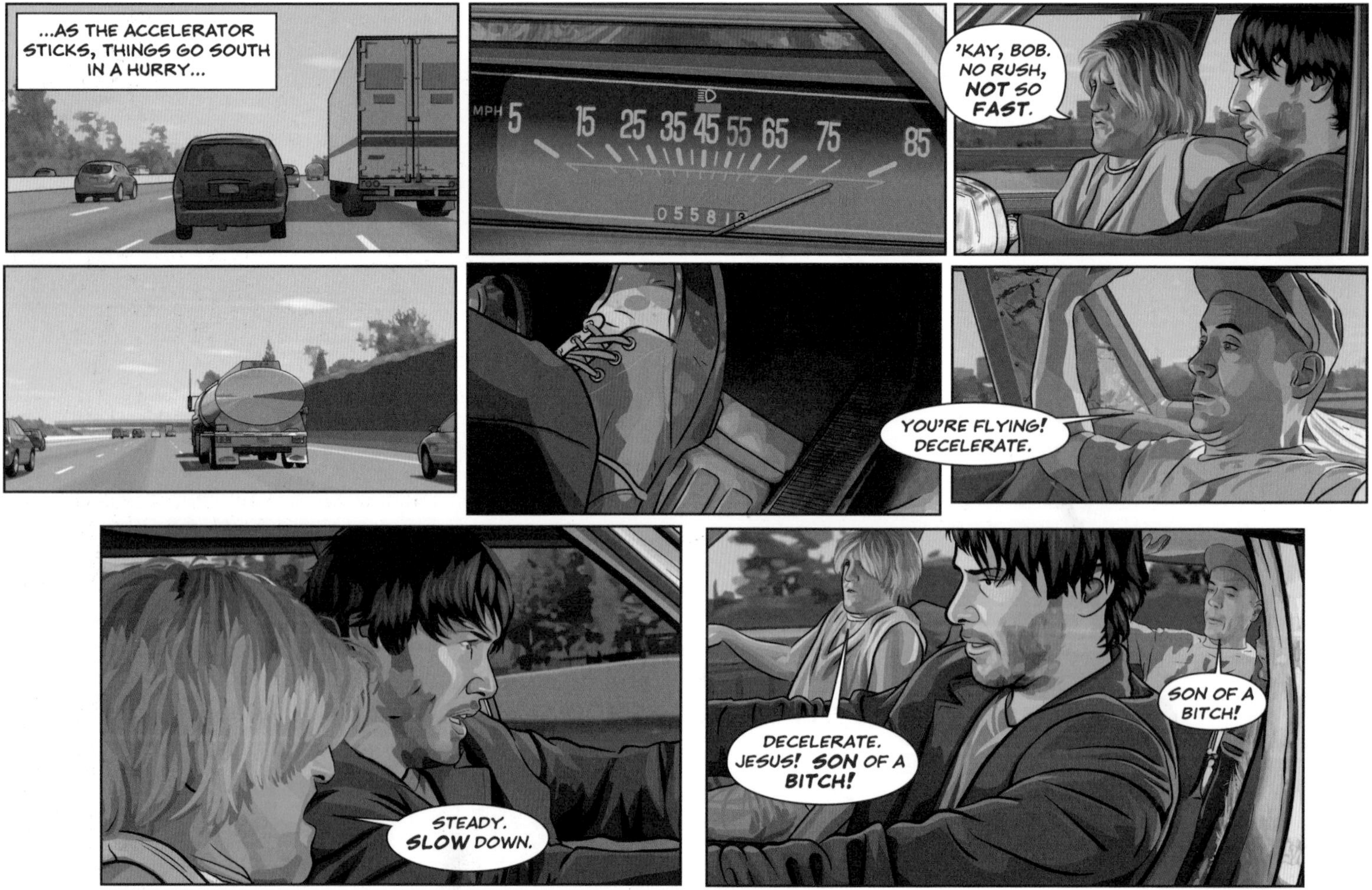
...AS THE ACCELERATOR STICKS, THINGS GO SOUTH IN A HURRY...
MPH 5 15 25 35 45 55 65 75 85
'KAY, BOB. NO RUSH, NOT SO FAST.
YOU'RE FLYING! DECELERATE.
STEADY. SLOW DOWN.
DECELERATE. JESUS! SON OF A BITCH!
SON OF A BITCH!

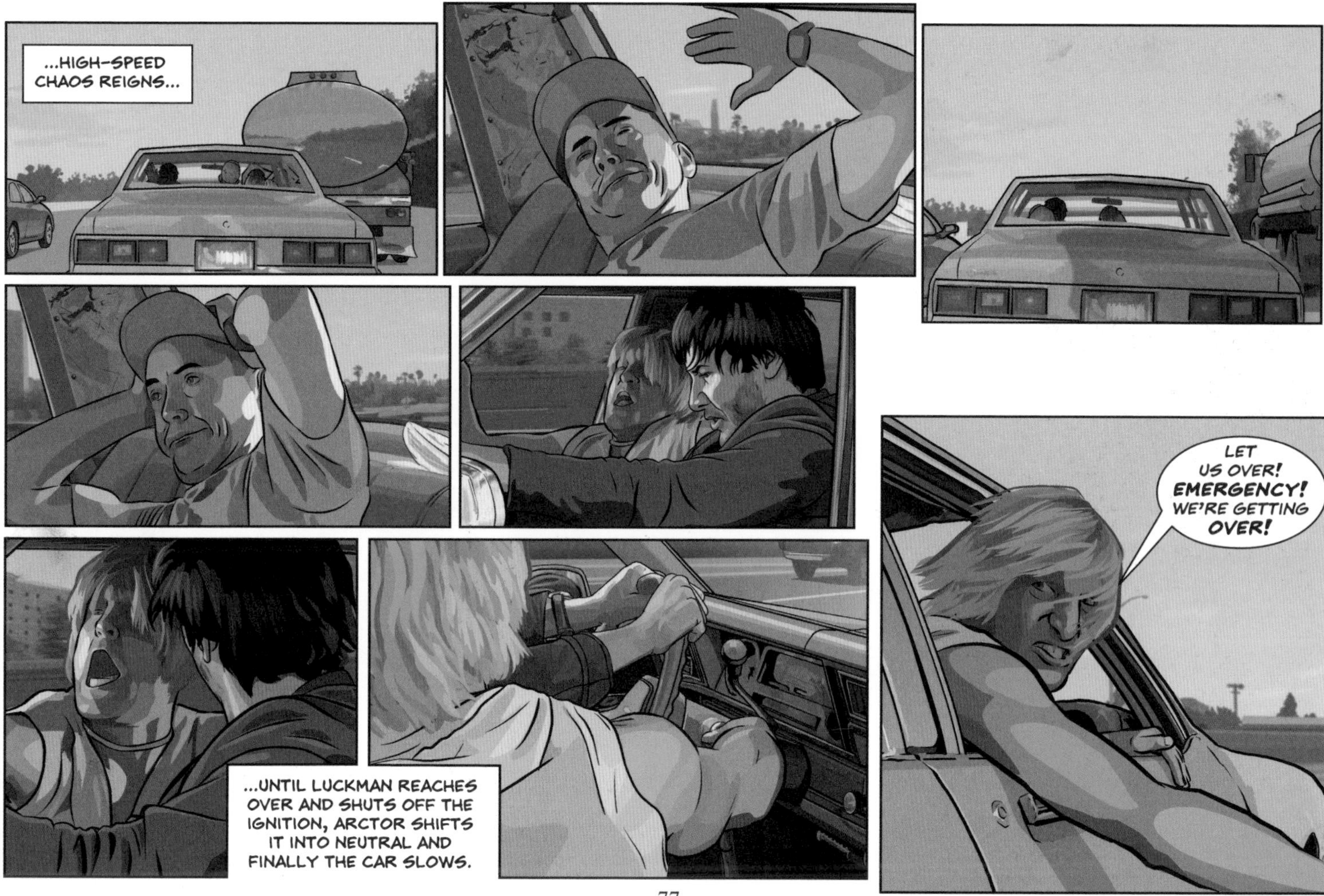
...HIGH-SPEED CHAOS REIGNS...
LET US OVER! EMERGENCY! WE'RE GETTING OVER!
...UNTIL LUCKMAN REACHES OVER AND SHUTS OFF THE IGNITION, ARCTOR SHIFTS IT INTO NEUTRAL AND FINALLY THE CAR SLOWS.

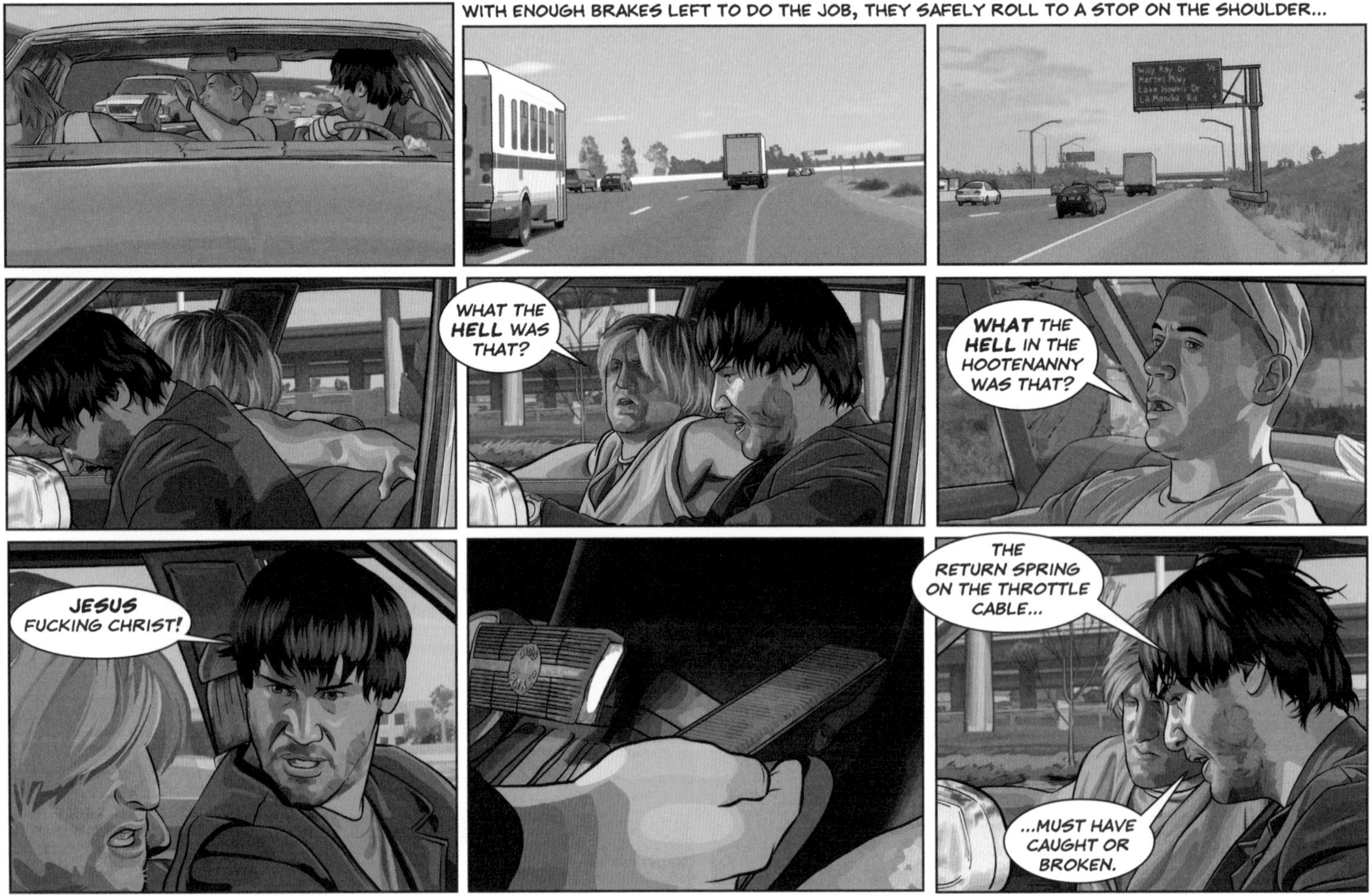
WITH ENOUGH BRAKES LEFT TO DO THE JOB, THEY SAFELY ROLL TO A STOP ON THE SHOULDER...
WHAT THE HELL WAS THAT?
WHAT THE HELL IN THE HOOTENANNY WAS THAT?
JESUS FUCKING CHRIST!
THE RETURN SPRING ON THE THROTTLE CABLE...
...MUST HAVE CAUGHT OR BROKEN.

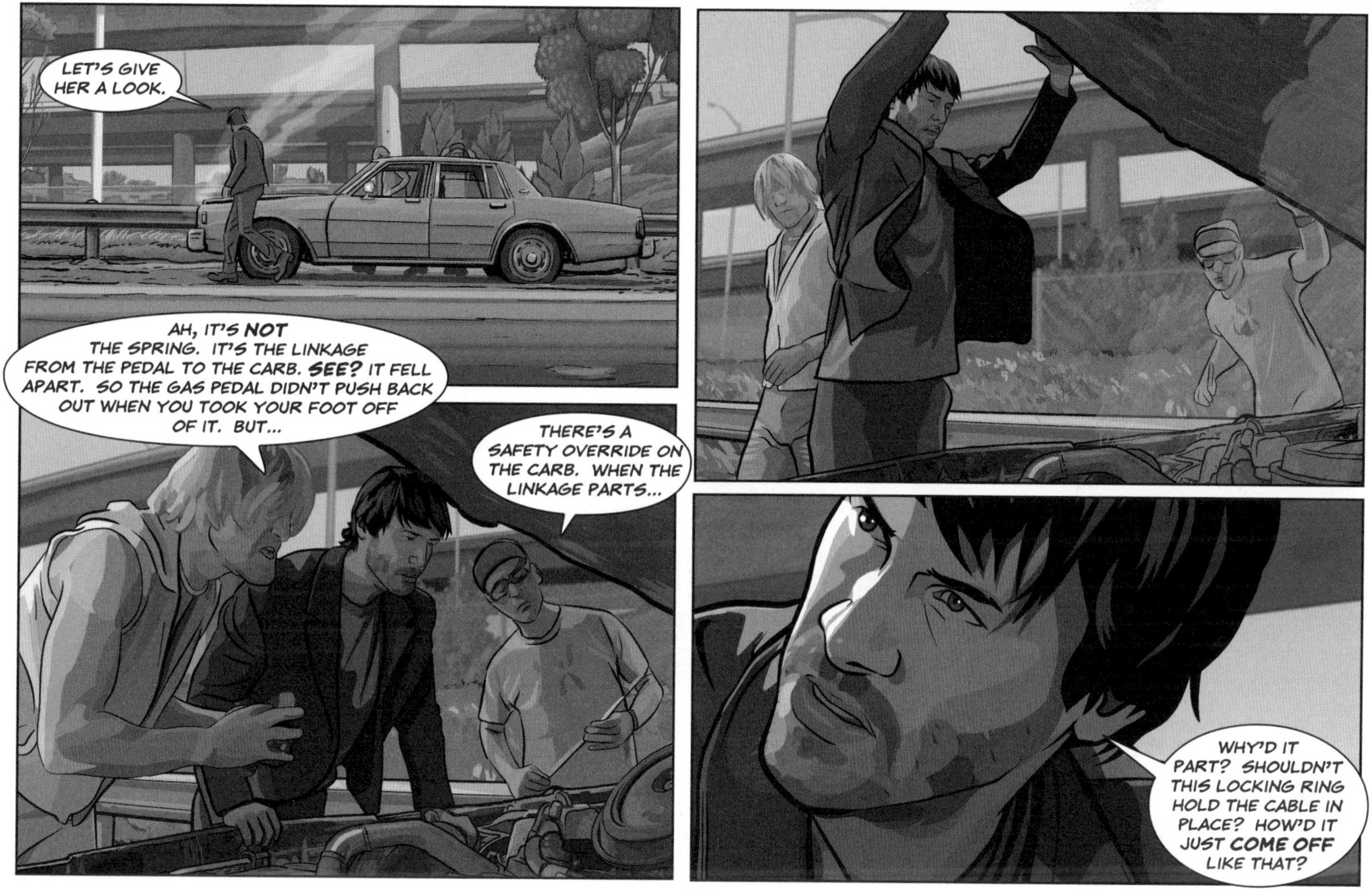
LET'S GIVE HER A LOOK.
AH, IT'S NOT THE SPRING. IT'S THE LINKAGE FROM THE PEDAL TO THE CARB. SEE? IT FELL APART. SO THE GAS PEDAL DIDN'T PUSH BACK OUT WHEN YOU TOOK YOUR FOOT OFF OF IT. BUT...
THERE'S A SAFETY OVERRIDE ON THE CARB. WHEN THE LINKAGE PARTS...
WHY'D IT PART? SHOULDN'T THIS LOCKING RING HOLD THE CABLE IN PLACE? HOW'D IT JUST COME OFF LIKE THAT?

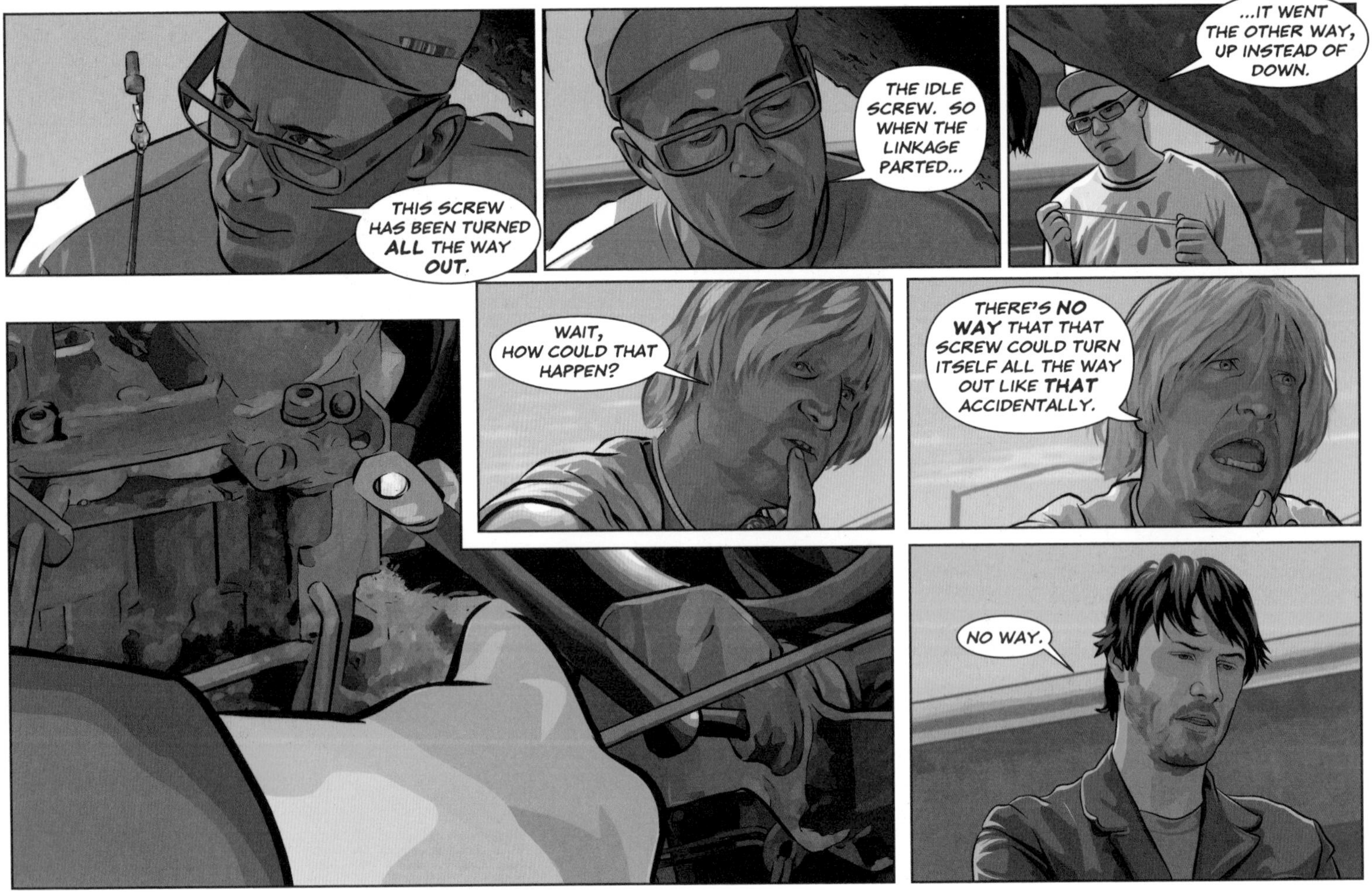
THIS SCREW HAS BEEN TURNED ALL THE WAY OUT.
THE IDLE SCREW. SO WHEN THE LINKAGE PARTED...
...IT WENT THE OTHER WAY, UP INSTEAD OF DOWN.
WAIT, HOW COULD THAT HAPPEN?
THERE'S NO WAY THAT THAT SCREW COULD TURN ITSELF ALL THE WAY OUT LIKE THAT ACCIDENTALLY.
NO WAY.

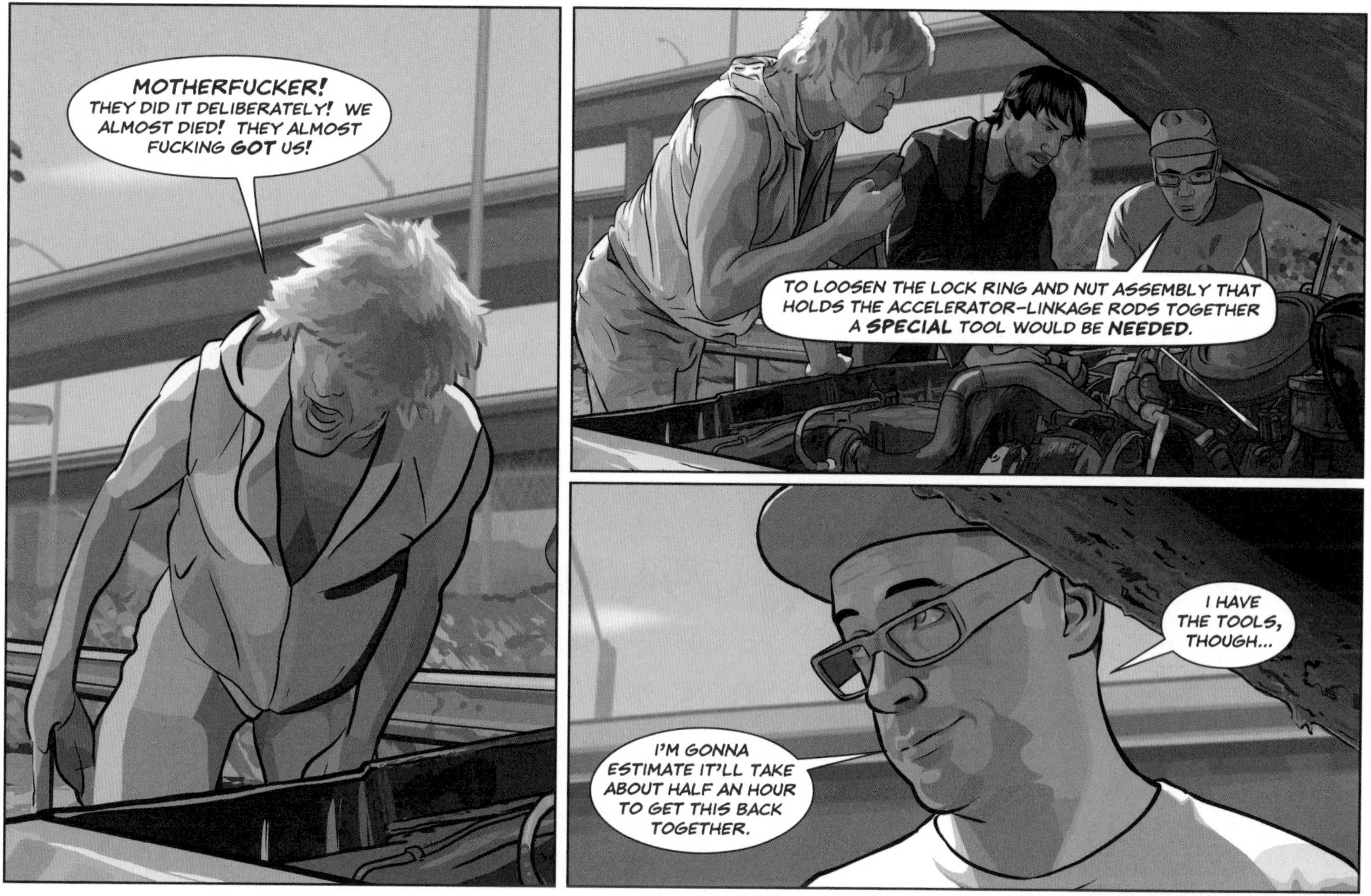
MOTHERFUCKER! THEY DID IT DELIBERATELY! WE ALMOST DIED! THEY ALMOST FUCKING GOT US!
TO LOOSEN THE LOCK RING AND NUT ASSEMBLY THAT HOLDS THE ACCELERATOR-LINKAGE RODS TOGETHER A SPECIAL TOOL WOULD BE NEEDED.
I HAVE THE TOOLS, THOUGH...
I'M GONNA ESTIMATE IT'LL TAKE ABOUT HALF AN HOUR TO GET THIS BACK TOGETHER.

...**BACK** AT THE HOUSE.

WELL, WE CAN ALWAYS GO TO A **REPAIRS** CENTER AND BORROW THEIRS OR GET A **TOW TRUCK** OUT HERE.

TO HELP PASS THE TIME BARRIS OPENS A CANISTER OF DEATH AND TAPS OUT TWO FOR LUCKMAN.

HE TAPS OUT TWO MORE FOR ARCTOR, WHO FOR THE MOMENT DECLINES.

YOU KNOW, I THINK THAT'S WHAT'S FUCKING **US** UP. FUCKING UP OUR BRAINS. WE'RE GONNA WIND UP LIKE **FRECK** SOON.

NO.

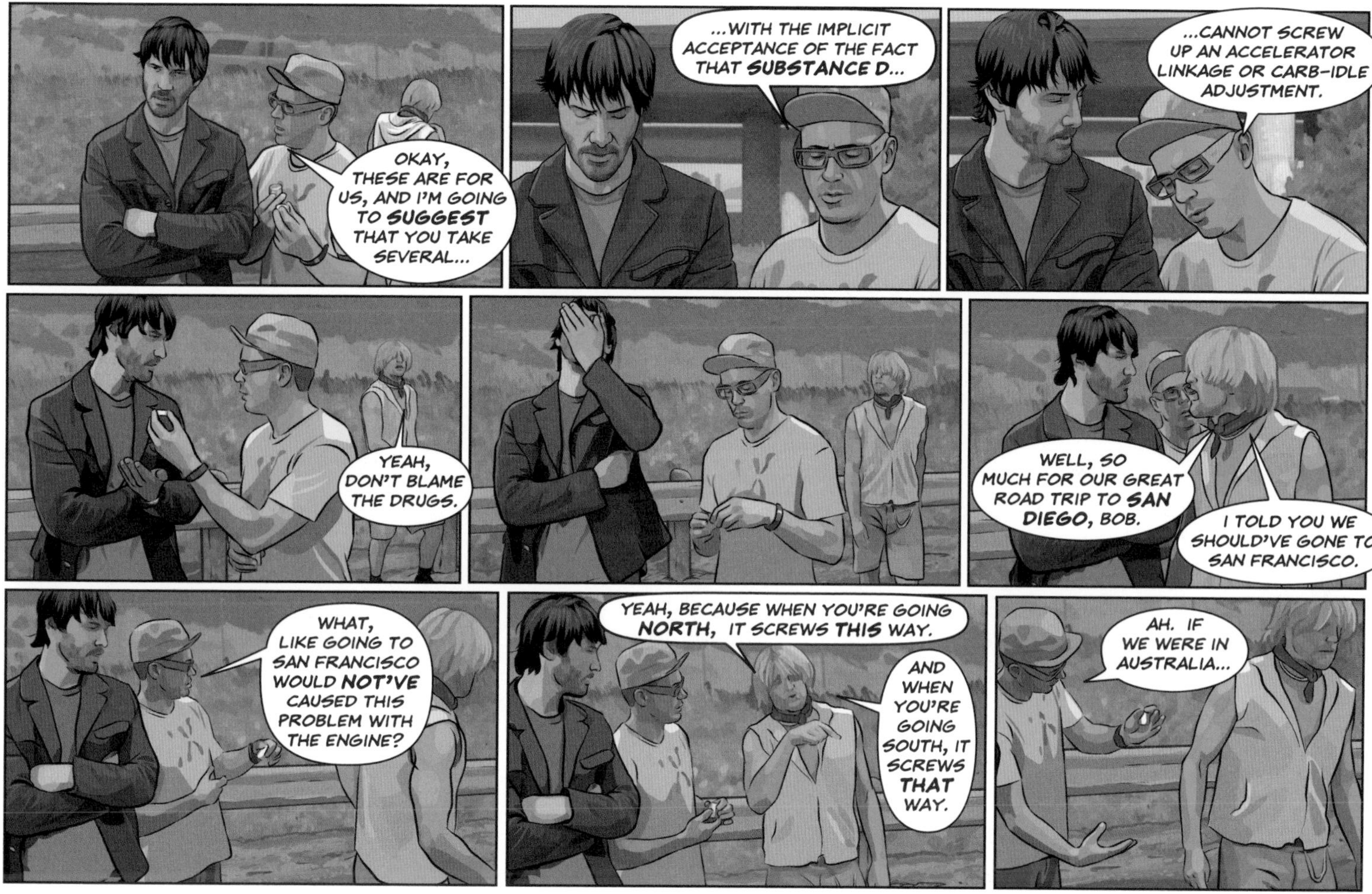
OKAY, THESE ARE FOR US, AND I'M GOING TO SUGGEST THAT YOU TAKE SEVERAL...
...WITH THE IMPLICIT ACCEPTANCE OF THE FACT THAT SUBSTANCE D...
...CANNOT SCREW UP AN ACCELERATOR LINKAGE OR CARB-IDLE ADJUSTMENT.
YEAH, DON'T BLAME THE DRUGS.
WELL, SO MUCH FOR OUR GREAT ROAD TRIP TO SAN DIEGO, BOB.
I TOLD YOU WE SHOULD'VE GONE TO SAN FRANCISCO.
WHAT, LIKE GOING TO SAN FRANCISCO WOULD NOT'VE CAUSED THIS PROBLEM WITH THE ENGINE?
YEAH, BECAUSE WHEN YOU'RE GOING NORTH, IT SCREWS THIS WAY.
AND WHEN YOU'RE GOING SOUTH, IT SCREWS THAT WAY.
AH. IF WE WERE IN AUSTRALIA...

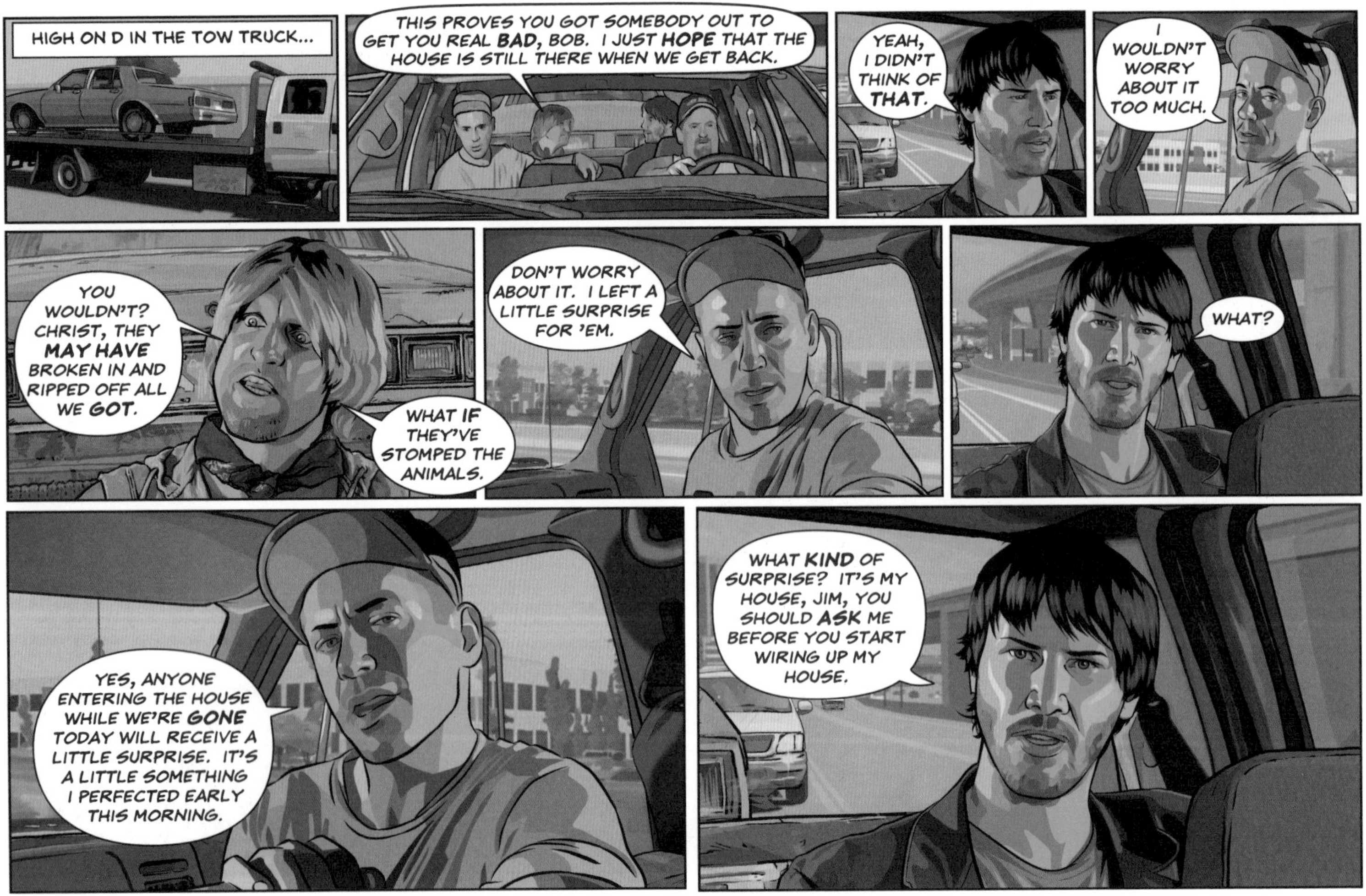
HIGH ON D IN THE TOW TRUCK...
THIS PROVES YOU GOT SOMEBODY OUT TO GET YOU REAL BAD, BOB. I JUST HOPE THAT THE HOUSE IS STILL THERE WHEN WE GET BACK.
YEAH, I DIDN'T THINK OF THAT.
I WOULDN'T WORRY ABOUT IT TOO MUCH.
YOU WOULDN'T? CHRIST, THEY MAY HAVE BROKEN IN AND RIPPED OFF ALL WE GOT.
WHAT IF THEY'VE STOMPED THE ANIMALS.
DON'T WORRY ABOUT IT. I LEFT A LITTLE SURPRISE FOR 'EM.
WHAT?
YES, ANYONE ENTERING THE HOUSE WHILE WE'RE GONE TODAY WILL RECEIVE A LITTLE SURPRISE. IT'S A LITTLE SOMETHING I PERFECTED EARLY THIS MORNING.
WHAT KIND OF SURPRISE? IT'S MY HOUSE, JIM, YOU SHOULD ASK ME BEFORE YOU START WIRING UP MY HOUSE.

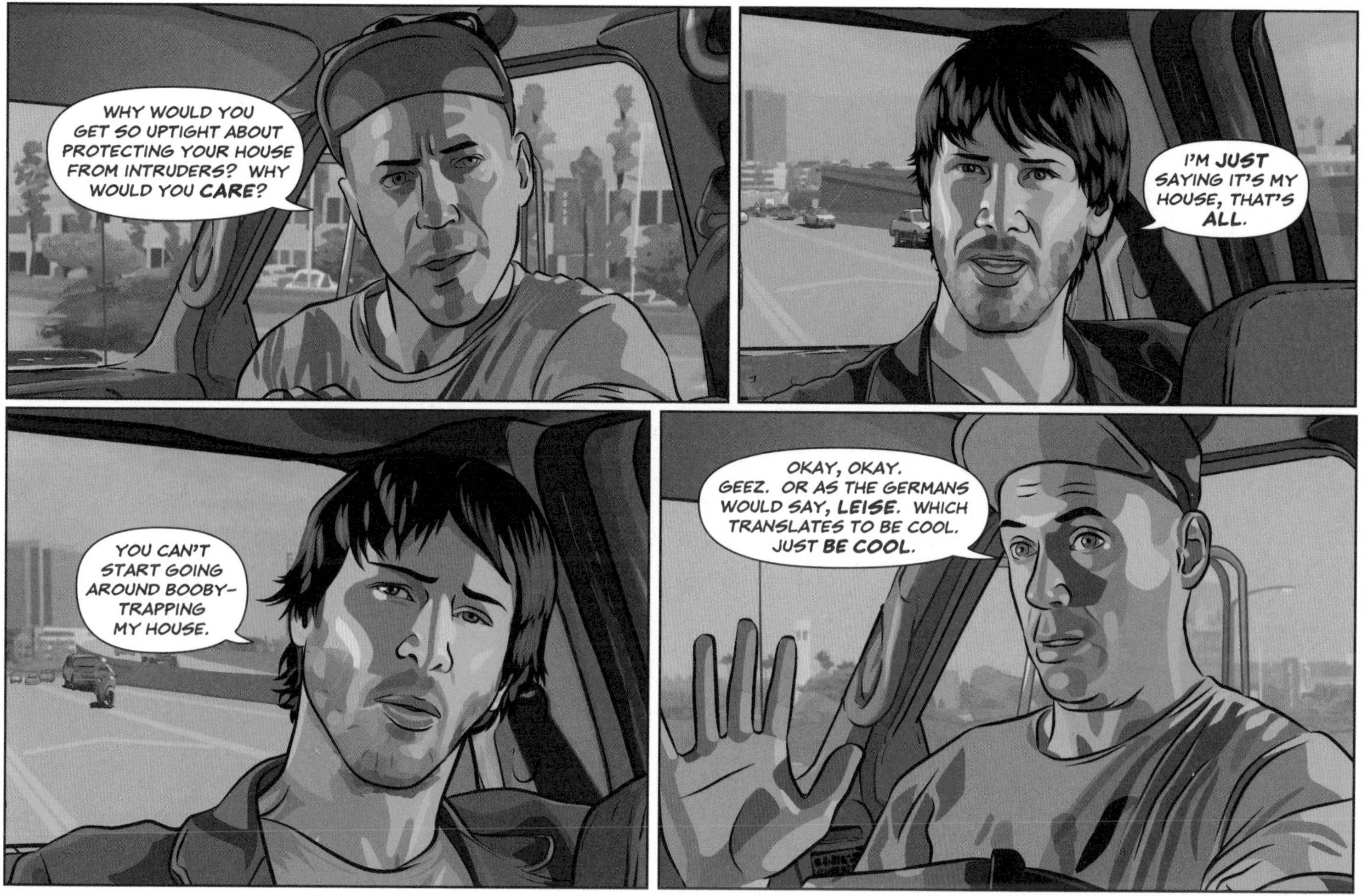
WHY WOULD YOU GET SO UPTIGHT ABOUT PROTECTING YOUR HOUSE FROM INTRUDERS? WHY WOULD YOU **CARE**?
I'M **JUST** SAYING IT'S MY HOUSE, THAT'S **ALL**.
YOU CAN'T START GOING AROUND BOOBY-TRAPPING MY HOUSE.
OKAY, OKAY. GEEZ. OR AS THE GERMANS WOULD SAY, **LEISE**. WHICH TRANSLATES TO BE COOL. JUST **BE COOL**.

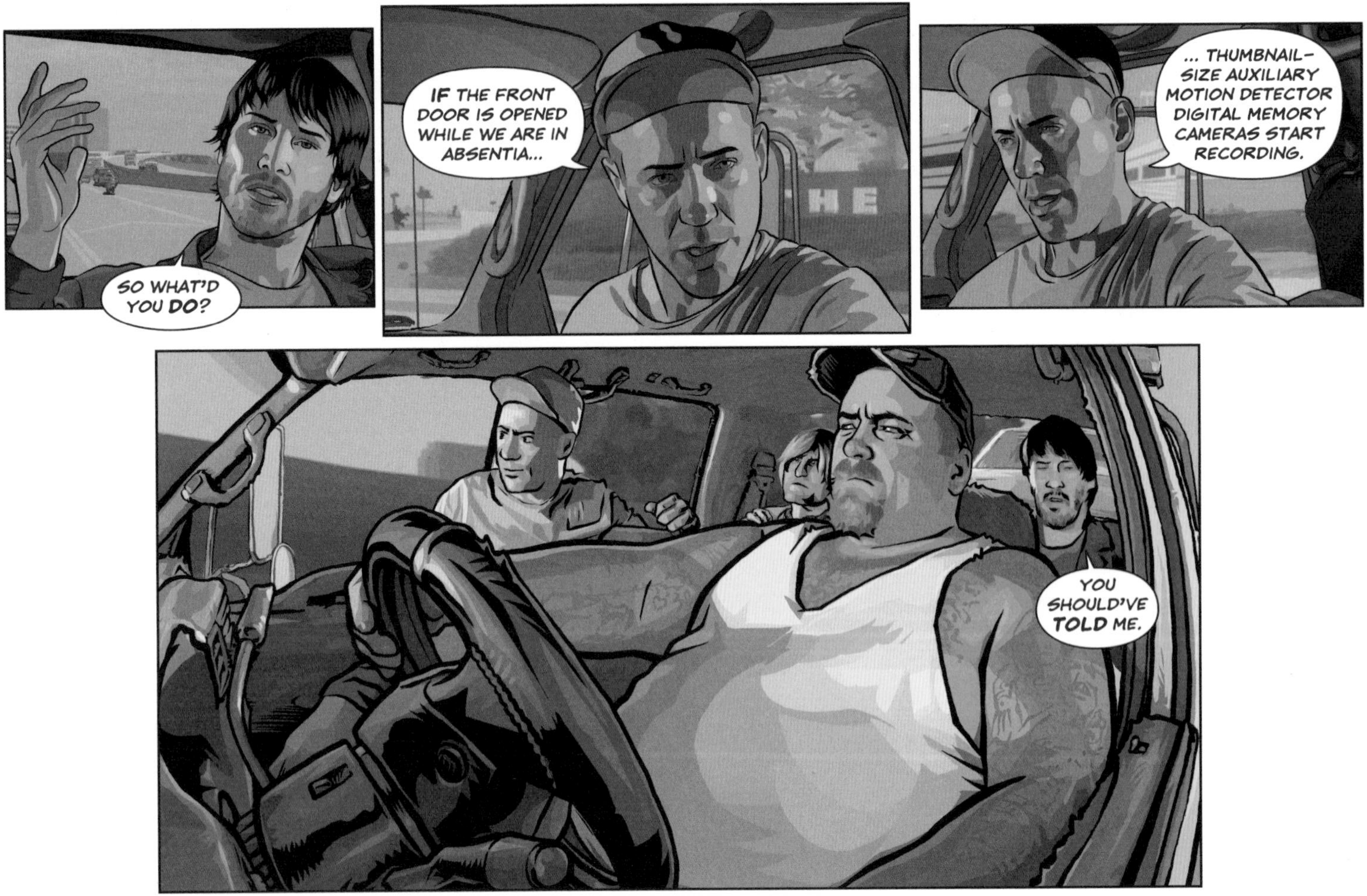
SO WHAT'D YOU DO?
IF THE FRONT DOOR IS OPENED WHILE WE ARE IN ABSENTIA...
... THUMBNAIL-SIZE AUXILIARY MOTION DETECTOR DIGITAL MEMORY CAMERAS START RECORDING.
YOU SHOULD'VE TOLD ME.

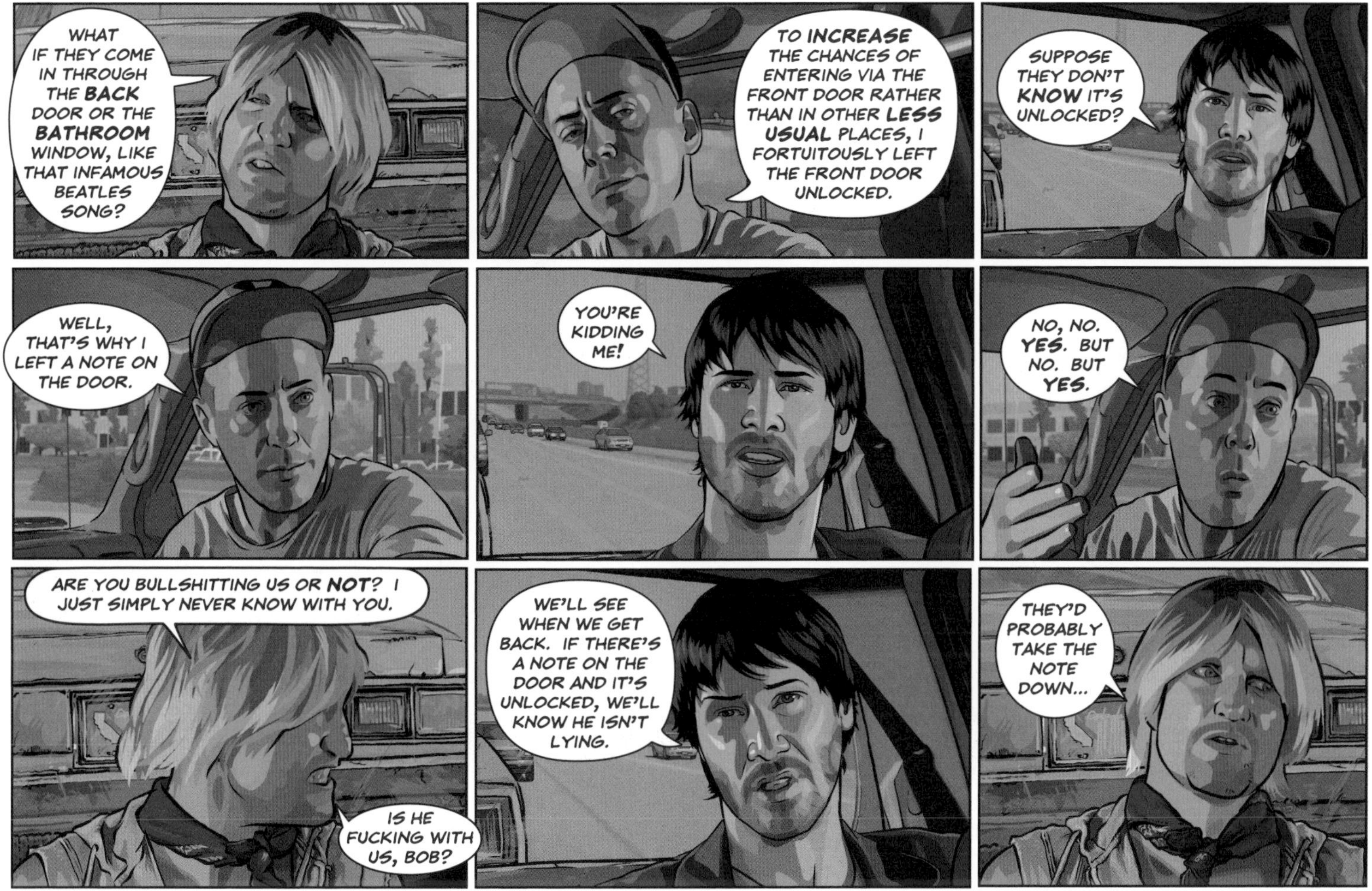
WHAT IF THEY COME IN THROUGH THE BACK DOOR OR THE BATHROOM WINDOW, LIKE THAT INFAMOUS BEATLES SONG?
TO INCREASE THE CHANCES OF ENTERING VIA THE FRONT DOOR RATHER THAN IN OTHER LESS USUAL PLACES, I FORTUITOUSLY LEFT THE FRONT DOOR UNLOCKED.
SUPPOSE THEY DON'T KNOW IT'S UNLOCKED?
WELL, THAT'S WHY I LEFT A NOTE ON THE DOOR.
YOU'RE KIDDING ME!
NO, NO. YES. BUT NO. BUT YES.
ARE YOU BULLSHITTING US OR NOT? I JUST SIMPLY NEVER KNOW WITH YOU.
IS HE FUCKING WITH US, BOB?
WE'LL SEE WHEN WE GET BACK. IF THERE'S A NOTE ON THE DOOR AND IT'S UNLOCKED, WE'LL KNOW HE ISN'T LYING.
THEY'D PROBABLY TAKE THE NOTE DOWN...

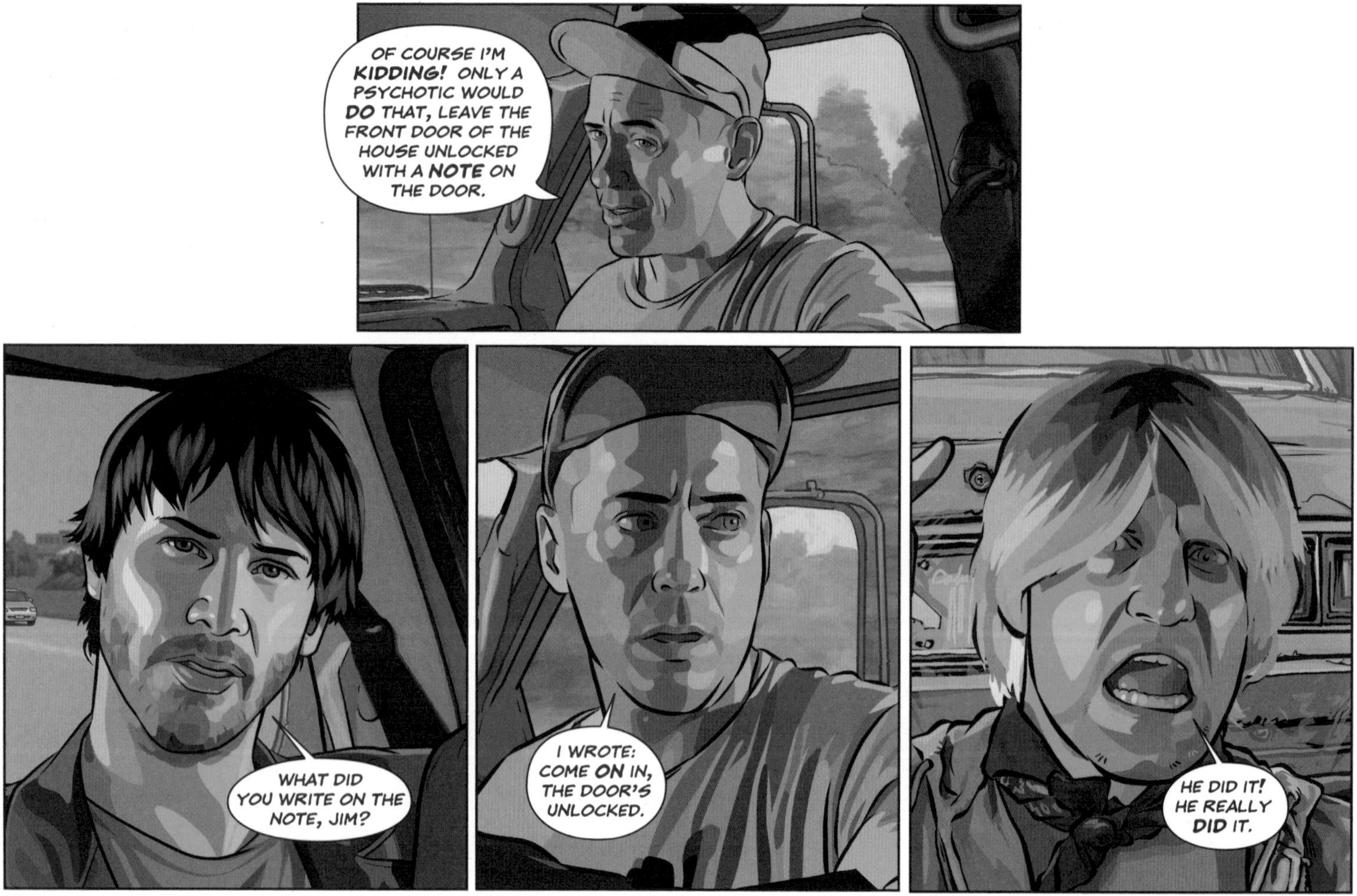
OF COURSE I'M KIDDING! ONLY A PSYCHOTIC WOULD DO THAT, LEAVE THE FRONT DOOR OF THE HOUSE UNLOCKED WITH A NOTE ON THE DOOR.
WHAT DID YOU WRITE ON THE NOTE, JIM?
I WROTE: COME ON IN, THE DOOR'S UNLOCKED.
HE DID IT! HE REALLY DID IT.

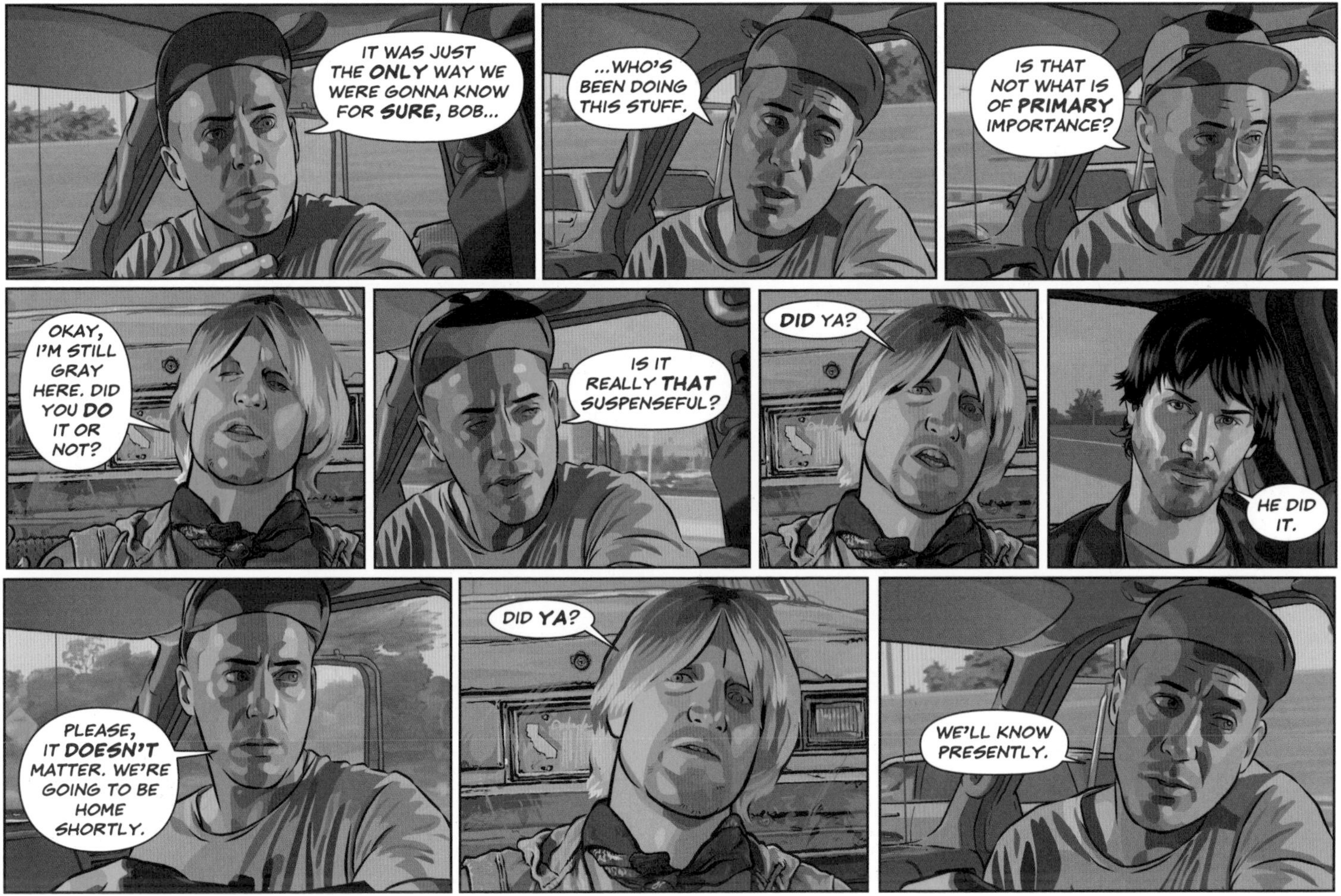
IT WAS JUST THE ONLY WAY WE WERE GONNA KNOW FOR SURE, BOB...
...WHO'S BEEN DOING THIS STUFF.
IS THAT NOT WHAT IS OF PRIMARY IMPORTANCE?
OKAY, I'M STILL GRAY HERE. DID YOU DO IT OR NOT?
IS IT REALLY THAT SUSPENSEFUL?
DID YA?
HE DID IT.
PLEASE, IT DOESN'T MATTER. WE'RE GOING TO BE HOME SHORTLY.
DID YA?
WE'LL KNOW PRESENTLY.

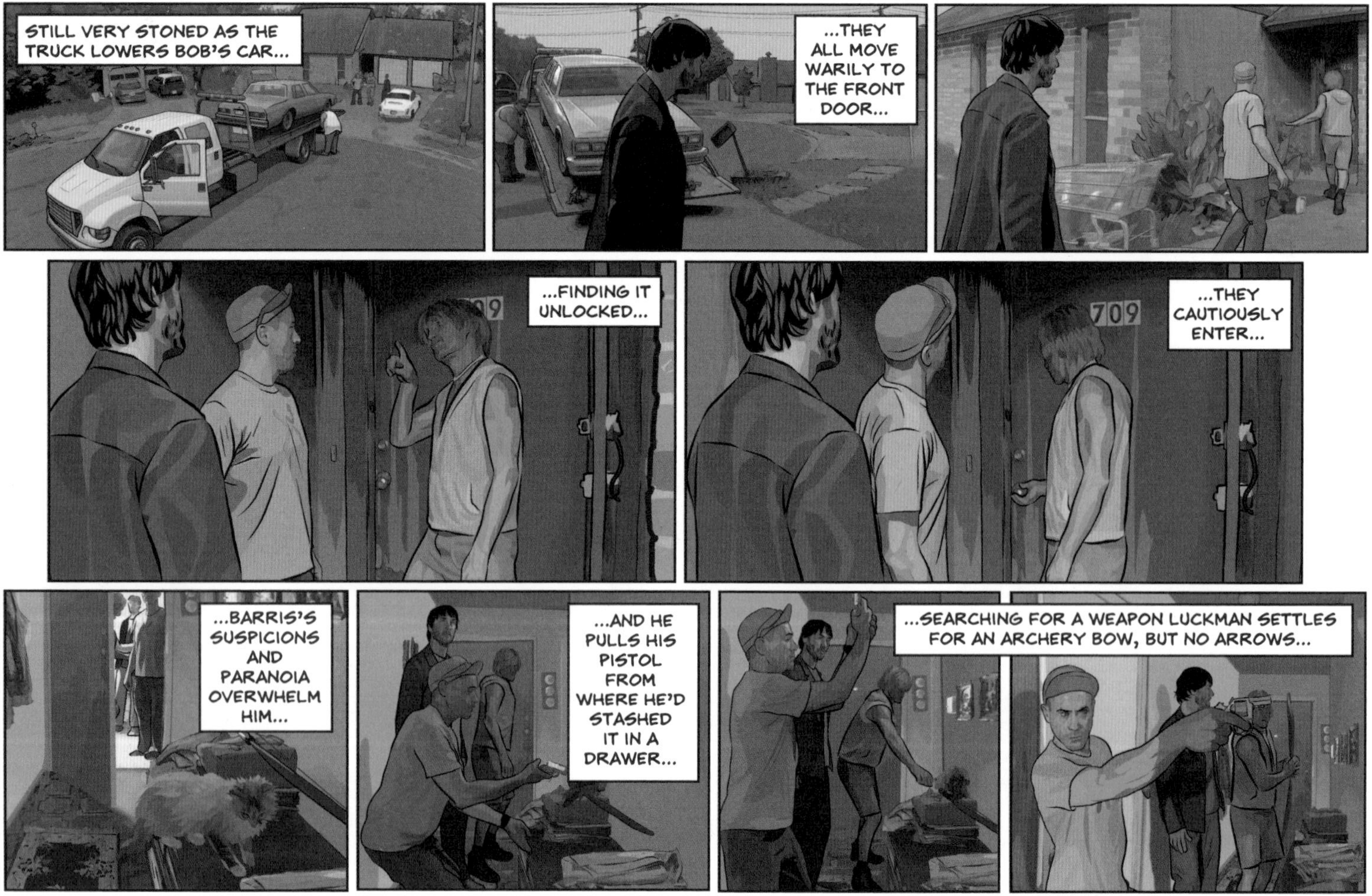
STILL VERY STONED AS THE TRUCK LOWERS BOB'S CAR...
...THEY ALL MOVE WARILY TO THE FRONT DOOR...
...FINDING IT UNLOCKED...
709
...THEY CAUTIOUSLY ENTER...
...BARRIS'S SUSPICIONS AND PARANOIA OVERWHELM HIM...
...AND HE PULLS HIS PISTOL FROM WHERE HE'D STASHED IT IN A DRAWER...
...SEARCHING FOR A WEAPON LUCKMAN SETTLES FOR AN ARCHERY BOW, BUT NO ARROWS...

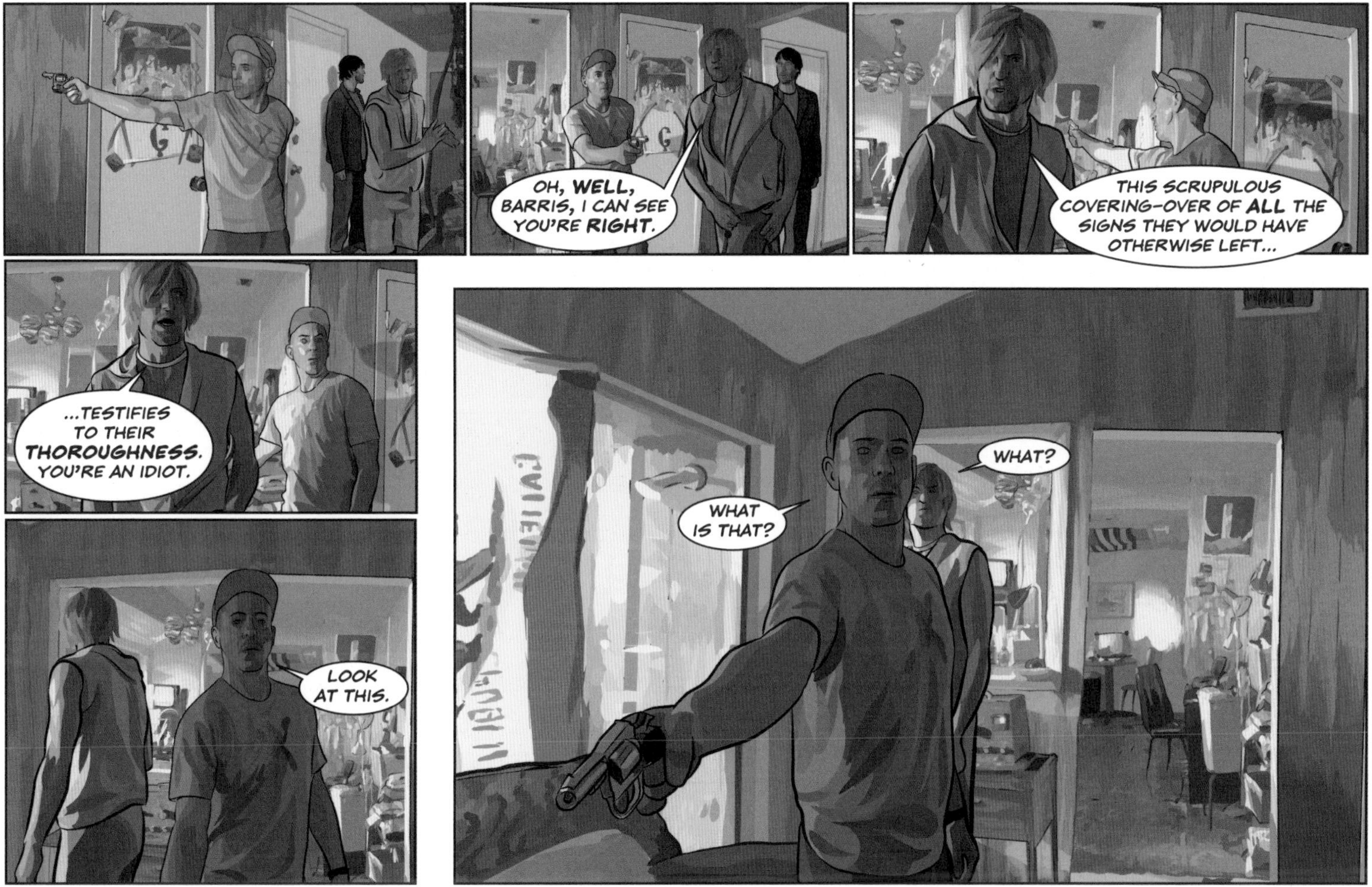
OH, WELL, BARRIS, I CAN SEE YOU'RE RIGHT.
THIS SCRUPULOUS COVERING-OVER OF ALL THE SIGNS THEY WOULD HAVE OTHERWISE LEFT...
...TESTIFIES TO THEIR THOROUGHNESS. YOU'RE AN IDIOT.
LOOK AT THIS.
WHAT IS THAT?
WHAT?

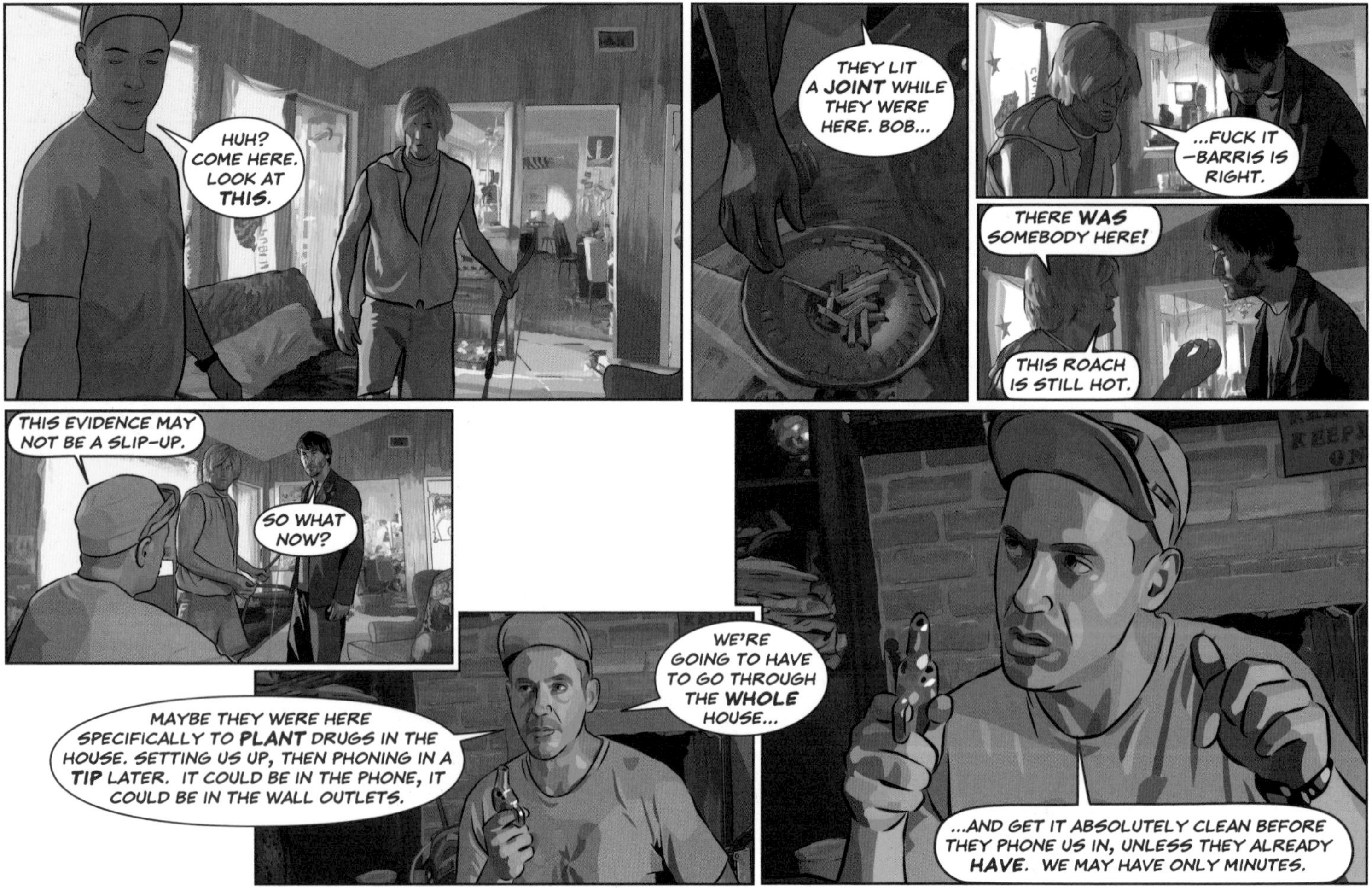
HUH? COME HERE. LOOK AT THIS.
THEY LIT A JOINT WHILE THEY WERE HERE. BOB...
...FUCK IT —BARRIS IS RIGHT.
THERE WAS SOMEBODY HERE!
THIS ROACH IS STILL HOT.
THIS EVIDENCE MAY NOT BE A SLIP-UP.
SO WHAT NOW?
MAYBE THEY WERE HERE SPECIFICALLY TO PLANT DRUGS IN THE HOUSE. SETTING US UP, THEN PHONING IN A TIP LATER. IT COULD BE IN THE PHONE, IT COULD BE IN THE WALL OUTLETS.
WE'RE GOING TO HAVE TO GO THROUGH THE WHOLE HOUSE...
...AND GET IT ABSOLUTELY CLEAN BEFORE THEY PHONE US IN, UNLESS THEY ALREADY HAVE. WE MAY HAVE ONLY MINUTES.

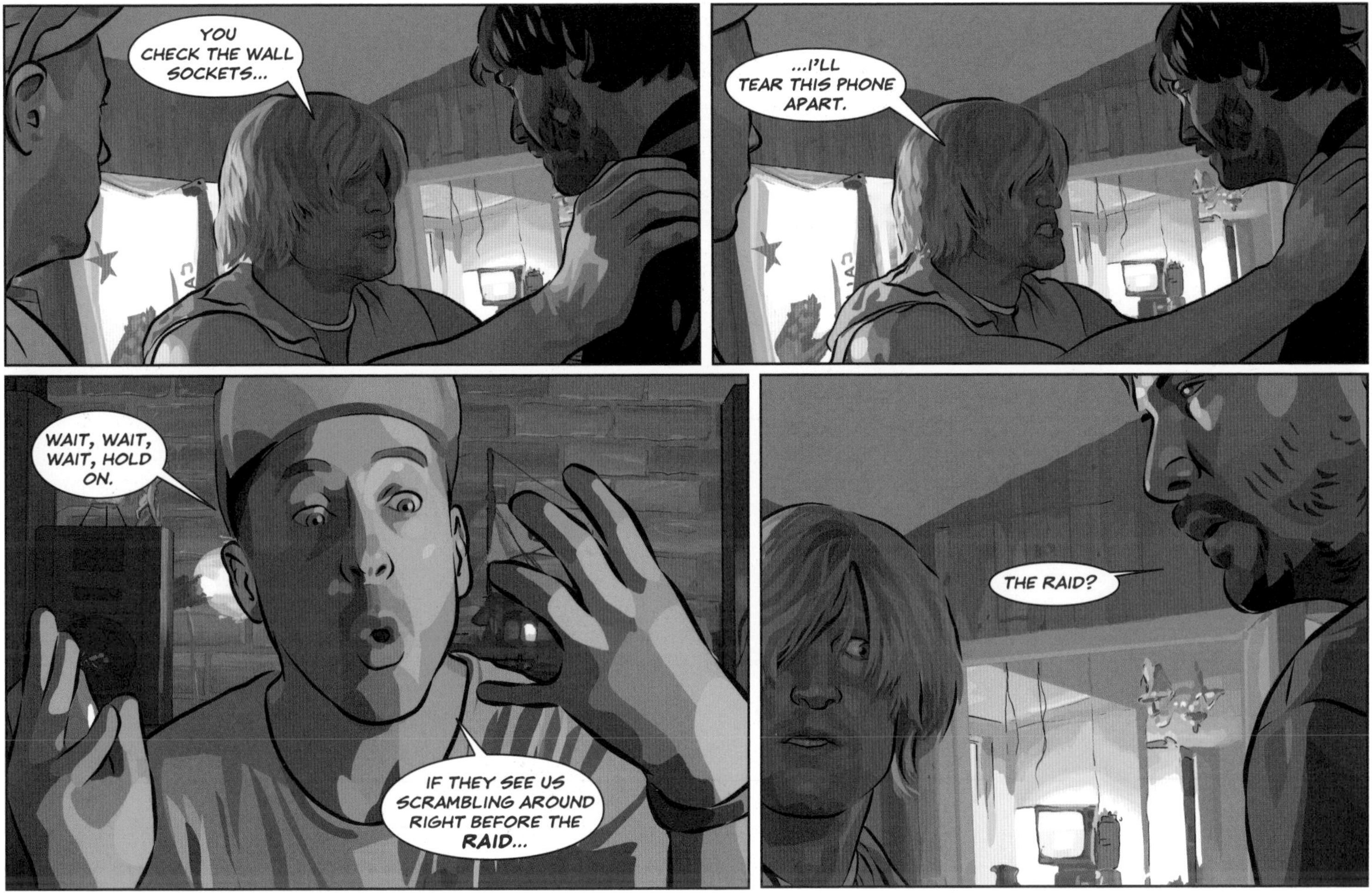
YOU CHECK THE WALL SOCKETS...
...I'LL TEAR THIS PHONE APART.
WAIT, WAIT, WAIT, HOLD ON.
IF THEY SEE US SCRAMBLING AROUND RIGHT BEFORE THE RAID...
THE RAID?

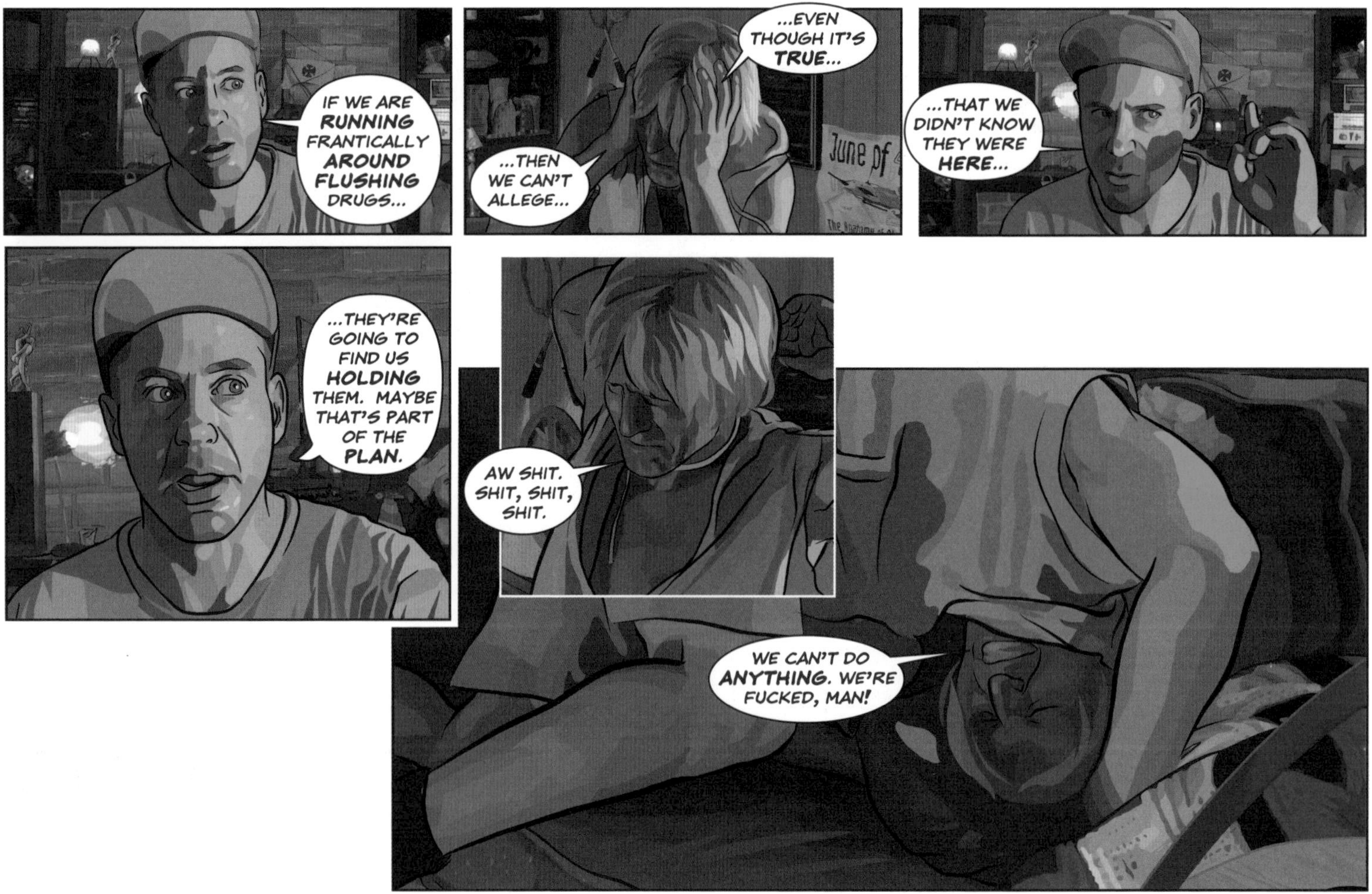
IF WE ARE RUNNING FRANTICALLY AROUND FLUSHING DRUGS...
...THEN WE CAN'T ALLEGE...
...EVEN THOUGH IT'S TRUE...
June of
...THAT WE DIDN'T KNOW THEY WERE HERE...
...THEY'RE GOING TO FIND US HOLDING THEM. MAYBE THAT'S PART OF THE PLAN.
AW SHIT. SHIT, SHIT, SHIT.
WE CAN'T DO ANYTHING. WE'RE FUCKED, MAN!

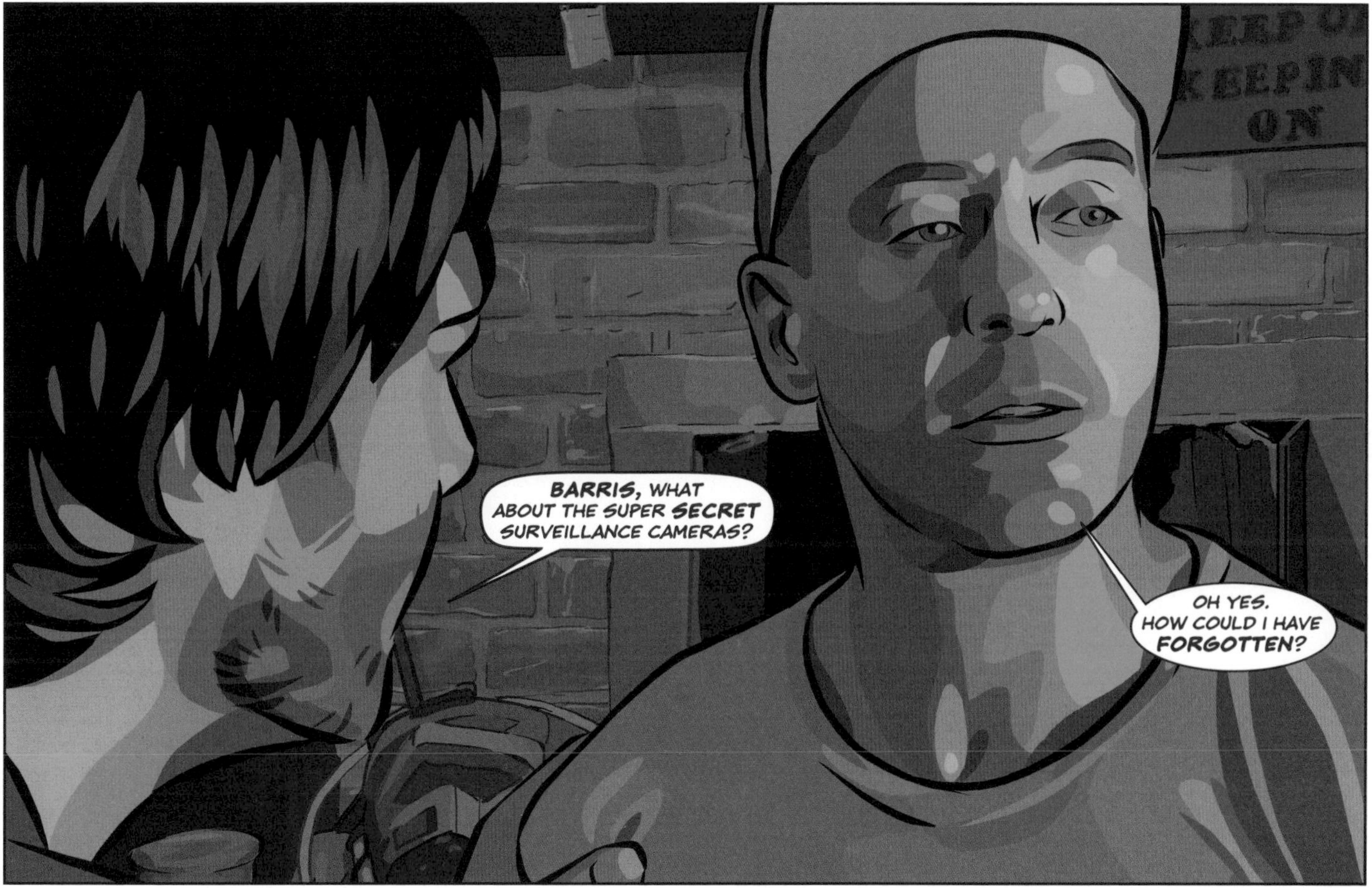
KEEP ON KEEPING ON
BARRIS, WHAT ABOUT THE SUPER SECRET SURVEILLANCE CAMERAS?
OH YES. HOW COULD I HAVE FORGOTTEN?

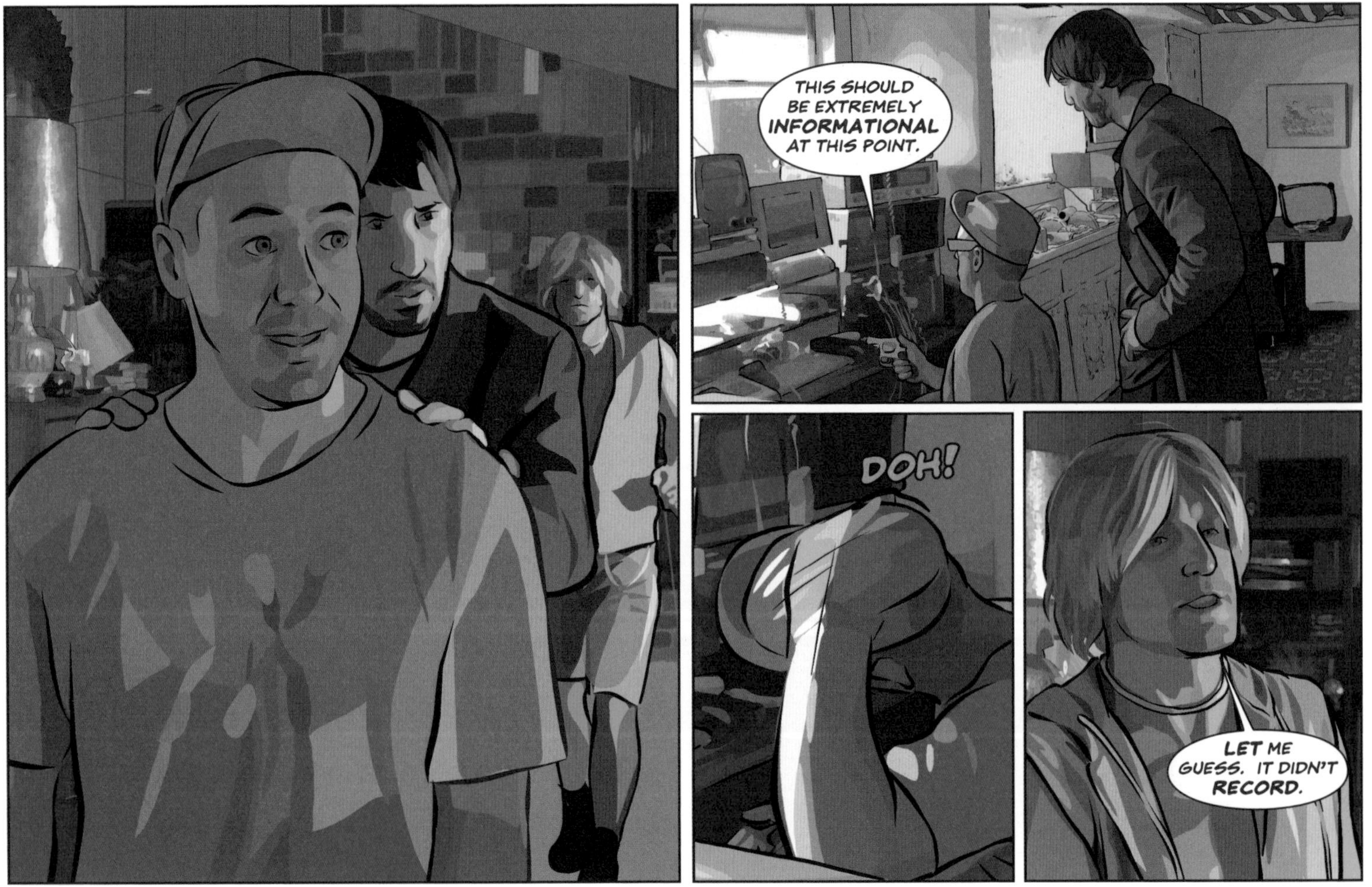
THIS SHOULD BE EXTREMELY INFORMATIONAL AT THIS POINT.
DOH!
LET ME GUESS. IT DIDN'T RECORD.

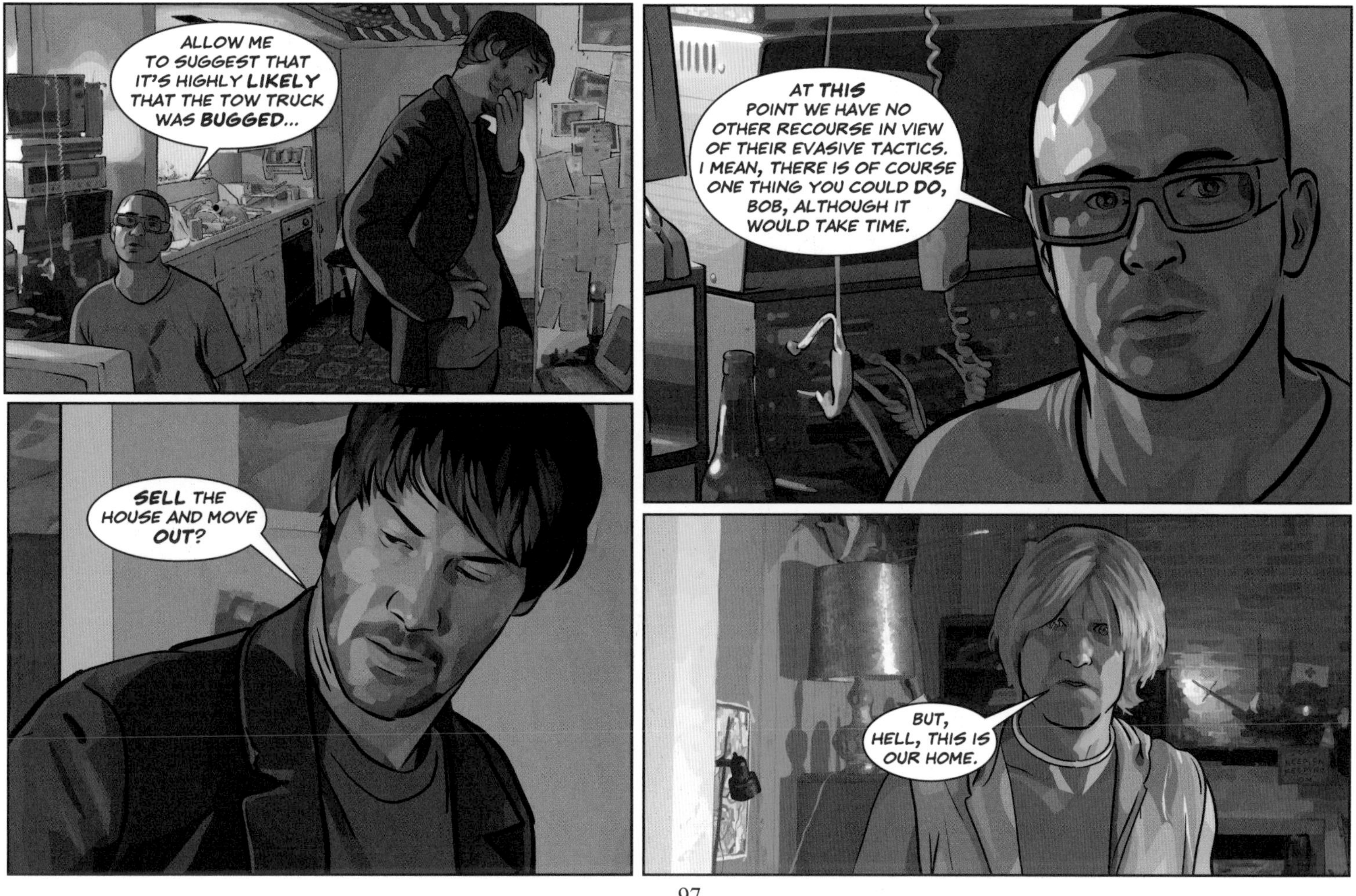
ALLOW ME TO SUGGEST THAT IT'S HIGHLY LIKELY THAT THE TOW TRUCK WAS BUGGED...
AT THIS POINT WE HAVE NO OTHER RECOURSE IN VIEW OF THEIR EVASIVE TACTICS. I MEAN, THERE IS OF COURSE ONE THING YOU COULD DO, BOB, ALTHOUGH IT WOULD TAKE TIME.
SELL THE HOUSE AND MOVE OUT?
BUT, HELL, THIS IS OUR HOME.

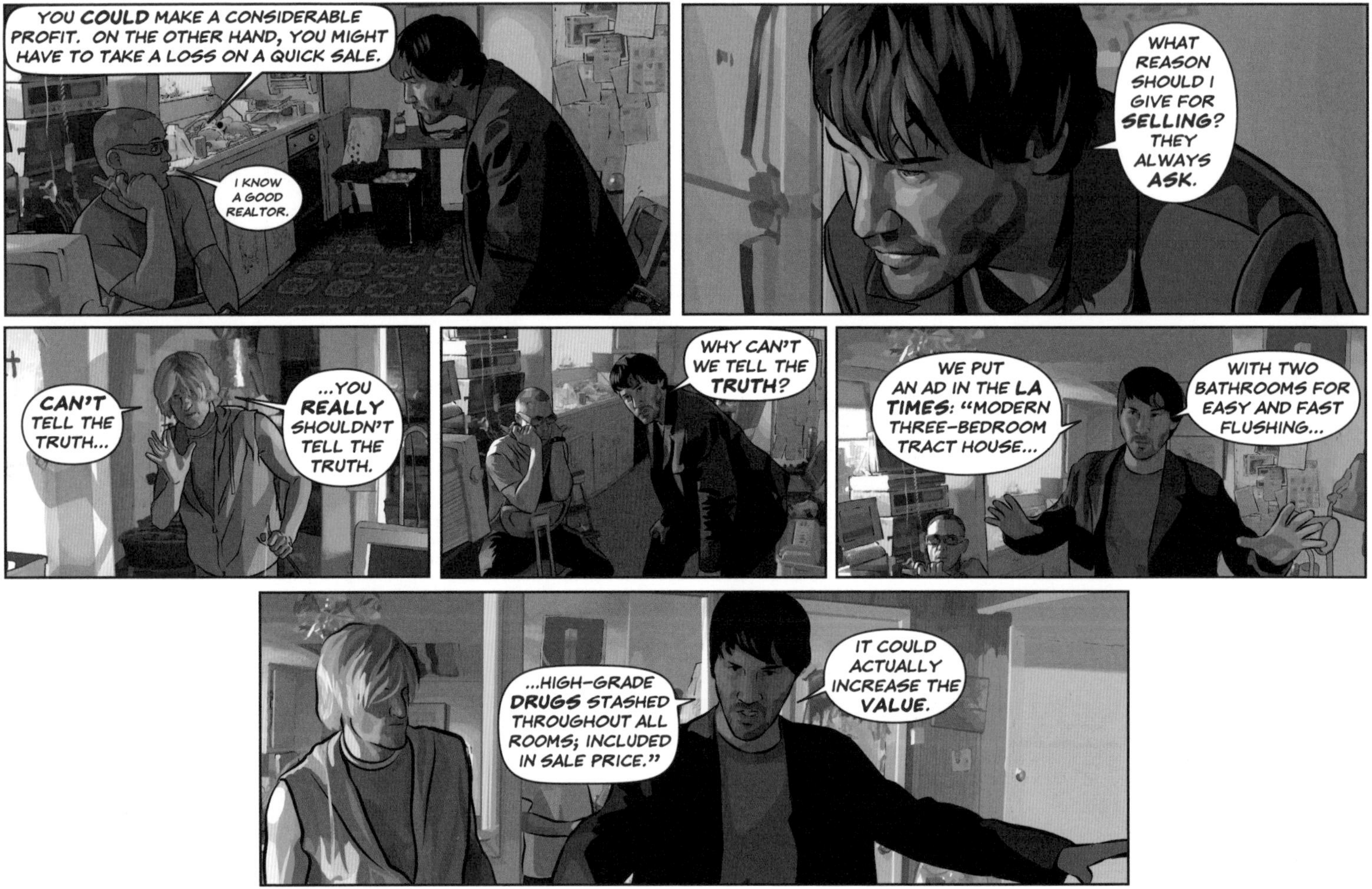
YOU COULD MAKE A CONSIDERABLE PROFIT. ON THE OTHER HAND, YOU MIGHT HAVE TO TAKE A LOSS ON A QUICK SALE.
I KNOW A GOOD REALTOR.
WHAT REASON SHOULD I GIVE FOR SELLING? THEY ALWAYS ASK.
CAN'T TELL THE TRUTH...
...YOU REALLY SHOULDN'T TELL THE TRUTH.
WHY CAN'T WE TELL THE TRUTH?
WE PUT AN AD IN THE LA TIMES: "MODERN THREE-BEDROOM TRACT HOUSE...
WITH TWO BATHROOMS FOR EASY AND FAST FLUSHING...
...HIGH-GRADE DRUGS STASHED THROUGHOUT ALL ROOMS; INCLUDED IN SALE PRICE."
IT COULD ACTUALLY INCREASE THE VALUE.

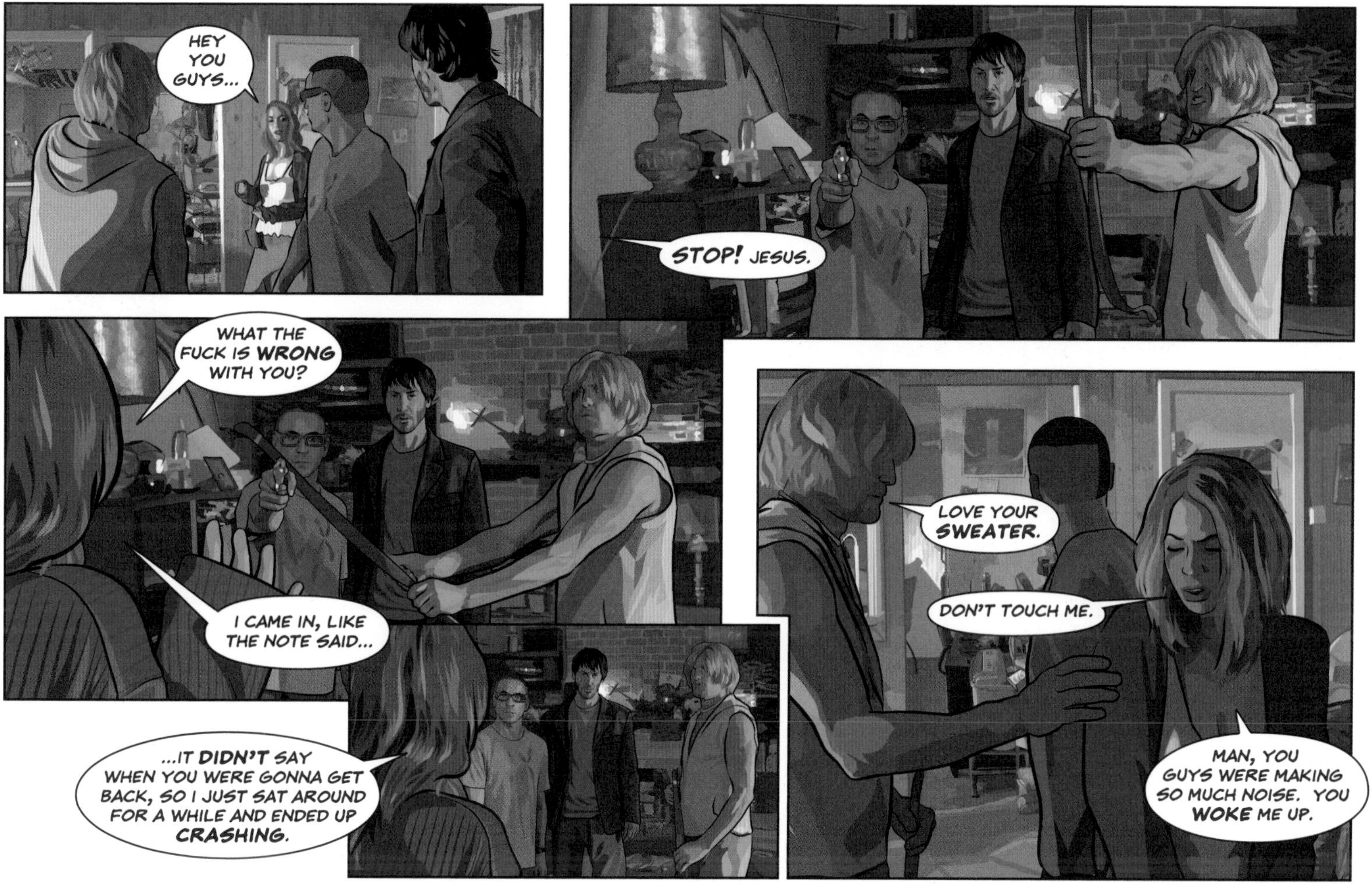
HEY YOU GUYS...
STOP! JESUS.
WHAT THE FUCK IS WRONG WITH YOU?
I CAME IN, LIKE THE NOTE SAID...
...IT DIDN'T SAY WHEN YOU WERE GONNA GET BACK, SO I JUST SAT AROUND FOR A WHILE AND ENDED UP CRASHING.
LOVE YOUR SWEATER.
DON'T TOUCH ME.
MAN, YOU GUYS WERE MAKING SO MUCH NOISE. YOU WOKE ME UP.

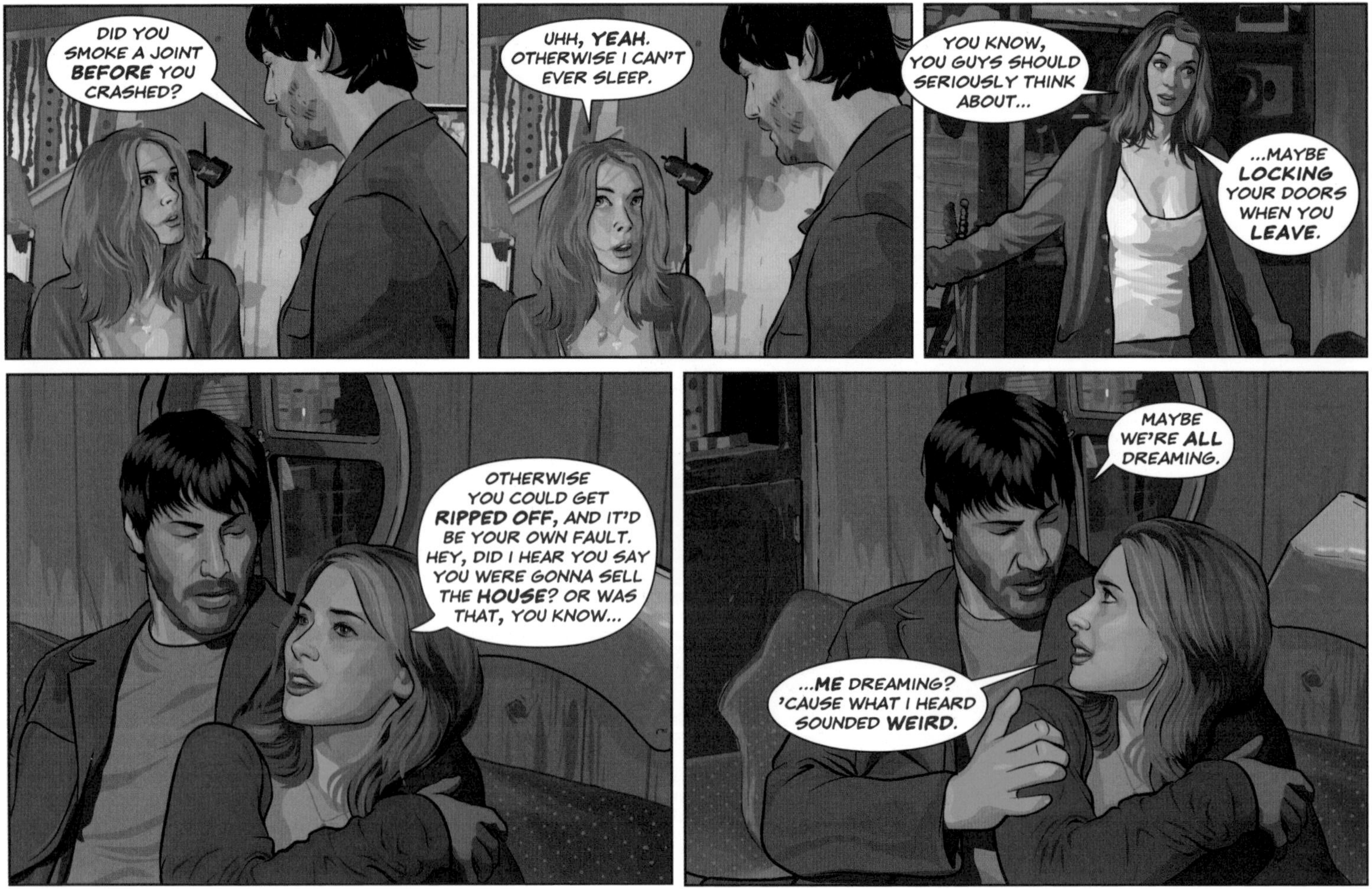
DID YOU SMOKE A JOINT BEFORE YOU CRASHED?
UHH, YEAH. OTHERWISE I CAN'T EVER SLEEP.
YOU KNOW, YOU GUYS SHOULD SERIOUSLY THINK ABOUT...
...MAYBE LOCKING YOUR DOORS WHEN YOU LEAVE.
OTHERWISE YOU COULD GET RIPPED OFF, AND IT'D BE YOUR OWN FAULT. HEY, DID I HEAR YOU SAY YOU WERE GONNA SELL THE HOUSE? OR WAS THAT, YOU KNOW...
MAYBE WE'RE ALL DREAMING.
...ME DREAMING? 'CAUSE WHAT I HEARD SOUNDED WEIRD.

THE NEXT DAY HANK WALKS FRED THROUGH A DUMPY ROOM FILLED WITH MONITORS AND COMPUTER STATIONS...

SO THE INFORMATION FROM THE HOLO-SCANNERS IN ARCTOR'S HOUSE ARE TRANSMITTED BACK **HERE**, TO STATION 12-879.

THIS'LL BE YOUR **NEW** HOME AWAY FROM HOME, PAL.

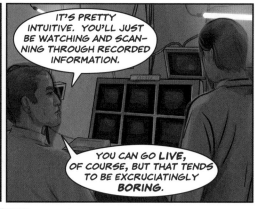

IT'S PRETTY INTUITIVE. YOU'LL JUST BE WATCHING AND SCANNING THROUGH RECORDED INFORMATION.

YOU CAN GO **LIVE**, OF COURSE, BUT THAT TENDS TO BE EXCRUCIATINGLY **BORING**.

YOU **SEE** WHERE THE HOLOS ARE PLACED? WHAT WOULD BE **GREAT** IS IF THEY EVER NEED SERVICING OR CHANGING OUT, IF YOU COULD DO THAT **YOURSELF** WHEN NO ONE ELSE IS AROUND.

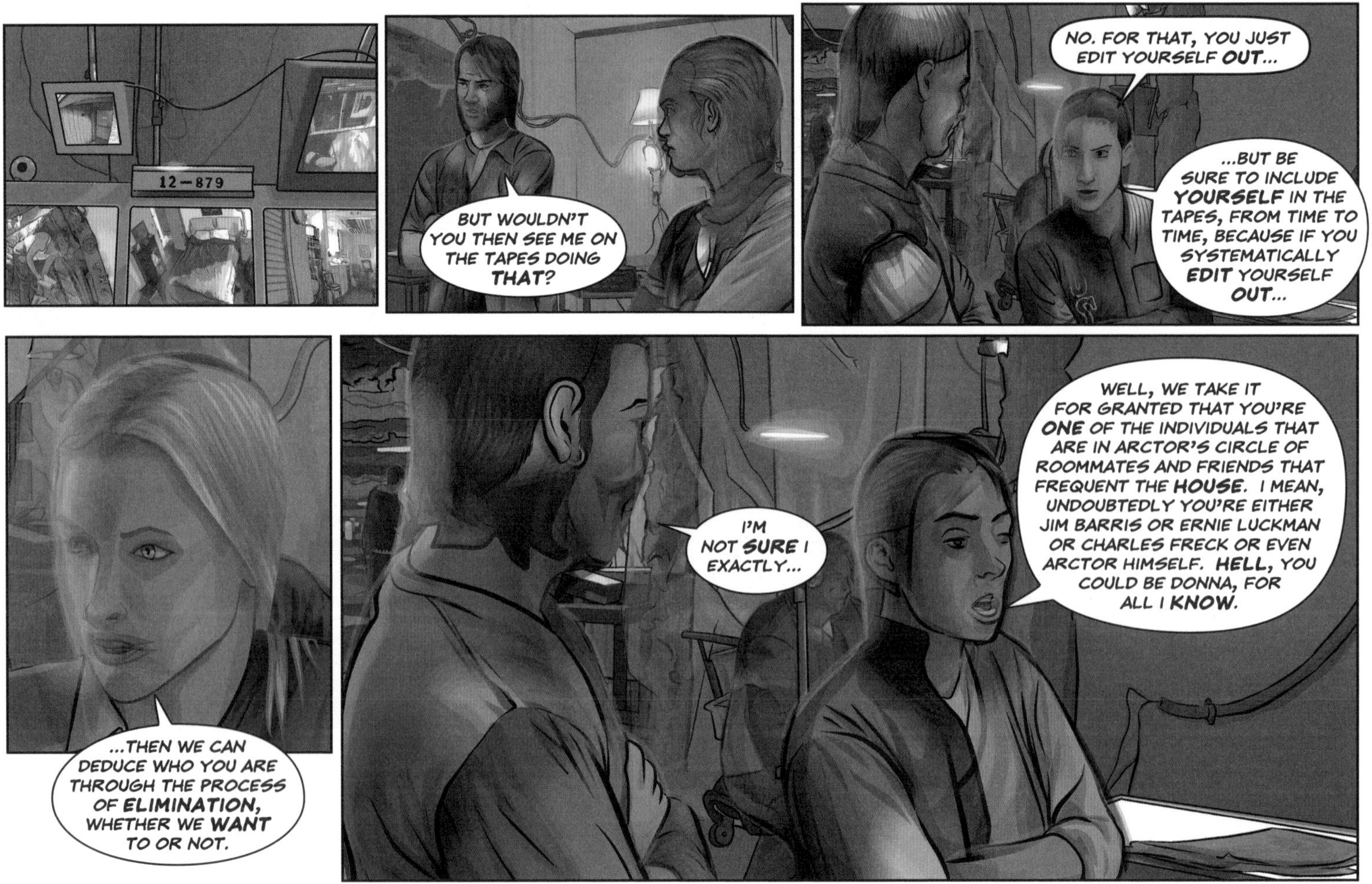
12-879
BUT WOULDN'T YOU THEN SEE ME ON THE TAPES DOING THAT?
NO. FOR THAT, YOU JUST EDIT YOURSELF OUT...
...BUT BE SURE TO INCLUDE YOURSELF IN THE TAPES, FROM TIME TO TIME, BECAUSE IF YOU SYSTEMATICALLY EDIT YOURSELF OUT...
...THEN WE CAN DEDUCE WHO YOU ARE THROUGH THE PROCESS OF ELIMINATION, WHETHER WE WANT TO OR NOT.
I'M NOT SURE I EXACTLY...
WELL, WE TAKE IT FOR GRANTED THAT YOU'RE ONE OF THE INDIVIDUALS THAT ARE IN ARCTOR'S CIRCLE OF ROOMMATES AND FRIENDS THAT FREQUENT THE HOUSE. I MEAN, UNDOUBTEDLY YOU'RE EITHER JIM BARRIS OR ERNIE LUCKMAN OR CHARLES FRECK OR EVEN ARCTOR HIMSELF. HELL, YOU COULD BE DONNA, FOR ALL I KNOW.

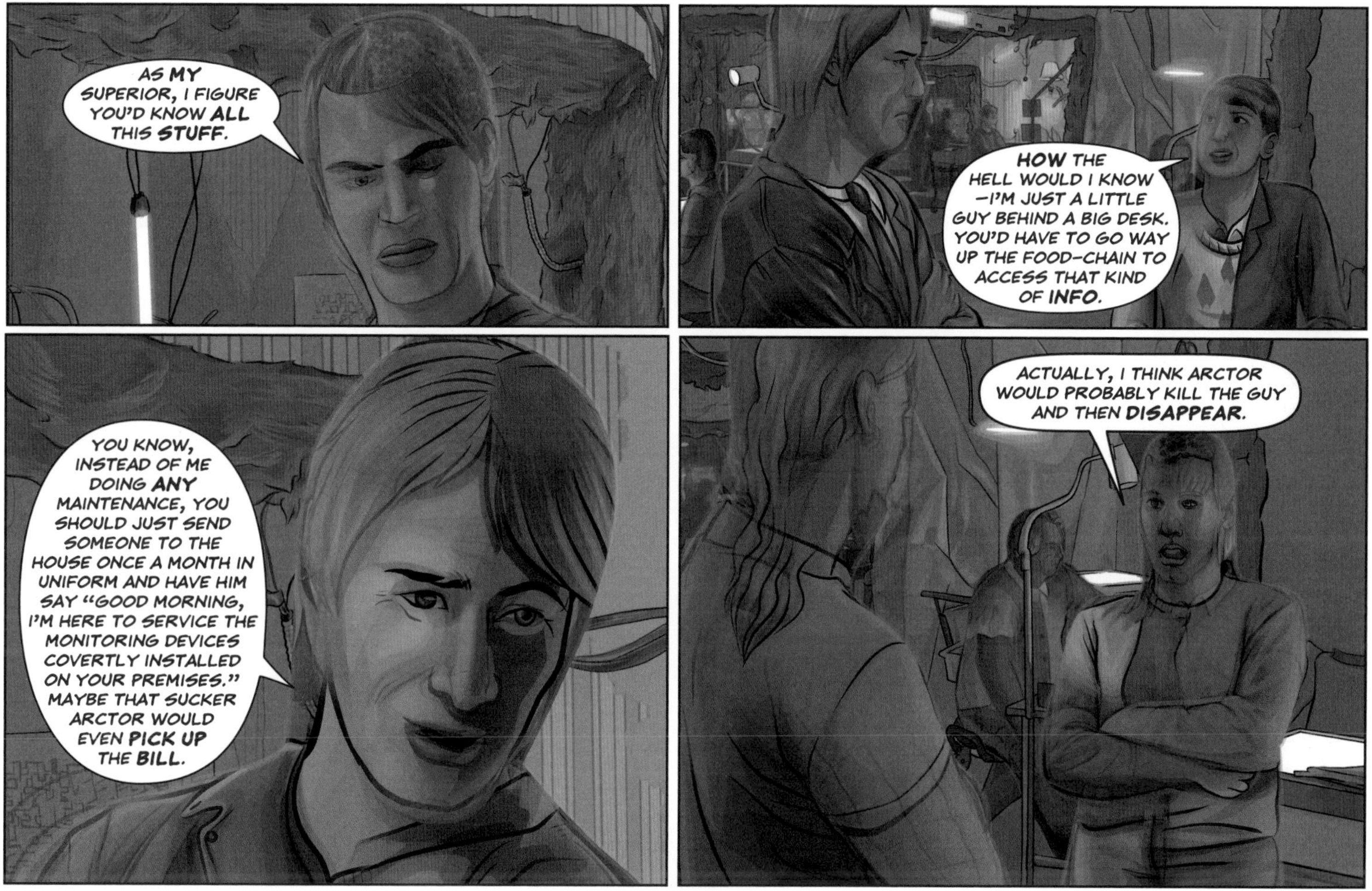
AS MY SUPERIOR, I FIGURE YOU'D KNOW ALL THIS STUFF.
HOW THE HELL WOULD I KNOW —I'M JUST A LITTLE GUY BEHIND A BIG DESK. YOU'D HAVE TO GO WAY UP THE FOOD-CHAIN TO ACCESS THAT KIND OF INFO.
YOU KNOW, INSTEAD OF ME DOING ANY MAINTENANCE, YOU SHOULD JUST SEND SOMEONE TO THE HOUSE ONCE A MONTH IN UNIFORM AND HAVE HIM SAY "GOOD MORNING, I'M HERE TO SERVICE THE MONITORING DEVICES COVERTLY INSTALLED ON YOUR PREMISES." MAYBE THAT SUCKER ARCTOR WOULD EVEN PICK UP THE BILL.
ACTUALLY, I THINK ARCTOR WOULD PROBABLY KILL THE GUY AND THEN DISAPPEAR.

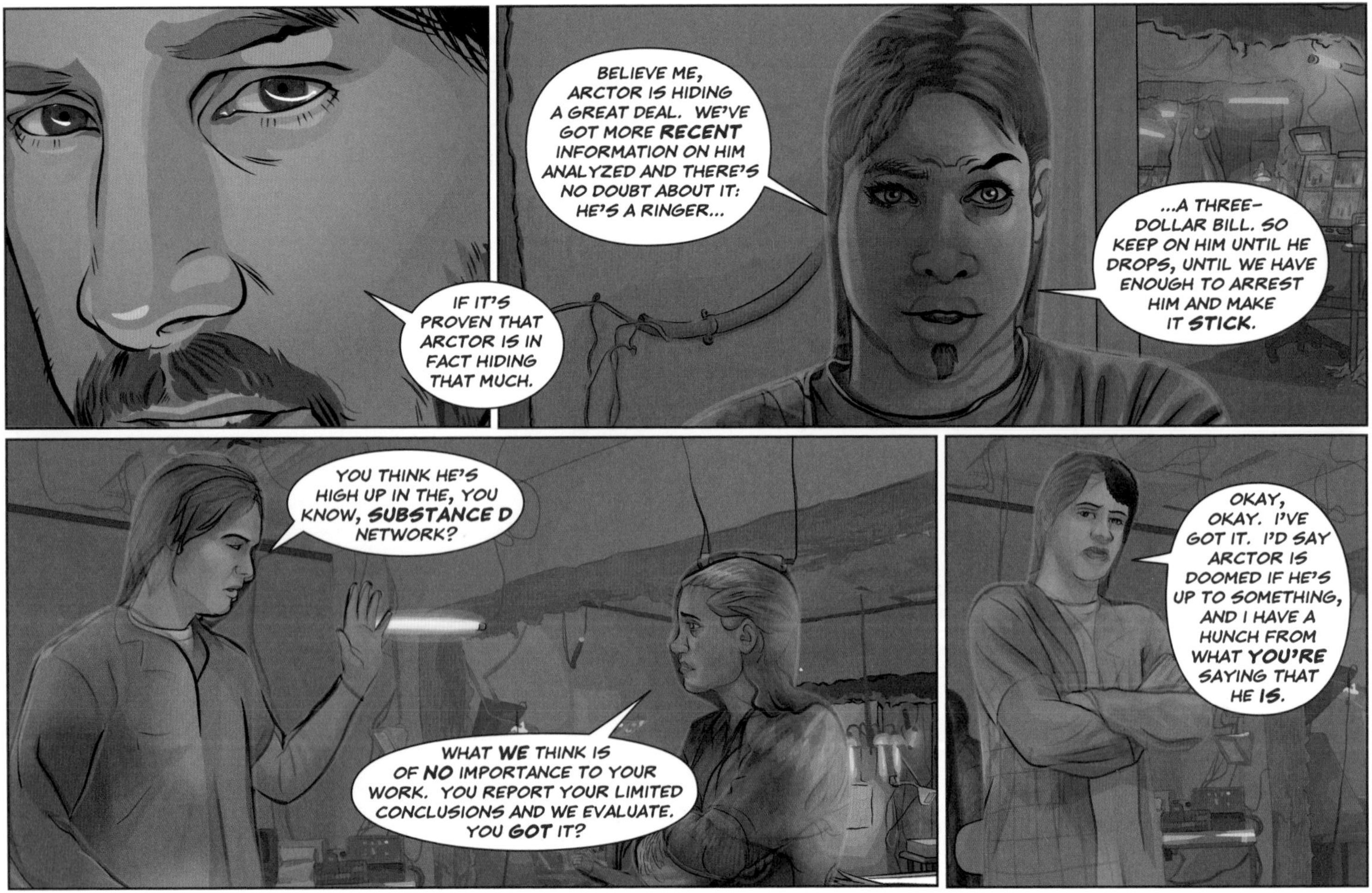
BELIEVE ME, ARCTOR IS HIDING A GREAT DEAL. WE'VE GOT MORE RECENT INFORMATION ON HIM ANALYZED AND THERE'S NO DOUBT ABOUT IT: HE'S A RINGER...
IF IT'S PROVEN THAT ARCTOR IS IN FACT HIDING THAT MUCH.
...A THREE-DOLLAR BILL. SO KEEP ON HIM UNTIL HE DROPS, UNTIL WE HAVE ENOUGH TO ARREST HIM AND MAKE IT STICK.
YOU THINK HE'S HIGH UP IN THE, YOU KNOW, SUBSTANCE D NETWORK?
WHAT WE THINK IS OF NO IMPORTANCE TO YOUR WORK. YOU REPORT YOUR LIMITED CONCLUSIONS AND WE EVALUATE. YOU GOT IT?
OKAY, OKAY. I'VE GOT IT. I'D SAY ARCTOR IS DOOMED IF HE'S UP TO SOMETHING, AND I HAVE A HUNCH FROM WHAT YOU'RE SAYING THAT HE IS.

BURNING DAYLIGHT AT BOB'S HOUSE, TRYING TO FIX HIS CAR.

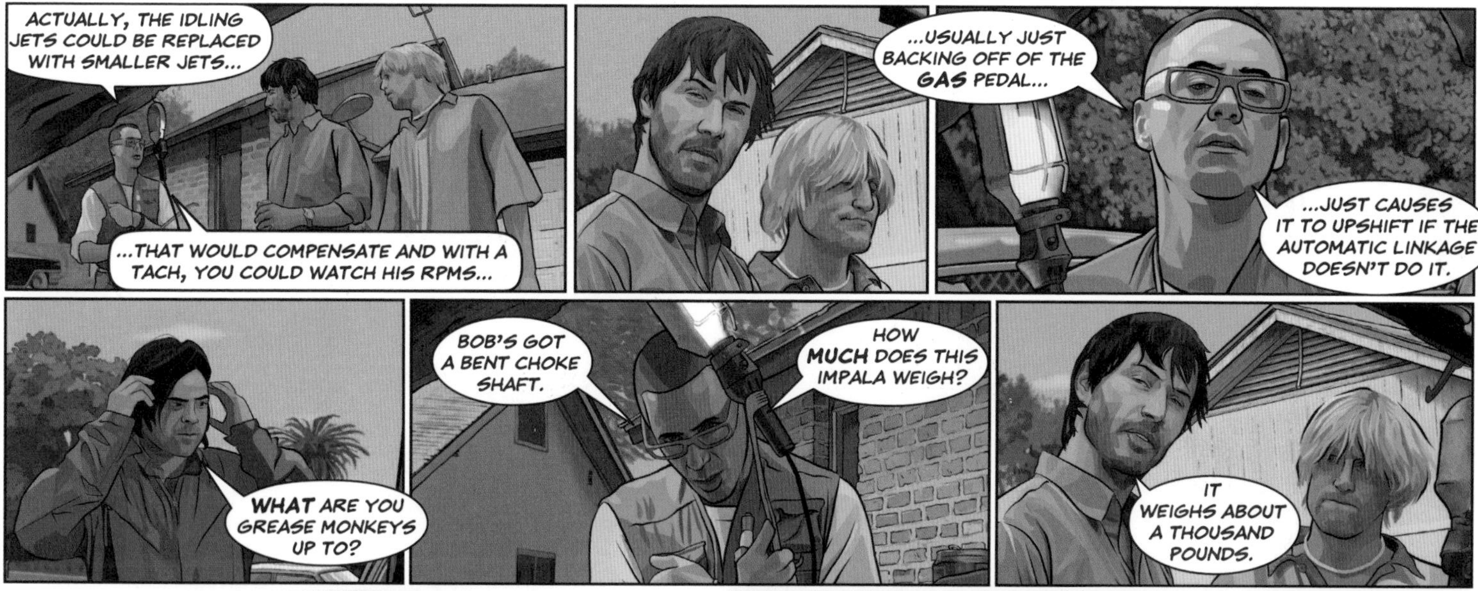
ACTUALLY, THE IDLING JETS COULD BE REPLACED WITH SMALLER JETS...
...THAT WOULD COMPENSATE AND WITH A TACH, YOU COULD WATCH HIS RPMS...
...USUALLY JUST BACKING OFF OF THE GAS PEDAL...
...JUST CAUSES IT TO UPSHIFT IF THE AUTOMATIC LINKAGE DOESN'T DO IT.
WHAT ARE YOU GREASE MONKEYS UP TO?
BOB'S GOT A BENT CHOKE SHAFT.
HOW MUCH DOES THIS IMPALA WEIGH?
IT WEIGHS ABOUT A THOUSAND POUNDS.

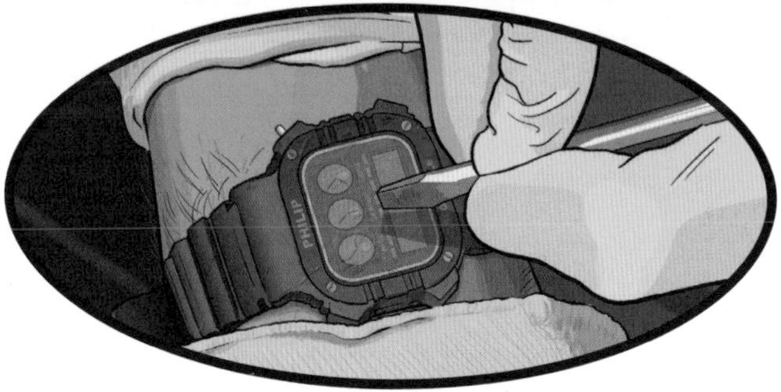
PHILIP

BARRIS DOES SOME CALCULATIONS, USING HIS WATCHFACE.

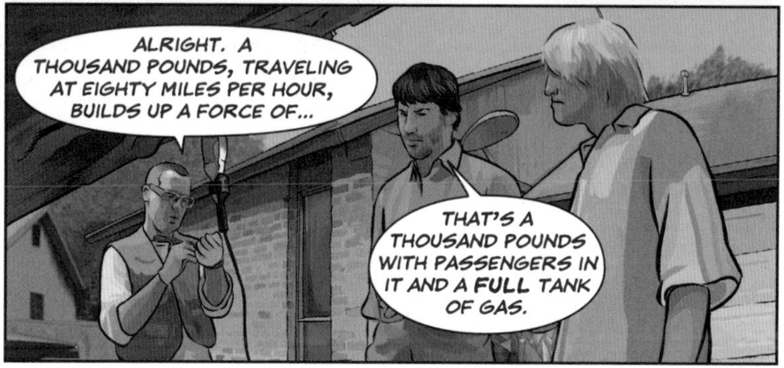
ALRIGHT. A THOUSAND POUNDS, TRAVELING AT EIGHTY MILES PER HOUR, BUILDS UP A FORCE OF...
THAT'S A THOUSAND POUNDS WITH PASSENGERS IN IT AND A FULL TANK OF GAS.

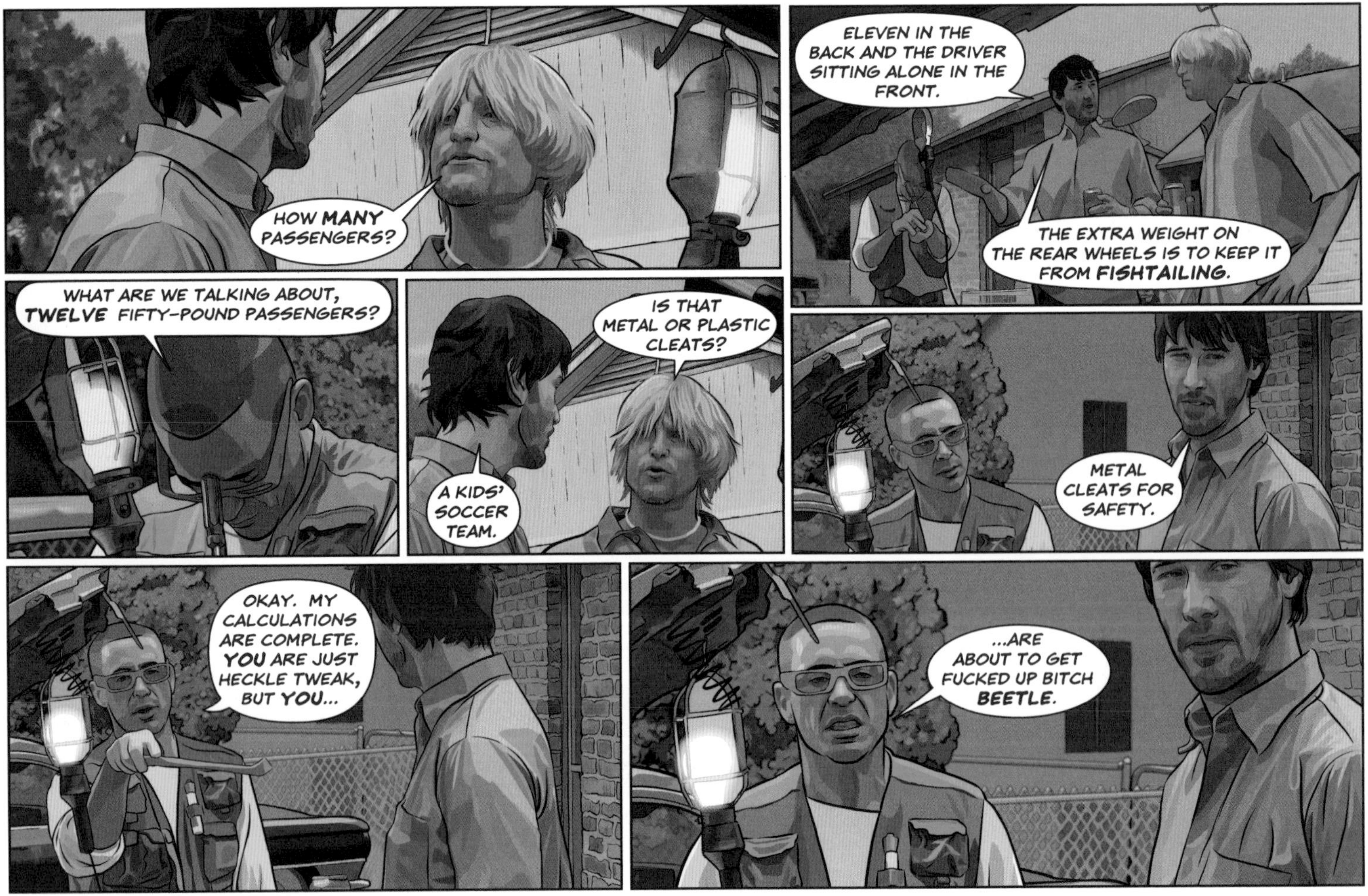
HOW MANY PASSENGERS?
ELEVEN IN THE BACK AND THE DRIVER SITTING ALONE IN THE FRONT.
THE EXTRA WEIGHT ON THE REAR WHEELS IS TO KEEP IT FROM FISHTAILING.
WHAT ARE WE TALKING ABOUT, TWELVE FIFTY-POUND PASSENGERS?
A KIDS' SOCCER TEAM.
IS THAT METAL OR PLASTIC CLEATS?
METAL CLEATS FOR SAFETY.
OKAY. MY CALCULATIONS ARE COMPLETE. YOU ARE JUST HECKLE TWEAK, BUT YOU...
...ARE ABOUT TO GET FUCKED UP BITCH BEETLE.

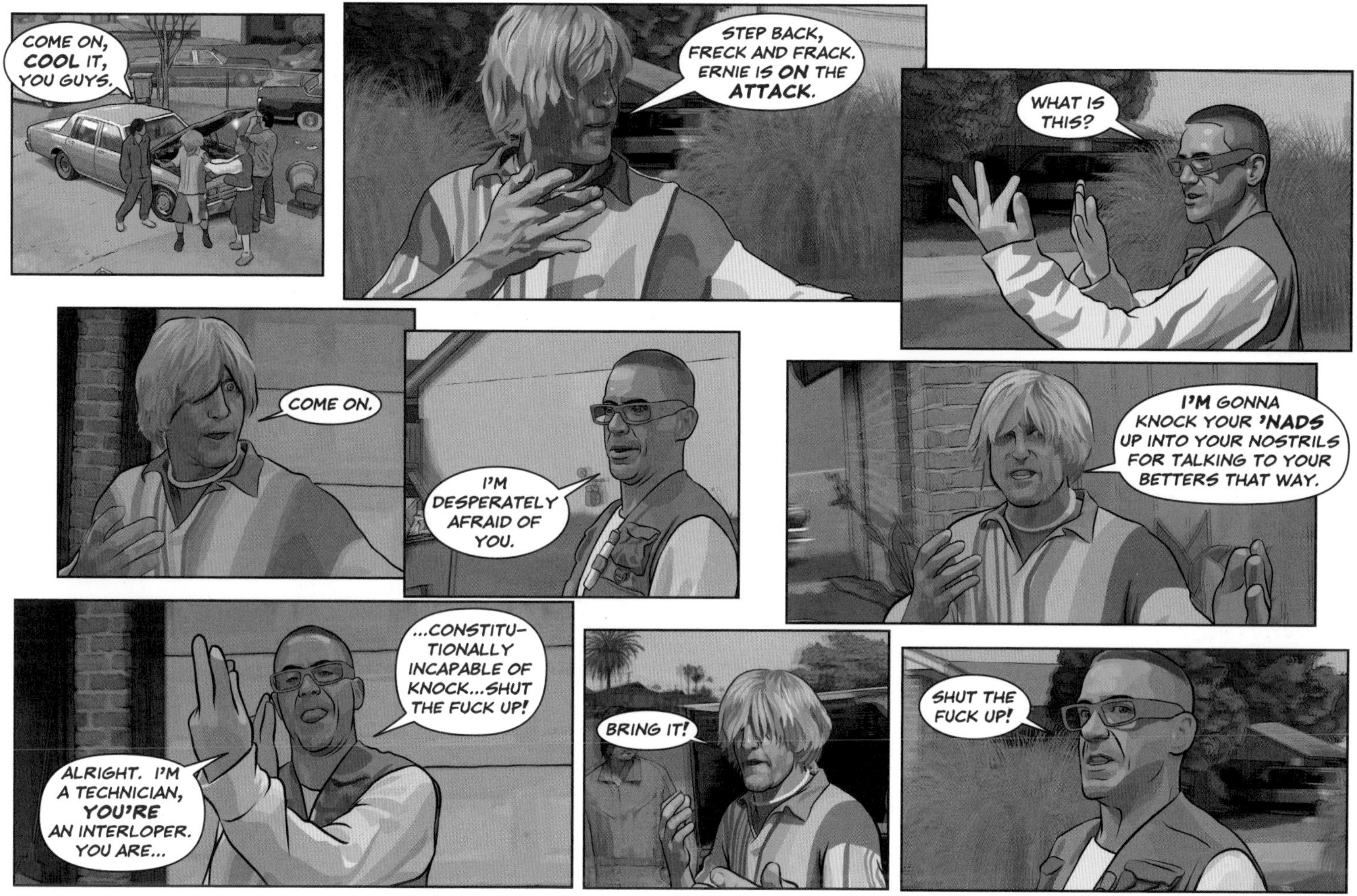
COME ON, COOL IT, YOU GUYS.
STEP BACK, FRECK AND FRACK. ERNIE IS ON THE ATTACK.
WHAT IS THIS?
COME ON.
I'M DESPERATELY AFRAID OF YOU.
I'M GONNA KNOCK YOUR 'NADS UP INTO YOUR NOSTRILS FOR TALKING TO YOUR BETTERS THAT WAY.
ALRIGHT. I'M A TECHNICIAN, YOU'RE AN INTERLOPER. YOU ARE...
...CONSTITUTIONALLY INCAPABLE OF KNOCK...SHUT THE FUCK UP!
BRING IT!
SHUT THE FUCK UP!

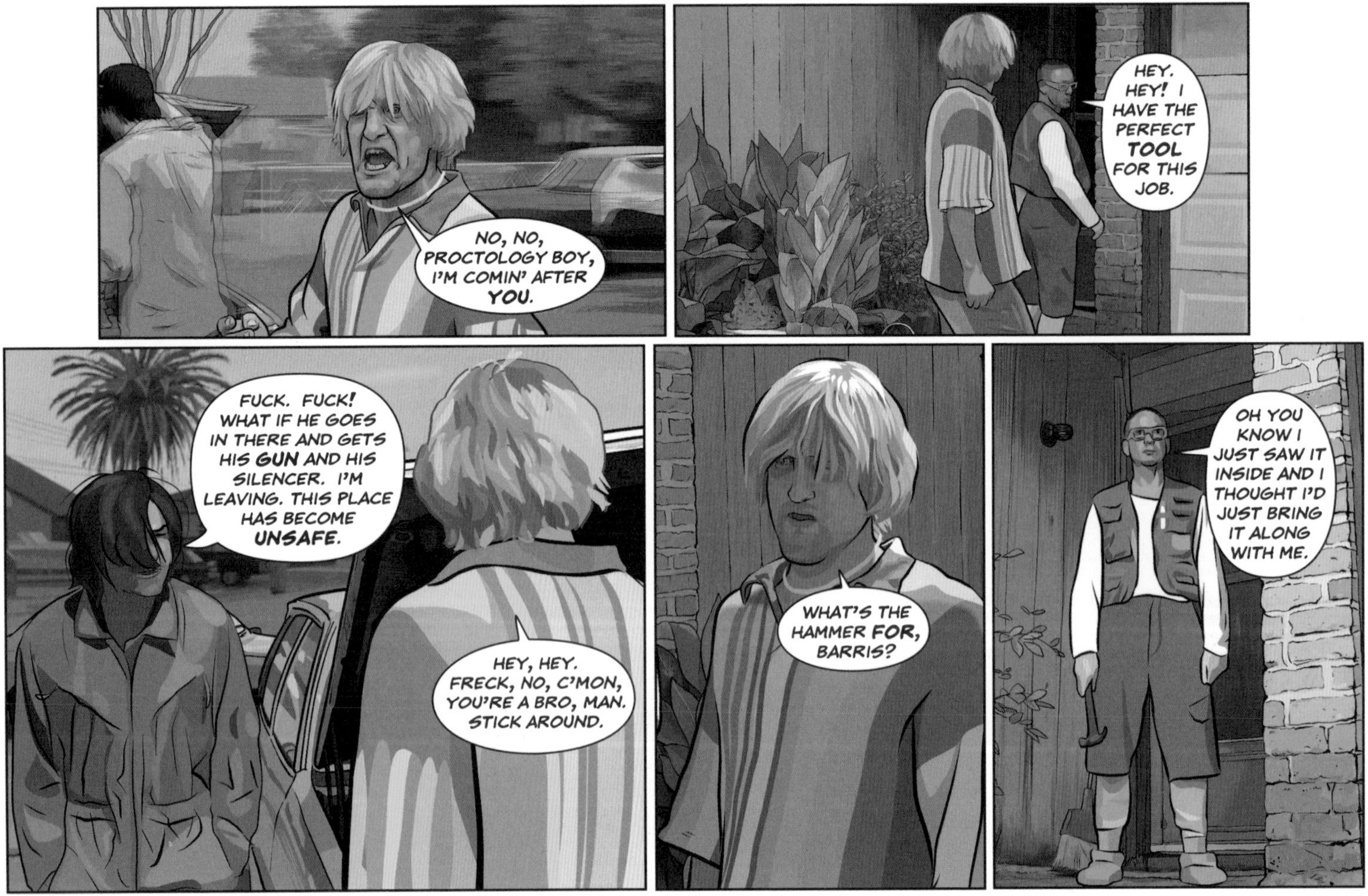
NO, NO, PROCTOLOGY BOY, I'M COMIN' AFTER YOU.
HEY. HEY! I HAVE THE PERFECT TOOL FOR THIS JOB.
FUCK. FUCK! WHAT IF HE GOES IN THERE AND GETS HIS GUN AND HIS SILENCER. I'M LEAVING. THIS PLACE HAS BECOME UNSAFE.
HEY, HEY. FRECK, NO, C'MON, YOU'RE A BRO, MAN. STICK AROUND.
WHAT'S THE HAMMER FOR, BARRIS?
OH YOU KNOW I JUST SAW IT INSIDE AND I THOUGHT I'D JUST BRING IT ALONG WITH ME.

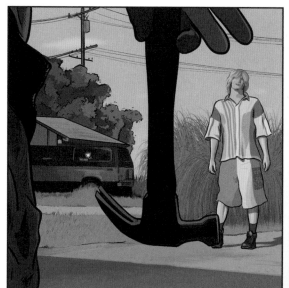

SAME WITH **THIS.**

YOU GUYS ARE FUCKED UP.

YOU READY?

OH, YEAH, YEAH, WHAT DO YOU WANT? **COME ON,** HAMMERHEAD.

MAKE A MOVE.

OKAY, IF YOU GUYS ARE GOING TO **KILL** EACH OTHER, I'M SPLITTING. IT'S GETTING REALLY FUCKED UP **OVER HERE.**

BARRIS, LUCKMAN, AND ARCTOR ARE SITTING AROUND THE LIVING ROOM. LUCKMAN IS ROLLING A JOINT AS HE TALKS...

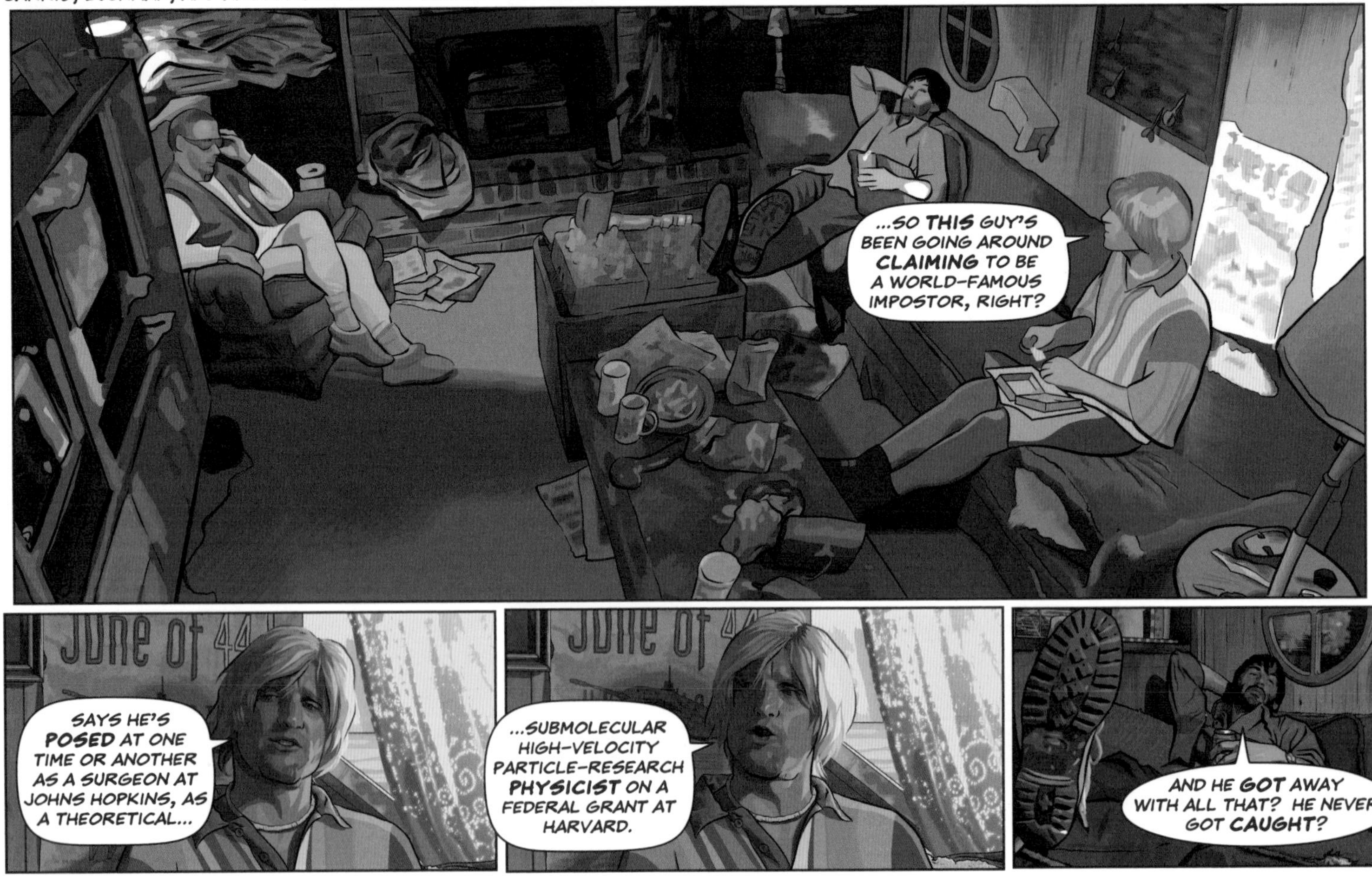
...SO THIS GUY'S BEEN GOING AROUND CLAIMING TO BE A WORLD-FAMOUS IMPOSTOR, RIGHT?
SAYS HE'S POSED AT ONE TIME OR ANOTHER AS A SURGEON AT JOHNS HOPKINS, AS A THEORETICAL...
...SUBMOLECULAR HIGH-VELOCITY PARTICLE-RESEARCH PHYSICIST ON A FEDERAL GRANT AT HARVARD.
AND HE GOT AWAY WITH ALL THAT? HE NEVER GOT CAUGHT?

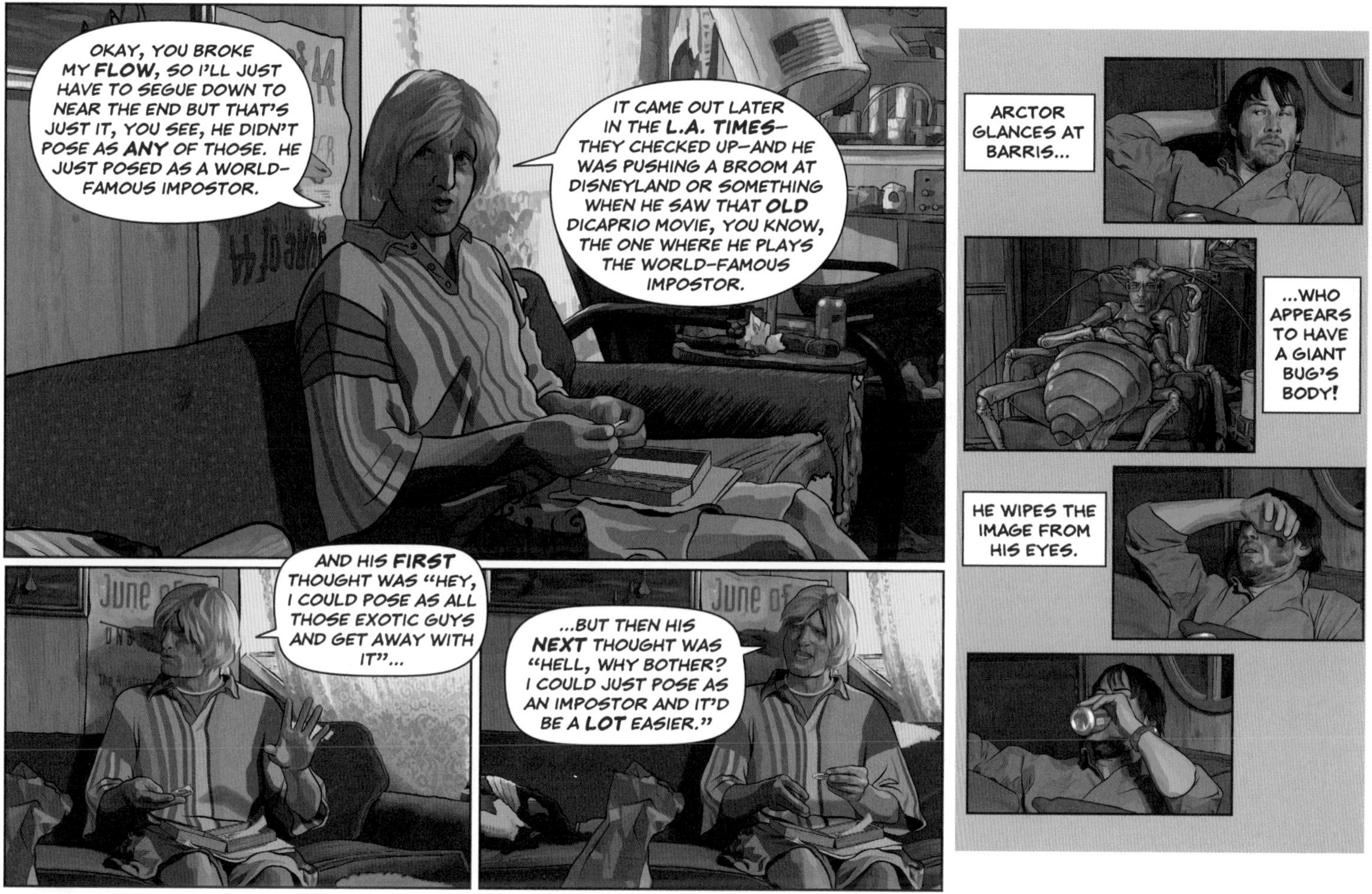
OKAY, YOU BROKE MY FLOW, SO I'LL JUST HAVE TO SEGUE DOWN TO NEAR THE END BUT THAT'S JUST IT, YOU SEE, HE DIDN'T POSE AS ANY OF THOSE. HE JUST POSED AS A WORLD-FAMOUS IMPOSTOR.
IT CAME OUT LATER IN THE L.A. TIMES—THEY CHECKED UP—AND HE WAS PUSHING A BROOM AT DISNEYLAND OR SOMETHING WHEN HE SAW THAT OLD DICAPRIO MOVIE, YOU KNOW, THE ONE WHERE HE PLAYS THE WORLD-FAMOUS IMPOSTOR.
AND HIS FIRST THOUGHT WAS "HEY, I COULD POSE AS ALL THOSE EXOTIC GUYS AND GET AWAY WITH IT"...
...BUT THEN HIS NEXT THOUGHT WAS "HELL, WHY BOTHER? I COULD JUST POSE AS AN IMPOSTOR AND IT'D BE A LOT EASIER."
ARCTOR GLANCES AT BARRIS...
...WHO APPEARS TO HAVE A GIANT BUG'S BODY!
HE WIPES THE IMAGE FROM HIS EYES.

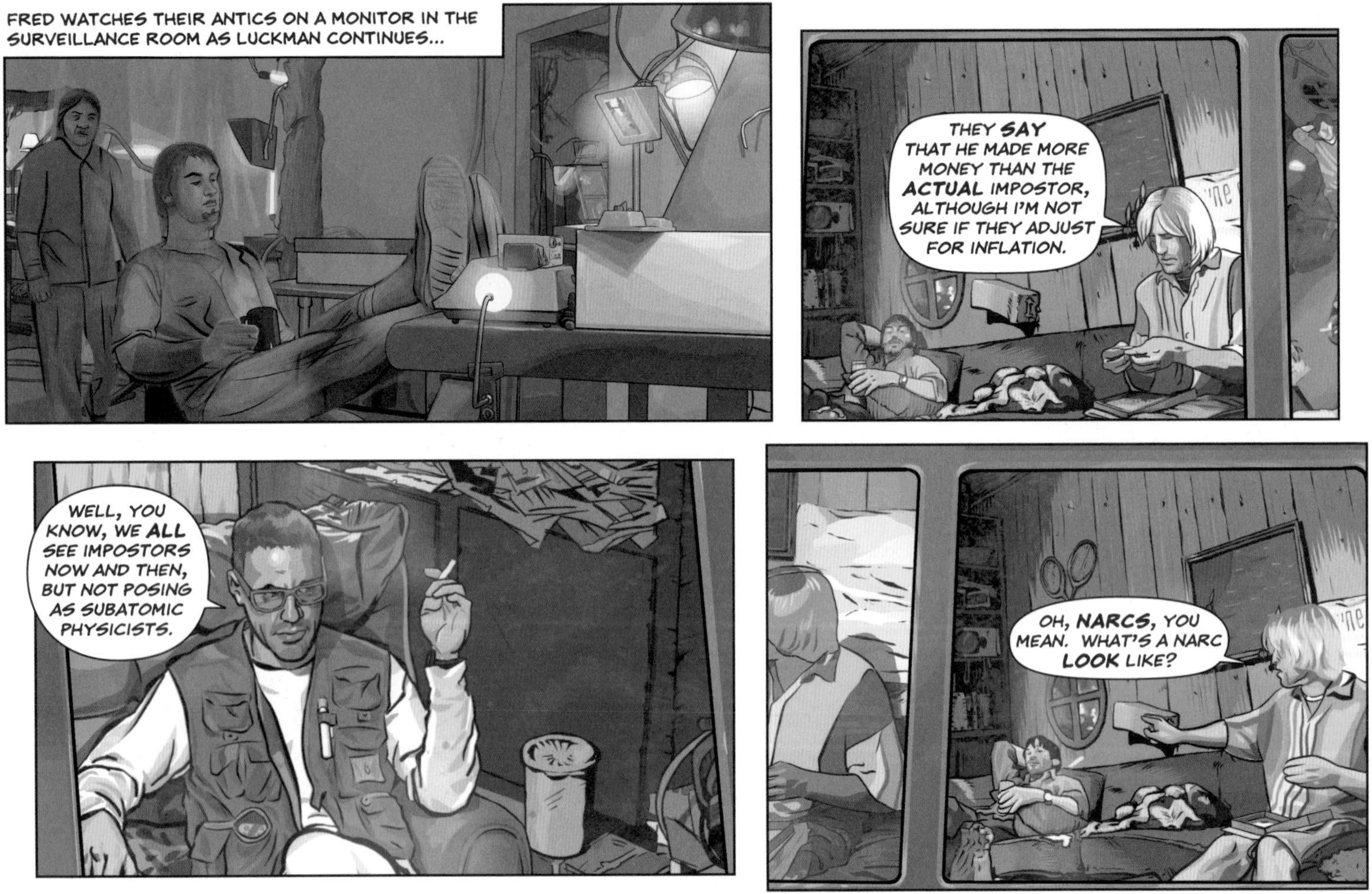
FRED WATCHES THEIR ANTICS ON A MONITOR IN THE SURVEILLANCE ROOM AS LUCKMAN CONTINUES...
THEY SAY THAT HE MADE MORE MONEY THAN THE ACTUAL IMPOSTOR, ALTHOUGH I'M NOT SURE IF THEY ADJUST FOR INFLATION.
WELL, YOU KNOW, WE ALL SEE IMPOSTORS NOW AND THEN, BUT NOT POSING AS SUBATOMIC PHYSICISTS.
OH, NARCS, YOU MEAN. WHAT'S A NARC LOOK LIKE?

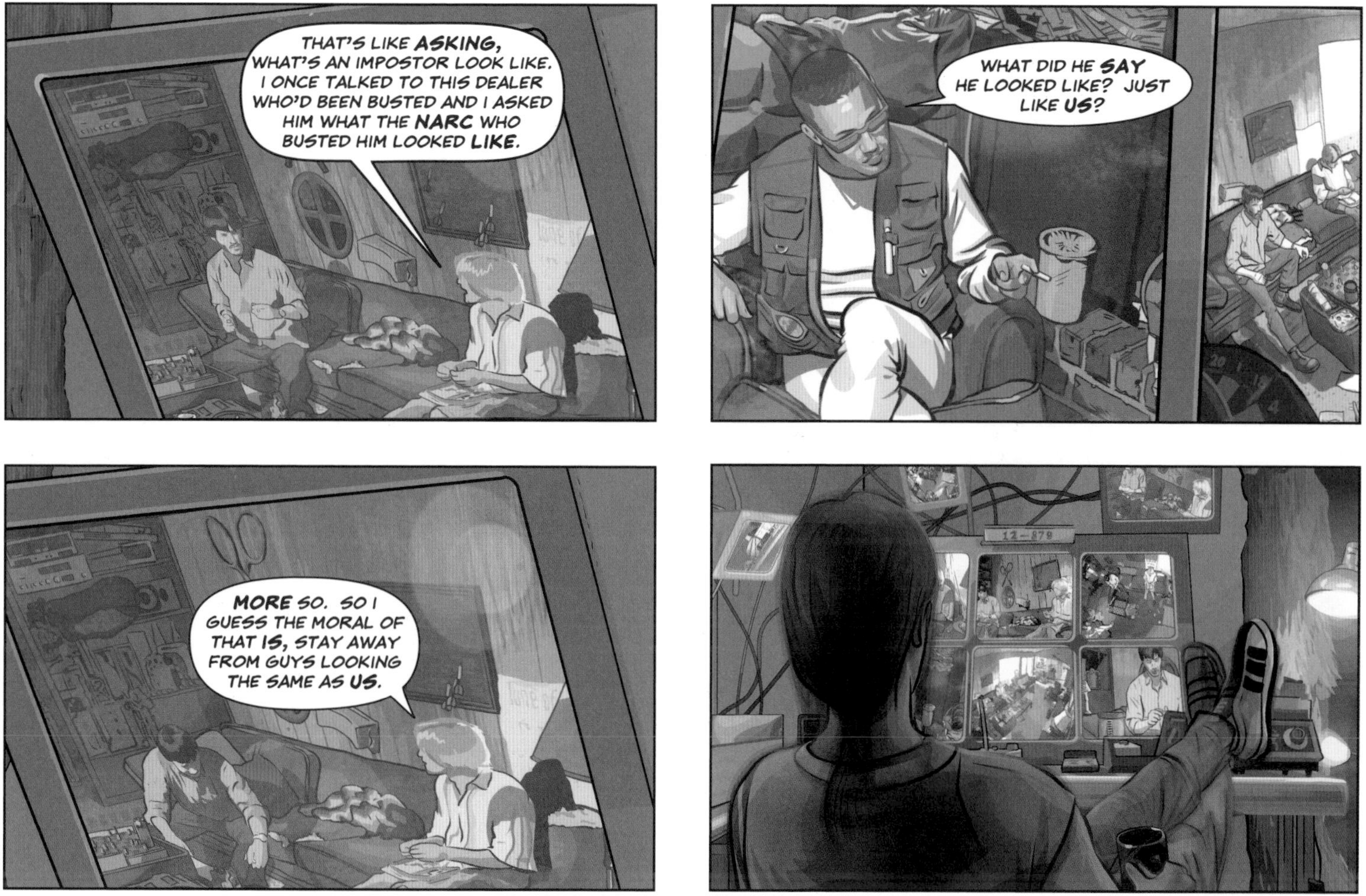
THAT'S LIKE ASKING, WHAT'S AN IMPOSTOR LOOK LIKE. I ONCE TALKED TO THIS DEALER WHO'D BEEN BUSTED AND I ASKED HIM WHAT THE NARC WHO BUSTED HIM LOOKED LIKE.
WHAT DID HE SAY HE LOOKED LIKE? JUST LIKE US?
MORE SO. SO I GUESS THE MORAL OF THAT IS, STAY AWAY FROM GUYS LOOKING THE SAME AS US.
12-879

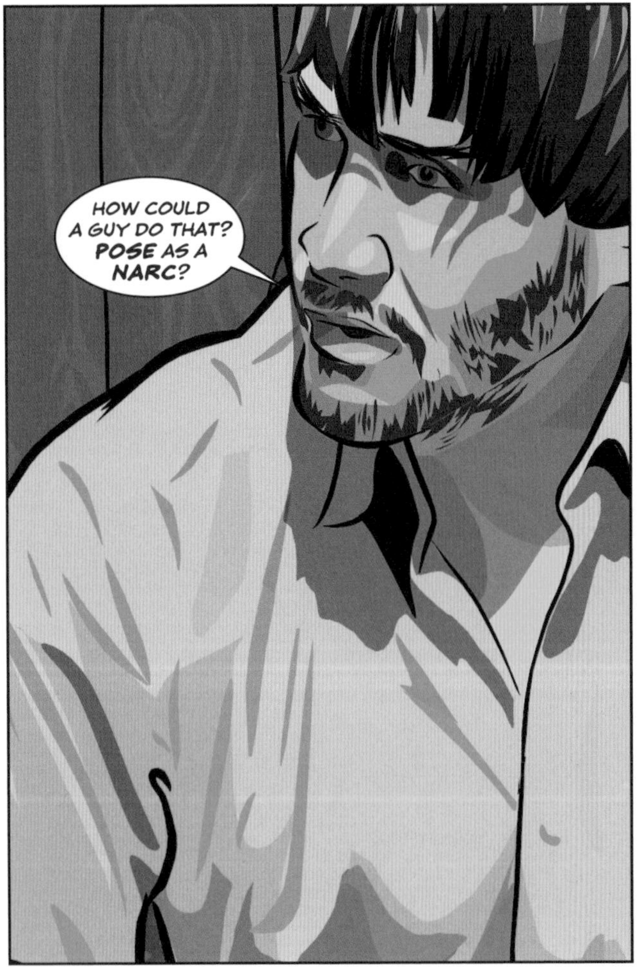
HOW COULD A GUY DO THAT? **POSE** AS A NARC?

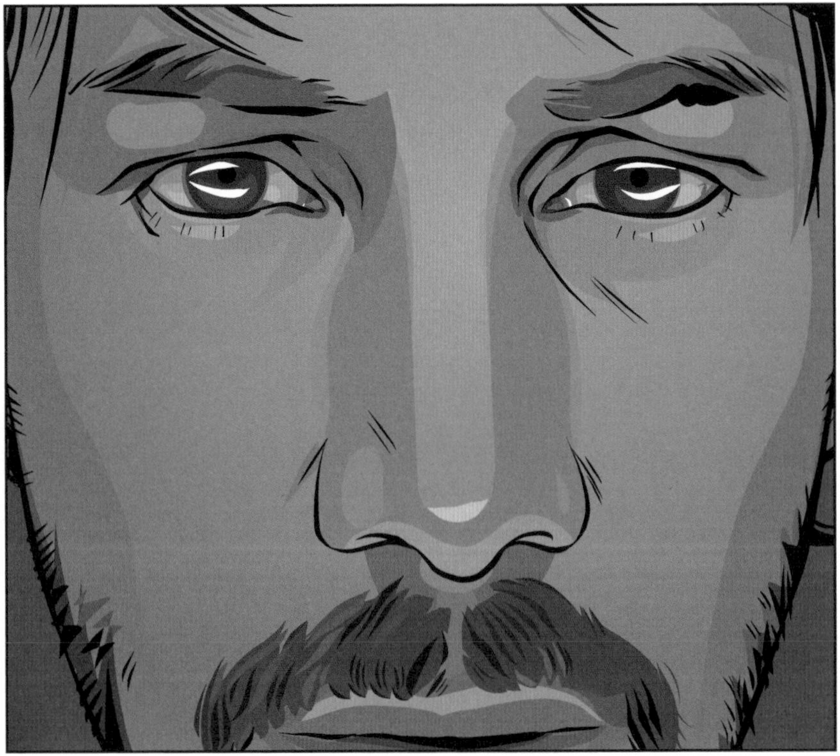

INSIDE HIS SUIT ARCTOR IS PAYING SPECIAL ATTENTION TO THEIR DRUGGIE RAP AND LETS THE FOOTAGE ROLL.

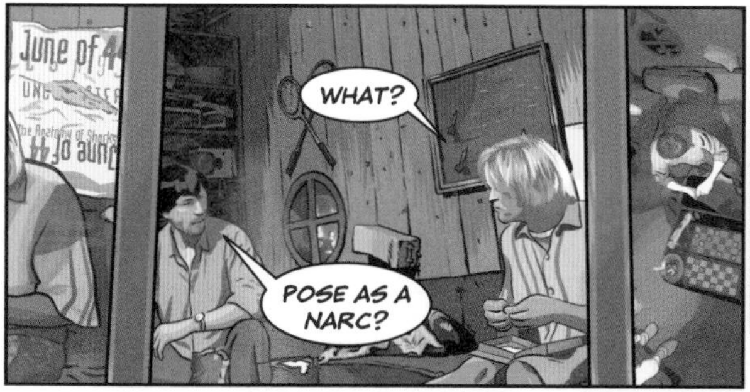
WHAT?
POSE AS A NARC?

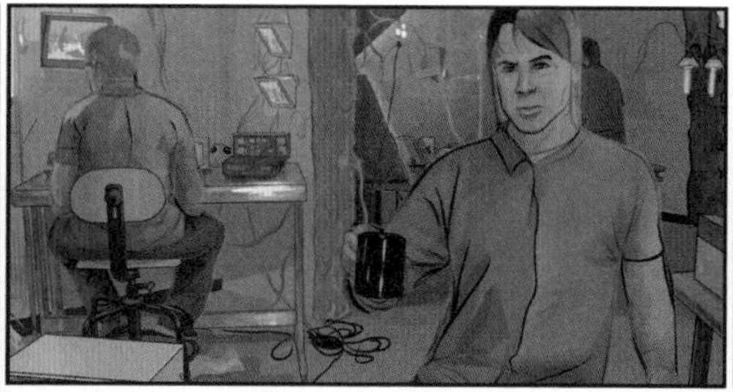

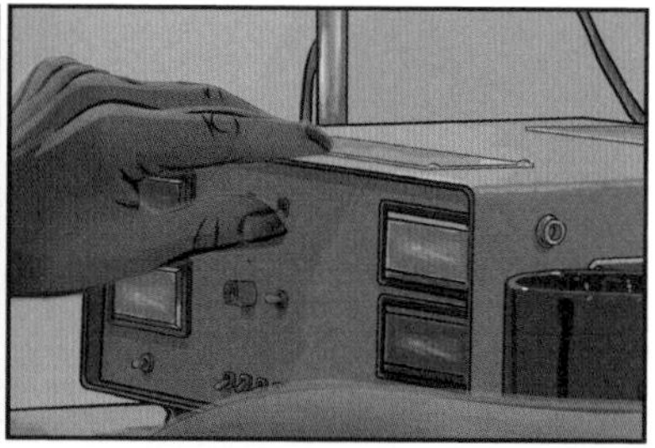

FRED LEANS OVER AND FLIPS A SWITCH. BOB'S IMAGE IS SPREAD OUT OVER ALL SIX MONITORS.

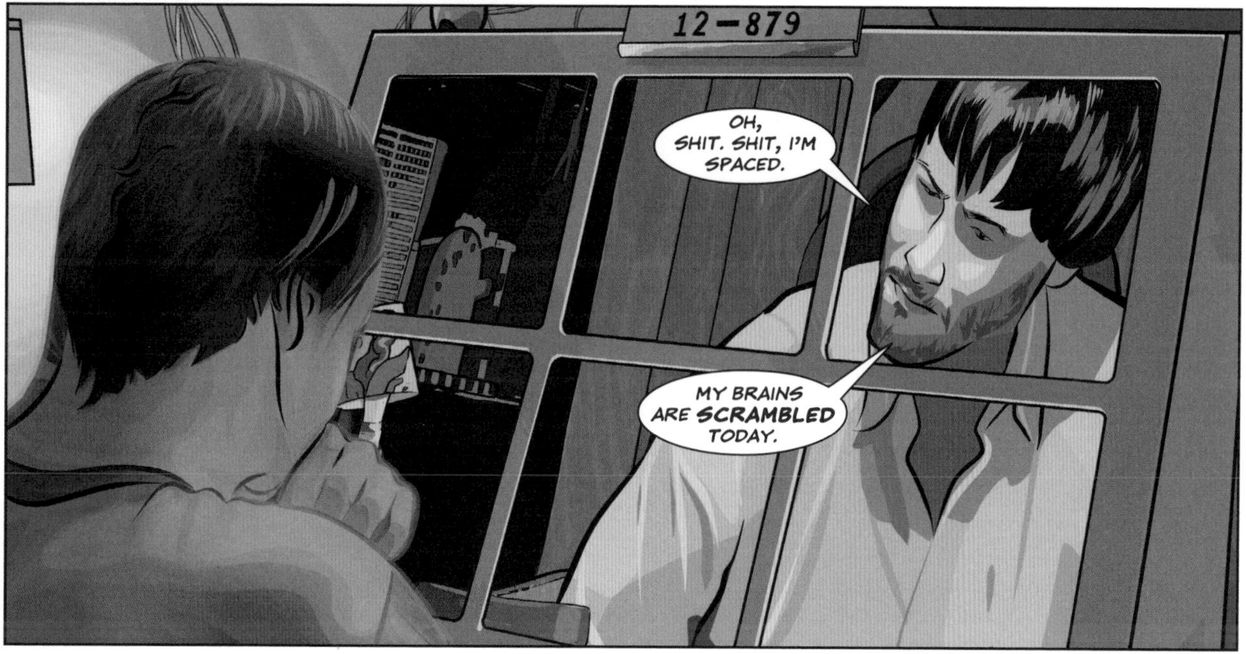
12-879
OH, SHIT. SHIT, I'M SPACED.
MY BRAINS ARE **SCRAMBLED** TODAY.

THEN HE FREEZES THE FRAME, LINGERING, PONDERING WHAT HE'S JUST HEARD.

FRED FAST-FORWARDS THE TAPE, PAST BOB'S LEAVING. IN AN ACCELERATED/DIGITAL MODE HE IS ABLE TO MAKE OUT EVERYDAY NONSENSE.

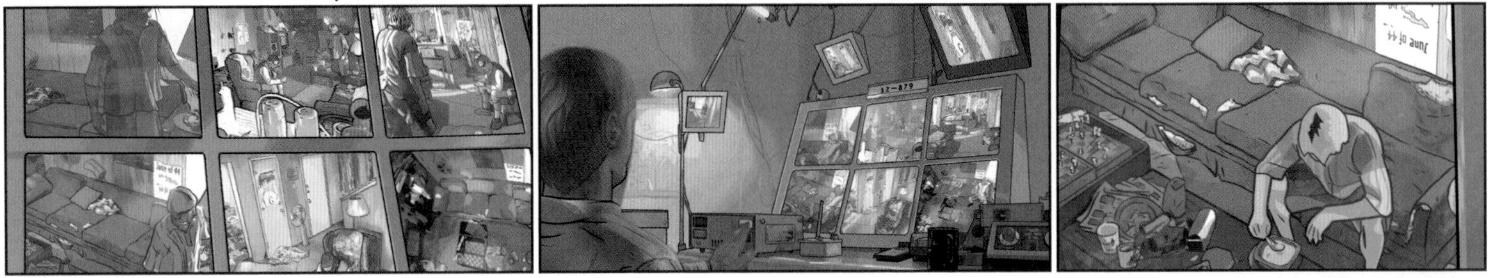

SWITCHING OVER, FRED WATCHES THE "LIVE" FEED TRANSMITTED FROM BOB'S HOUSE...

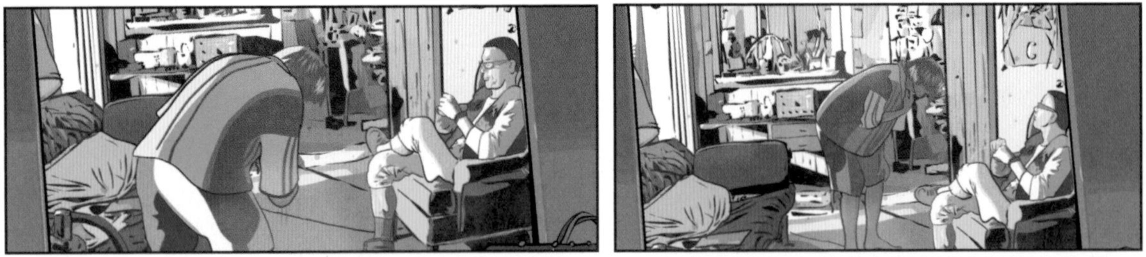

AFTER SHOVELING DOWN A MOUTHFUL OF HIS TV DINNER, LUCKMAN DROPS HIS SPOON, STAGGERING TO HIS FEET.

HE MAKES A "CHOKING" GESTURE IN FRONT OF BARRIS, WHO GAZES AT HIM BLANKLY.

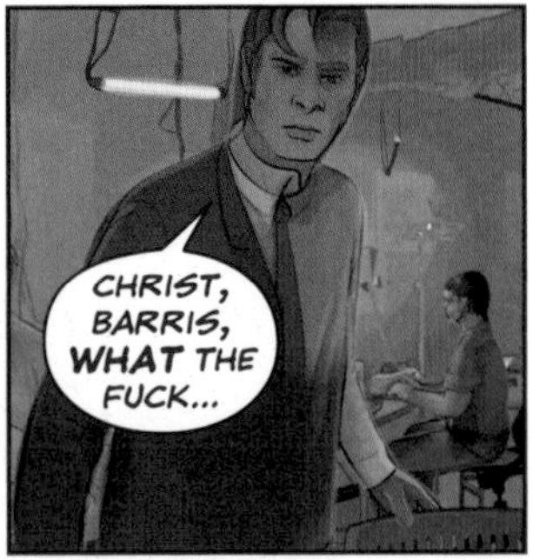
CHRIST, BARRIS, WHAT THE FUCK...

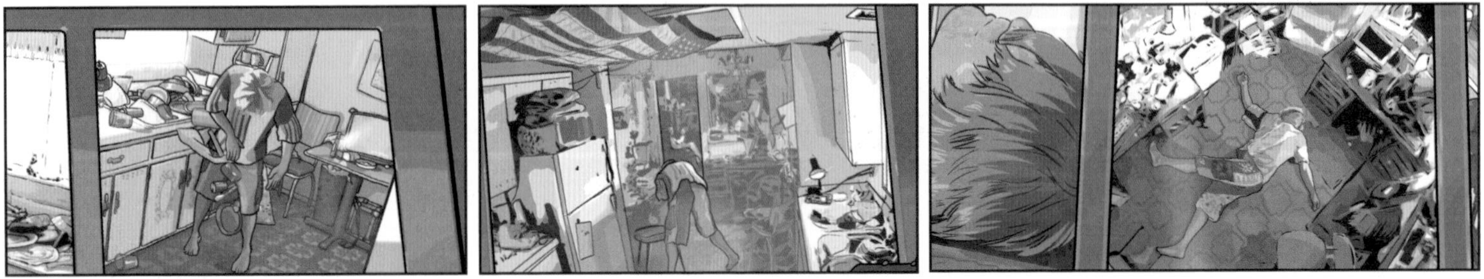

AS LUCKMAN LAYS ON THE FLOOR WITHOUT MOVING. BARRIS CONTINUES TO DO NOTHING, BUT HAS A CREEPY GRIN ON HIS FACE. THIS IS TOO MUCH FOR FRED, WHO PICKS UP A CORDLESS PHONE AT THE WORKSTATION BUT AS HE'S DIALING HE SEES BARRIS PICK UP THE PHONE AND DIAL.

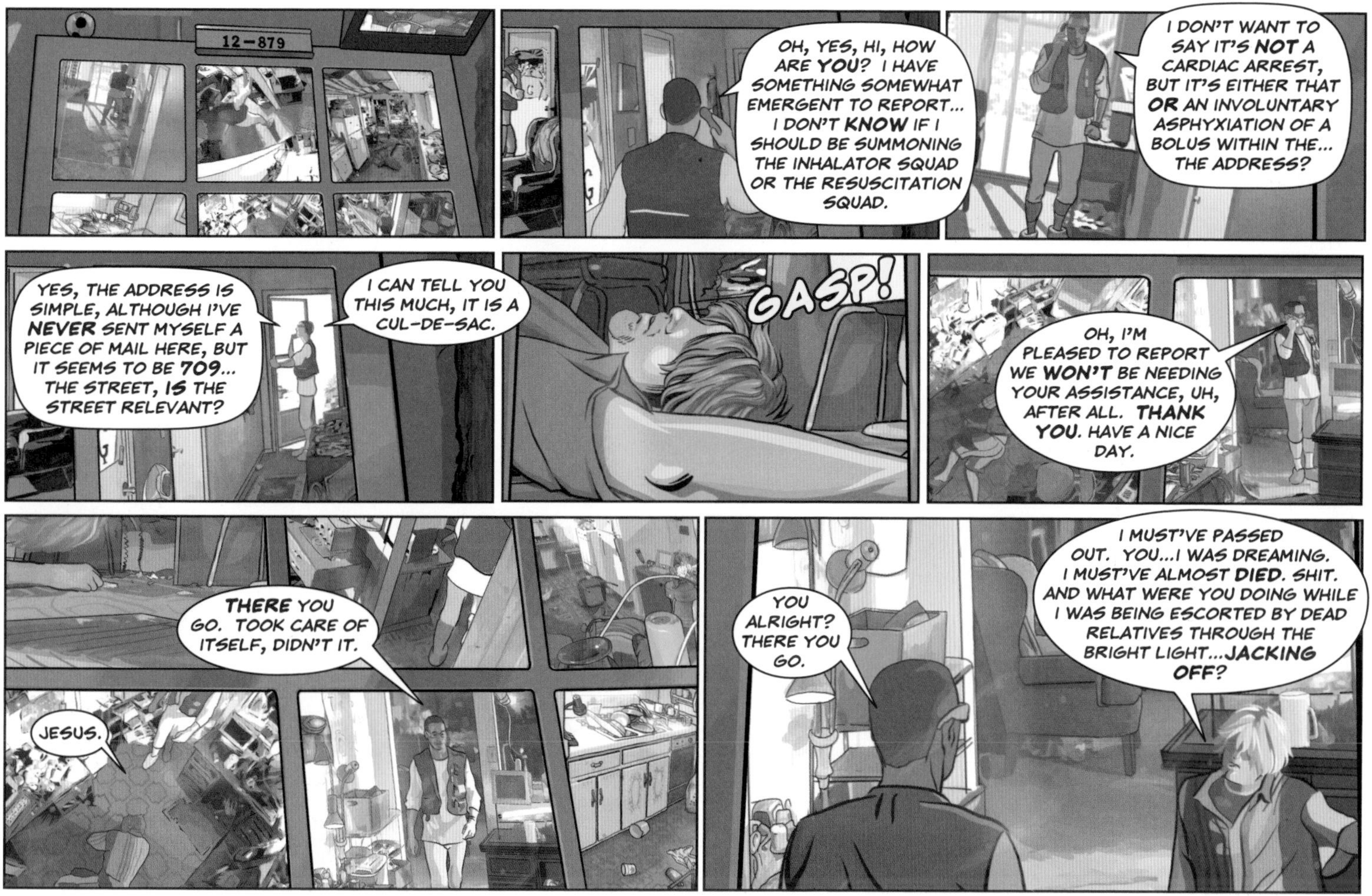
12-879
OH, YES, HI, HOW ARE YOU? I HAVE SOMETHING SOMEWHAT EMERGENT TO REPORT... I DON'T KNOW IF I SHOULD BE SUMMONING THE INHALATOR SQUAD OR THE RESUSCITATION SQUAD.
I DON'T WANT TO SAY IT'S NOT A CARDIAC ARREST, BUT IT'S EITHER THAT OR AN INVOLUNTARY ASPHYXIATION OF A BOLUS WITHIN THE... THE ADDRESS?
YES, THE ADDRESS IS SIMPLE, ALTHOUGH I'VE NEVER SENT MYSELF A PIECE OF MAIL HERE, BUT IT SEEMS TO BE 709... THE STREET, IS THE STREET RELEVANT?
I CAN TELL YOU THIS MUCH, IT IS A CUL-DE-SAC.
GASP!
OH, I'M PLEASED TO REPORT WE WON'T BE NEEDING YOUR ASSISTANCE, UH, AFTER ALL. THANK YOU. HAVE A NICE DAY.
THERE YOU GO. TOOK CARE OF ITSELF, DIDN'T IT.
JESUS.
YOU ALRIGHT? THERE YOU GO.
I MUST'VE PASSED OUT. YOU...I WAS DREAMING. I MUST'VE ALMOST DIED. SHIT. AND WHAT WERE YOU DOING WHILE I WAS BEING ESCORTED BY DEAD RELATIVES THROUGH THE BRIGHT LIGHT...JACKING OFF?

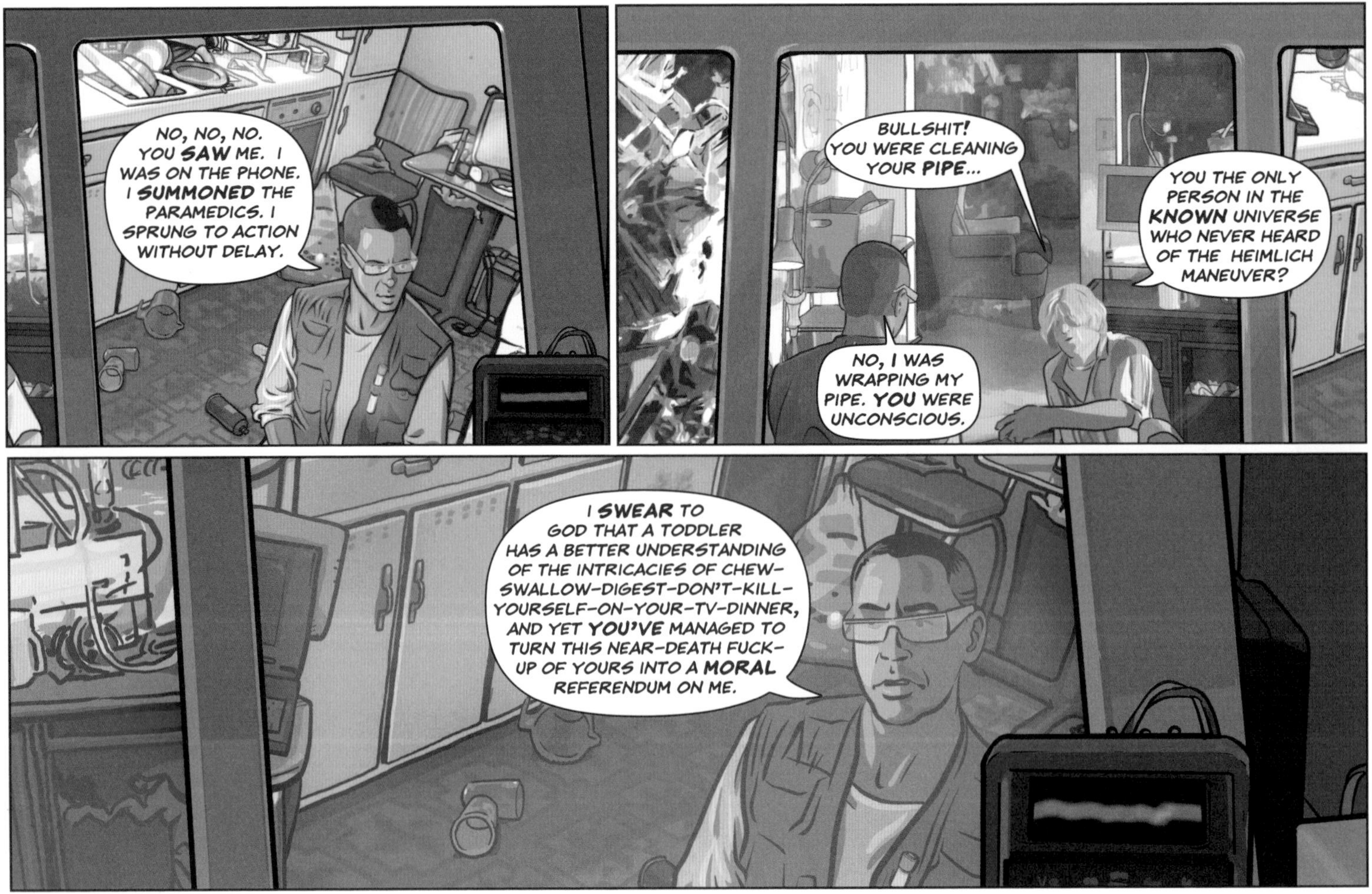
NO, NO, NO. YOU SAW ME. I WAS ON THE PHONE. I SUMMONED THE PARAMEDICS. I SPRUNG TO ACTION WITHOUT DELAY.
BULLSHIT! YOU WERE CLEANING YOUR PIPE...
NO, I WAS WRAPPING MY PIPE. YOU WERE UNCONSCIOUS.
YOU THE ONLY PERSON IN THE KNOWN UNIVERSE WHO NEVER HEARD OF THE HEIMLICH MANEUVER?
I SWEAR TO GOD THAT A TODDLER HAS A BETTER UNDERSTANDING OF THE INTRICACIES OF CHEW-SWALLOW-DIGEST-DON'T-KILL-YOURSELF-ON-YOUR-TV-DINNER, AND YET YOU'VE MANAGED TO TURN THIS NEAR-DEATH FUCK-UP OF YOURS INTO A MORAL REFERENDUM ON ME.

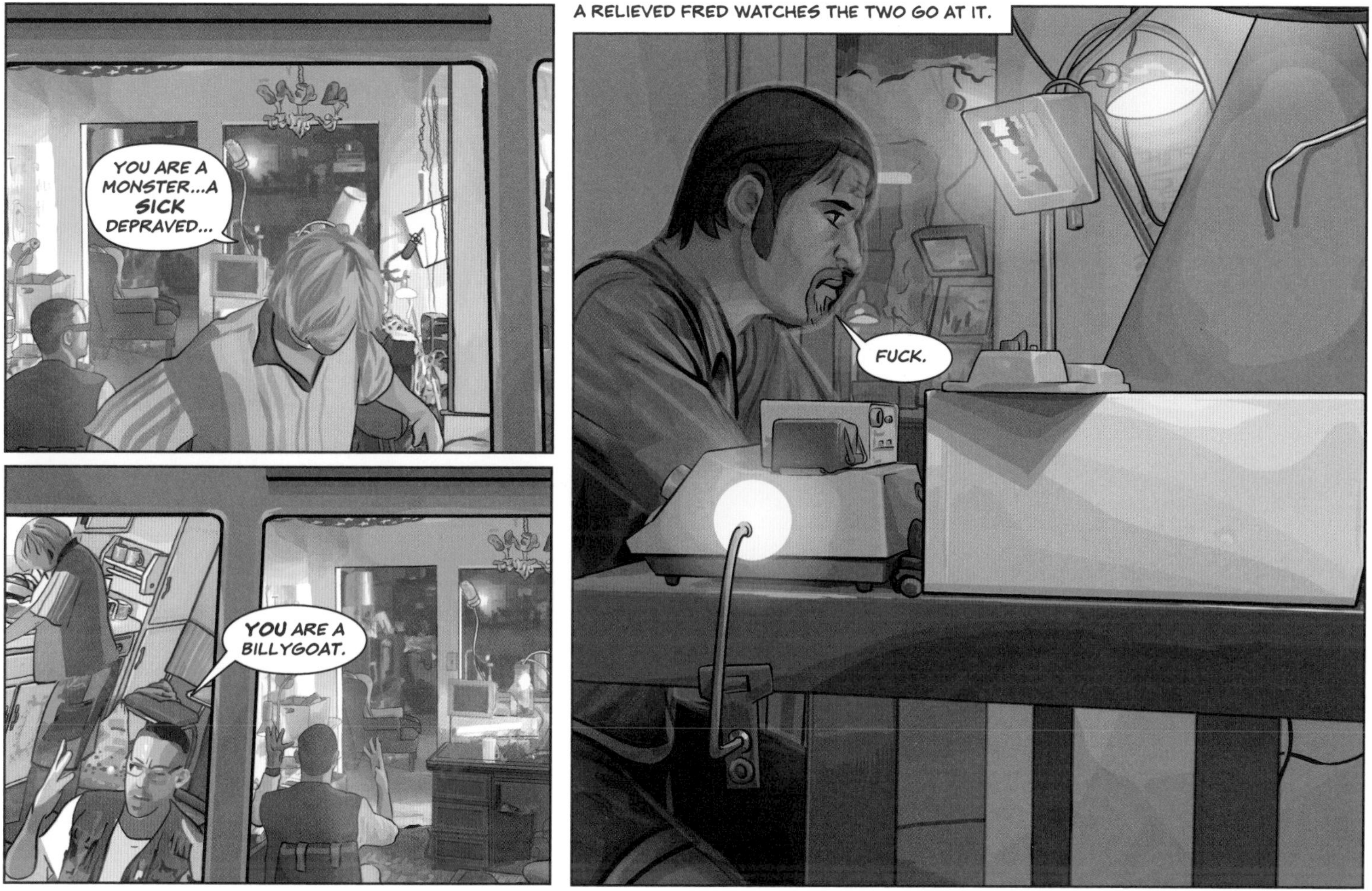
YOU ARE A MONSTER...A SICK DEPRAVED...
YOU ARE A BILLYGOAT.
A RELIEVED FRED WATCHES THE TWO GO AT IT.
FUCK.

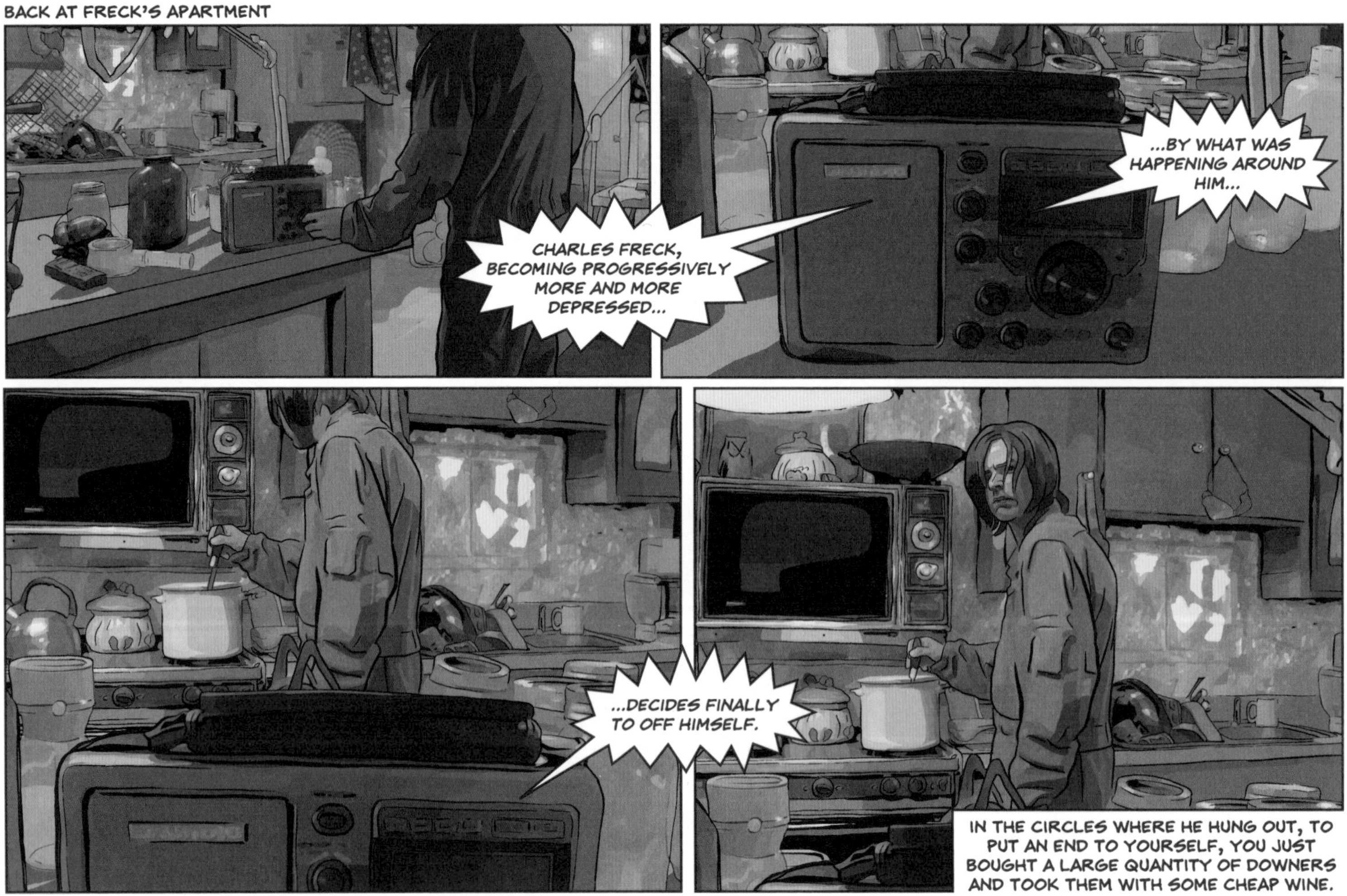
BACK AT FRECK'S APARTMENT
CHARLES FRECK, BECOMING PROGRESSIVELY MORE AND MORE DEPRESSED...
...BY WHAT WAS HAPPENING AROUND HIM...
...DECIDES FINALLY TO OFF HIMSELF.
IN THE CIRCLES WHERE HE HUNG OUT, TO PUT AN END TO YOURSELF, YOU JUST BOUGHT A LARGE QUANTITY OF DOWNERS AND TOOK THEM WITH SOME CHEAP WINE.

THE PLANNING PART HAD TO DO WITH THE ARTIFACTS HE WANTED FOUND ON HIM BY LATER ARCHEOLOGISTS.

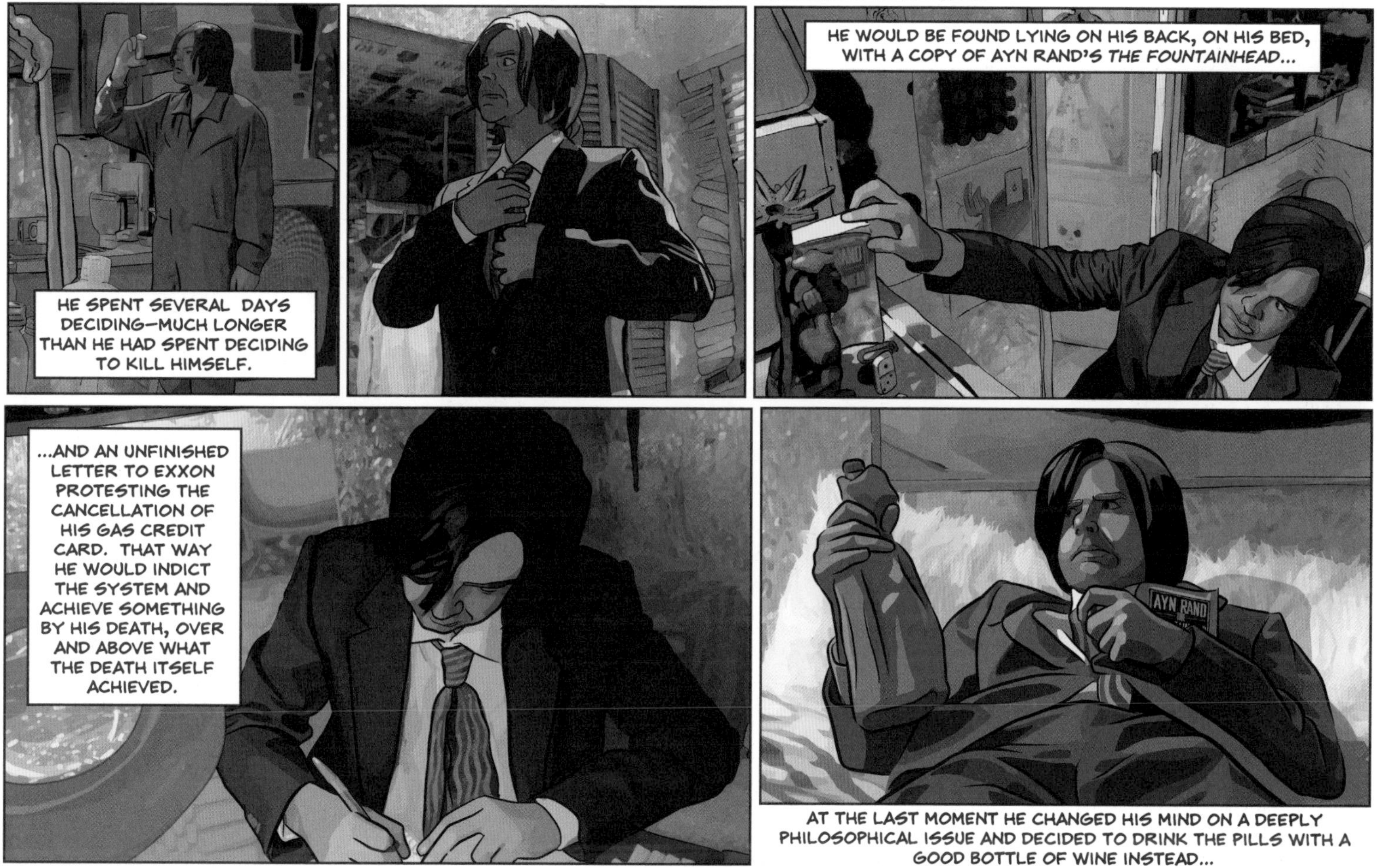
HE SPENT SEVERAL DAYS DECIDING—MUCH LONGER THAN HE HAD SPENT DECIDING TO KILL HIMSELF.
HE WOULD BE FOUND LYING ON HIS BACK, ON HIS BED, WITH A COPY OF AYN RAND'S *THE FOUNTAINHEAD*...
...AND AN UNFINISHED LETTER TO EXXON PROTESTING THE CANCELLATION OF HIS GAS CREDIT CARD. THAT WAY HE WOULD INDICT THE SYSTEM AND ACHIEVE SOMETHING BY HIS DEATH, OVER AND ABOVE WHAT THE DEATH ITSELF ACHIEVED.
AYN RAND

AT THE LAST MOMENT HE CHANGED HIS MIND ON A DEEPLY PHILOSOPHICAL ISSUE AND DECIDED TO DRINK THE PILLS WITH A GOOD BOTTLE OF WINE INSTEAD...

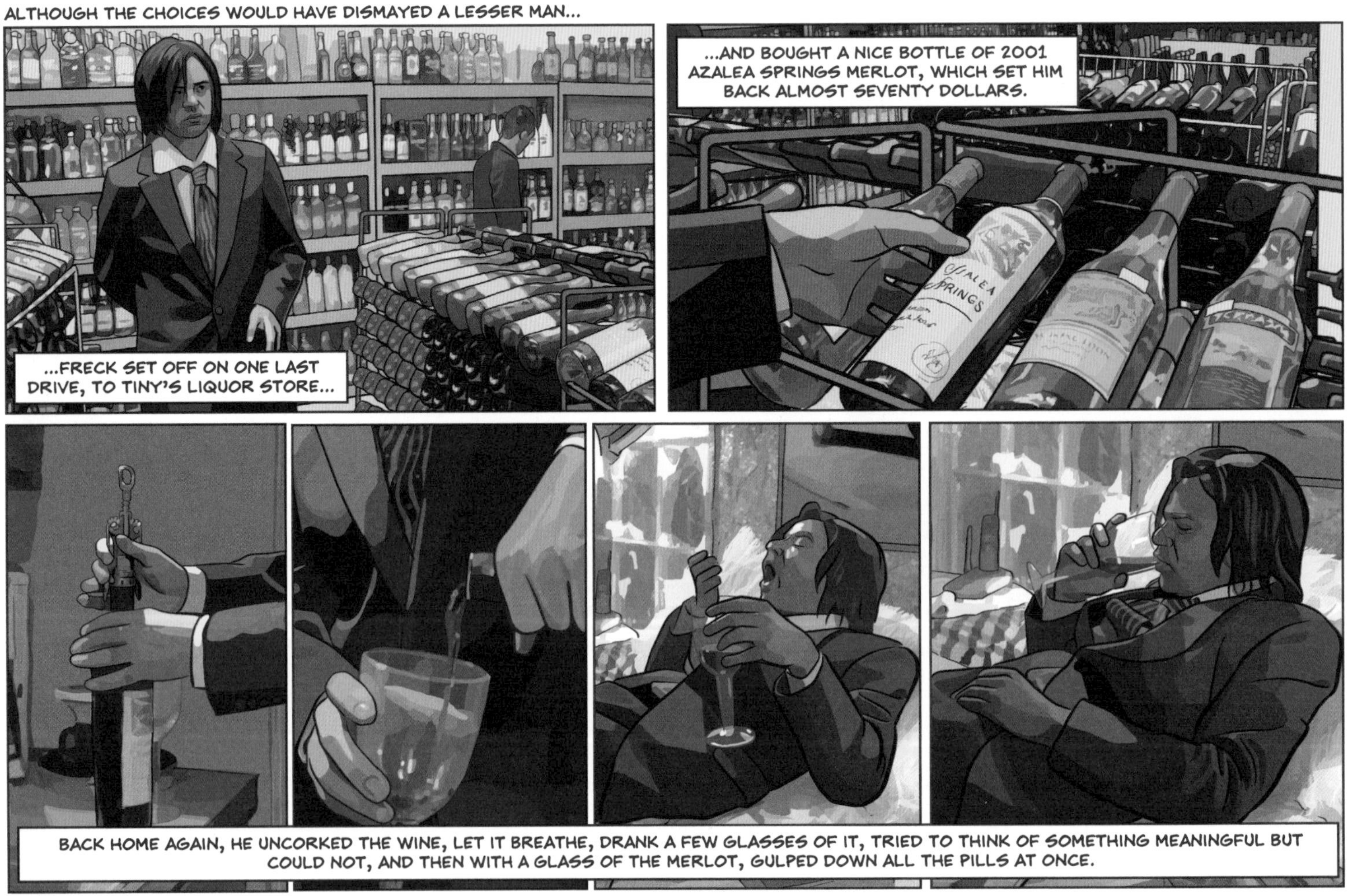
ALTHOUGH THE CHOICES WOULD HAVE DISMAYED A LESSER MAN...
...FRECK SET OFF ON ONE LAST DRIVE, TO TINY'S LIQUOR STORE...
...AND BOUGHT A NICE BOTTLE OF 2001 AZALEA SPRINGS MERLOT, WHICH SET HIM BACK ALMOST SEVENTY DOLLARS.
BACK HOME AGAIN, HE UNCORKED THE WINE, LET IT BREATHE, DRANK A FEW GLASSES OF IT, TRIED TO THINK OF SOMETHING MEANINGFUL BUT COULD NOT, AND THEN WITH A GLASS OF THE MERLOT, GULPED DOWN ALL THE PILLS AT ONCE.

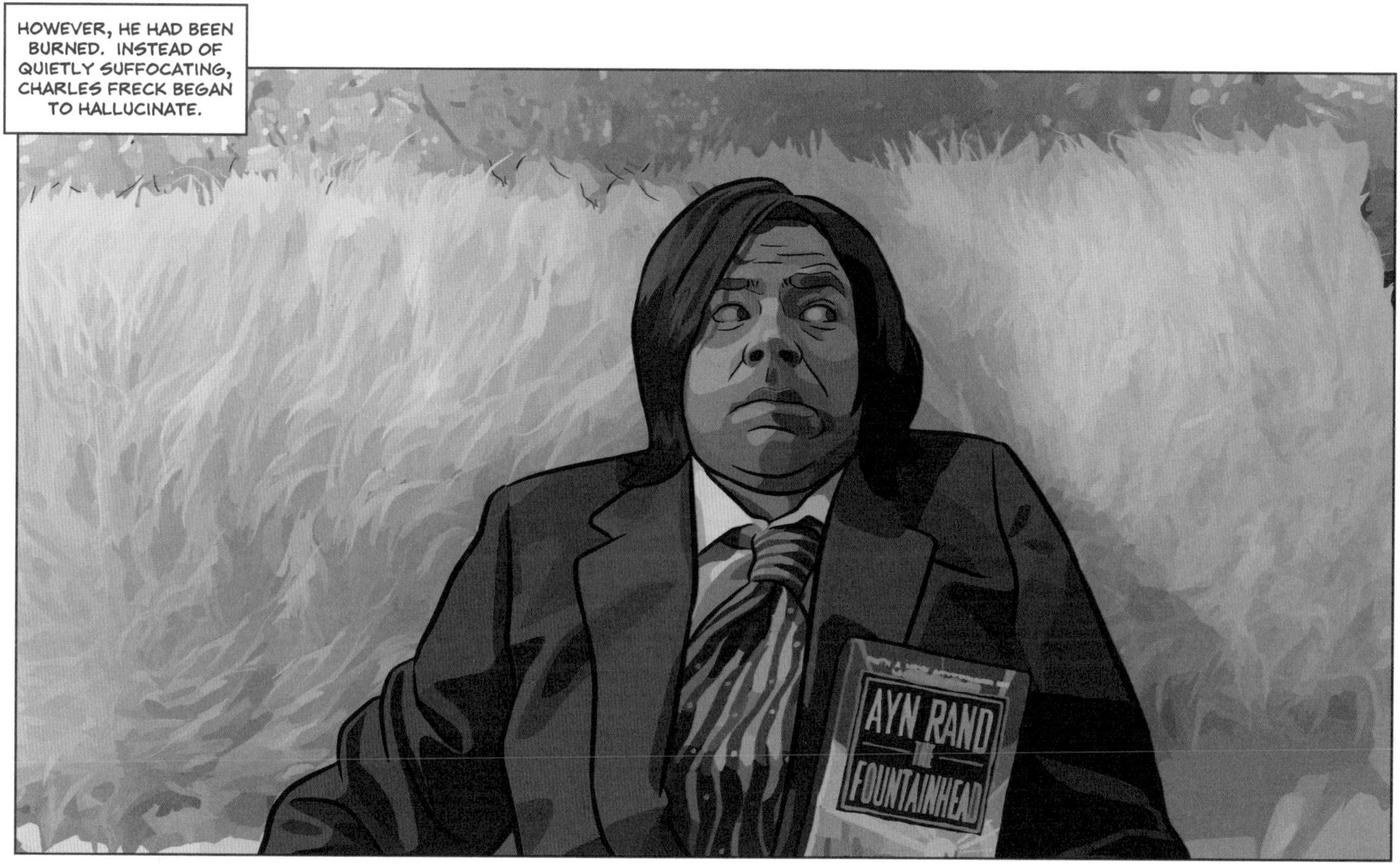
HOWEVER, HE HAD BEEN BURNED. INSTEAD OF QUIETLY SUFFOCATING, CHARLES FRECK BEGAN TO HALLUCINATE.
AYN RAND
FOUNTAINHEAD

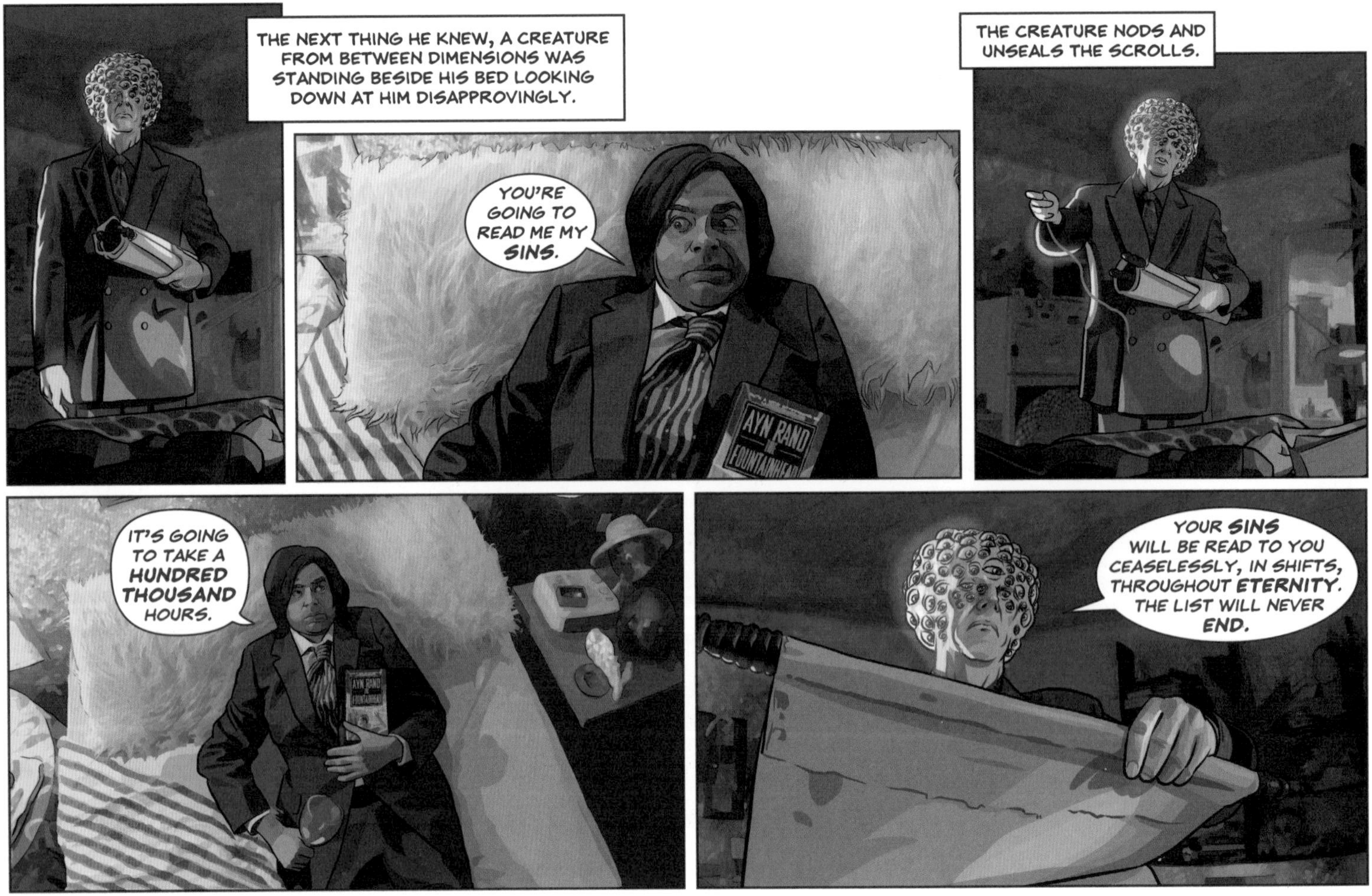
THE NEXT THING HE KNEW, A CREATURE FROM BETWEEN DIMENSIONS WAS STANDING BESIDE HIS BED LOOKING DOWN AT HIM DISAPPROVINGLY.
YOU'RE GOING TO READ ME MY **SINS**.
AYN RAND
FOUNTAINHEAD
THE CREATURE NODS AND UNSEALS THE SCROLLS.
IT'S GOING TO TAKE A **HUNDRED THOUSAND** HOURS.
YOUR **SINS** WILL BE READ TO YOU CEASELESSLY, IN SHIFTS, THROUGHOUT **ETERNITY**. THE LIST WILL NEVER **END**.

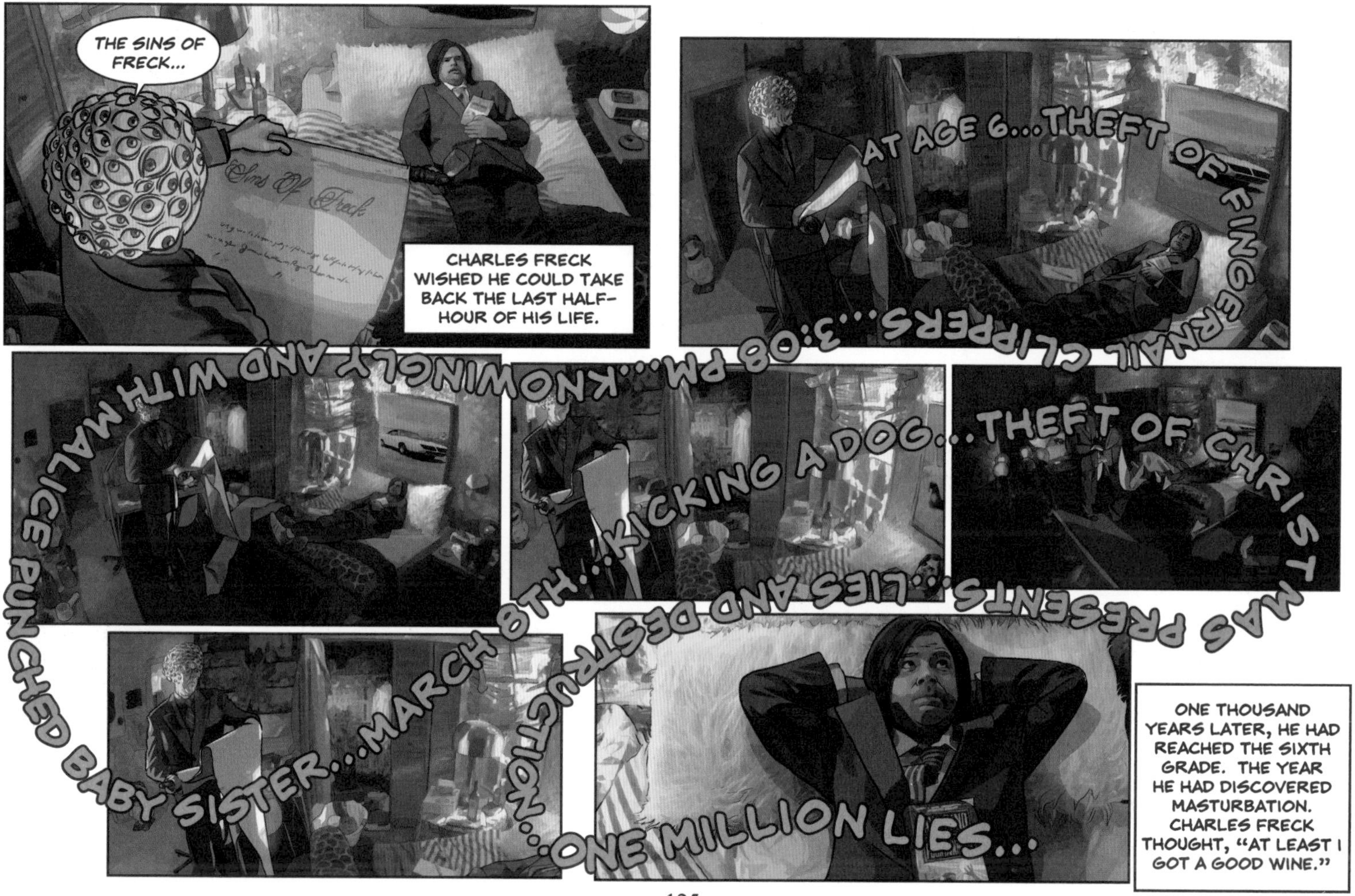
THE SINS OF FRECK...
Sins Of Freck
CHARLES FRECK WISHED HE COULD TAKE BACK THE LAST HALF-HOUR OF HIS LIFE.
AT AGE 6...THEFT OF FINGERNAIL CLIPPERS...3:08 PM...KNOWINGLY AND WITH MALICE PUNCHED BABY SISTER...MARCH 8TH...KICKING A DOG...THEFT OF CHRISTMAS PRESENTS...LIES AND DESTRUCTION...ONE MILLION LIES...
ONE THOUSAND YEARS LATER, HE HAD REACHED THE SIXTH GRADE. THE YEAR HE HAD DISCOVERED MASTURBATION. CHARLES FRECK THOUGHT, "AT LEAST I GOT A GOOD WINE."

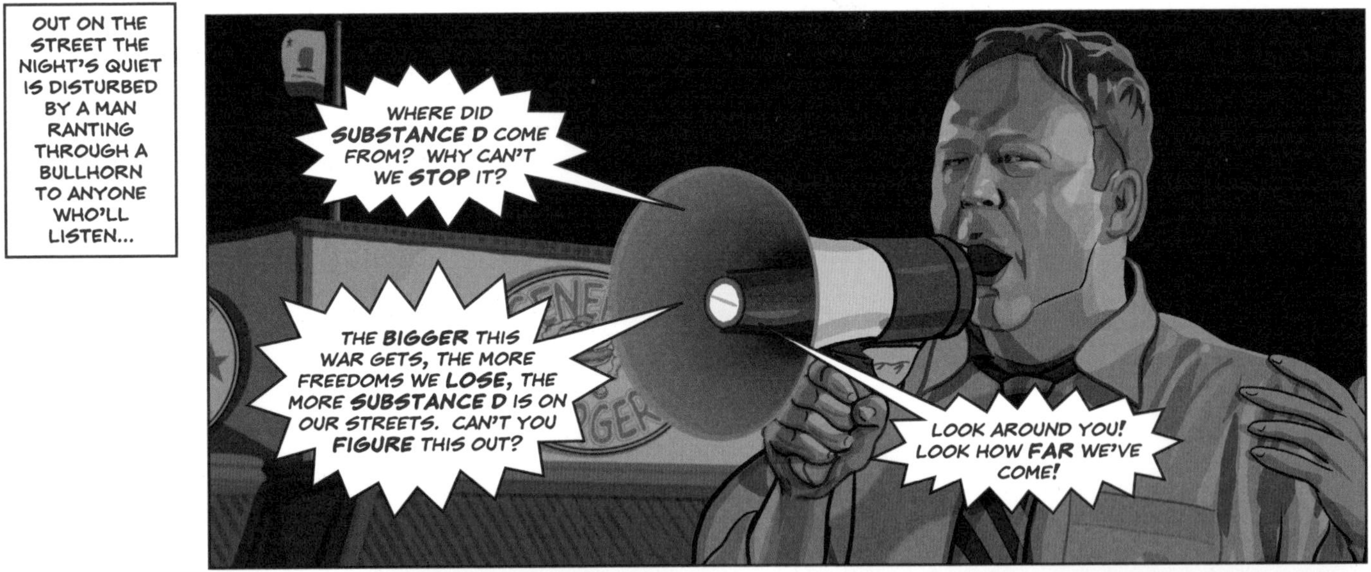
OUT ON THE STREET THE NIGHT'S QUIET IS DISTURBED BY A MAN RANTING THROUGH A BULLHORN TO ANYONE WHO'LL LISTEN...
WHERE DID SUBSTANCE D COME FROM? WHY CAN'T WE STOP IT?
THE BIGGER THIS WAR GETS, THE MORE FREEDOMS WE LOSE, THE MORE SUBSTANCE D IS ON OUR STREETS. CAN'T YOU FIGURE THIS OUT?
LOOK AROUND YOU! LOOK HOW FAR WE'VE COME!

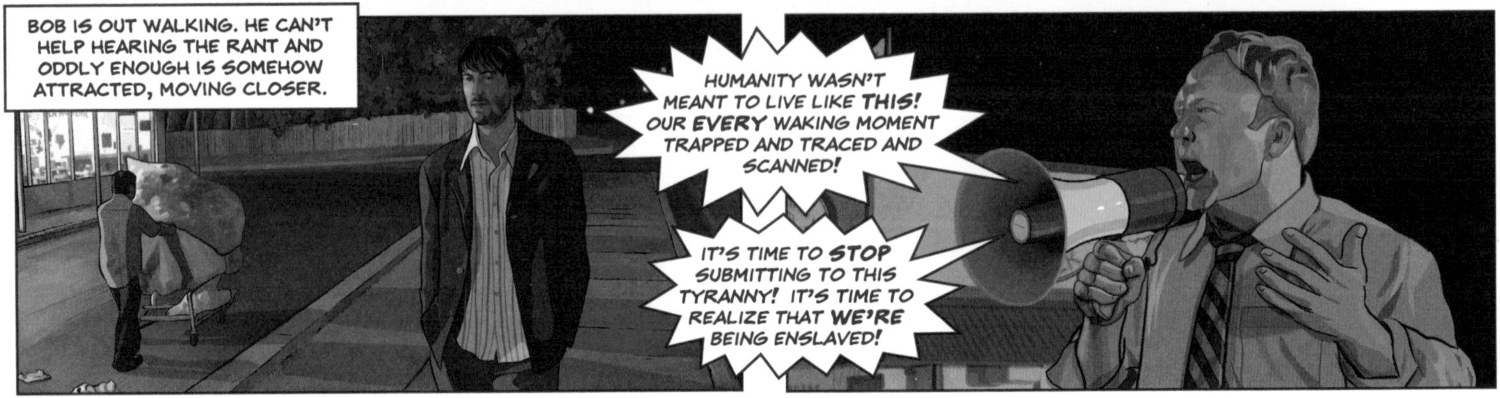
BOB IS OUT WALKING. HE CAN'T HELP HEARING THE RANT AND ODDLY ENOUGH IS SOMEHOW ATTRACTED, MOVING CLOSER.
HUMANITY WASN'T MEANT TO LIVE LIKE THIS! OUR EVERY WAKING MOMENT TRAPPED AND TRACED AND SCANNED!
IT'S TIME TO STOP SUBMITTING TO THIS TYRANNY! IT'S TIME TO REALIZE THAT WE'RE BEING ENSLAVED!

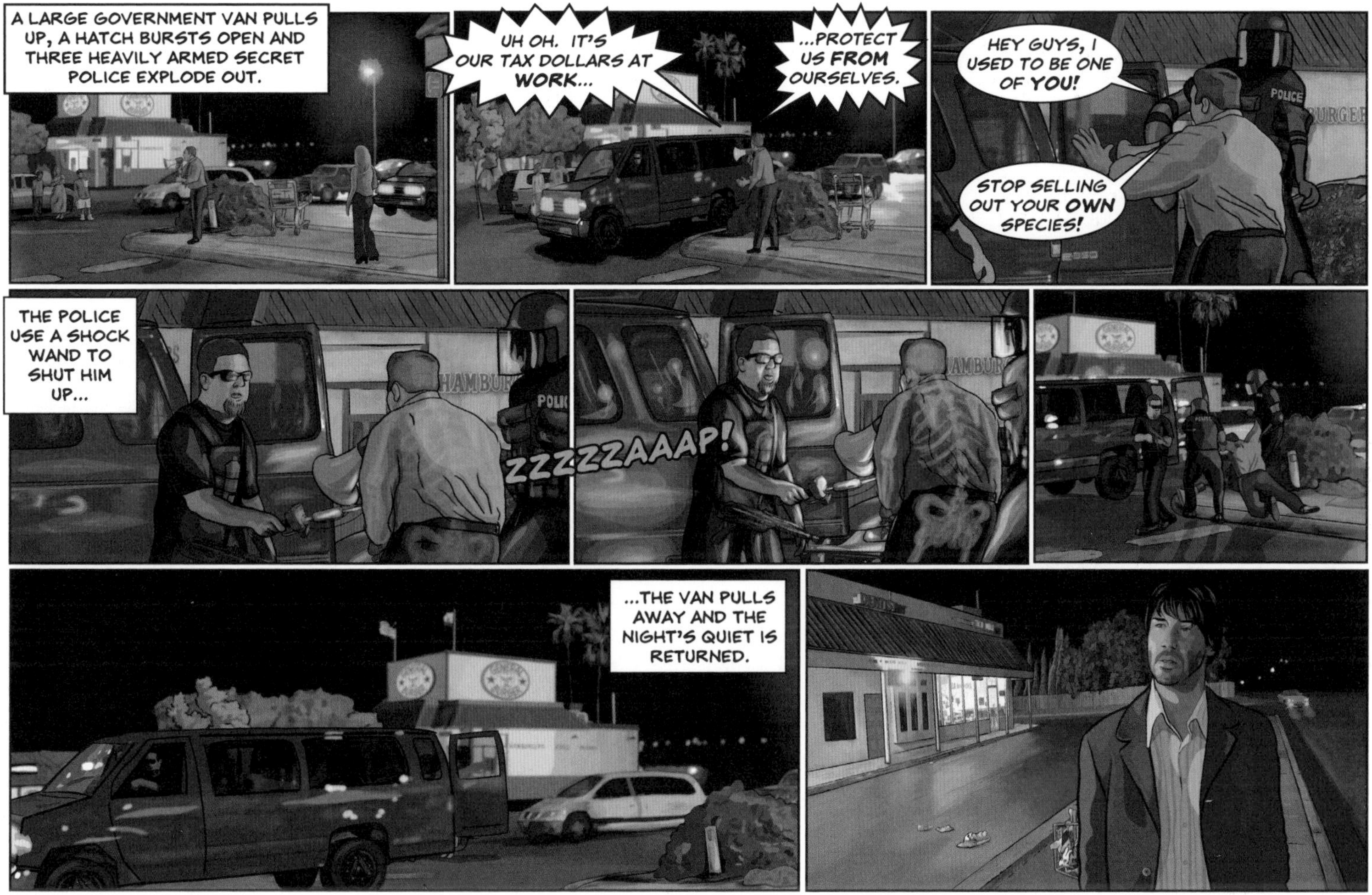
A LARGE GOVERNMENT VAN PULLS UP, A HATCH BURSTS OPEN AND THREE HEAVILY ARMED SECRET POLICE EXPLODE OUT.
UH OH. IT'S OUR TAX DOLLARS AT WORK...
...PROTECT US FROM OURSELVES.
HEY GUYS, I USED TO BE ONE OF YOU!
STOP SELLING OUT YOUR OWN SPECIES!
THE POLICE USE A SHOCK WAND TO SHUT HIM UP...
ZZZZZAAAP!
...THE VAN PULLS AWAY AND THE NIGHT'S QUIET IS RETURNED.

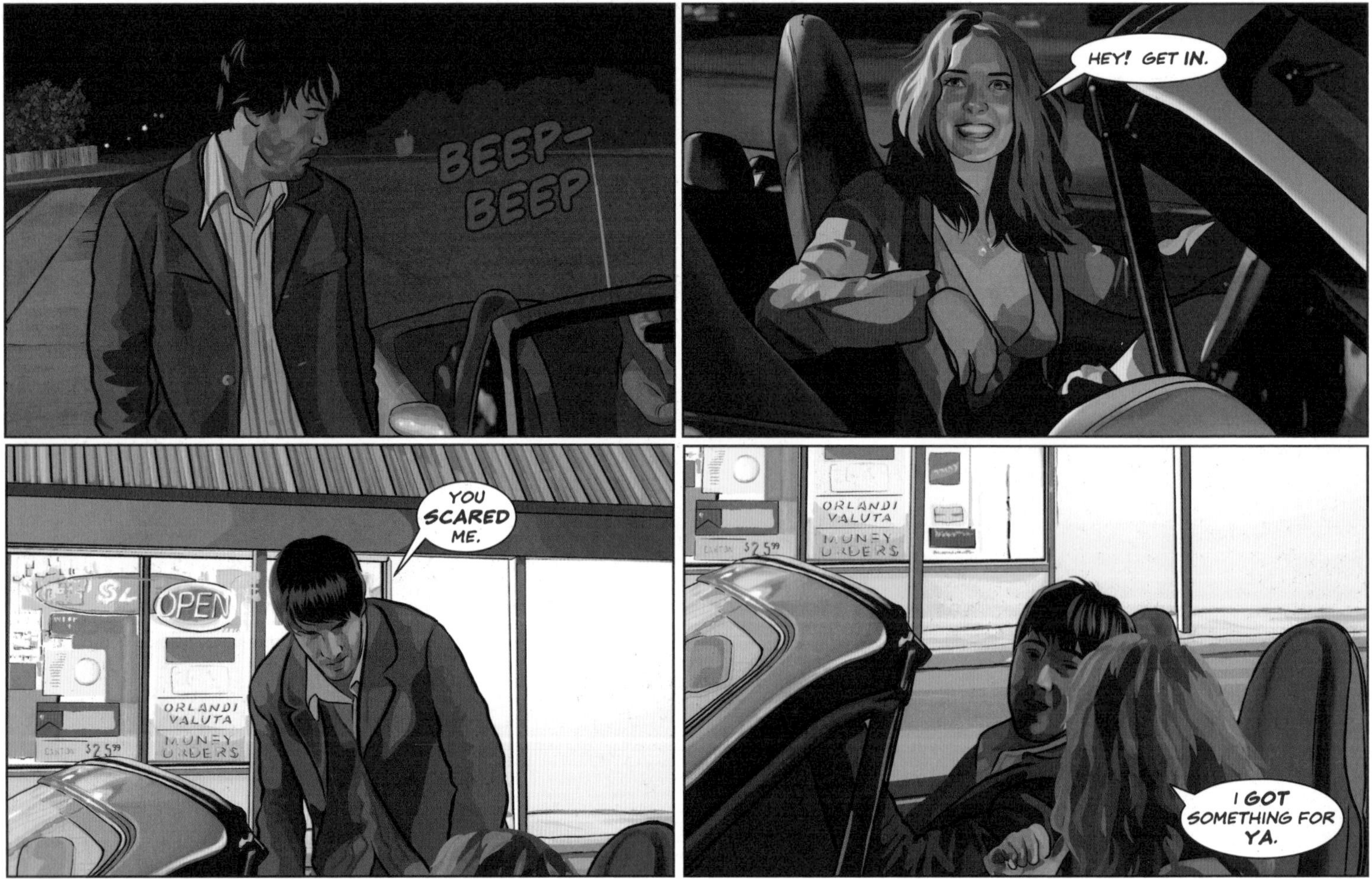
BEEP-
BEEP
HEY! GET IN.
YOU SCARED ME.
OPEN
ORLANDI VALUTA
I GOT SOMETHING FOR YA.

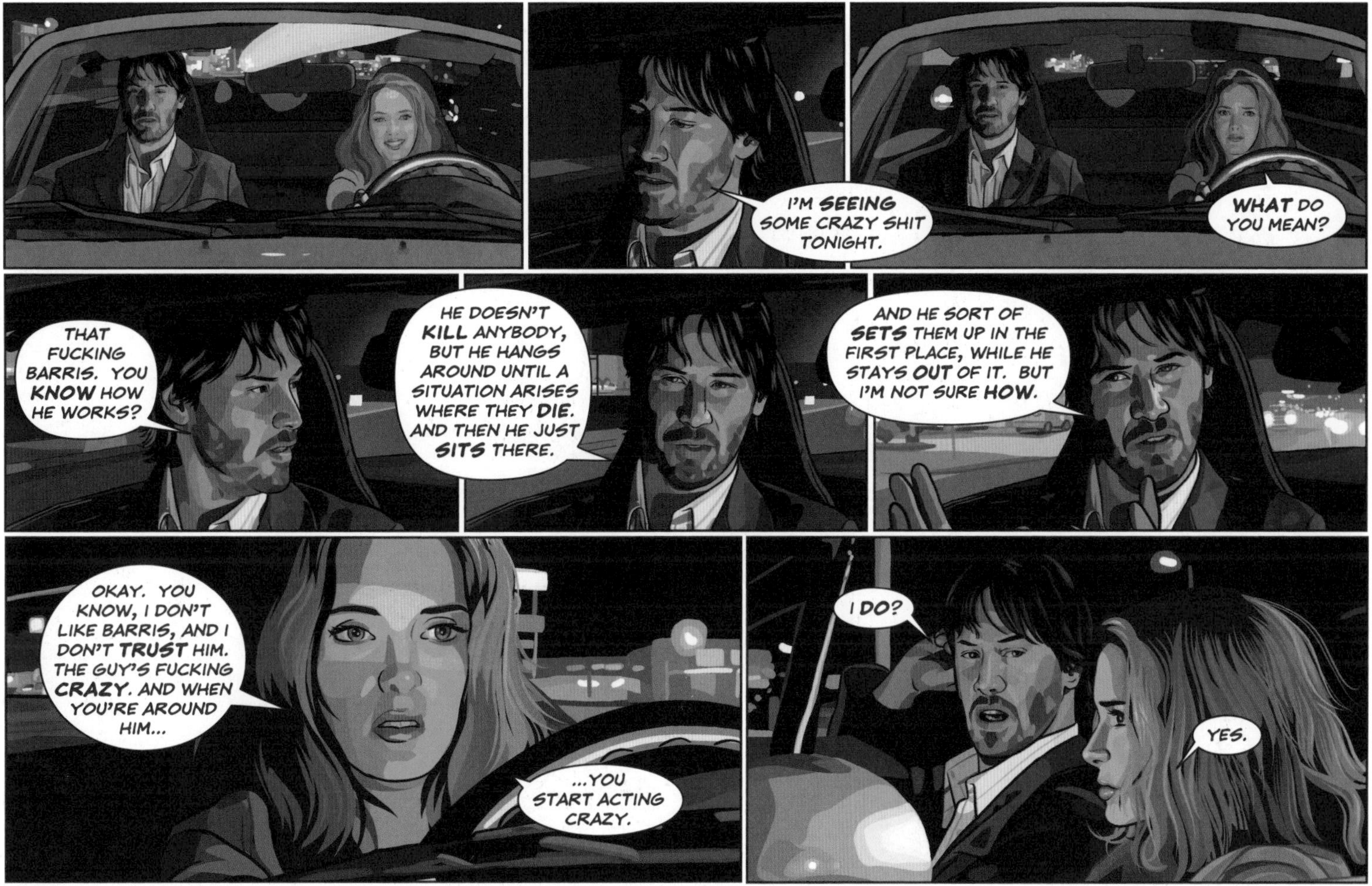
I'M SEEING SOME CRAZY SHIT TONIGHT.
WHAT DO YOU MEAN?
THAT FUCKING BARRIS. YOU KNOW HOW HE WORKS?
HE DOESN'T KILL ANYBODY, BUT HE HANGS AROUND UNTIL A SITUATION ARISES WHERE THEY DIE. AND THEN HE JUST SITS THERE.
AND HE SORT OF SETS THEM UP IN THE FIRST PLACE, WHILE HE STAYS OUT OF IT. BUT I'M NOT SURE HOW.
OKAY. YOU KNOW, I DON'T LIKE BARRIS, AND I DON'T TRUST HIM. THE GUY'S FUCKING CRAZY. AND WHEN YOU'RE AROUND HIM...
...YOU START ACTING CRAZY.
I DO?
YES.

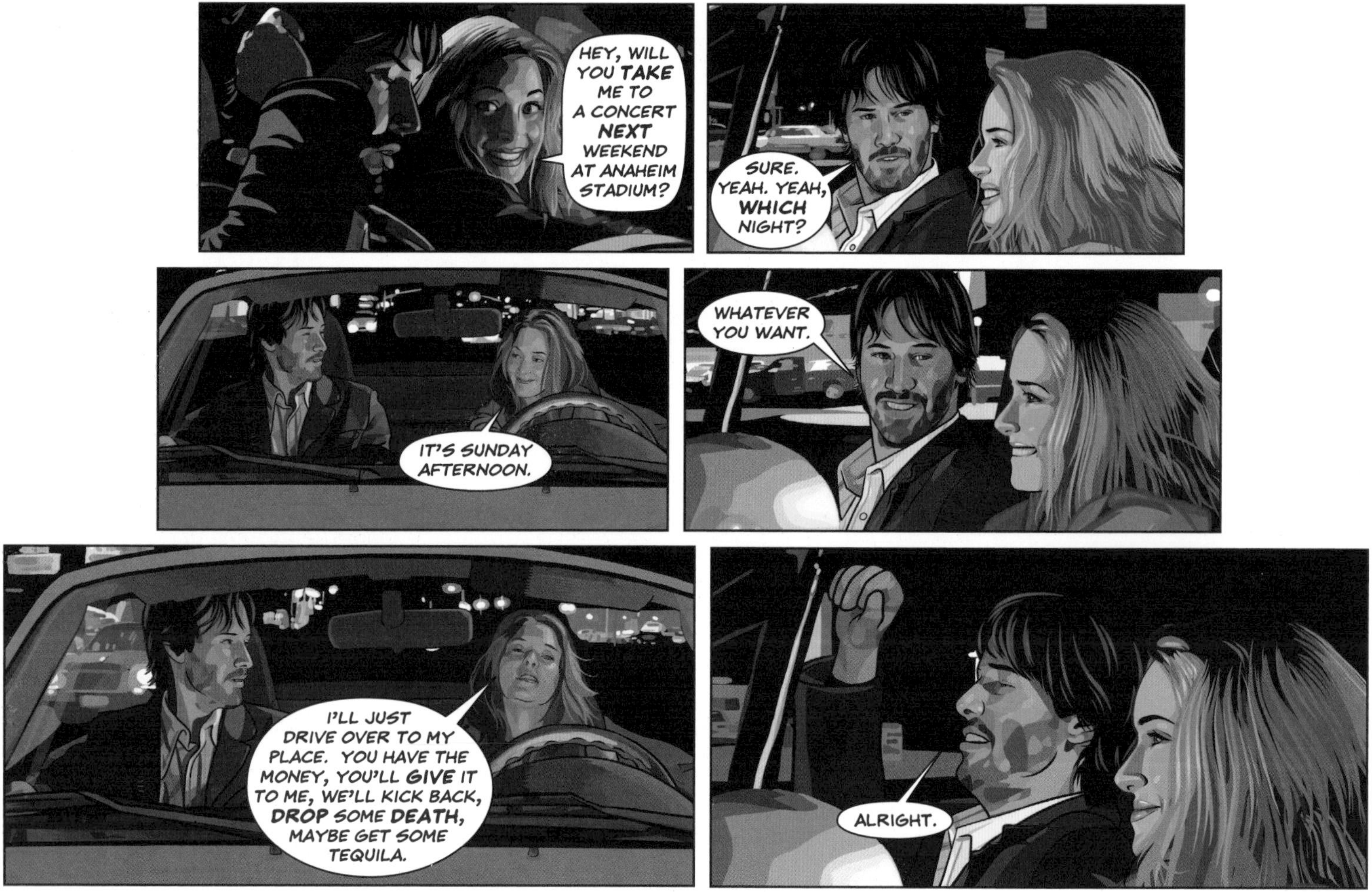
HEY, WILL YOU TAKE ME TO A CONCERT NEXT WEEKEND AT ANAHEIM STADIUM?
SURE. YEAH. YEAH, WHICH NIGHT?
IT'S SUNDAY AFTERNOON.
WHATEVER YOU WANT.
I'LL JUST DRIVE OVER TO MY PLACE. YOU HAVE THE MONEY, YOU'LL GIVE IT TO ME, WE'LL KICK BACK, DROP SOME DEATH, MAYBE GET SOME TEQUILA.
ALRIGHT.

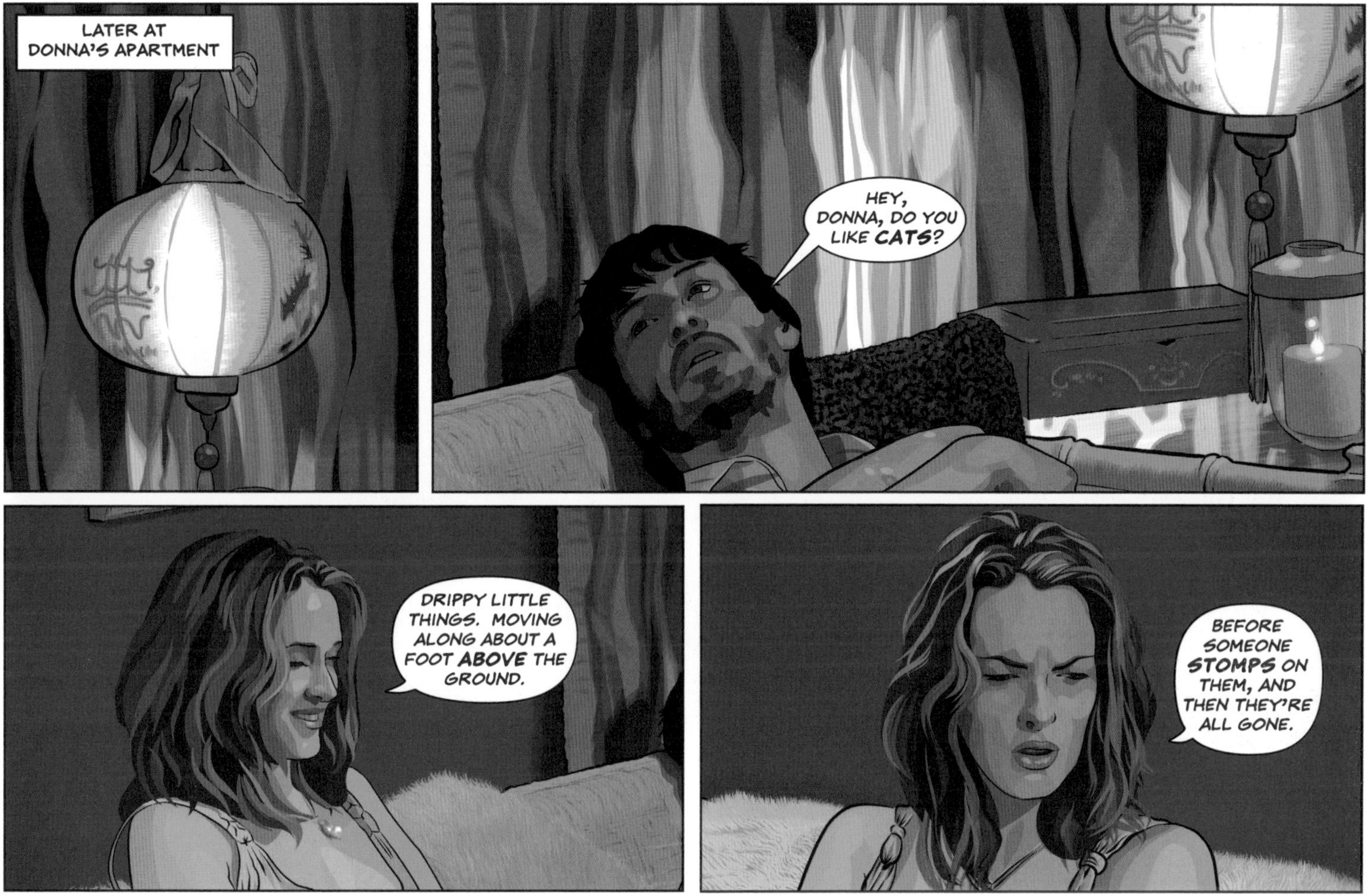
LATER AT DONNA'S APARTMENT
HEY, DONNA, DO YOU LIKE **CATS**?
DRIPPY LITTLE THINGS. MOVING ALONG ABOUT A FOOT **ABOVE** THE GROUND.
BEFORE SOMEONE **STOMPS** ON THEM, AND THEN THEY'RE ALL GONE.

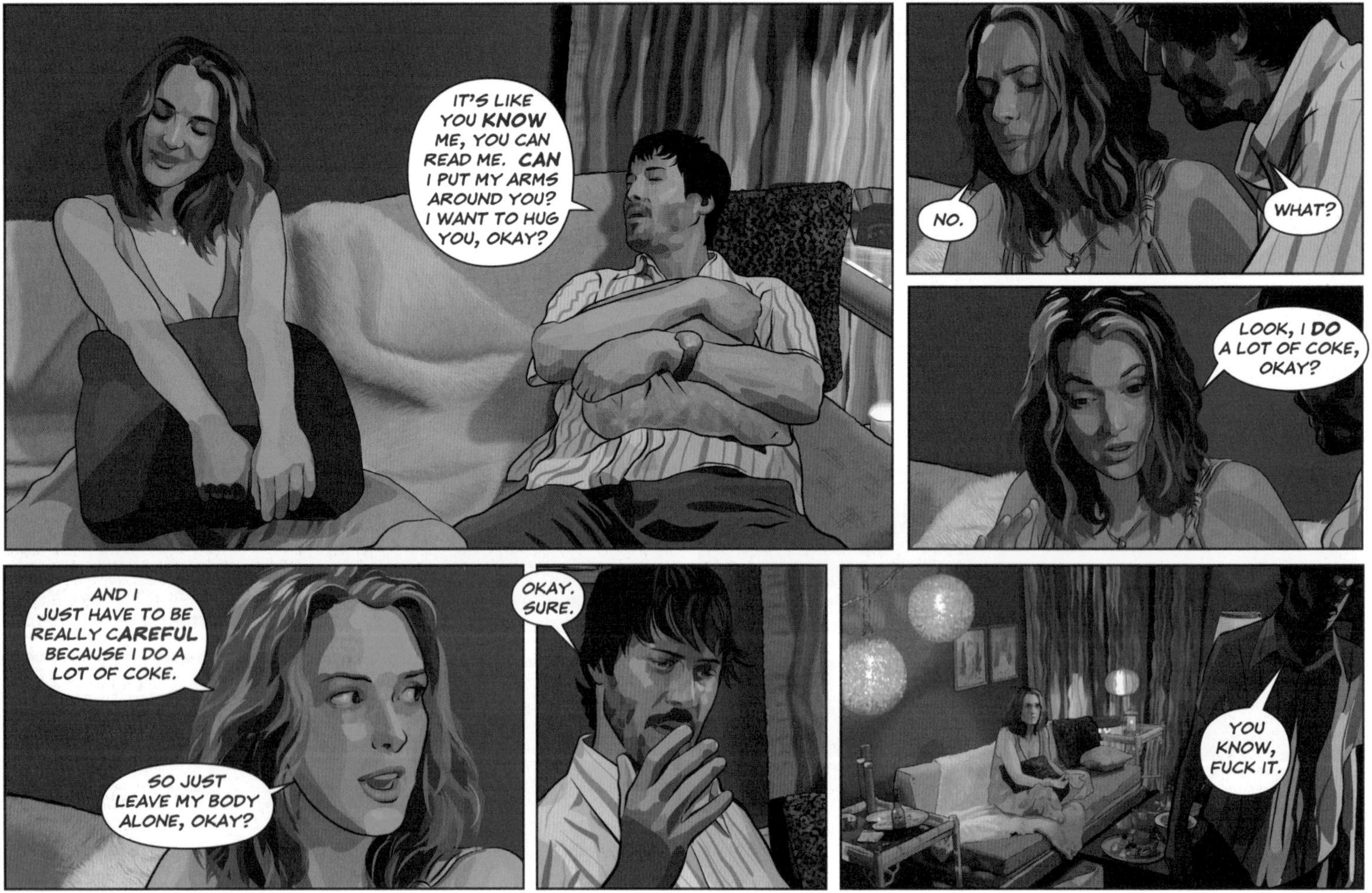
IT'S LIKE YOU KNOW ME, YOU CAN READ ME. CAN I PUT MY ARMS AROUND YOU? I WANT TO HUG YOU, OKAY?
NO.
WHAT?
LOOK, I DO A LOT OF COKE, OKAY?
AND I JUST HAVE TO BE REALLY CAREFUL BECAUSE I DO A LOT OF COKE.
SO JUST LEAVE MY BODY ALONE, OKAY?
OKAY. SURE.
YOU KNOW, FUCK IT.

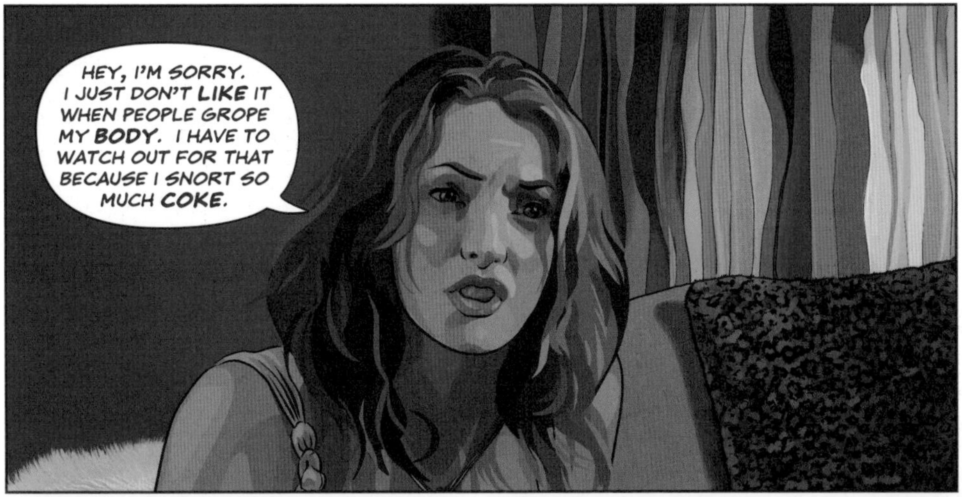
HEY, I'M SORRY. I JUST DON'T **LIKE** IT WHEN PEOPLE GROPE MY **BODY**. I HAVE TO WATCH OUT FOR THAT BECAUSE I SNORT SO MUCH **COKE**.

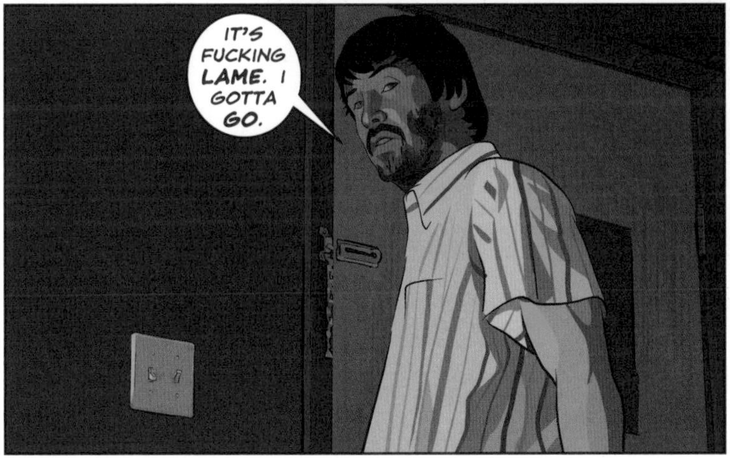
IT'S FUCKING **LAME**. I GOTTA **GO**.

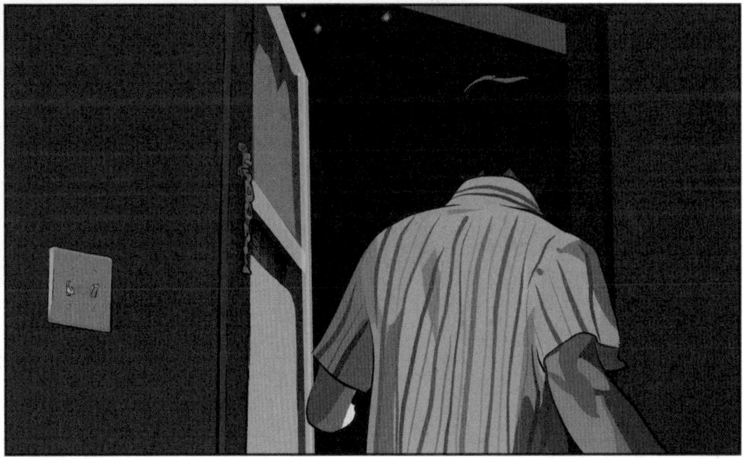

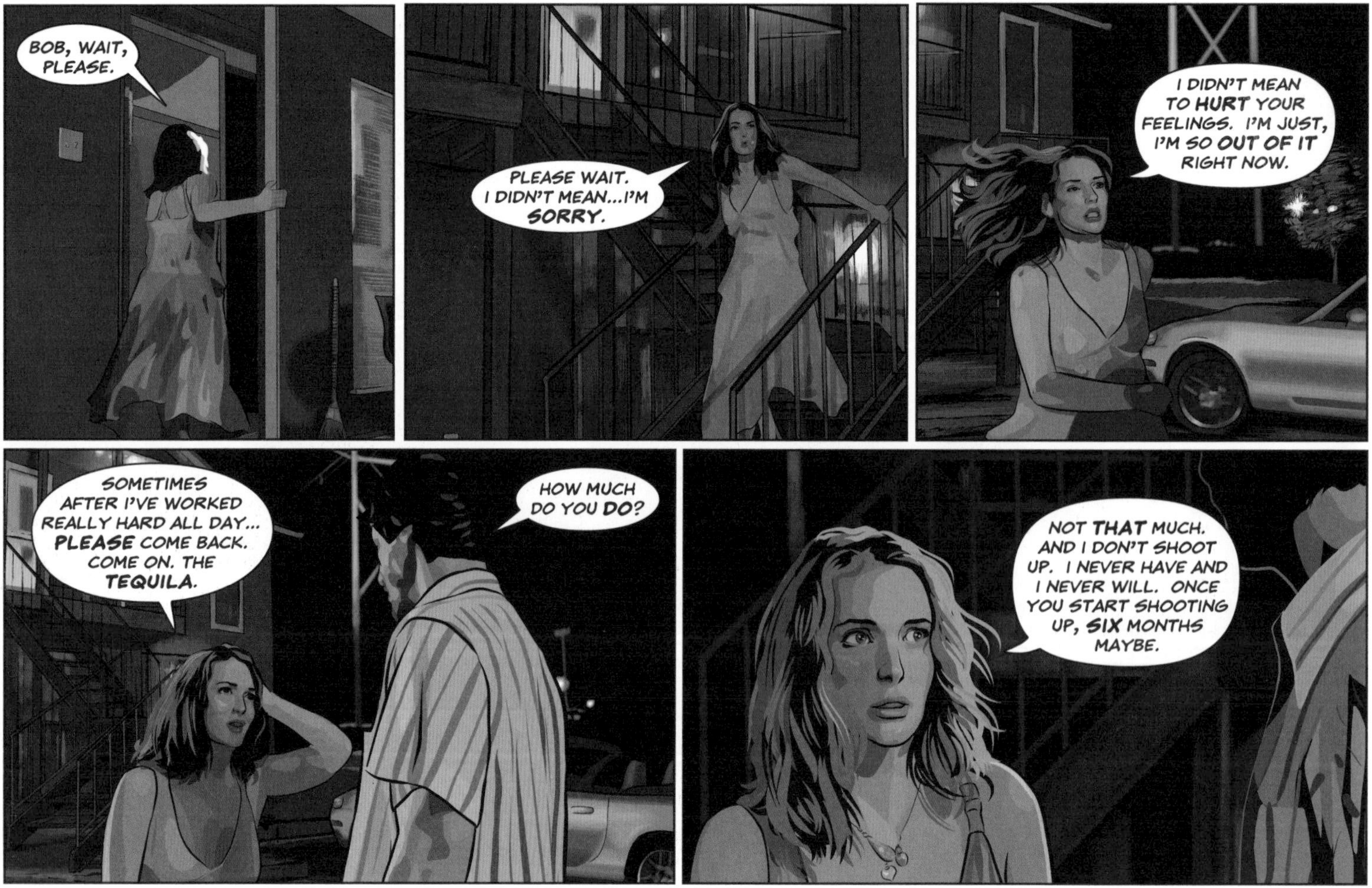
BOB, WAIT, PLEASE.
PLEASE WAIT. I DIDN'T MEAN...I'M SORRY.
I DIDN'T MEAN TO HURT YOUR FEELINGS. I'M JUST, I'M SO OUT OF IT RIGHT NOW.
SOMETIMES AFTER I'VE WORKED REALLY HARD ALL DAY... PLEASE COME BACK. COME ON. THE TEQUILA.
HOW MUCH DO YOU DO?
NOT THAT MUCH. AND I DON'T SHOOT UP. I NEVER HAVE AND I NEVER WILL. ONCE YOU START SHOOTING UP, SIX MONTHS MAYBE.

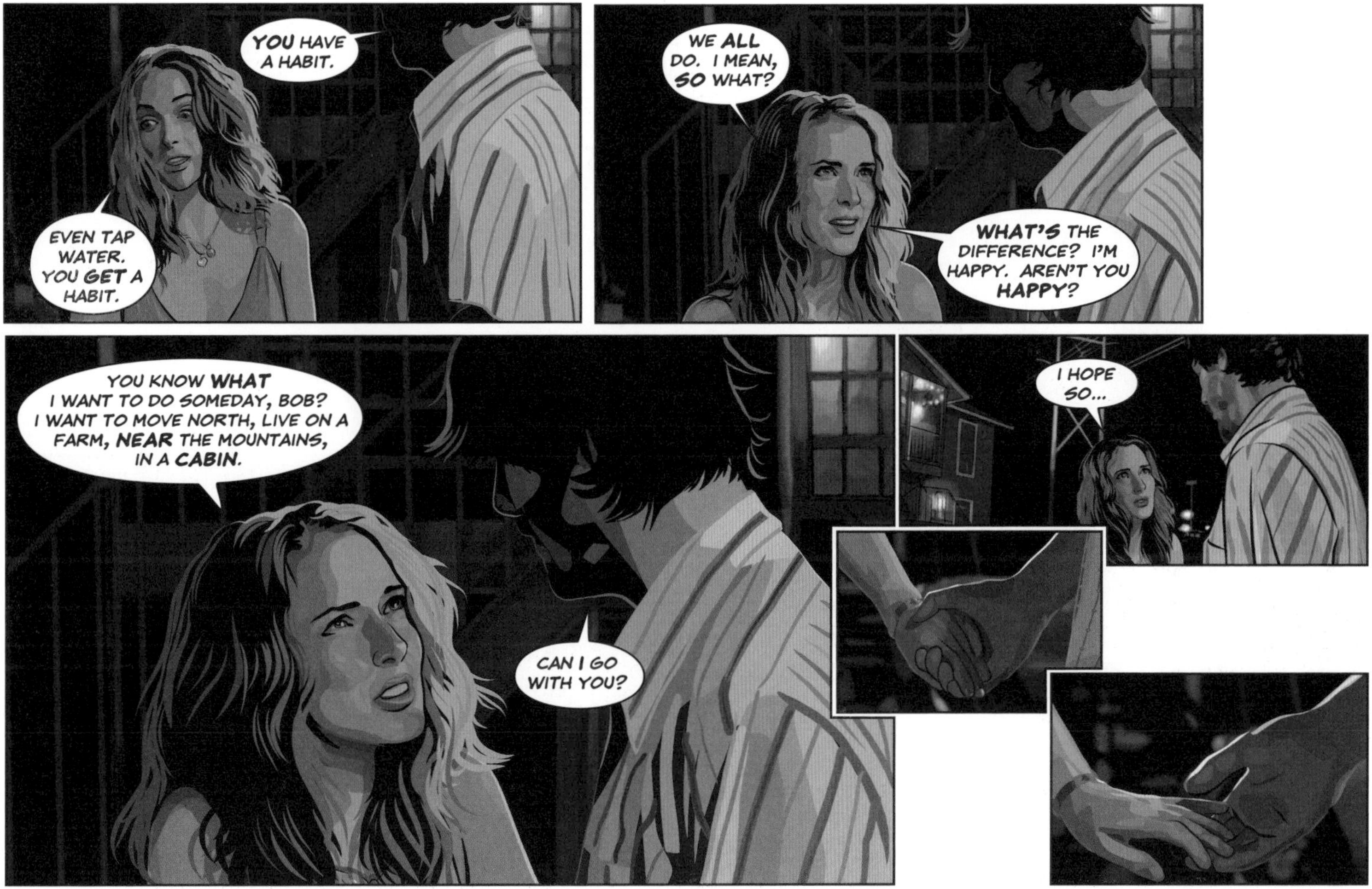
YOU HAVE A HABIT.
EVEN TAP WATER. YOU GET A HABIT.
WE ALL DO. I MEAN, SO WHAT?
WHAT'S THE DIFFERENCE? I'M HAPPY. AREN'T YOU HAPPY?
YOU KNOW WHAT I WANT TO DO SOMEDAY, BOB? I WANT TO MOVE NORTH, LIVE ON A FARM, NEAR THE MOUNTAINS, IN A CABIN.
CAN I GO WITH YOU?
I HOPE SO...

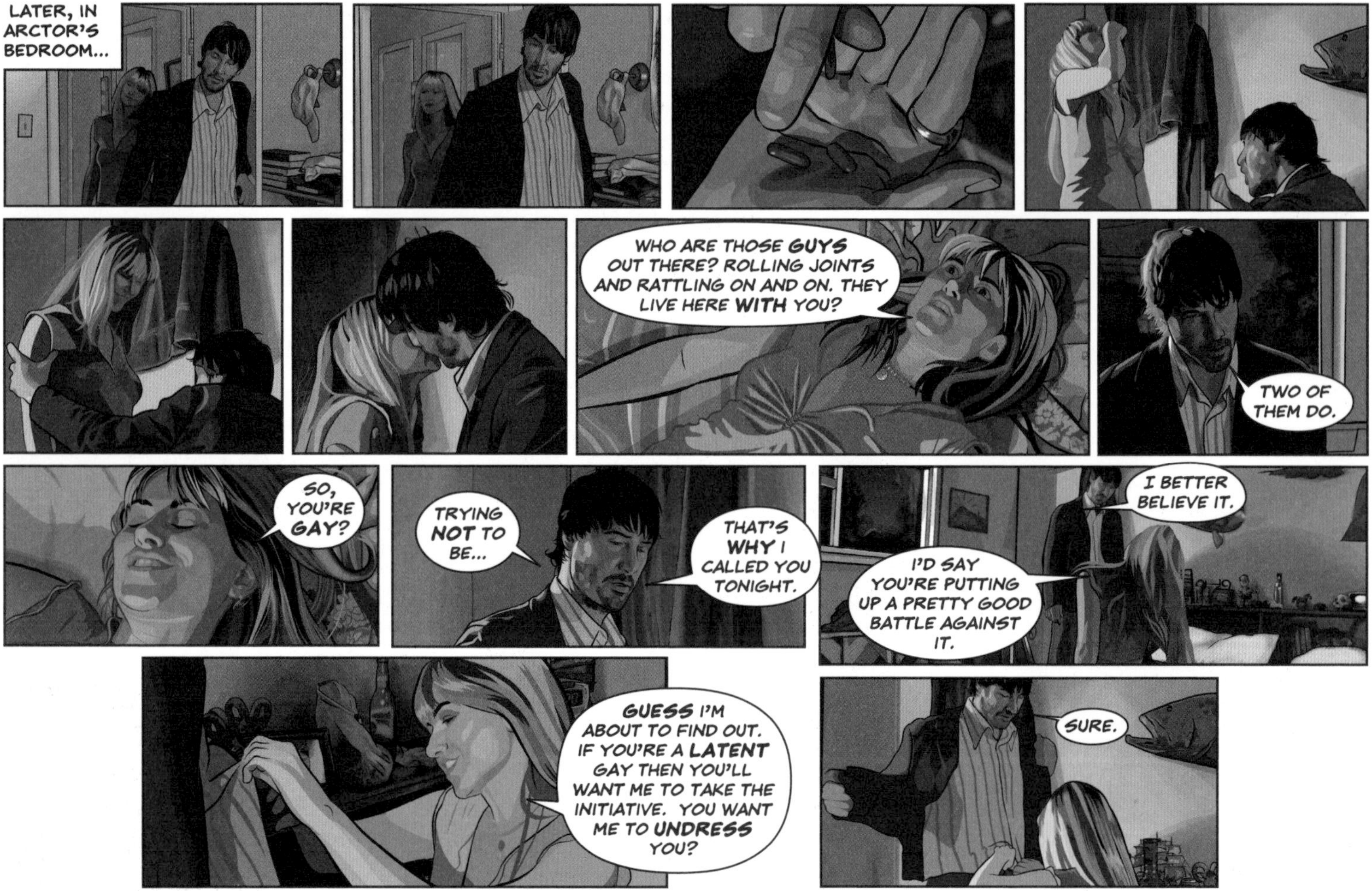
LATER, IN ARCTOR'S BEDROOM...
WHO ARE THOSE GUYS OUT THERE? ROLLING JOINTS AND RATTLING ON AND ON. THEY LIVE HERE WITH YOU?
TWO OF THEM DO.
SO, YOU'RE GAY?
TRYING NOT TO BE...
THAT'S WHY I CALLED YOU TONIGHT.
I'D SAY YOU'RE PUTTING UP A PRETTY GOOD BATTLE AGAINST IT.
I BETTER BELIEVE IT.
GUESS I'M ABOUT TO FIND OUT. IF YOU'RE A LATENT GAY THEN YOU'LL WANT ME TO TAKE THE INITIATIVE. YOU WANT ME TO UNDRESS YOU?
SURE.

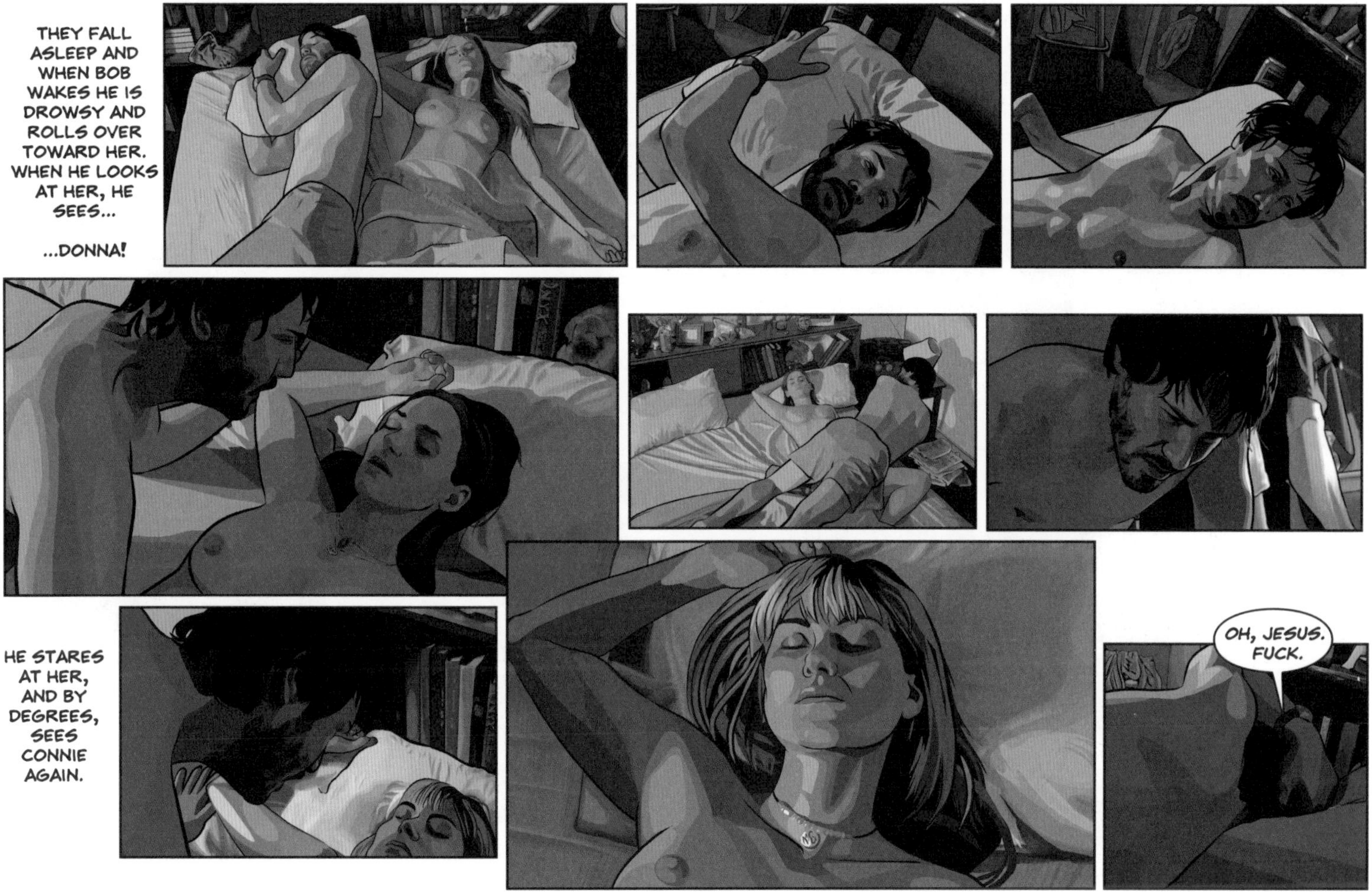
THEY FALL ASLEEP AND WHEN BOB WAKES HE IS DROWSY AND ROLLS OVER TOWARD HER. WHEN HE LOOKS AT HER, HE SEES...
...DONNA!
HE STARES AT HER, AND BY DEGREES, SEES CONNIE AGAIN.
OH, JESUS. FUCK.

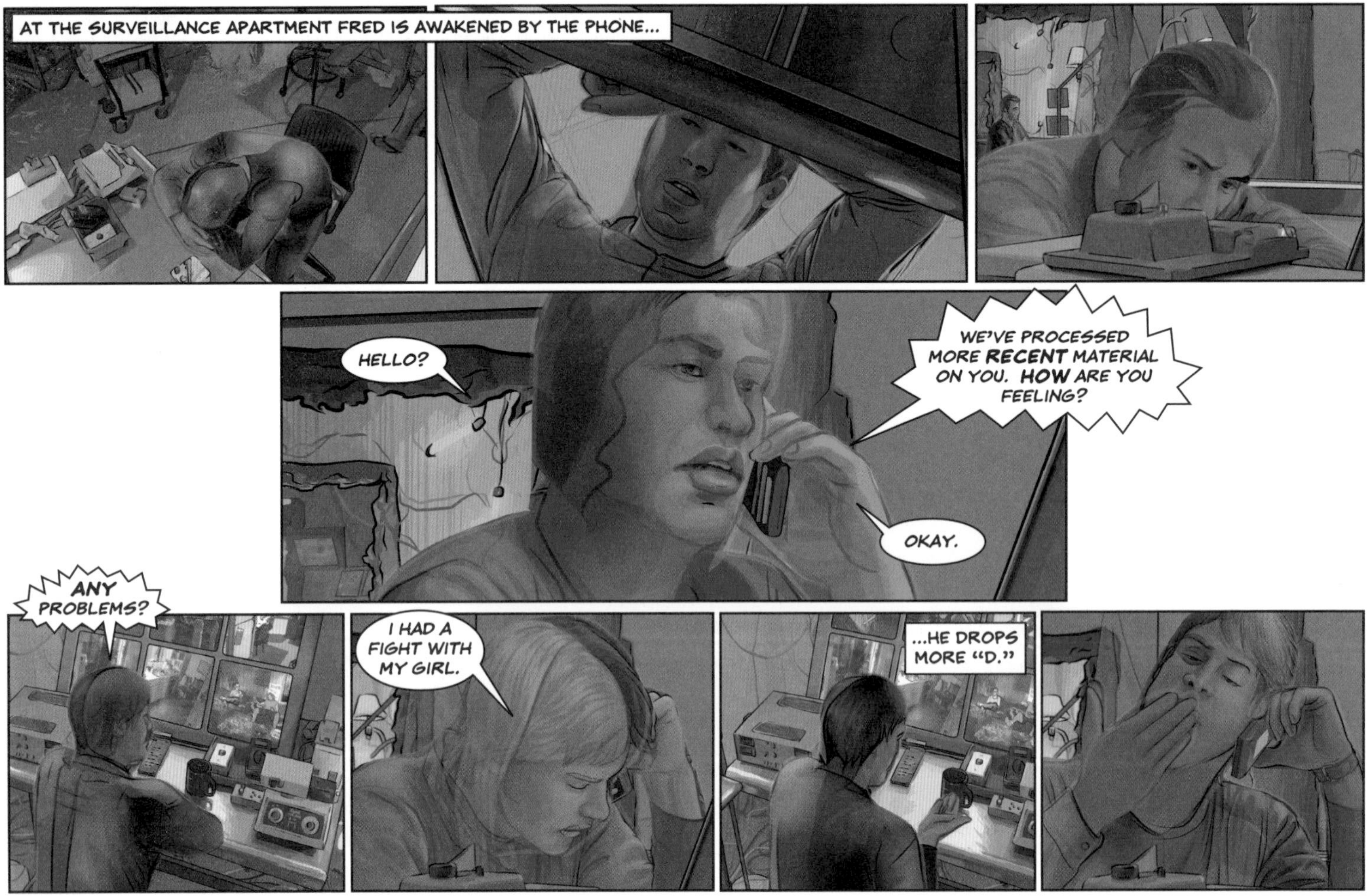
AT THE SURVEILLANCE APARTMENT FRED IS AWAKENED BY THE PHONE...
HELLO?
WE'VE PROCESSED MORE **RECENT** MATERIAL ON YOU. **HOW** ARE YOU FEELING?
OKAY.
ANY PROBLEMS?
I HAD A FIGHT WITH MY GIRL.
...HE DROPS MORE "D."

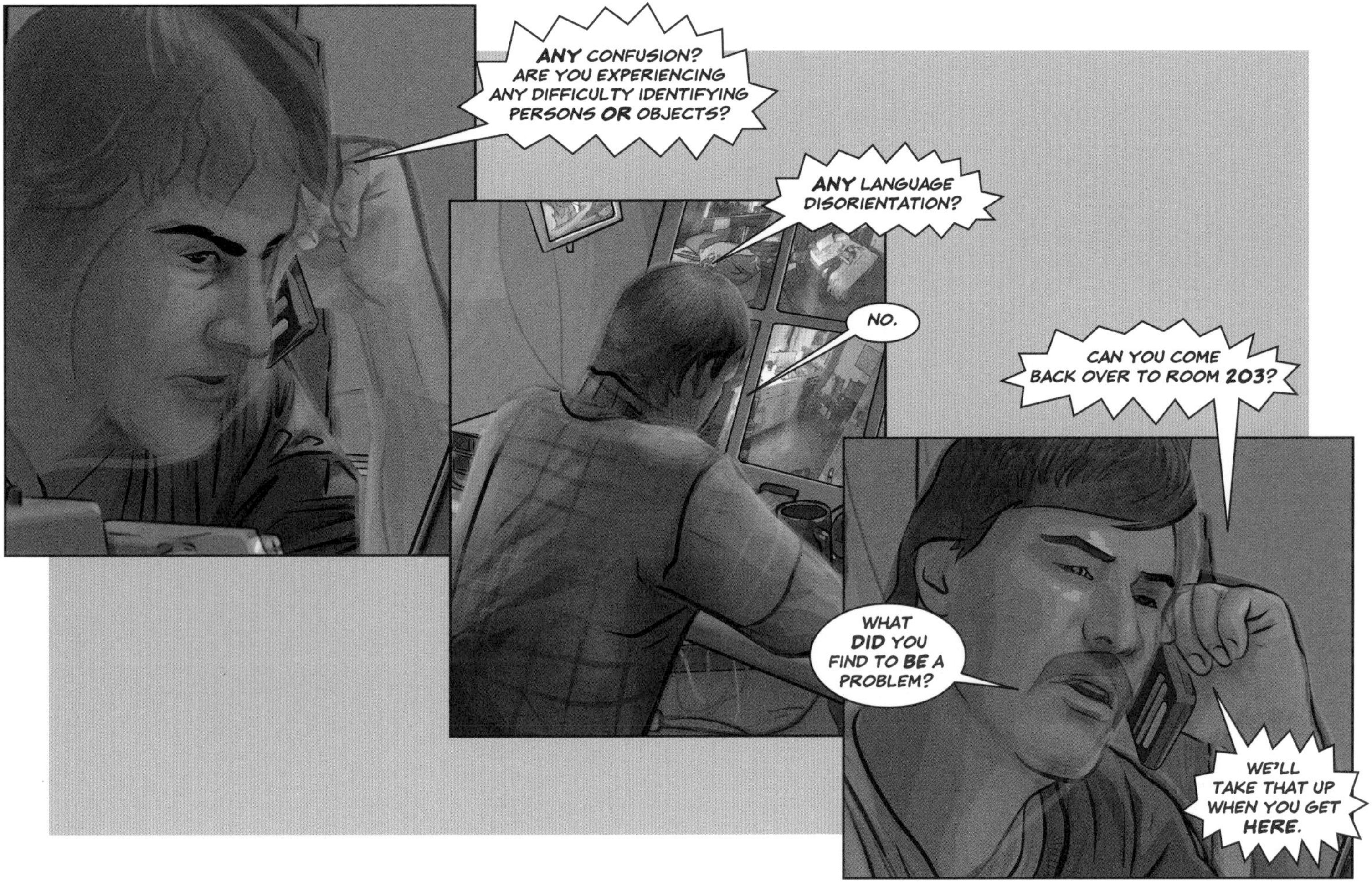
ANY CONFUSION? ARE YOU EXPERIENCING ANY DIFFICULTY IDENTIFYING PERSONS OR OBJECTS?
ANY LANGUAGE DISORIENTATION?
NO.
CAN YOU COME BACK OVER TO ROOM 203?
WHAT DID YOU FIND TO BE A PROBLEM?
WE'LL TAKE THAT UP WHEN YOU GET HERE.

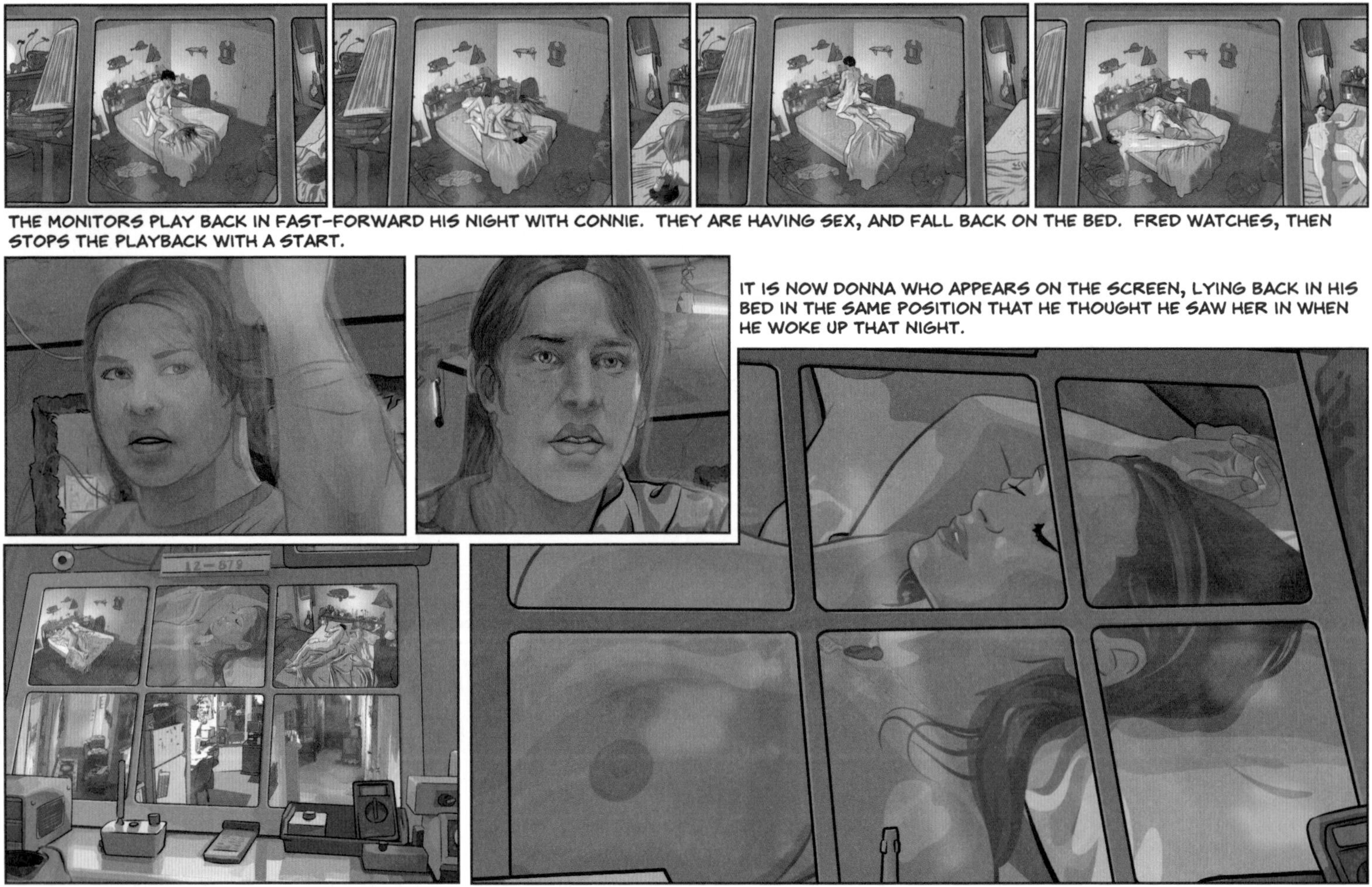
THE MONITORS PLAY BACK IN FAST-FORWARD HIS NIGHT WITH CONNIE. THEY ARE HAVING SEX, AND FALL BACK ON THE BED. FRED WATCHES, THEN STOPS THE PLAYBACK WITH A START.
IT IS NOW DONNA WHO APPEARS ON THE SCREEN, LYING BACK IN HIS BED IN THE SAME POSITION THAT HE THOUGHT HE SAW HER IN WHEN HE WOKE UP THAT NIGHT.

HE HITS THE STOP BUTTON AND TRANSFERS HER IMAGE TO THE LIGHTBOX NEXT TO THE MONITORS.

 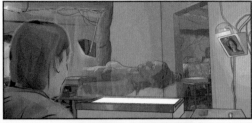 

HE STANDS UP, LOOKING DOWN AT THE IMAGE OF DONNA. WHEN HE HITS A BUTTON...

CONNIE...

DONNA.

...THE IMAGE SLOWLY TRANSFORMS INTO CONNIE. WHEN HE HITS ANOTHER BUTTON, IT SLOWLY REVERSES BACK INTO DONNA.

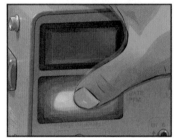

BACK IN ROOM 203, LATER, TWO MEDICAL OFFICERS ARE ADMINISTERING A SERIES OF TESTS.

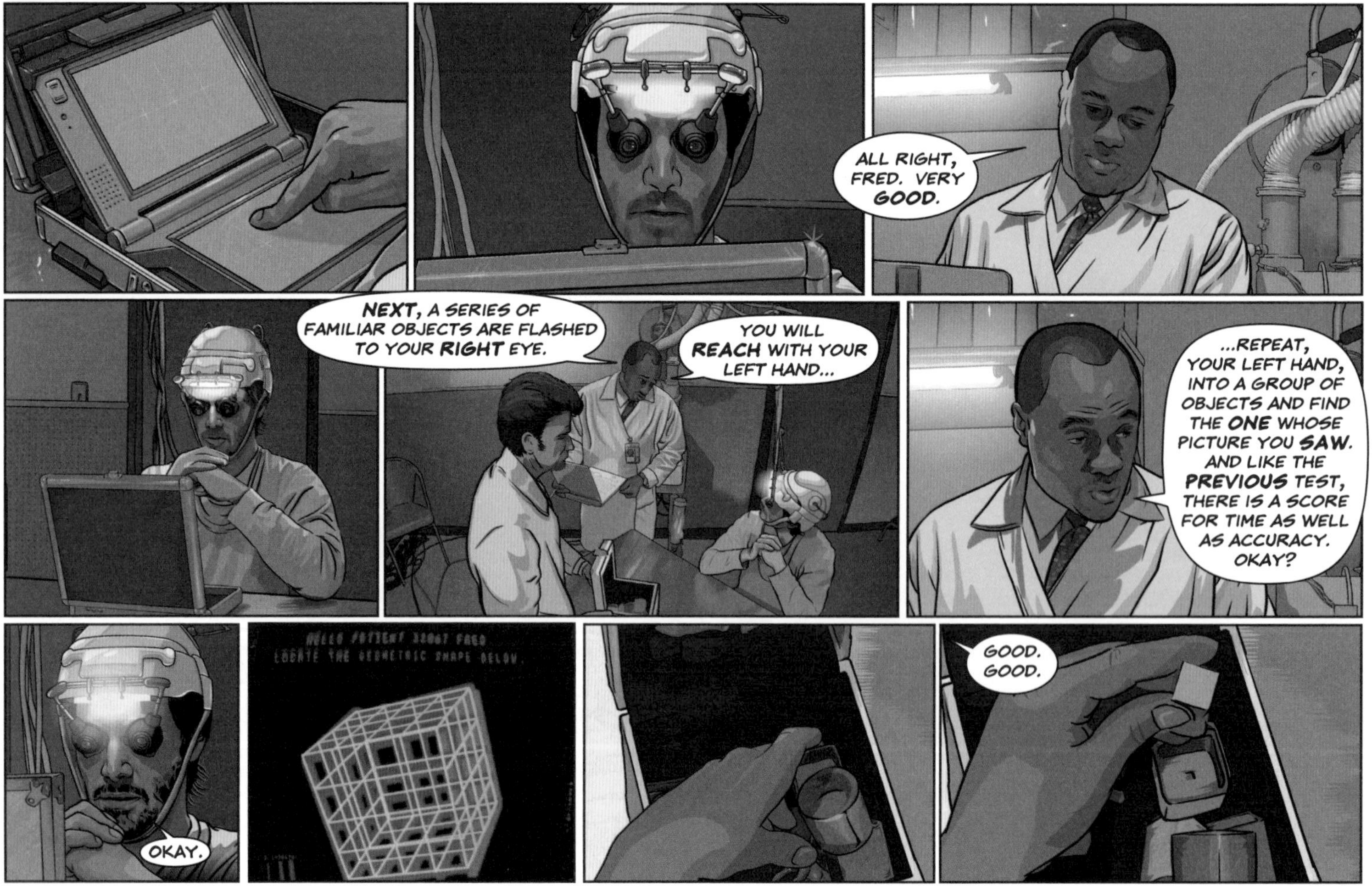
ALL RIGHT, FRED. VERY GOOD.
NEXT, A SERIES OF FAMILIAR OBJECTS ARE FLASHED TO YOUR RIGHT EYE.
YOU WILL REACH WITH YOUR LEFT HAND...
...REPEAT, YOUR LEFT HAND, INTO A GROUP OF OBJECTS AND FIND THE ONE WHOSE PICTURE YOU SAW. AND LIKE THE PREVIOUS TEST, THERE IS A SCORE FOR TIME AS WELL AS ACCURACY. OKAY?
OKAY.
GOOD. GOOD.

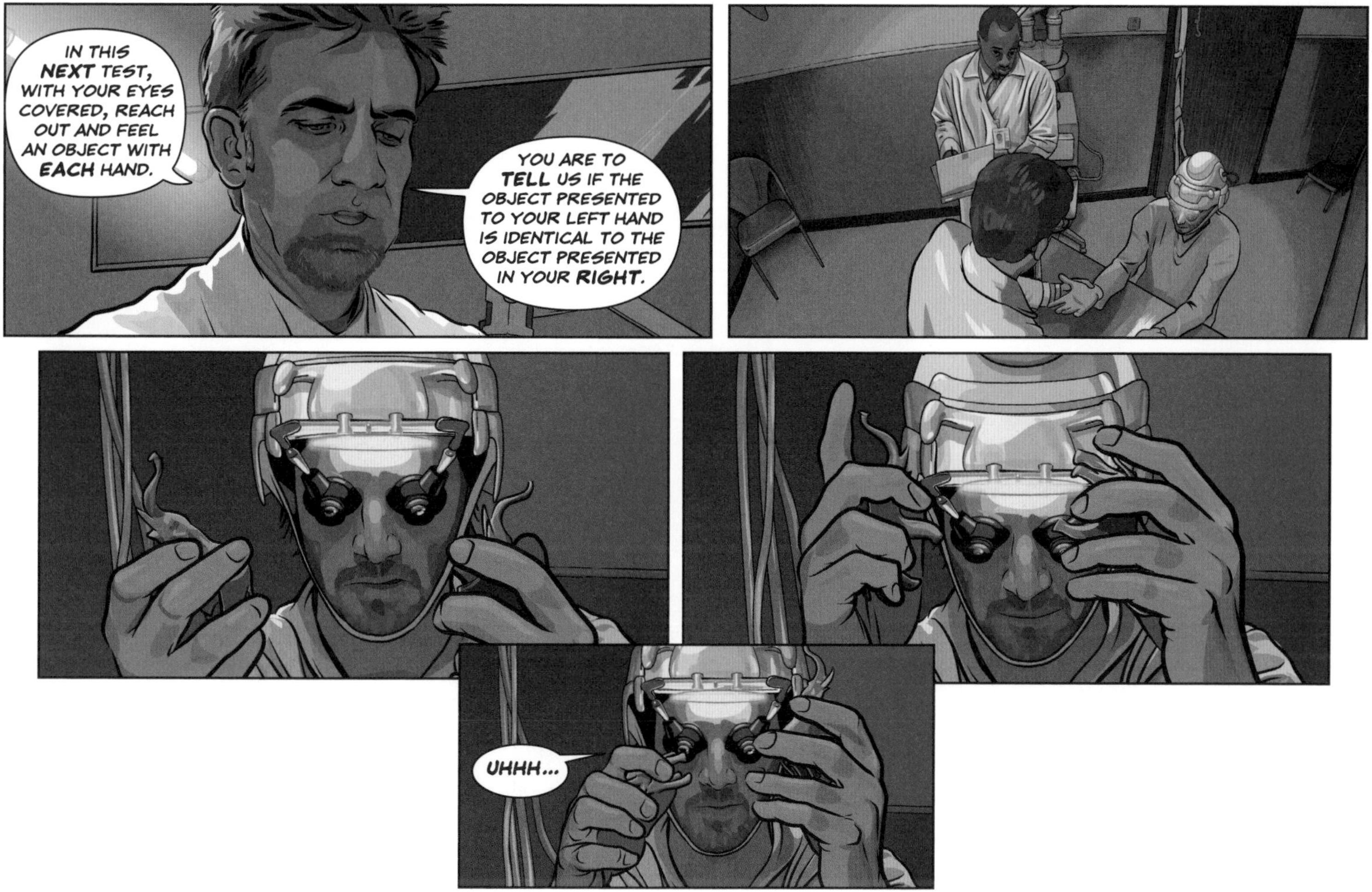
IN THIS NEXT TEST, WITH YOUR EYES COVERED, REACH OUT AND FEEL AN OBJECT WITH EACH HAND.
YOU ARE TO TELL US IF THE OBJECT PRESENTED TO YOUR LEFT HAND IS IDENTICAL TO THE OBJECT PRESENTED IN YOUR RIGHT.
UHHH...

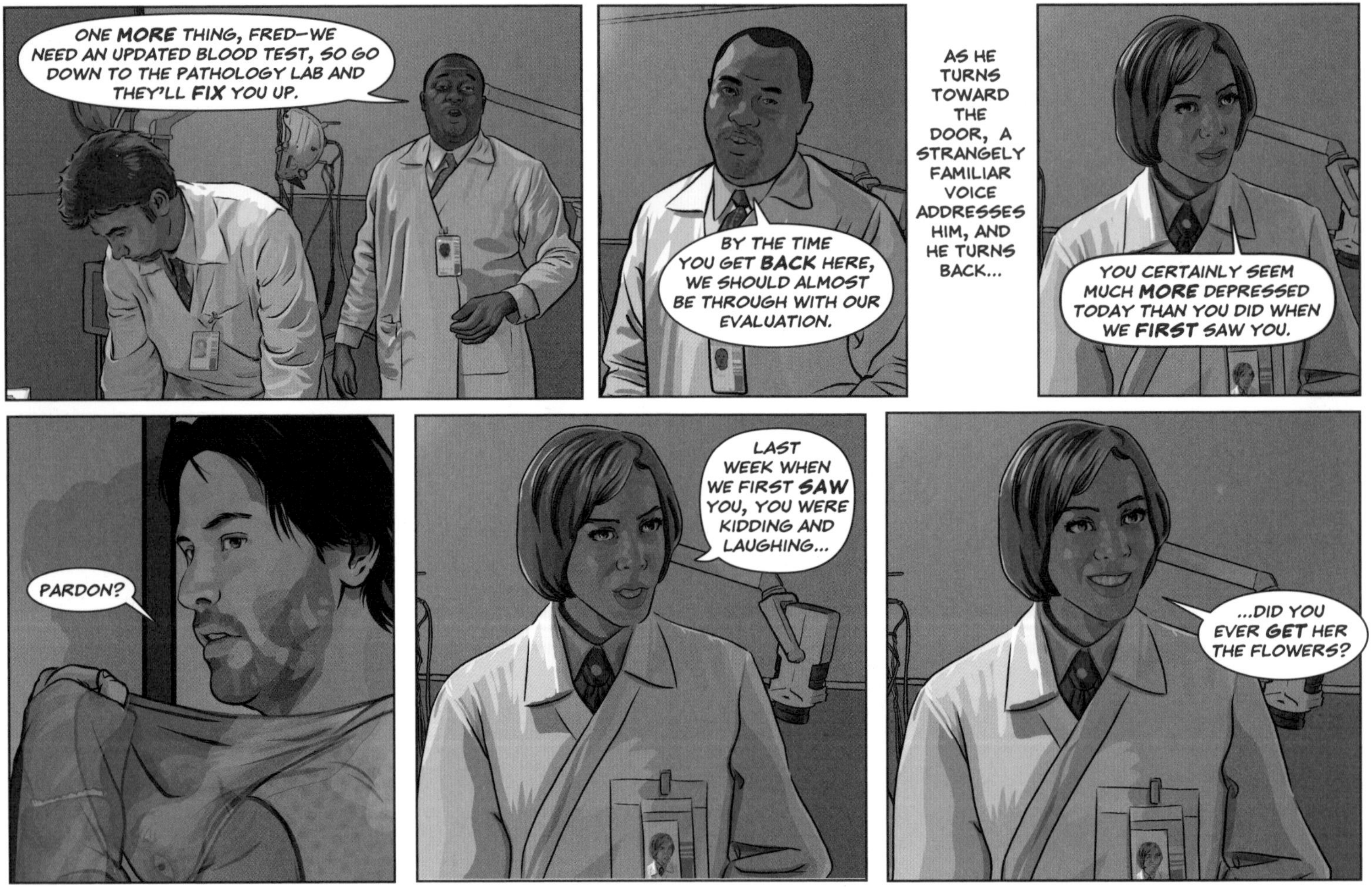

ONE MORE THING, FRED—WE NEED AN UPDATED BLOOD TEST, SO GO DOWN TO THE PATHOLOGY LAB AND THEY'LL FIX YOU UP.
BY THE TIME YOU GET BACK HERE, WE SHOULD ALMOST BE THROUGH WITH OUR EVALUATION.
AS HE TURNS TOWARD THE DOOR, A STRANGELY FAMILIAR VOICE ADDRESSES HIM, AND HE TURNS BACK...
YOU CERTAINLY SEEM MUCH MORE DEPRESSED TODAY THAN YOU DID WHEN WE FIRST SAW YOU.
PARDON?
LAST WEEK WHEN WE FIRST SAW YOU, YOU WERE KIDDING AND LAUGHING...
...DID YOU EVER GET HER THE FLOWERS?

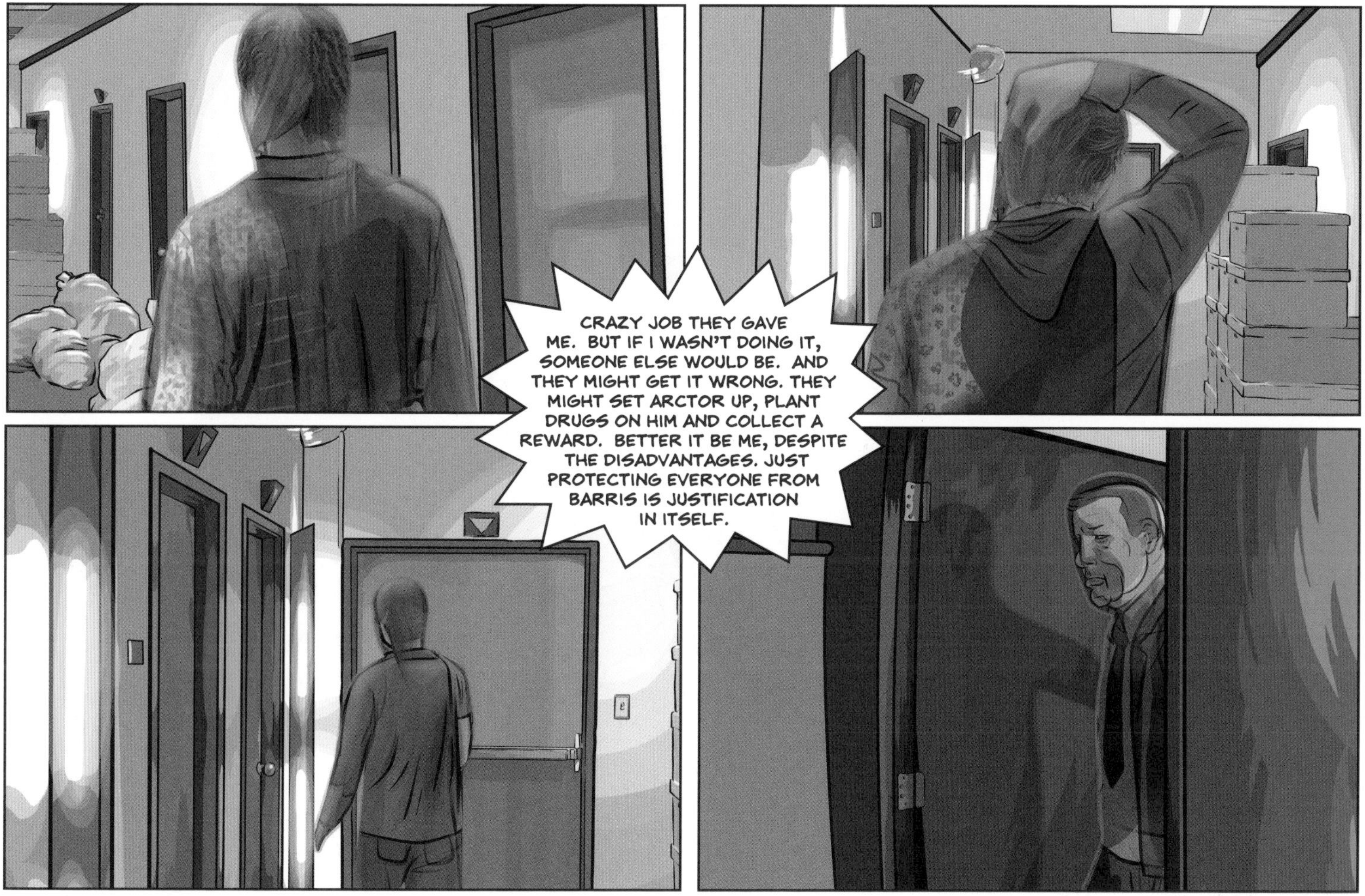
CRAZY JOB THEY GAVE ME. BUT IF I WASN'T DOING IT, SOMEONE ELSE WOULD BE. AND THEY MIGHT GET IT WRONG. THEY MIGHT SET ARCTOR UP, PLANT DRUGS ON HIM AND COLLECT A REWARD. BETTER IT BE ME, DESPITE THE DISADVANTAGES. JUST PROTECTING EVERYONE FROM BARRIS IS JUSTIFICATION IN ITSELF.

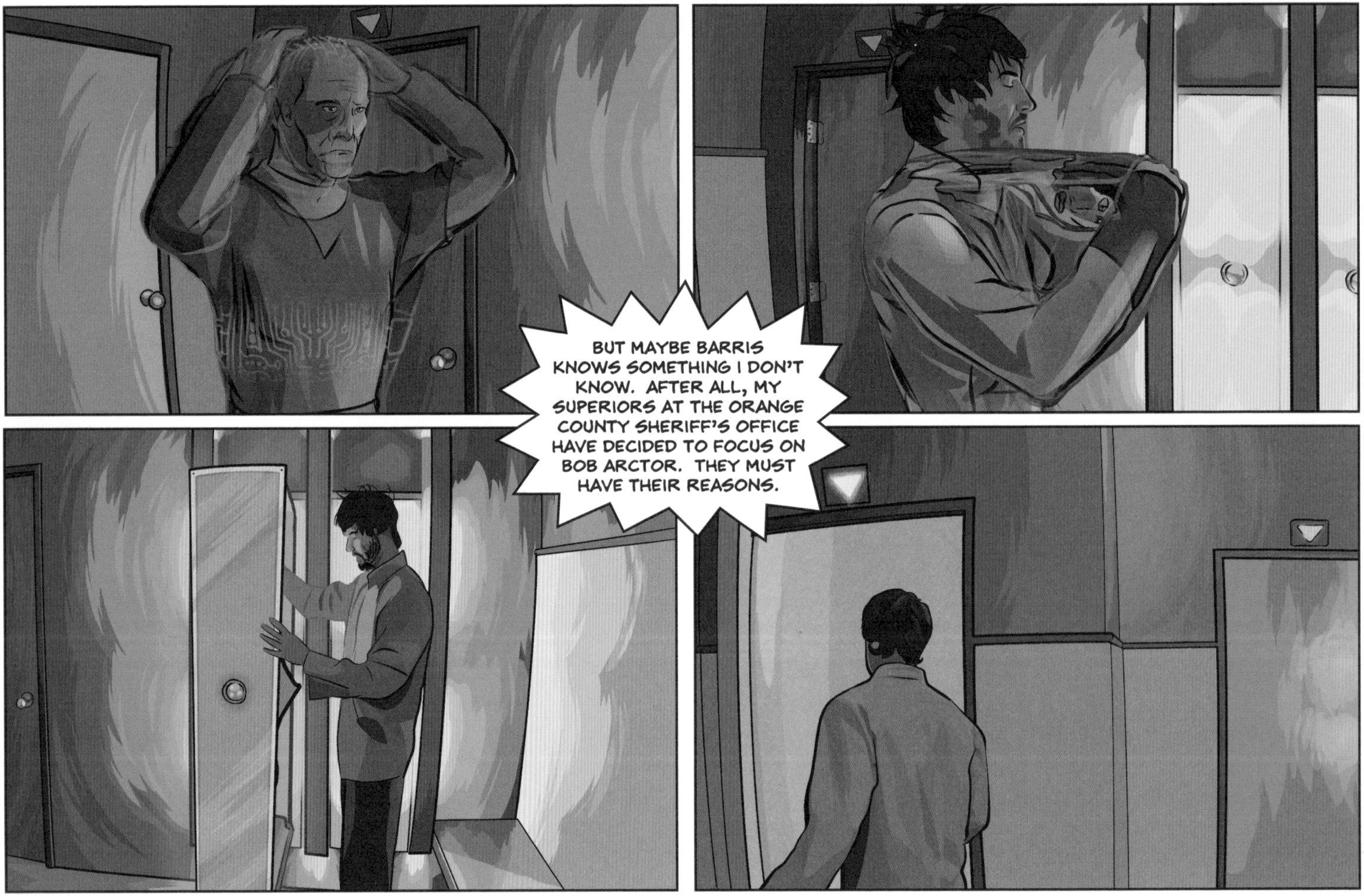
BUT MAYBE BARRIS KNOWS SOMETHING I DON'T KNOW. AFTER ALL, MY SUPERIORS AT THE ORANGE COUNTY SHERIFF'S OFFICE HAVE DECIDED TO FOCUS ON BOB ARCTOR. THEY MUST HAVE THEIR REASONS.

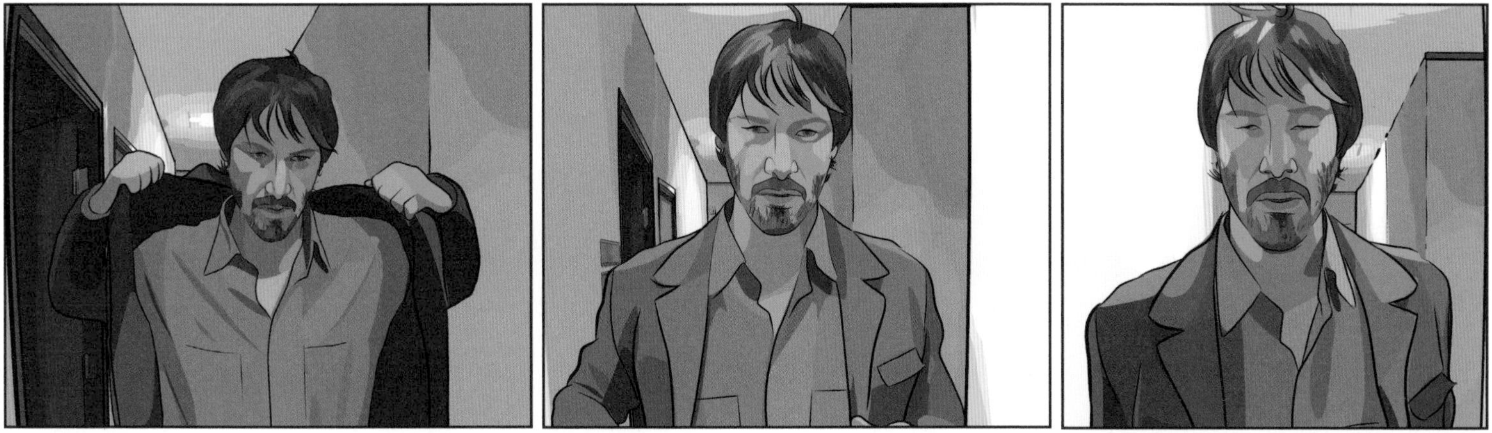

WHAT THE HELL AM I TALKING ABOUT? I MUST BE NUTS. I KNOW BOB ARCTOR. HE'S A GOOD PERSON. HE'S UP TO NOTHING, AT LEAST NOTHING TOO BAD. IN FACT HE WORKS FOR THE ORANGE COUNTY SHERIFF'S OFFICE COVERTLY, WHICH IS PROBABLY WHY BARRIS IS AFTER HIM.

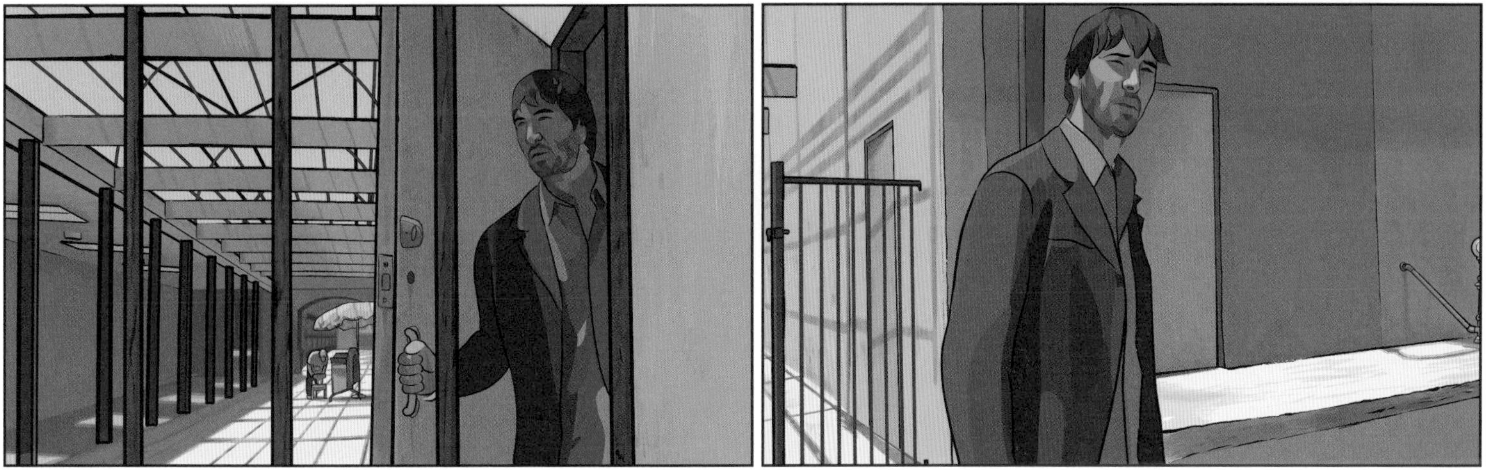

BUT, THAT WOULDN'T EXPLAIN WHY THE ORANGE COUNTY SHERIFF'S OFFICE IS AFTER HIM.

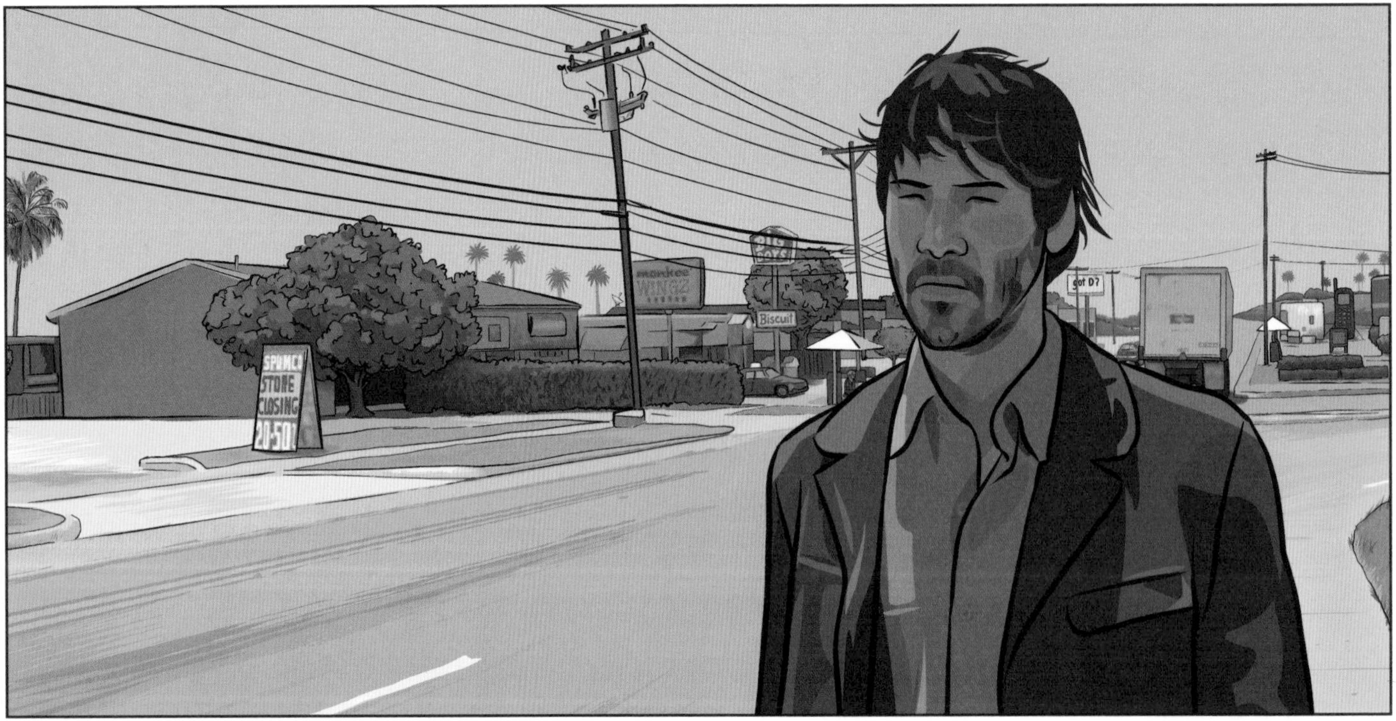
SPUMCO
STORE
CLOSING
monkee
WINGZ
BIG BOYS
Biscuit
got D?

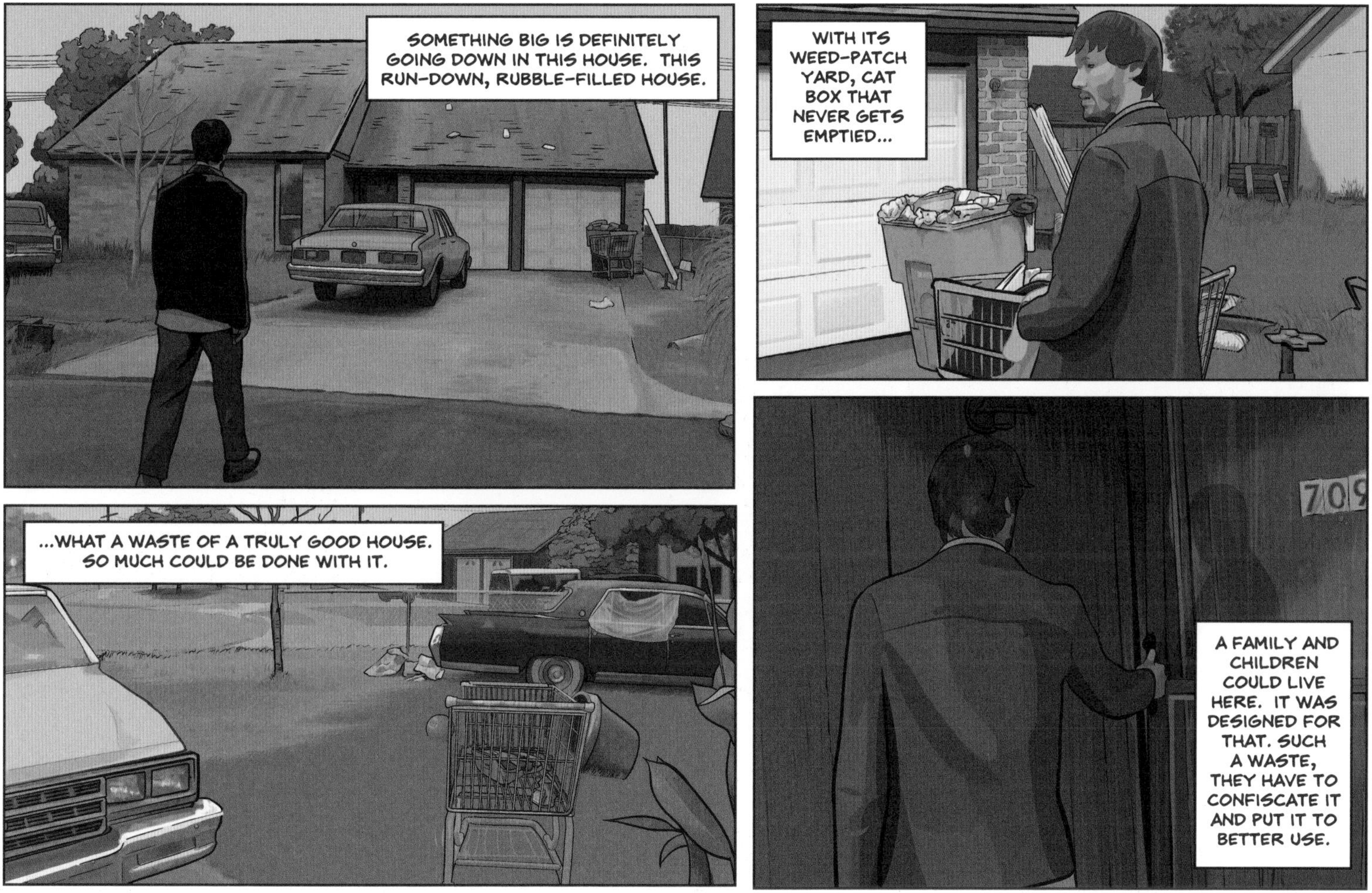
SOMETHING BIG IS DEFINITELY GOING DOWN IN THIS HOUSE. THIS RUN-DOWN, RUBBLE-FILLED HOUSE.
WITH ITS WEED-PATCH YARD, CAT BOX THAT NEVER GETS EMPTIED...
...WHAT A WASTE OF A TRULY GOOD HOUSE. SO MUCH COULD BE DONE WITH IT.
A FAMILY AND CHILDREN COULD LIVE HERE. IT WAS DESIGNED FOR THAT. SUCH A WASTE, THEY HAVE TO CONFISCATE IT AND PUT IT TO BETTER USE.

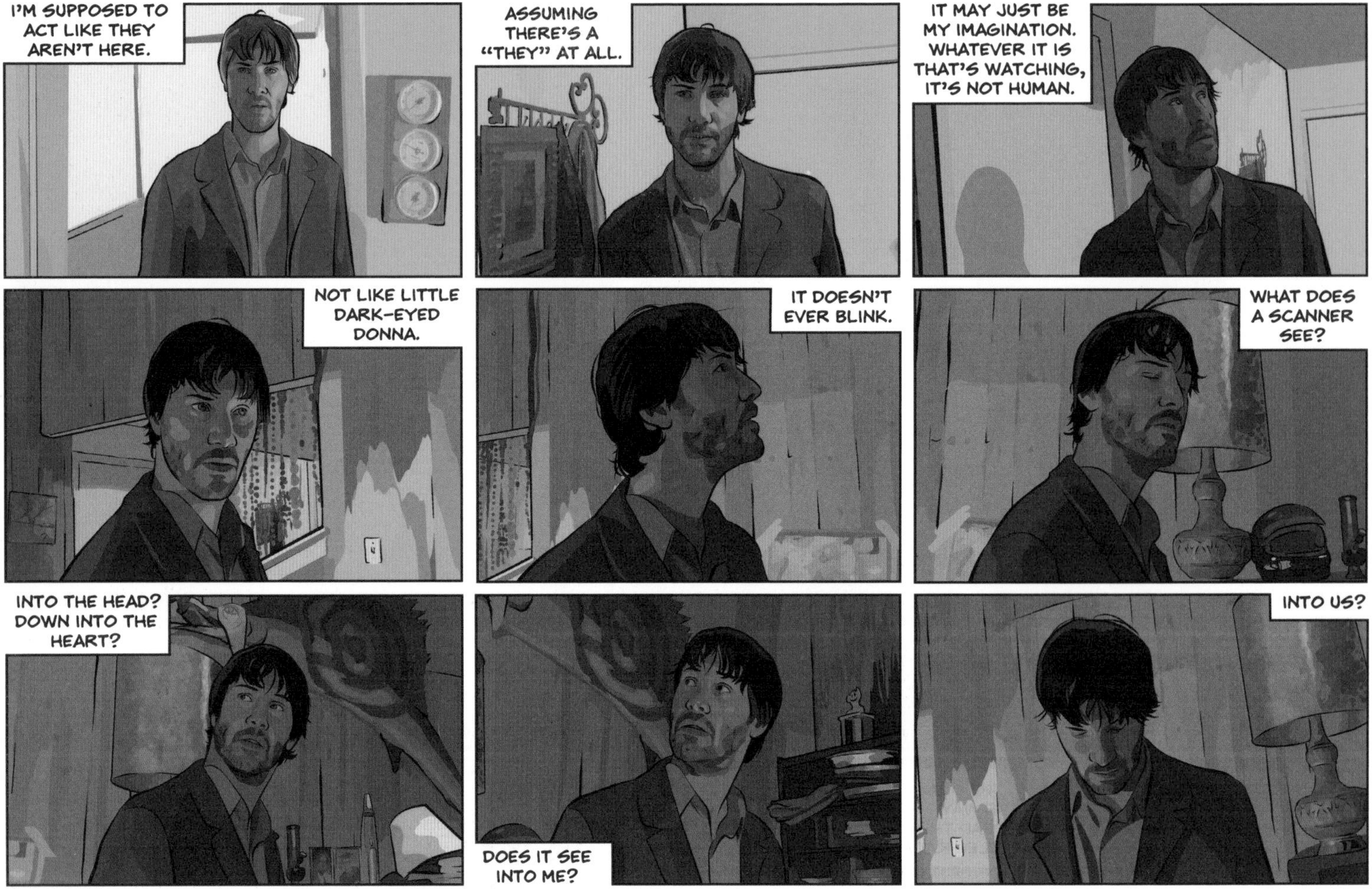
I'M SUPPOSED TO ACT LIKE THEY AREN'T HERE.
ASSUMING THERE'S A "THEY" AT ALL.
IT MAY JUST BE MY IMAGINATION. WHATEVER IT IS THAT'S WATCHING, IT'S NOT HUMAN.
NOT LIKE LITTLE DARK-EYED DONNA.
IT DOESN'T EVER BLINK.
WHAT DOES A SCANNER SEE?
INTO THE HEAD? DOWN INTO THE HEART?
DOES IT SEE INTO ME?
INTO US?

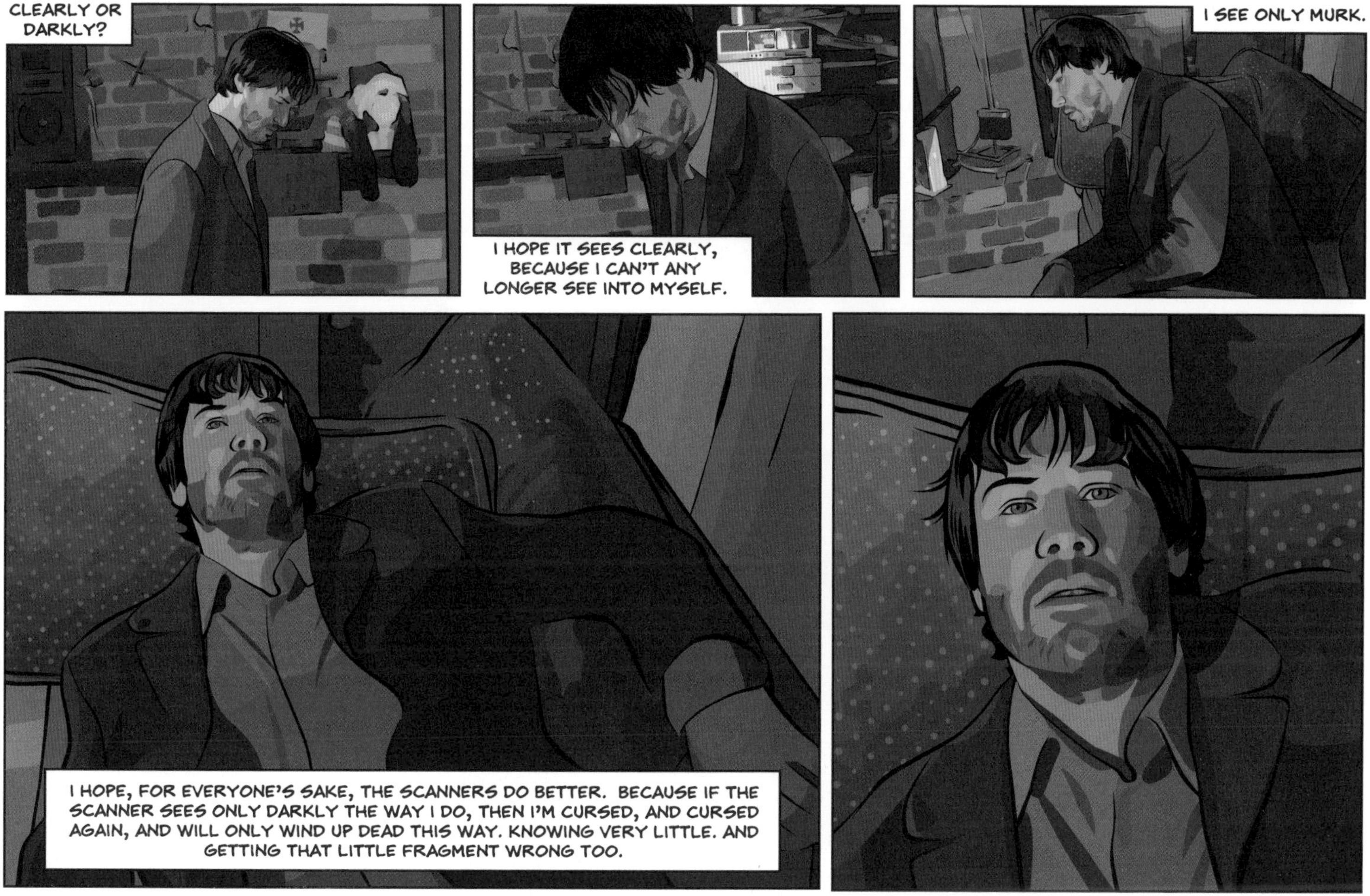
CLEARLY OR DARKLY?
I HOPE IT SEES CLEARLY, BECAUSE I CAN'T ANY LONGER SEE INTO MYSELF.
I SEE ONLY MURK.
I HOPE, FOR EVERYONE'S SAKE, THE SCANNERS DO BETTER. BECAUSE IF THE SCANNER SEES ONLY DARKLY THE WAY I DO, THEN I'M CURSED, AND CURSED AGAIN, AND WILL ONLY WIND UP DEAD THIS WAY. KNOWING VERY LITTLE. AND GETTING THAT LITTLE FRAGMENT WRONG TOO.

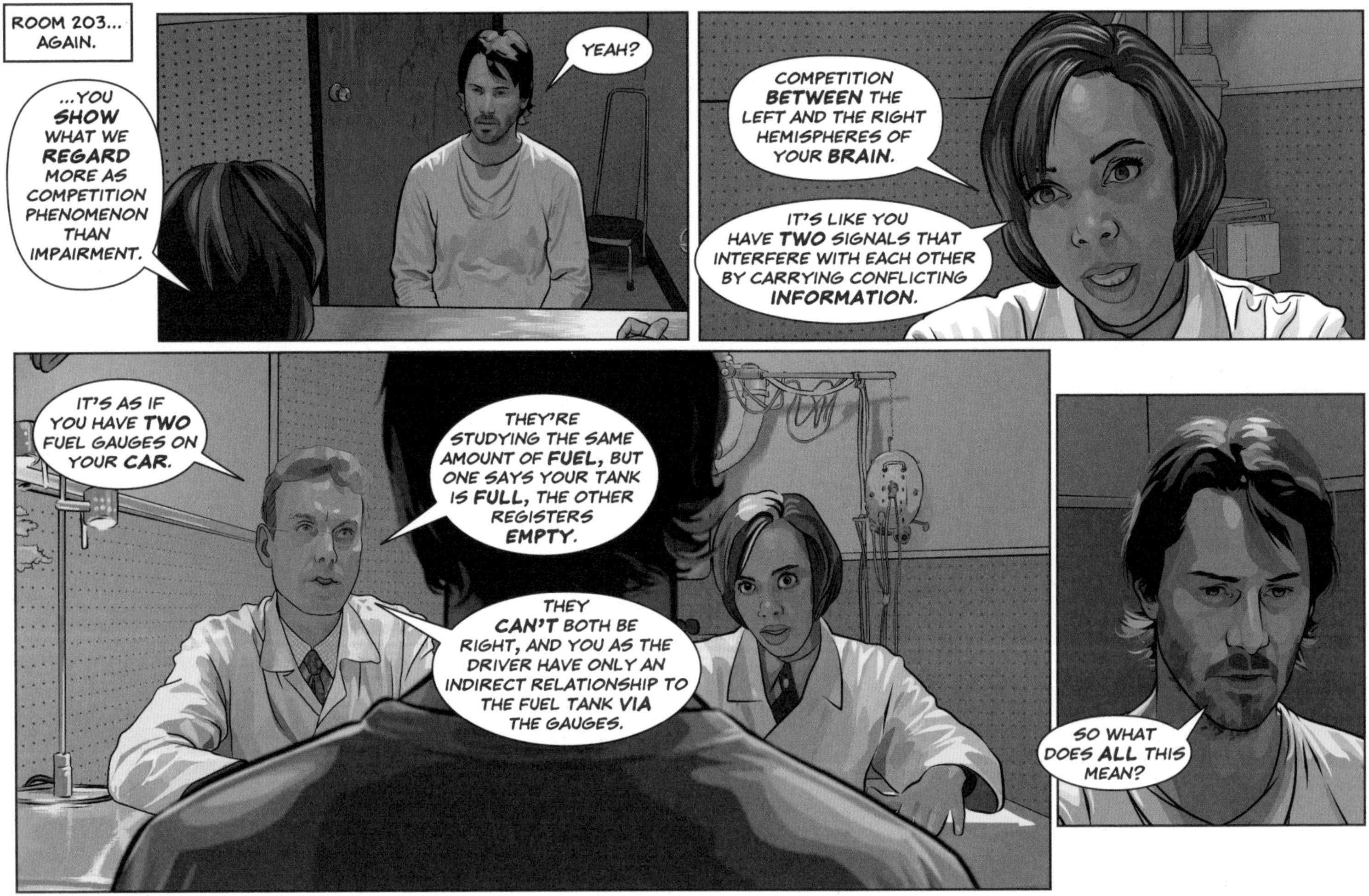
ROOM 203... AGAIN.
...YOU SHOW WHAT WE REGARD MORE AS COMPETITION PHENOMENON THAN IMPAIRMENT.
YEAH?
COMPETITION BETWEEN THE LEFT AND THE RIGHT HEMISPHERES OF YOUR BRAIN.
IT'S LIKE YOU HAVE TWO SIGNALS THAT INTERFERE WITH EACH OTHER BY CARRYING CONFLICTING INFORMATION.
IT'S AS IF YOU HAVE TWO FUEL GAUGES ON YOUR CAR.
THEY'RE STUDYING THE SAME AMOUNT OF FUEL, BUT ONE SAYS YOUR TANK IS FULL, THE OTHER REGISTERS EMPTY.
THEY CAN'T BOTH BE RIGHT, AND YOU AS THE DRIVER HAVE ONLY AN INDIRECT RELATIONSHIP TO THE FUEL TANK VIA THE GAUGES.
SO WHAT DOES ALL THIS MEAN?

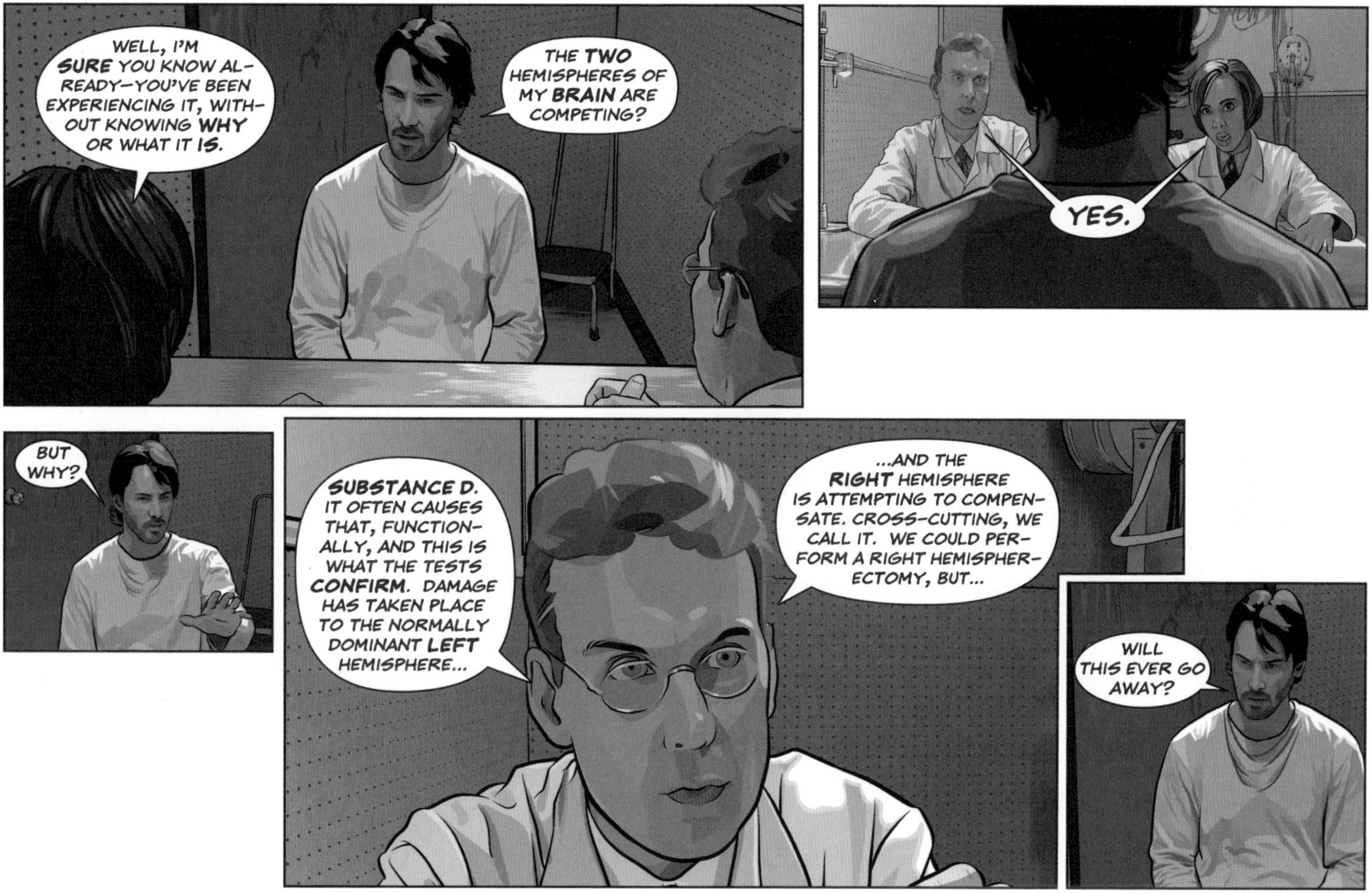
WELL, I'M SURE YOU KNOW AL-READY—YOU'VE BEEN EXPERIENCING IT, WITH-OUT KNOWING WHY OR WHAT IT IS.
THE TWO HEMISPHERES OF MY BRAIN ARE COMPETING?
YES.
BUT WHY?
SUBSTANCE D. IT OFTEN CAUSES THAT, FUNCTION-ALLY, AND THIS IS WHAT THE TESTS CONFIRM. DAMAGE HAS TAKEN PLACE TO THE NORMALLY DOMINANT LEFT HEMISPHERE...
...AND THE RIGHT HEMISPHERE IS ATTEMPTING TO COMPEN-SATE. CROSS-CUTTING, WE CALL IT. WE COULD PER-FORM A RIGHT HEMISPHER-ECTOMY, BUT...
WILL THIS EVER GO AWAY?

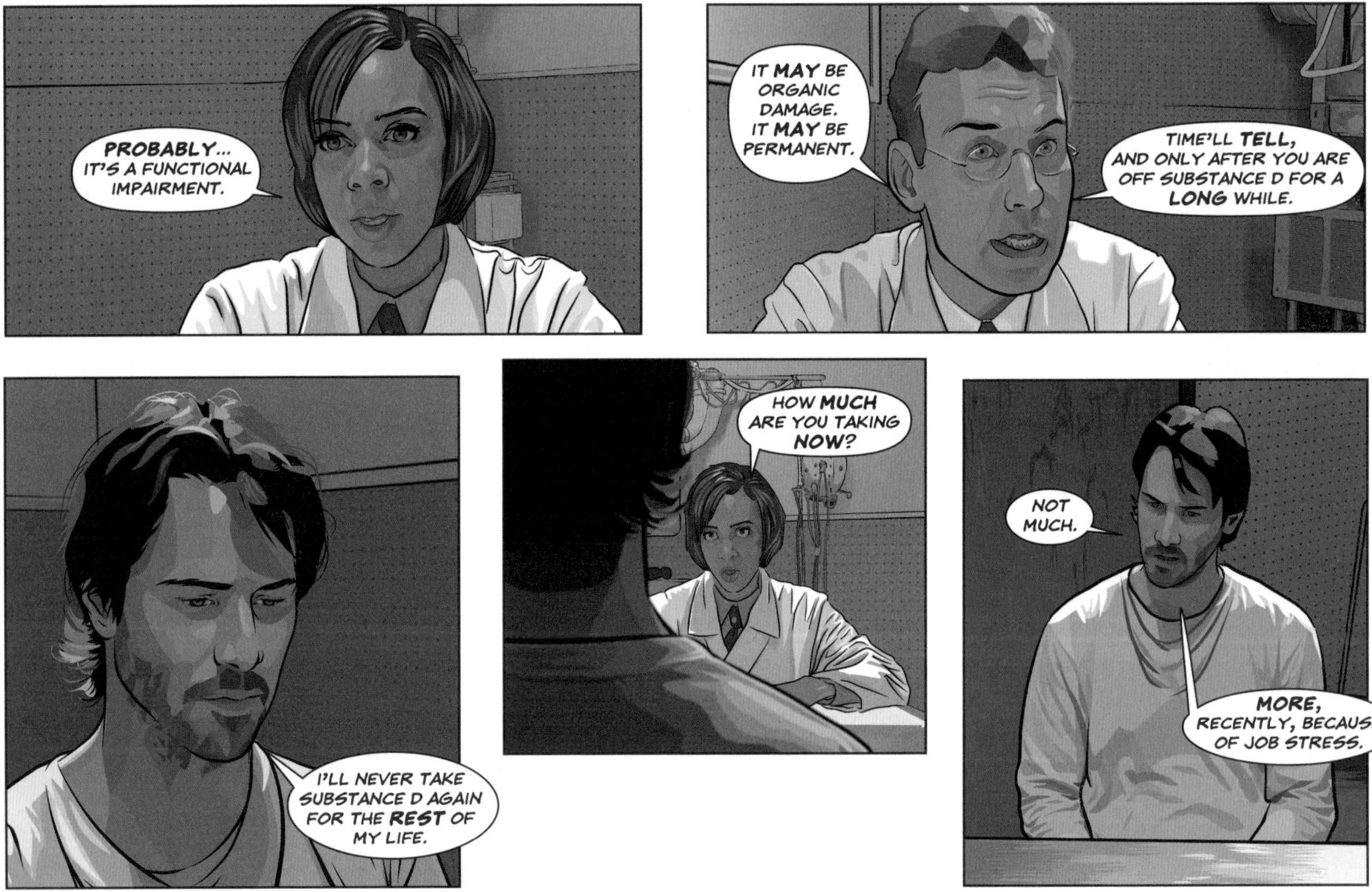
PROBABLY... IT'S A FUNCTIONAL IMPAIRMENT.
IT MAY BE ORGANIC DAMAGE. IT MAY BE PERMANENT.
TIME'LL TELL, AND ONLY AFTER YOU ARE OFF SUBSTANCE D FOR A LONG WHILE.
I'LL NEVER TAKE SUBSTANCE D AGAIN FOR THE REST OF MY LIFE.
HOW MUCH ARE YOU TAKING NOW?
NOT MUCH.
MORE, RECENTLY, BECAUSE OF JOB STRESS.

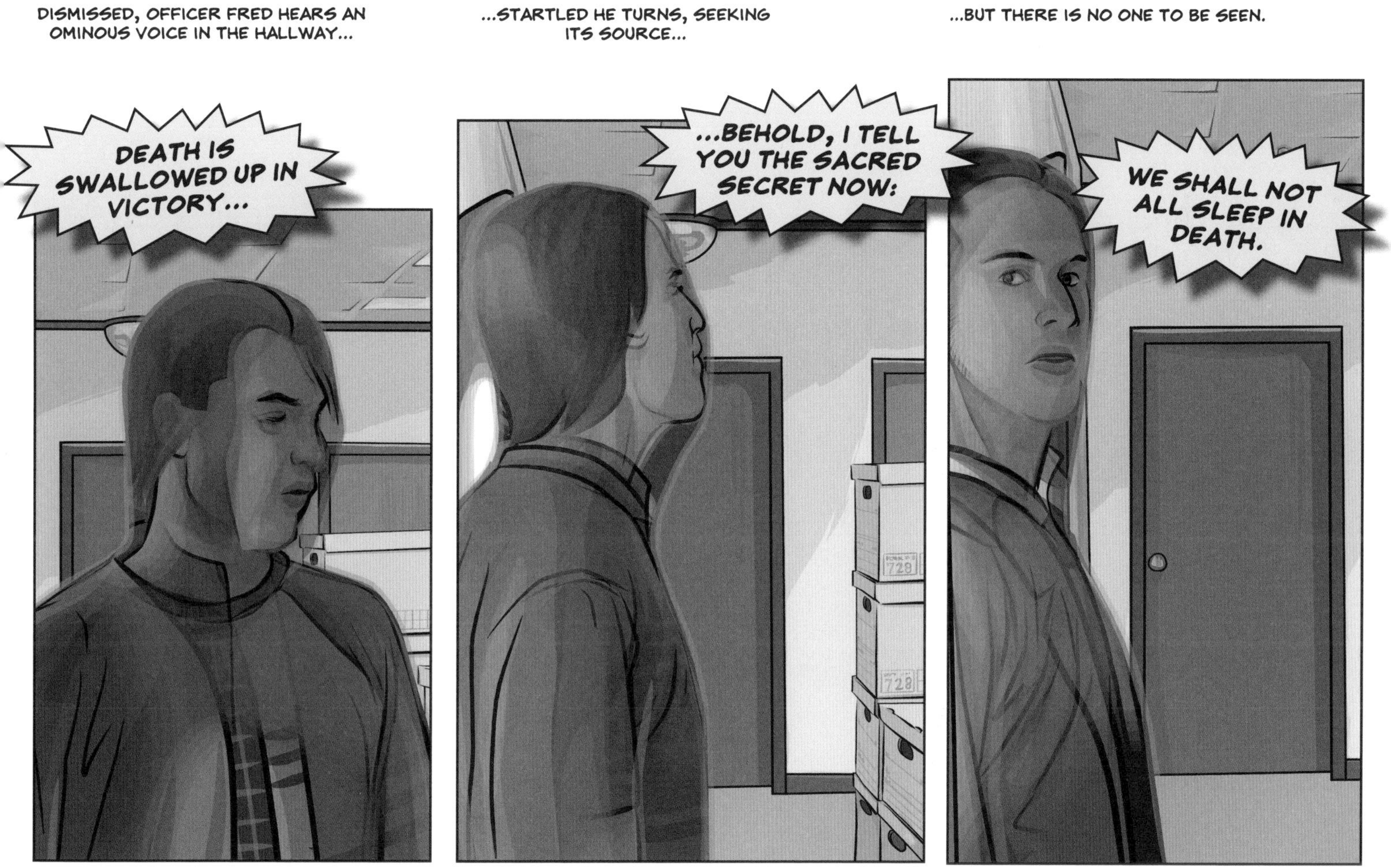
DISMISSED, OFFICER FRED HEARS AN OMINOUS VOICE IN THE HALLWAY...
DEATH IS SWALLOWED UP IN VICTORY...
...STARTLED HE TURNS, SEEKING ITS SOURCE...
...BEHOLD, I TELL YOU THE SACRED SECRET NOW:
...BUT THERE IS NO ONE TO BE SEEN.
WE SHALL NOT ALL SLEEP IN DEATH.

FRED SITS BY HANK'S DESK WHILE HANK LOOKS THROUGH FRED'S MEDICAL REPORT HALF-LISTENING TO THE EVIDENCE BARRIS IS PRESENTING TO THEM.

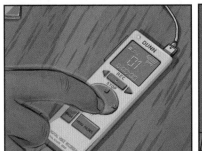

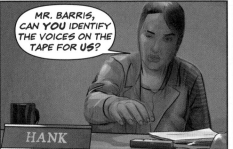

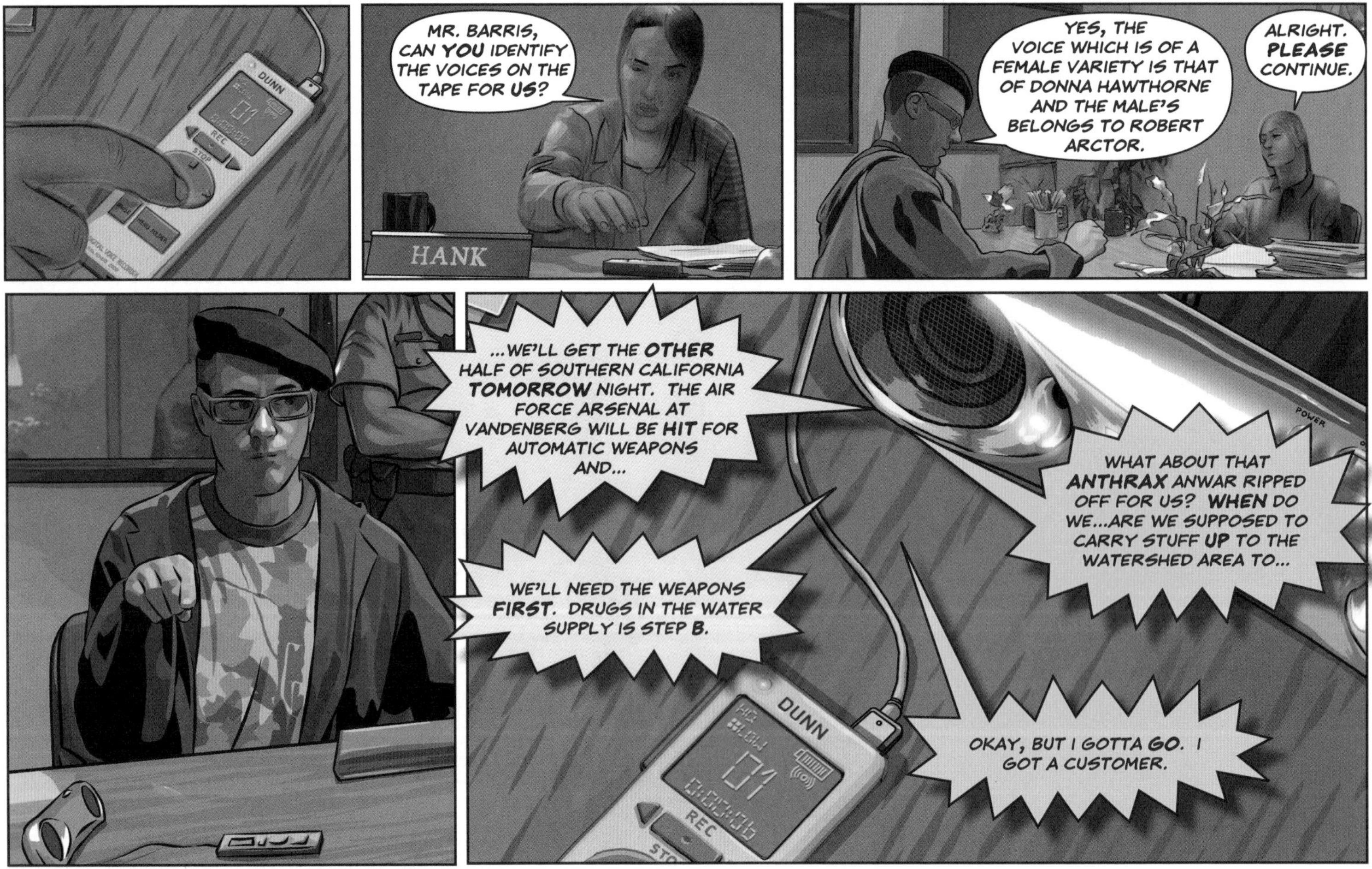

DUNN
REC
STOP
MR. BARRIS, CAN YOU IDENTIFY THE VOICES ON THE TAPE FOR US?
HANK
YES, THE VOICE WHICH IS OF A FEMALE VARIETY IS THAT OF DONNA HAWTHORNE AND THE MALE'S BELONGS TO ROBERT ARCTOR.
ALRIGHT. PLEASE CONTINUE.
...WE'LL GET THE OTHER HALF OF SOUTHERN CALIFORNIA TOMORROW NIGHT. THE AIR FORCE ARSENAL AT VANDENBERG WILL BE HIT FOR AUTOMATIC WEAPONS AND...
WHAT ABOUT THAT ANTHRAX ANWAR RIPPED OFF FOR US? WHEN DO WE...ARE WE SUPPOSED TO CARRY STUFF UP TO THE WATERSHED AREA TO...
WE'LL NEED THE WEAPONS FIRST. DRUGS IN THE WATER SUPPLY IS STEP B.
OKAY, BUT I GOTTA GO. I GOT A CUSTOMER.
POWER
DUNN
REC

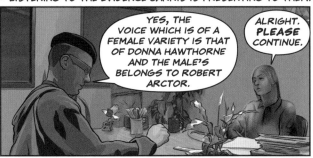

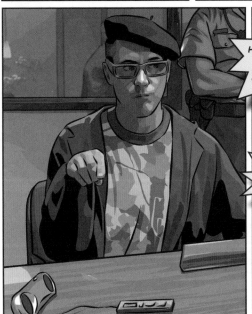

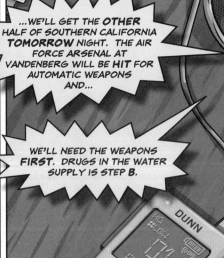

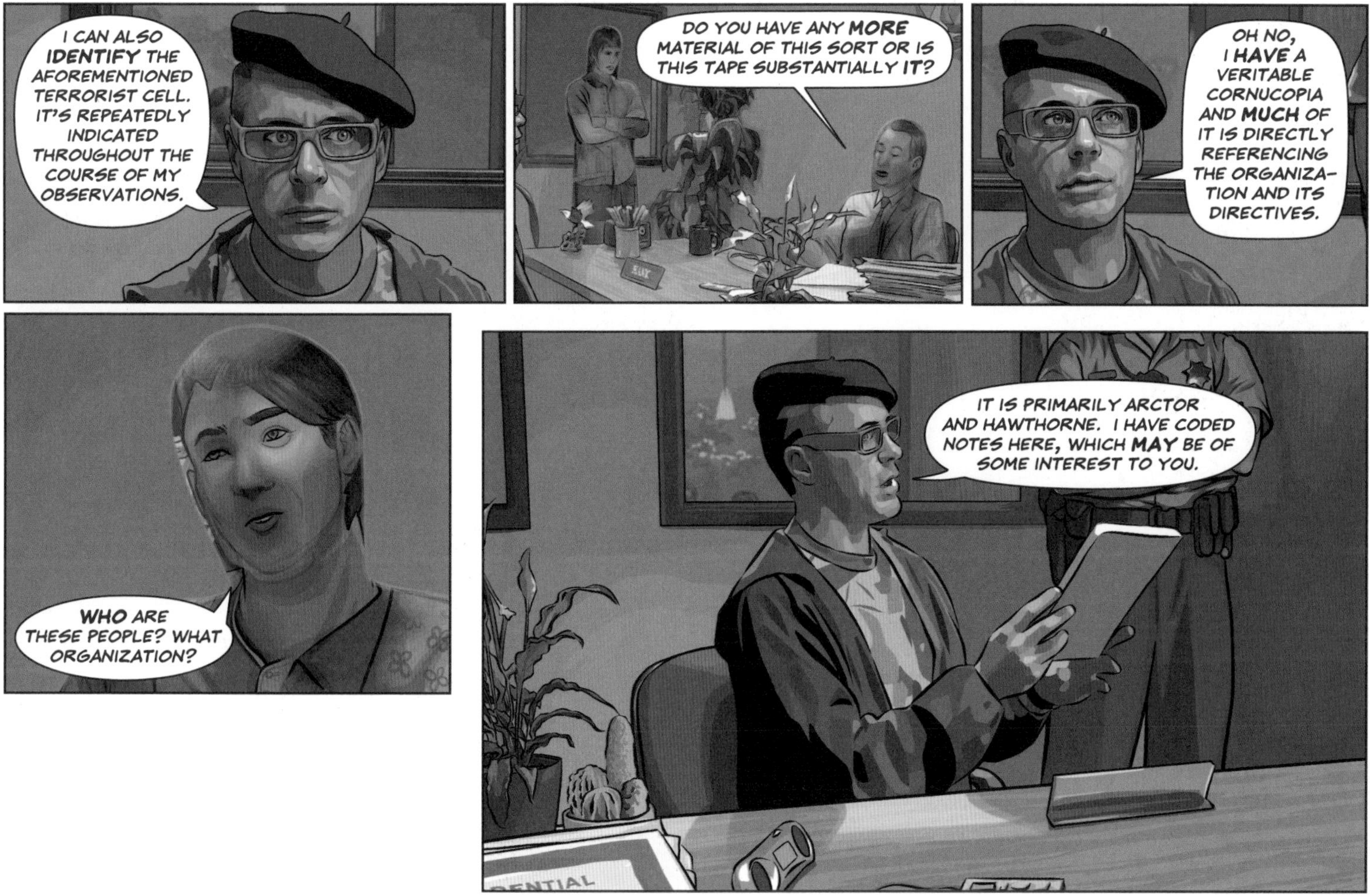
I CAN ALSO IDENTIFY THE AFOREMENTIONED TERRORIST CELL. IT'S REPEATEDLY INDICATED THROUGHOUT THE COURSE OF MY OBSERVATIONS.
DO YOU HAVE ANY MORE MATERIAL OF THIS SORT OR IS THIS TAPE SUBSTANTIALLY IT?
OH NO, I HAVE A VERITABLE CORNUCOPIA AND MUCH OF IT IS DIRECTLY REFERENCING THE ORGANIZATION AND ITS DIRECTIVES.
WHO ARE THESE PEOPLE? WHAT ORGANIZATION?
IT IS PRIMARILY ARCTOR AND HAWTHORNE. I HAVE CODED NOTES HERE, WHICH MAY BE OF SOME INTEREST TO YOU.

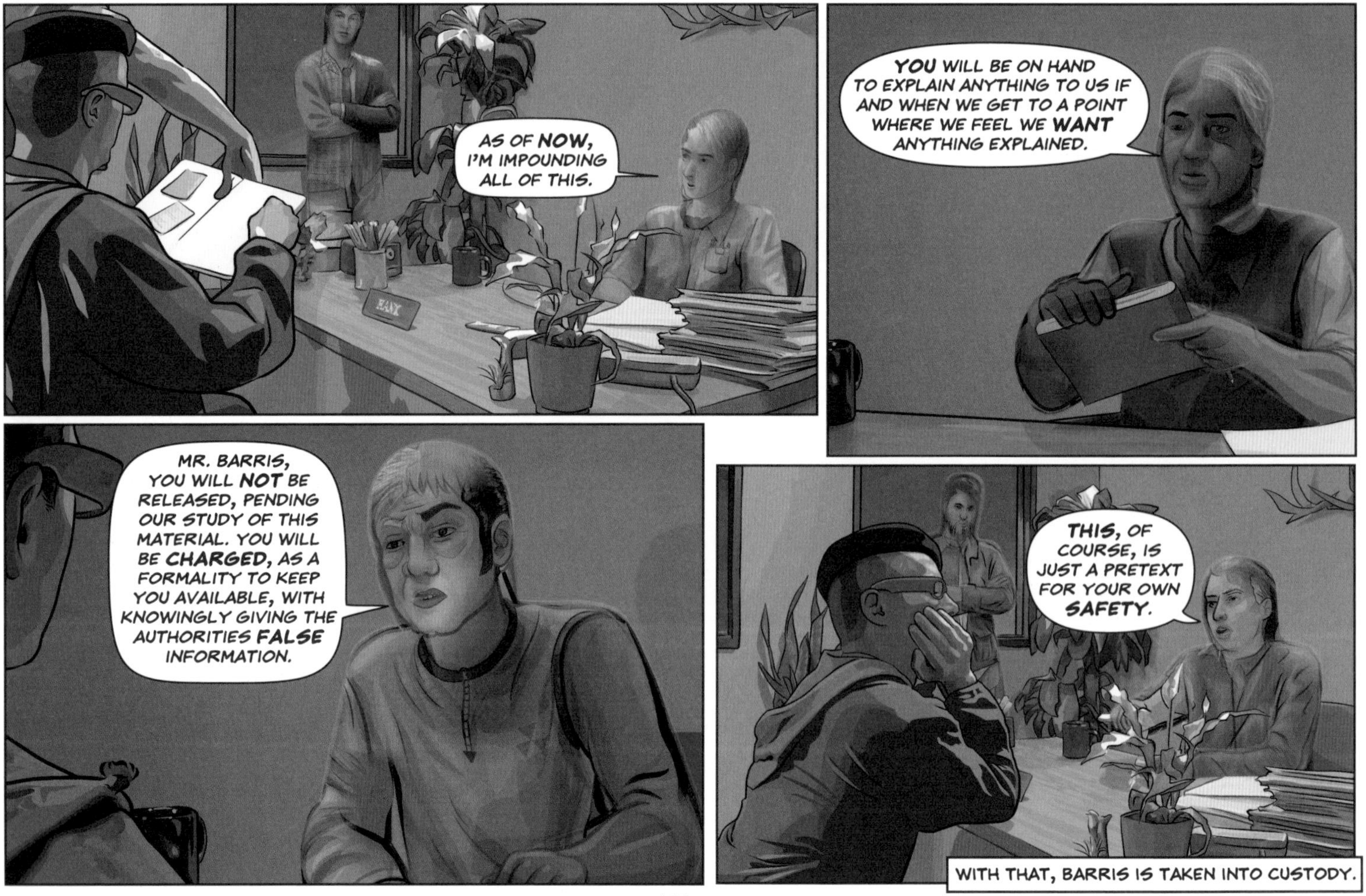
AS OF NOW, I'M IMPOUNDING ALL OF THIS.
YOU WILL BE ON HAND TO EXPLAIN ANYTHING TO US IF AND WHEN WE GET TO A POINT WHERE WE FEEL WE WANT ANYTHING EXPLAINED.
MR. BARRIS, YOU WILL NOT BE RELEASED, PENDING OUR STUDY OF THIS MATERIAL. YOU WILL BE CHARGED, AS A FORMALITY TO KEEP YOU AVAILABLE, WITH KNOWINGLY GIVING THE AUTHORITIES FALSE INFORMATION.
THIS, OF COURSE, IS JUST A PRETEXT FOR YOUR OWN SAFETY.
WITH THAT, BARRIS IS TAKEN INTO CUSTODY.

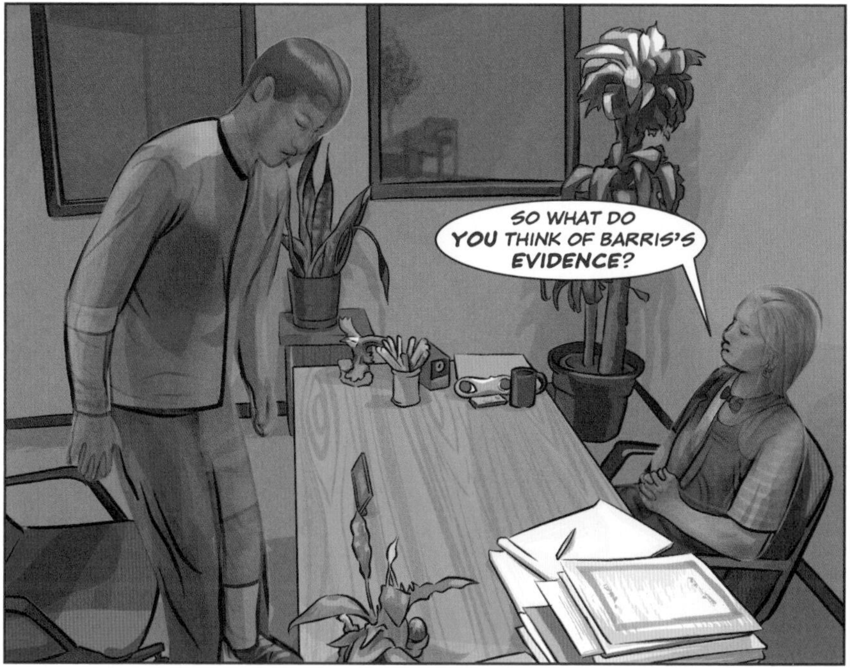
SO WHAT DO YOU THINK OF BARRIS'S EVIDENCE?

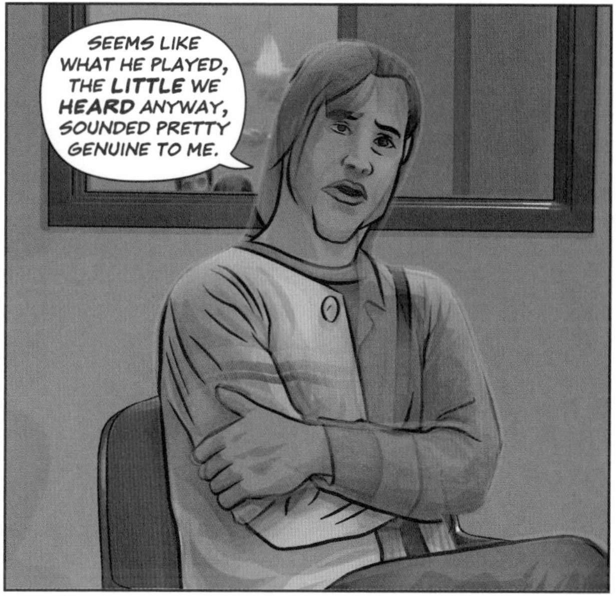
SEEMS LIKE WHAT HE PLAYED, THE LITTLE WE HEARD ANYWAY, SOUNDED PRETTY GENUINE TO ME.

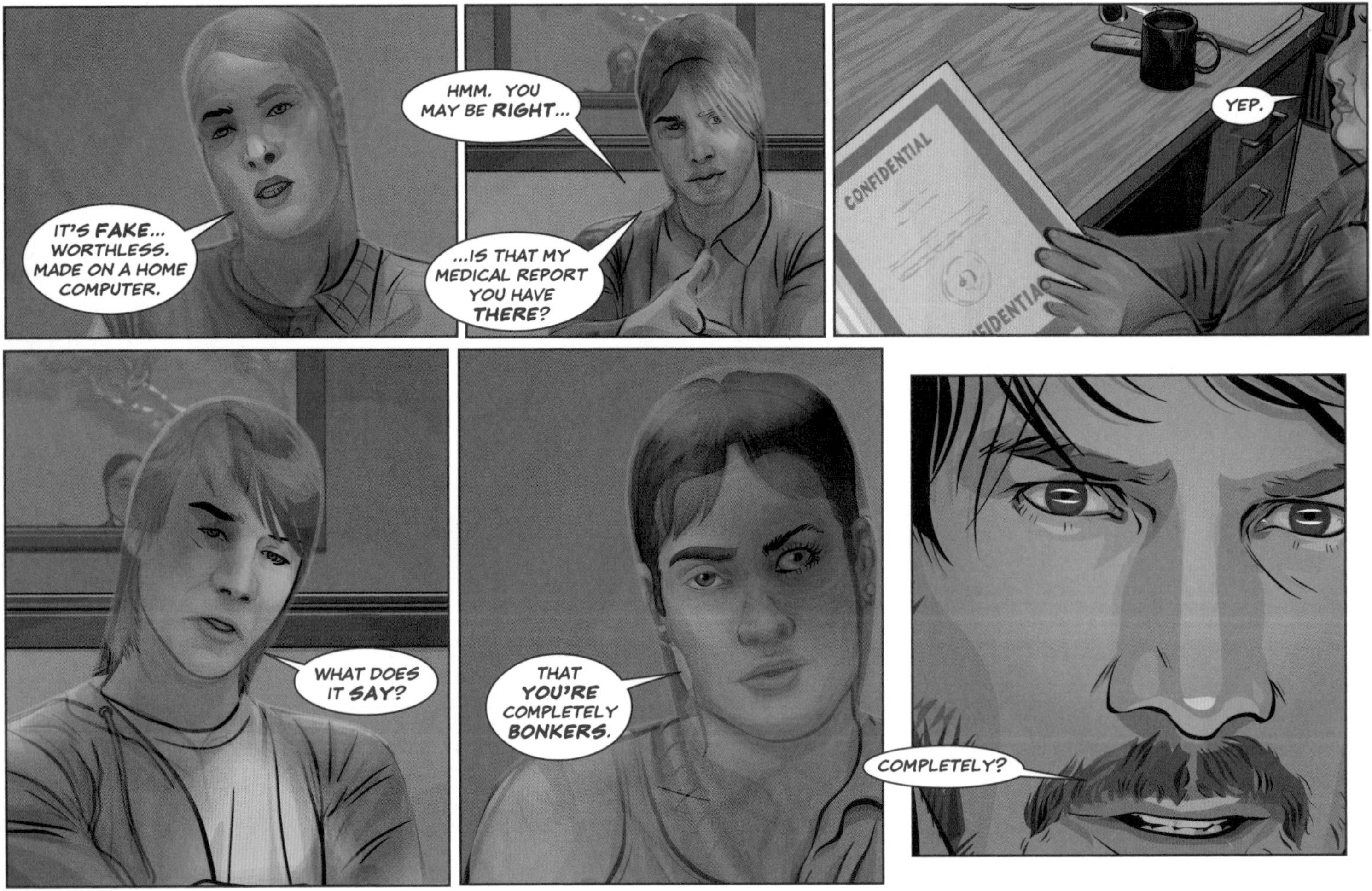
IT'S FAKE... WORTHLESS. MADE ON A HOME COMPUTER.
HMM. YOU MAY BE RIGHT...
...IS THAT MY MEDICAL REPORT YOU HAVE THERE?
YEP.
CONFIDENTIAL
WHAT DOES IT SAY?
THAT YOU'RE COMPLETELY BONKERS.
COMPLETELY?

THERE'S MAYBE **TWO** BRAIN CELLS THAT **STILL** LIGHT UP. THE REST IS JUST SHORT CIRCUITS AND SPARKS.

TWO.

LISTEN, WHEN YOU GO TO PICK UP YOUR NEXT **PAYCHECK**, THERE'LL BE A SUBSTANTIAL DIFFERENCE THIS TIME.

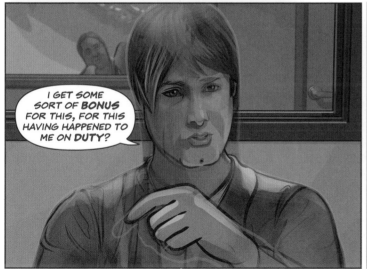

I GET SOME SORT OF **BONUS** FOR THIS, FOR THIS HAVING HAPPENED TO ME ON **DUTY**?

NO. **READ** YOUR PENAL CODE. AN OFFICER WHO WILLINGLY BECOMES AN **ADDICT** AND DOESN'T REPORT IT PROMPTLY IS SUBJECT TO A MISDEMEANOR **CHARGE**—A **FINE** AND/OR SIX MONTHS. YOU'LL PROBABLY JUST BE FINED.

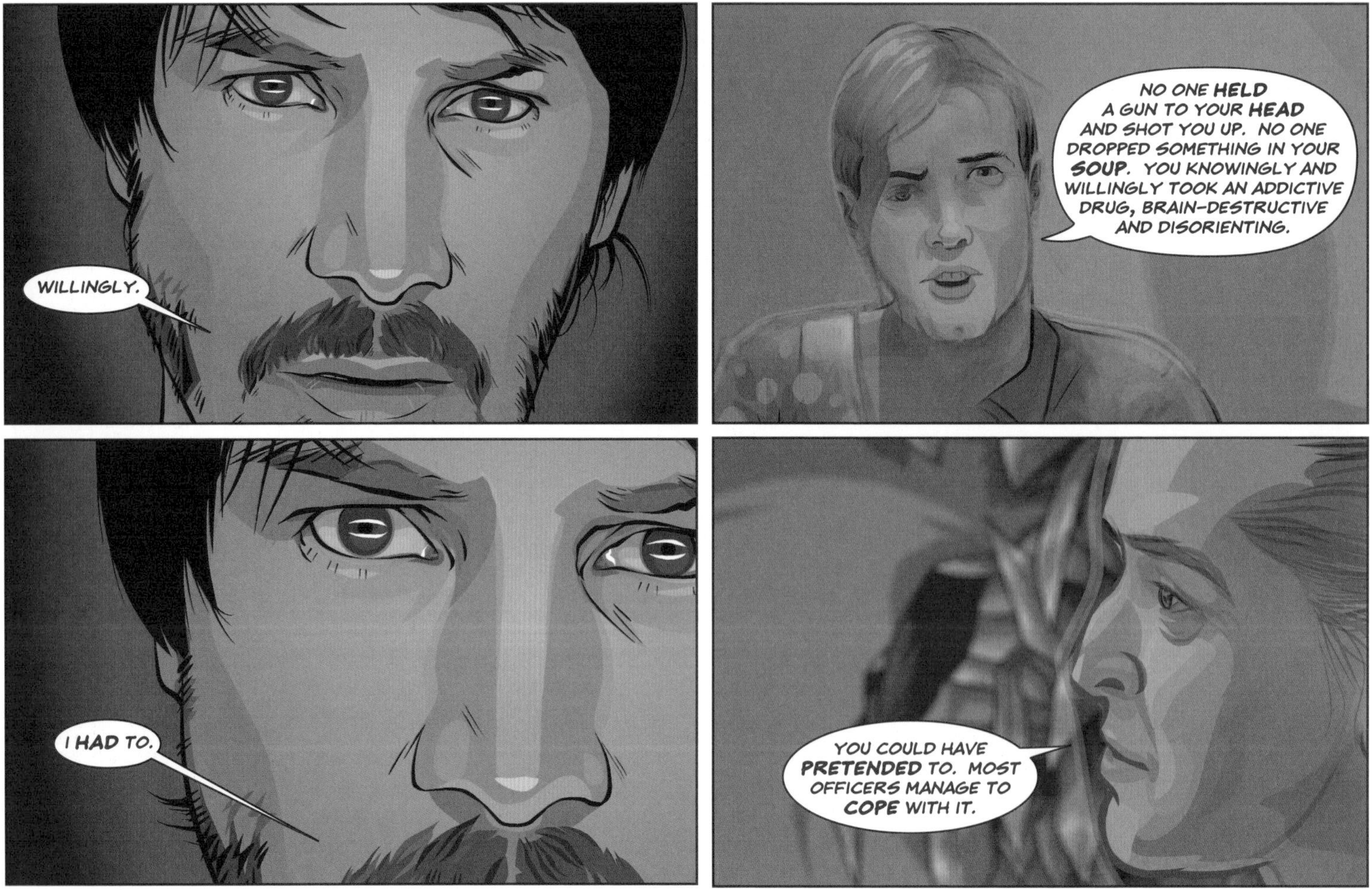
WILLINGLY.
NO ONE HELD A GUN TO YOUR HEAD AND SHOT YOU UP. NO ONE DROPPED SOMETHING IN YOUR SOUP. YOU KNOWINGLY AND WILLINGLY TOOK AN ADDICTIVE DRUG, BRAIN-DESTRUCTIVE AND DISORIENTING.
I HAD TO.
YOU COULD HAVE PRETENDED TO. MOST OFFICERS MANAGE TO COPE WITH IT.

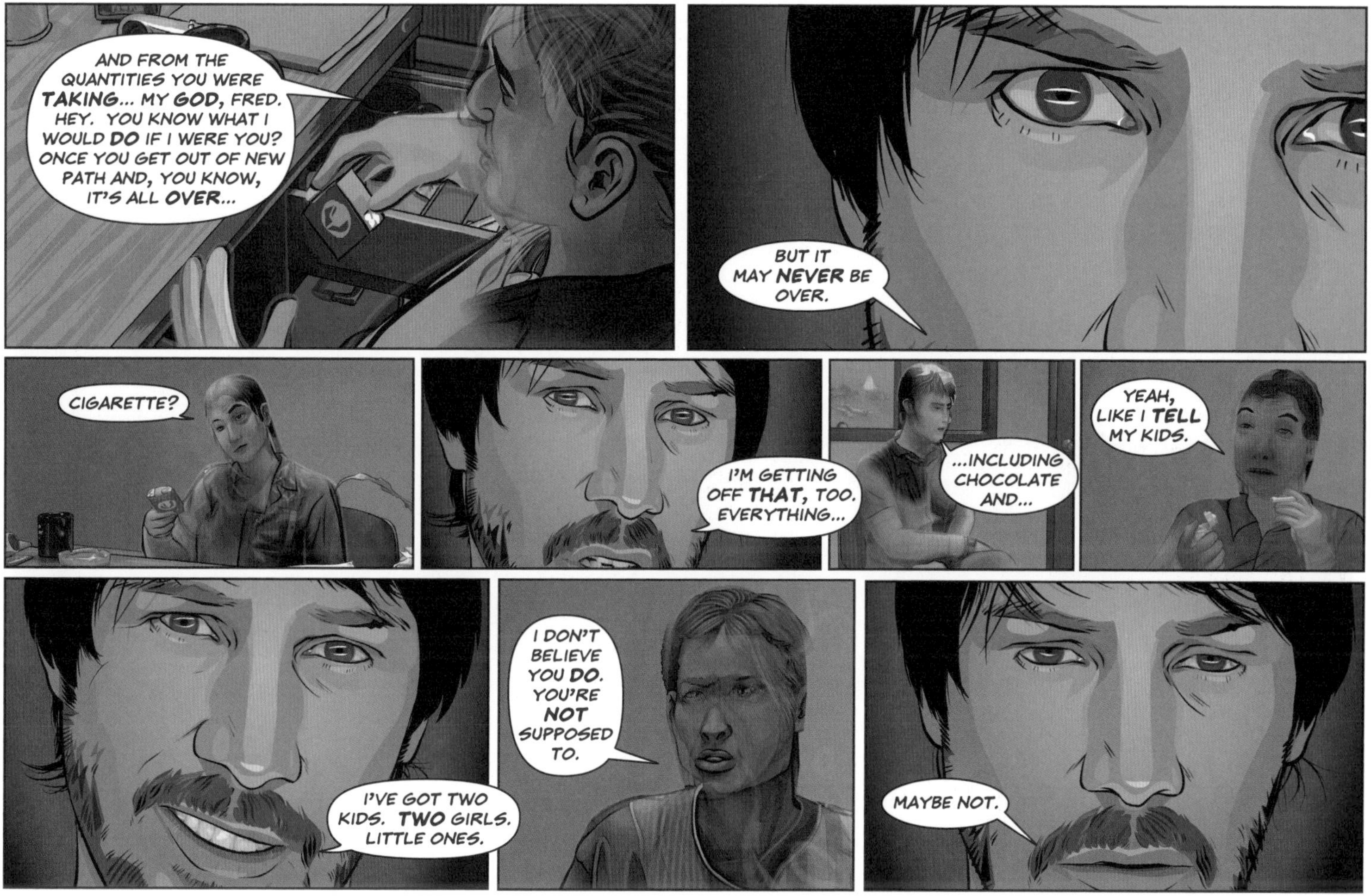
AND FROM THE QUANTITIES YOU WERE TAKING... MY GOD, FRED. HEY. YOU KNOW WHAT I WOULD DO IF I WERE YOU? ONCE YOU GET OUT OF NEW PATH AND, YOU KNOW, IT'S ALL OVER...
BUT IT MAY NEVER BE OVER.
CIGARETTE?
I'M GETTING OFF THAT, TOO. EVERYTHING...
...INCLUDING CHOCOLATE AND...
YEAH, LIKE I TELL MY KIDS.
I'VE GOT TWO KIDS. TWO GIRLS. LITTLE ONES.
I DON'T BELIEVE YOU DO. YOU'RE NOT SUPPOSED TO.
MAYBE NOT.

THEN, LIKE A BALLOON OVERFILLED WITH ANXIETY...EVERYTHING IN THE ROOM IS MOMENTARILY WRONG...

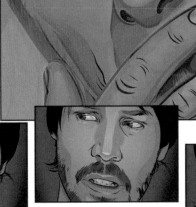

LISTEN, IS THERE ANYWHERE SPECIFIC YOU'D LIKE TO GO?

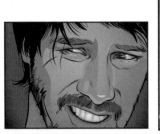

MAYBE OVER TO DONNA HAWTHORNE'S PLACE?

HANK

164

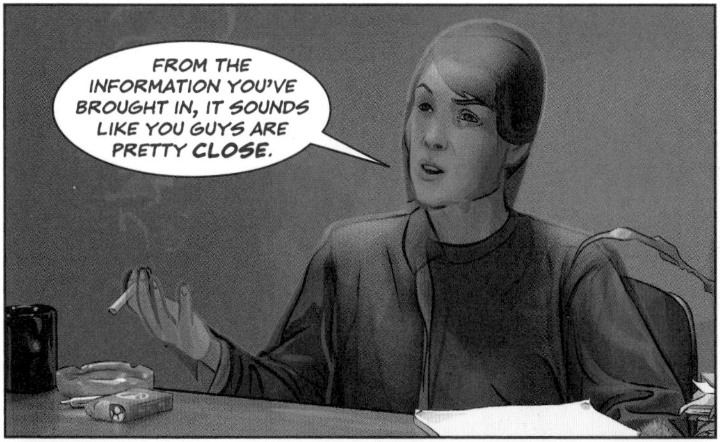
FROM THE INFORMATION YOU'VE BROUGHT IN, IT SOUNDS LIKE YOU GUYS ARE PRETTY **CLOSE**.

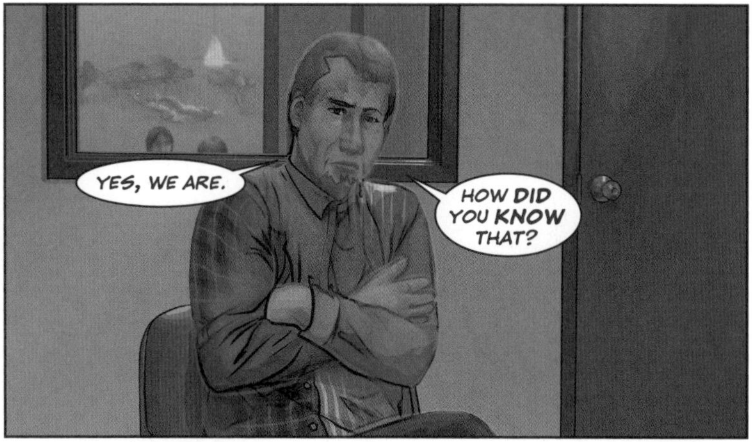
YES, WE ARE.
HOW **DID** YOU **KNOW** THAT?

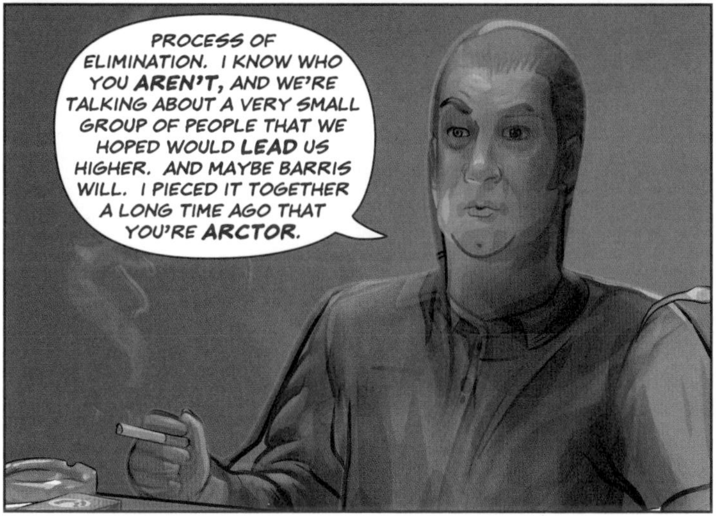
PROCESS OF ELIMINATION. I KNOW WHO YOU **AREN'T,** AND WE'RE TALKING ABOUT A VERY SMALL GROUP OF PEOPLE THAT WE HOPED WOULD **LEAD** US HIGHER. AND MAYBE BARRIS WILL. I PIECED IT TOGETHER A LONG TIME AGO THAT YOU'RE **ARCTOR**.

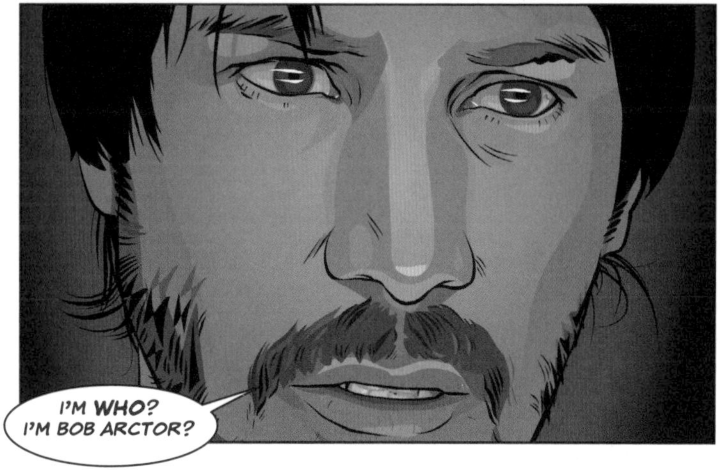
I'M **WHO?** I'M BOB ARCTOR?

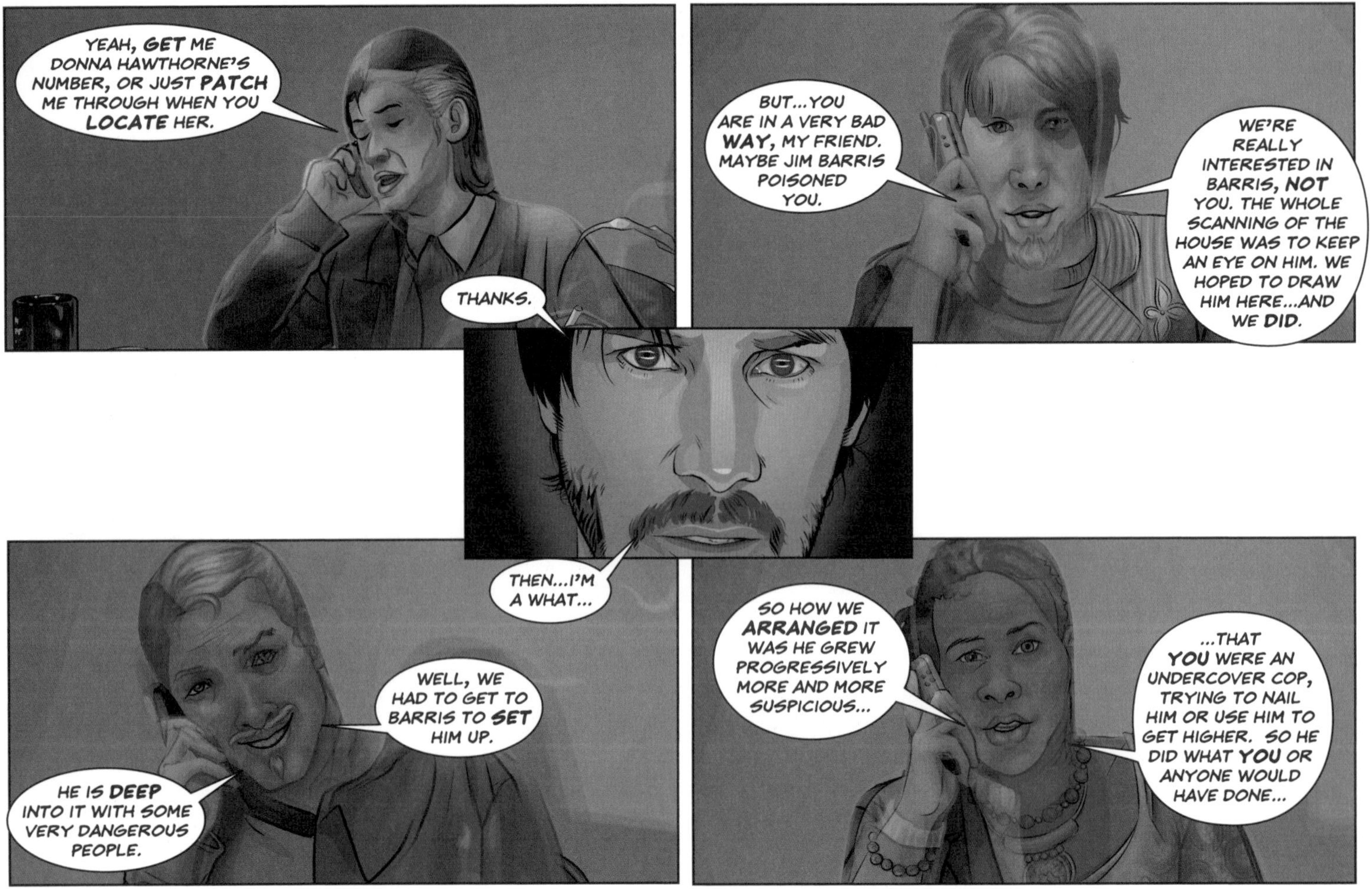
YEAH, GET ME DONNA HAWTHORNE'S NUMBER, OR JUST PATCH ME THROUGH WHEN YOU LOCATE HER.
BUT...YOU ARE IN A VERY BAD WAY, MY FRIEND. MAYBE JIM BARRIS POISONED YOU.
WE'RE REALLY INTERESTED IN BARRIS, NOT YOU. THE WHOLE SCANNING OF THE HOUSE WAS TO KEEP AN EYE ON HIM. WE HOPED TO DRAW HIM HERE...AND WE DID.
THANKS.
THEN...I'M A WHAT...
WELL, WE HAD TO GET TO BARRIS TO SET HIM UP.
HE IS DEEP INTO IT WITH SOME VERY DANGEROUS PEOPLE.
SO HOW WE ARRANGED IT WAS HE GREW PROGRESSIVELY MORE AND MORE SUSPICIOUS...
...THAT YOU WERE AN UNDERCOVER COP, TRYING TO NAIL HIM OR USE HIM TO GET HIGHER. SO HE DID WHAT YOU OR ANYONE WOULD HAVE DONE...

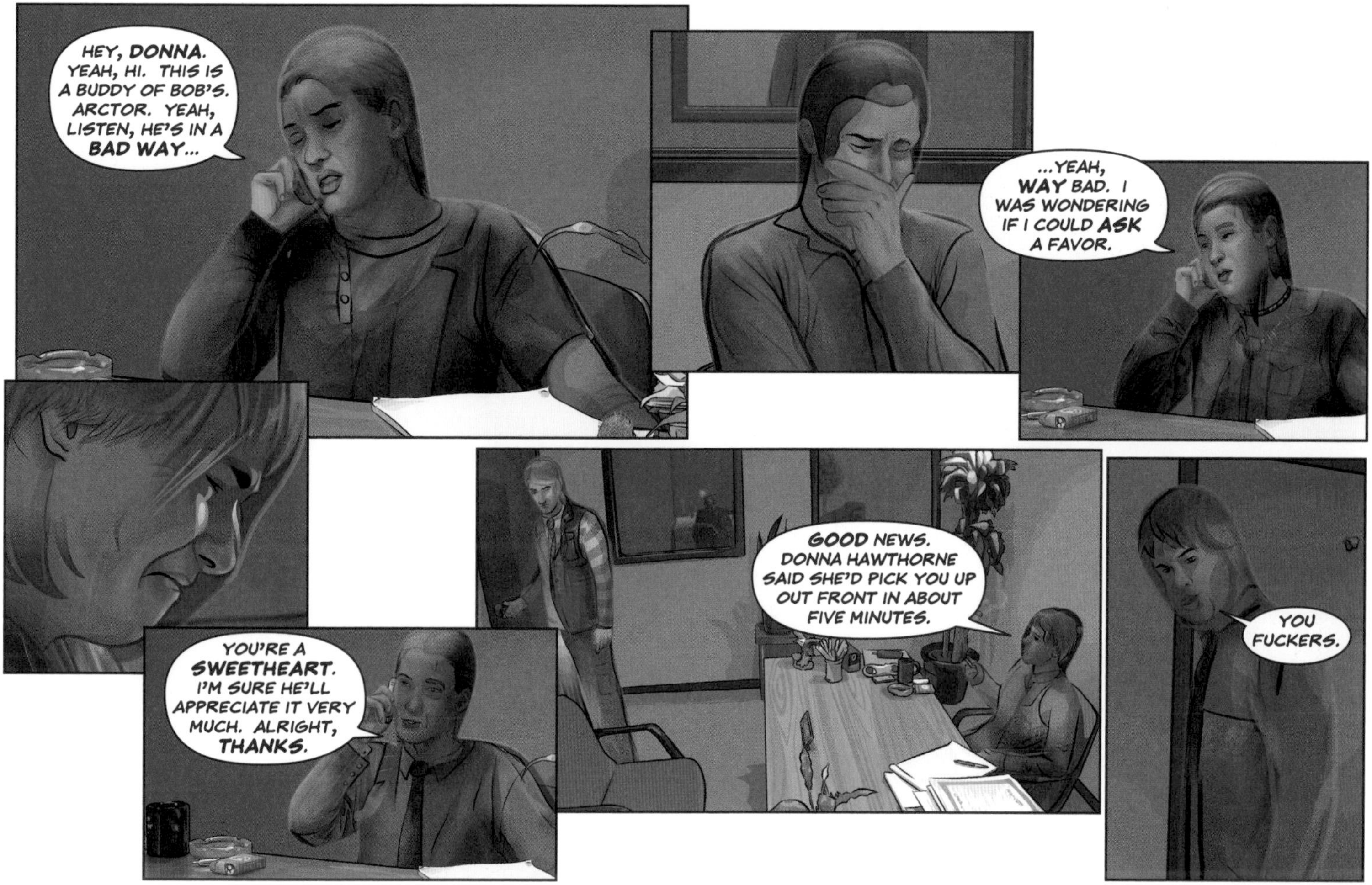
HEY, DONNA. YEAH, HI. THIS IS A BUDDY OF BOB'S. ARCTOR. YEAH, LISTEN, HE'S IN A BAD WAY...
...YEAH, WAY BAD. I WAS WONDERING IF I COULD ASK A FAVOR.
YOU'RE A SWEETHEART. I'M SURE HE'LL APPRECIATE IT VERY MUCH. ALRIGHT, THANKS.
GOOD NEWS. DONNA HAWTHORNE SAID SHE'D PICK YOU UP OUT FRONT IN ABOUT FIVE MINUTES.
YOU FUCKERS.

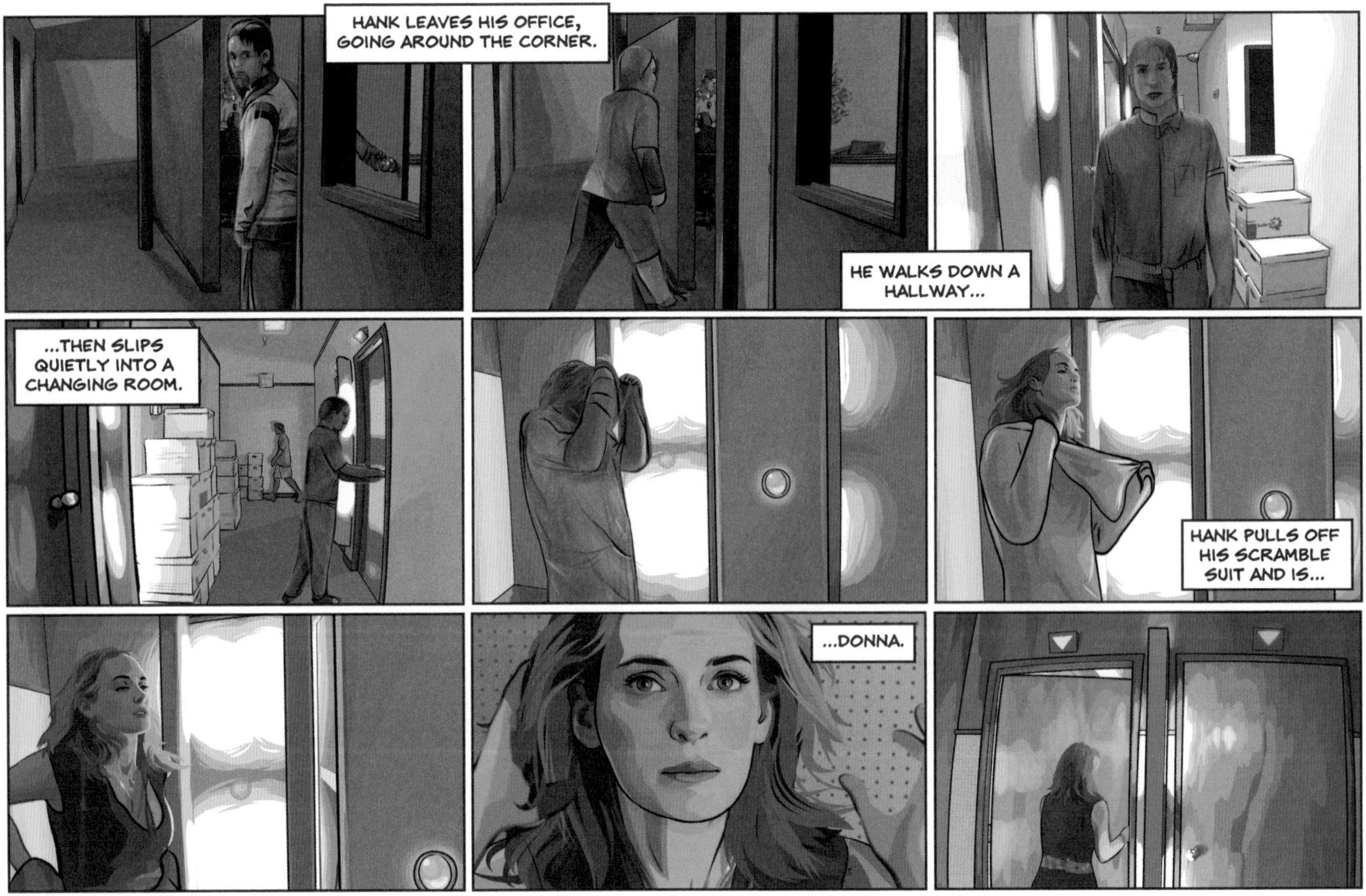
HANK LEAVES HIS OFFICE, GOING AROUND THE CORNER.
HE WALKS DOWN A HALLWAY...
...THEN SLIPS QUIETLY INTO A CHANGING ROOM.
HANK PULLS OFF HIS SCRAMBLE SUIT AND IS...
...DONNA.

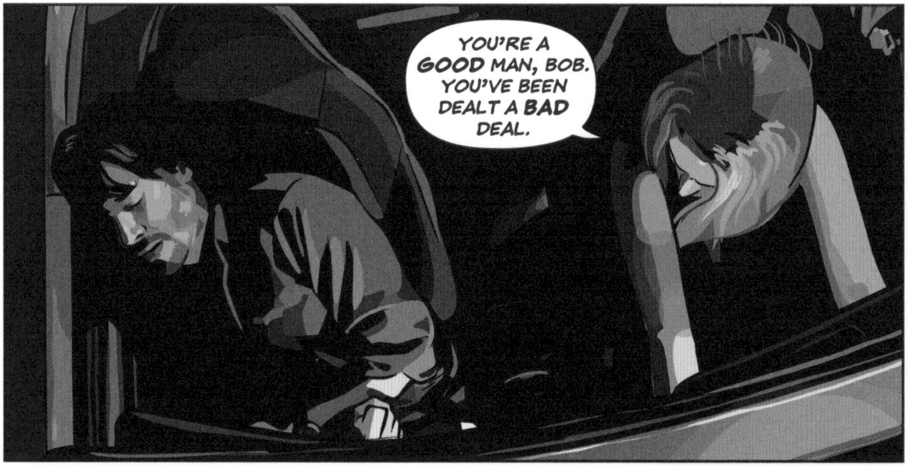
YOU'RE A GOOD MAN, BOB. YOU'VE BEEN DEALT A BAD DEAL.

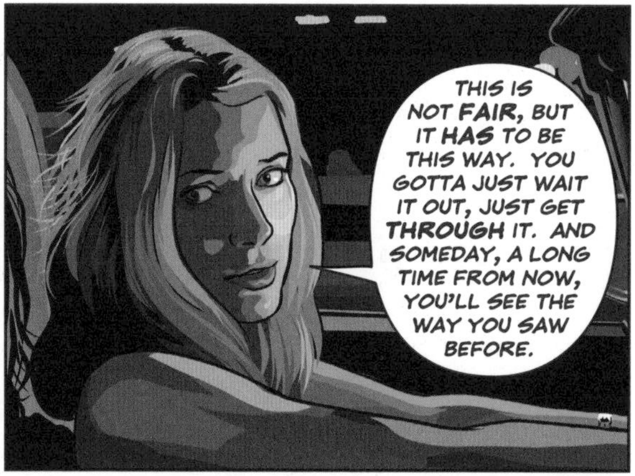
THIS IS NOT FAIR, BUT IT HAS TO BE THIS WAY. YOU GOTTA JUST WAIT IT OUT, JUST GET THROUGH IT. AND SOMEDAY, A LONG TIME FROM NOW, YOU'LL SEE THE WAY YOU SAW BEFORE.

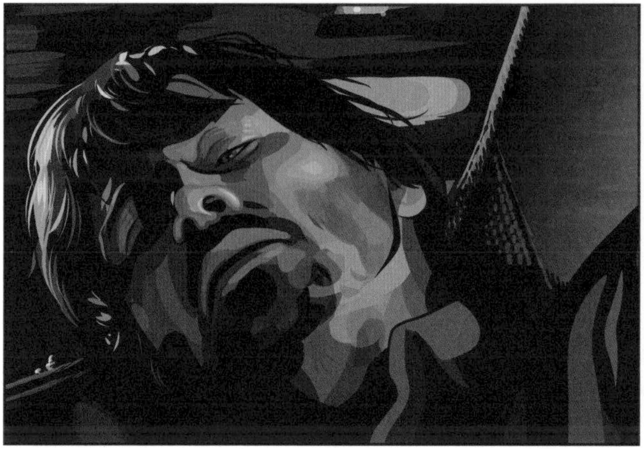

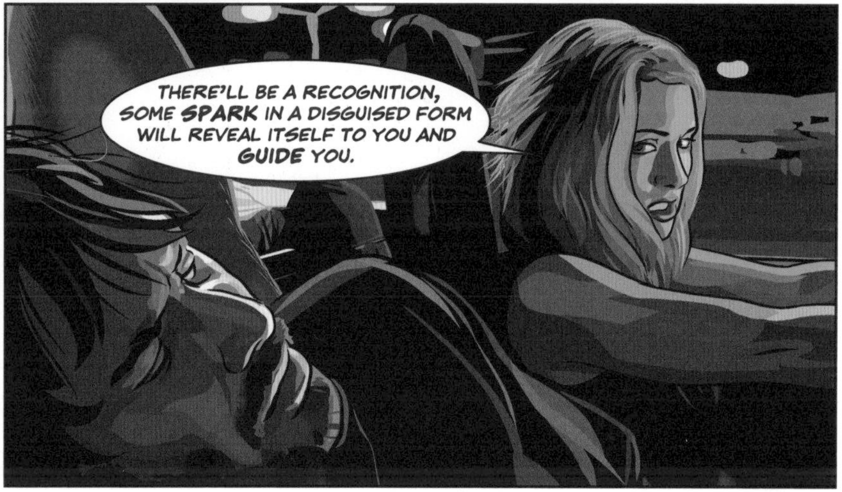
THERE'LL BE A RECOGNITION, SOME SPARK IN A DISGUISED FORM WILL REVEAL ITSELF TO YOU AND GUIDE YOU.

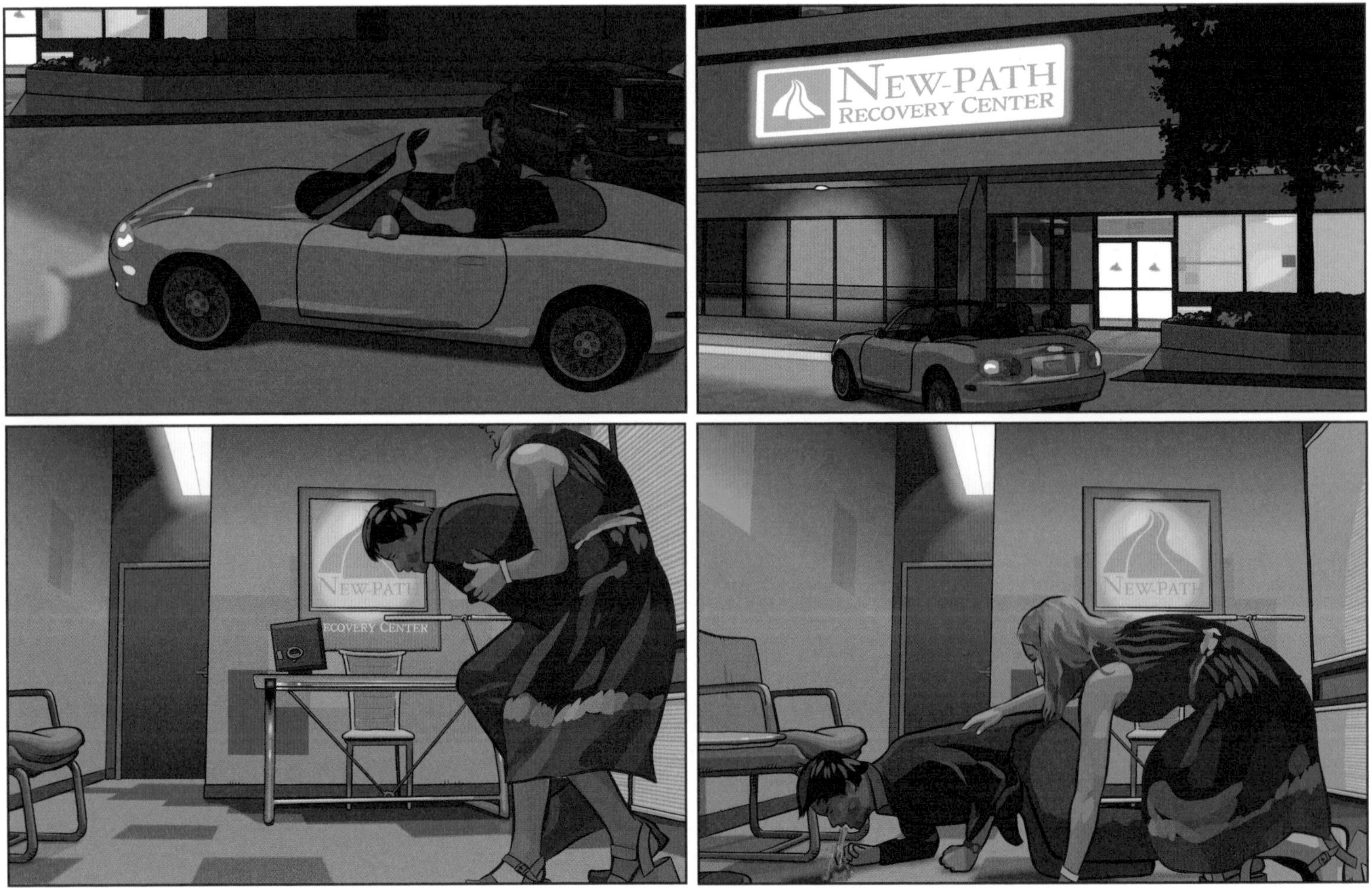
NEW-PATH
RECOVERY CENTER
NEW-PATH

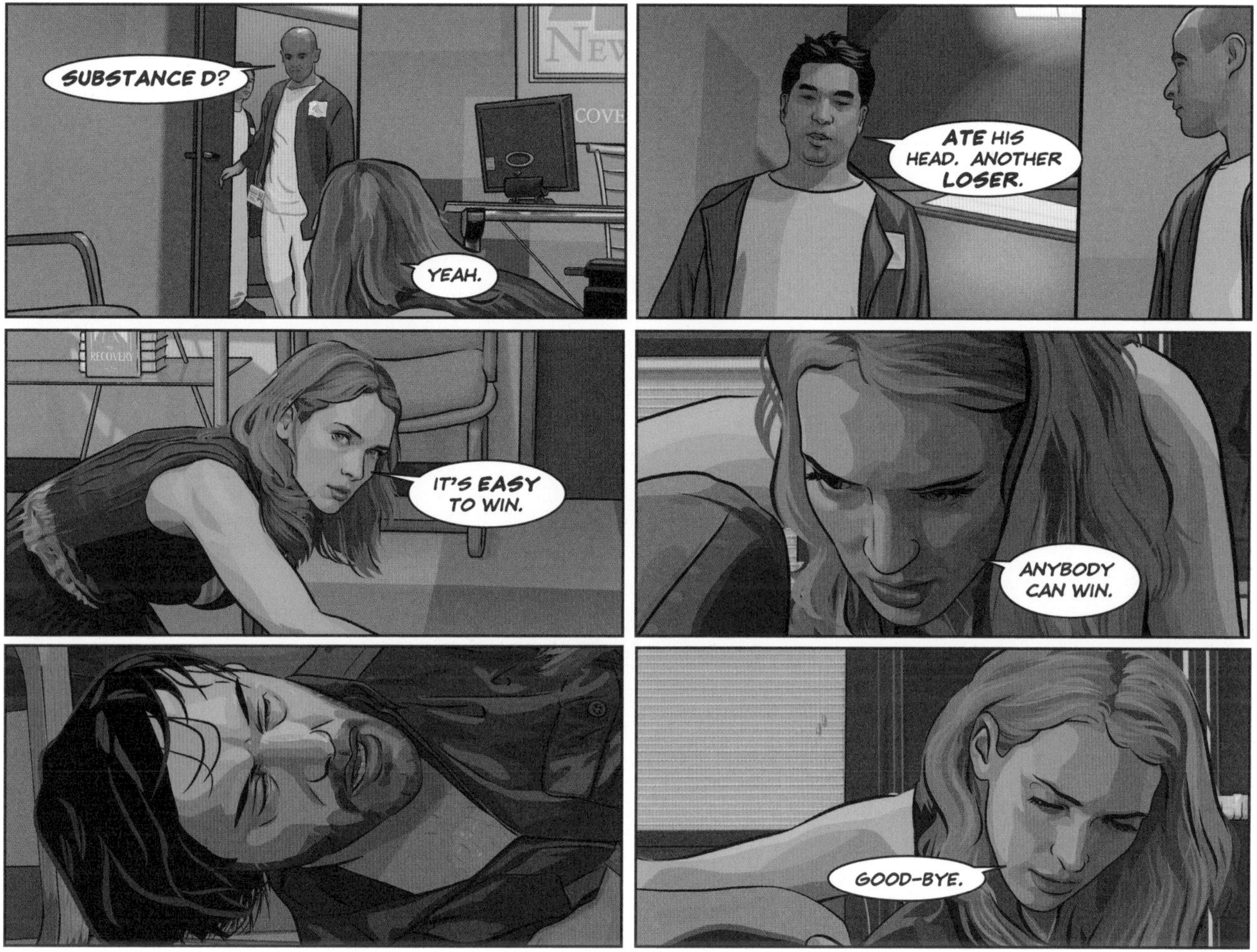
SUBSTANCE D?
YEAH.
ATE HIS HEAD. ANOTHER LOSER.
IT'S EASY TO WIN.
ANYBODY CAN WIN.
GOOD-BYE.

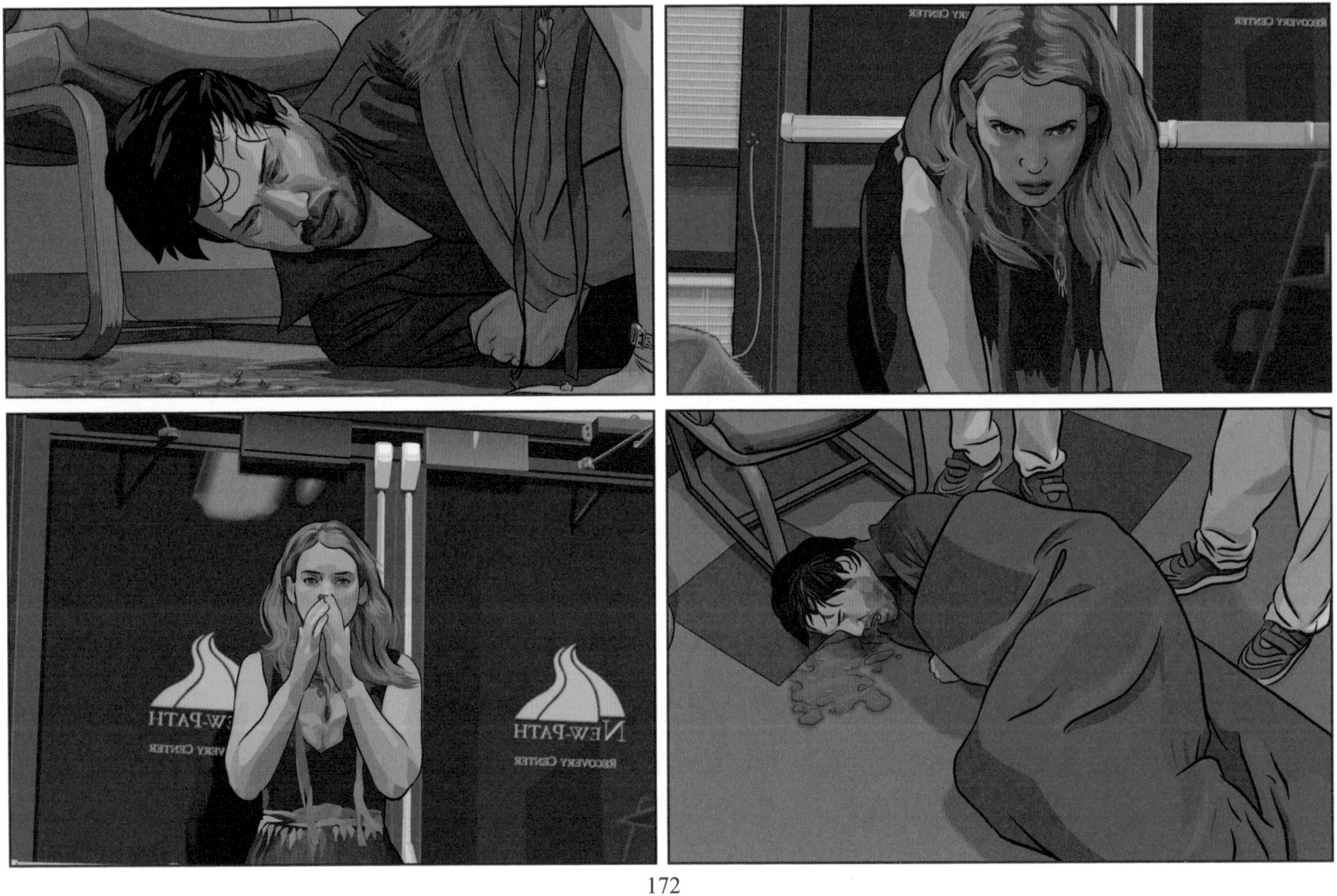
NEW-PATH
RECOVERY CENTER

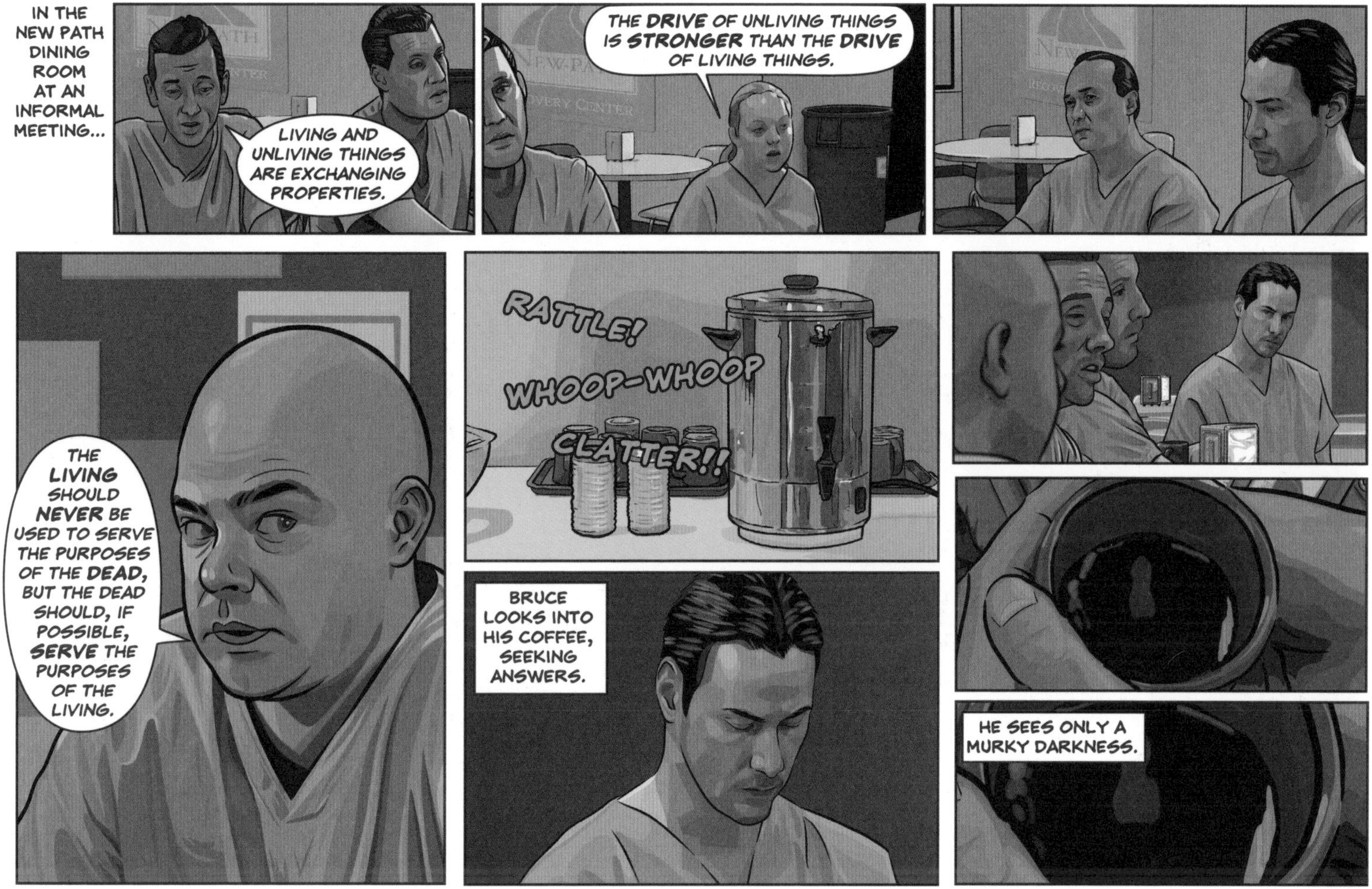
IN THE NEW PATH DINING ROOM AT AN INFORMAL MEETING...
LIVING AND UNLIVING THINGS ARE EXCHANGING PROPERTIES.
THE DRIVE OF UNLIVING THINGS IS STRONGER THAN THE DRIVE OF LIVING THINGS.
THE LIVING SHOULD NEVER BE USED TO SERVE THE PURPOSES OF THE DEAD, BUT THE DEAD SHOULD, IF POSSIBLE, SERVE THE PURPOSES OF THE LIVING.
RATTLE!
WHOOP-WHOOP
CLATTER!!
BRUCE LOOKS INTO HIS COFFEE, SEEKING ANSWERS.
HE SEES ONLY A MURKY DARKNESS.

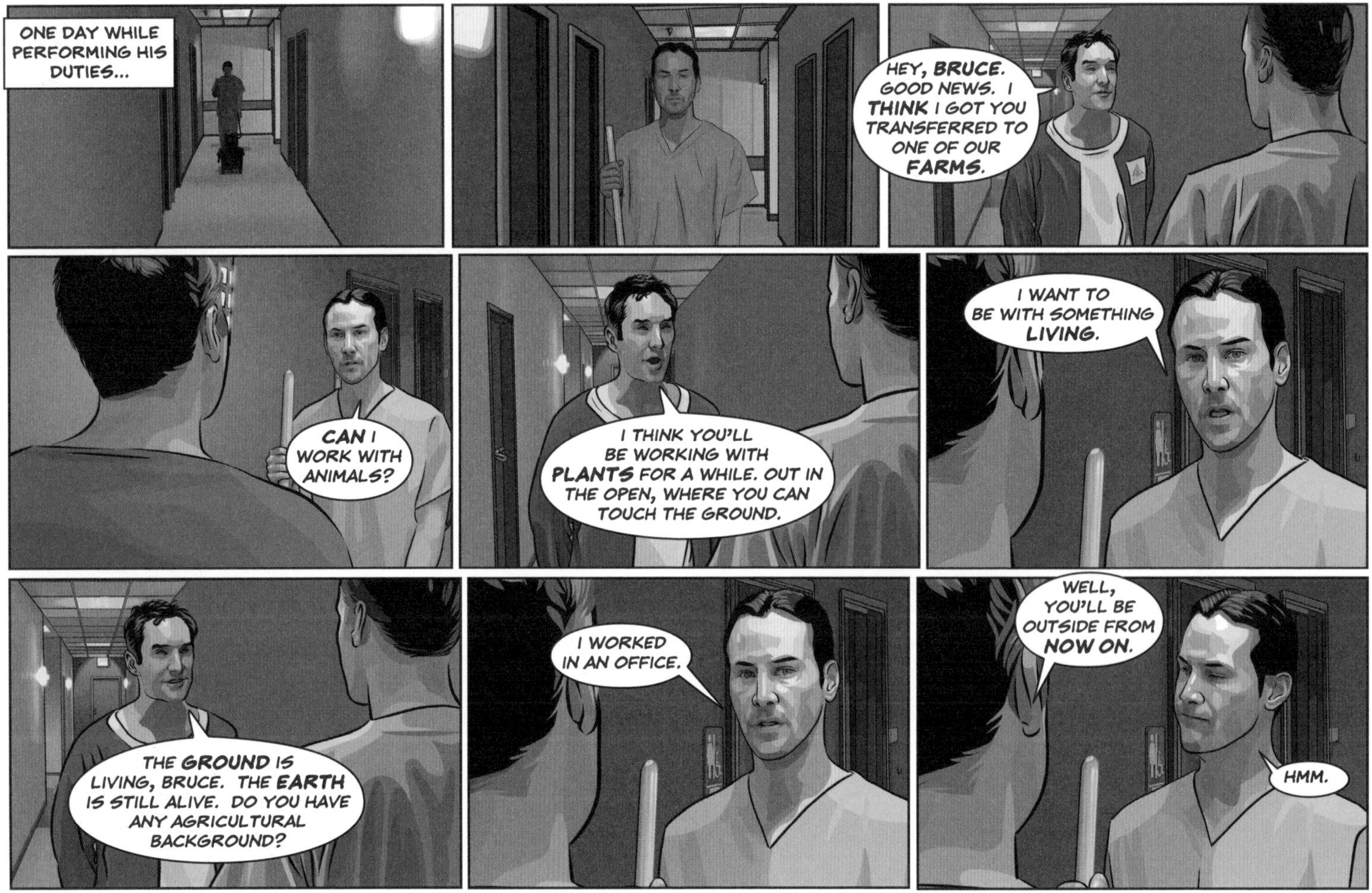
ONE DAY WHILE PERFORMING HIS DUTIES...
HEY, BRUCE. GOOD NEWS. I THINK I GOT YOU TRANSFERRED TO ONE OF OUR FARMS.
CAN I WORK WITH ANIMALS?
I THINK YOU'LL BE WORKING WITH PLANTS FOR A WHILE. OUT IN THE OPEN, WHERE YOU CAN TOUCH THE GROUND.
I WANT TO BE WITH SOMETHING LIVING.
THE GROUND IS LIVING, BRUCE. THE EARTH IS STILL ALIVE. DO YOU HAVE ANY AGRICULTURAL BACKGROUND?
I WORKED IN AN OFFICE.
WELL, YOU'LL BE OUTSIDE FROM NOW ON.
HMM.

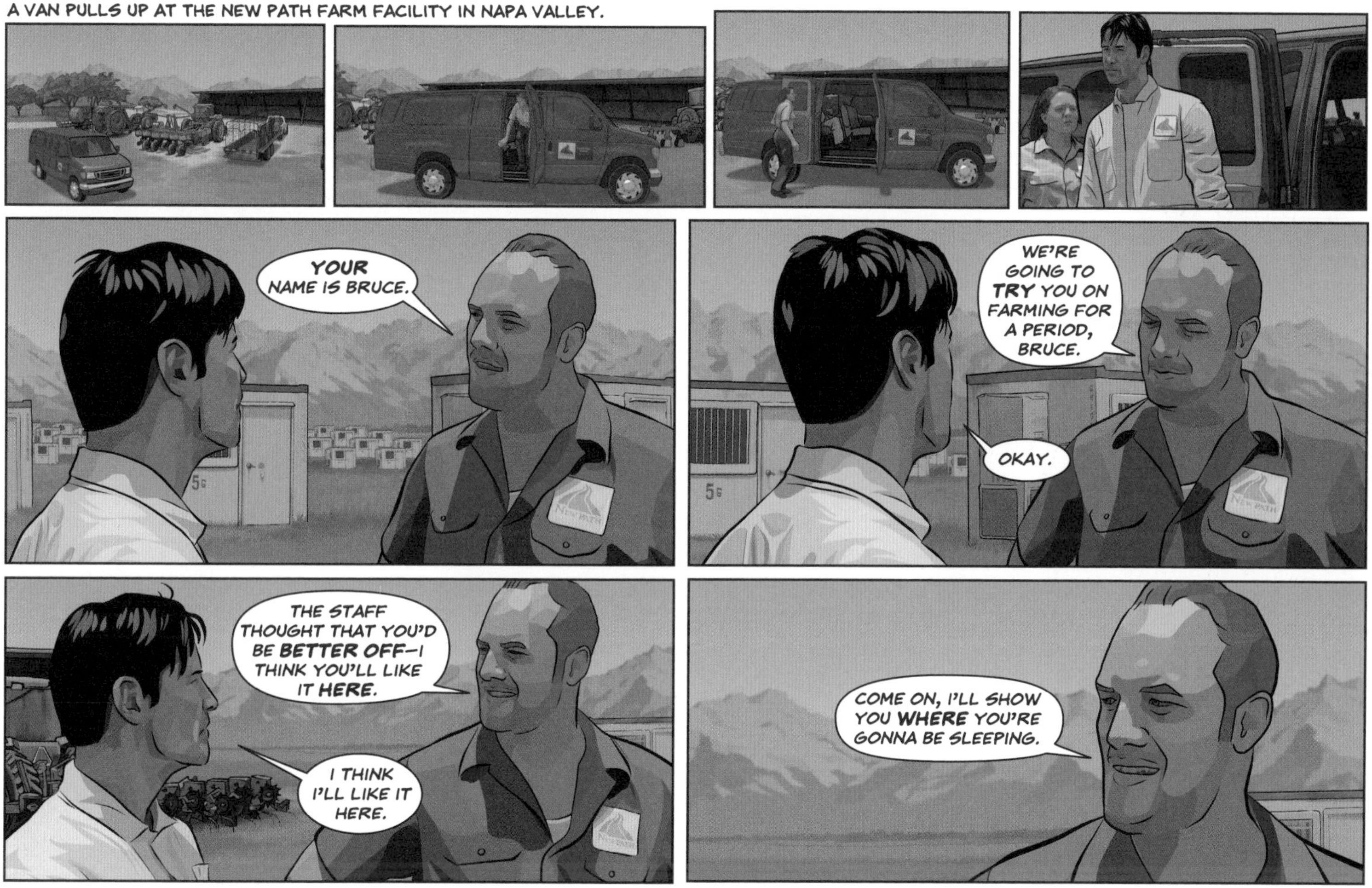
A VAN PULLS UP AT THE NEW PATH FARM FACILITY IN NAPA VALLEY.
YOUR NAME IS BRUCE.
WE'RE GOING TO TRY YOU ON FARMING FOR A PERIOD, BRUCE.
OKAY.
THE STAFF THOUGHT THAT YOU'D BE BETTER OFF—I THINK YOU'LL LIKE IT HERE.
I THINK I'LL LIKE IT HERE.
COME ON, I'LL SHOW YOU WHERE YOU'RE GONNA BE SLEEPING.

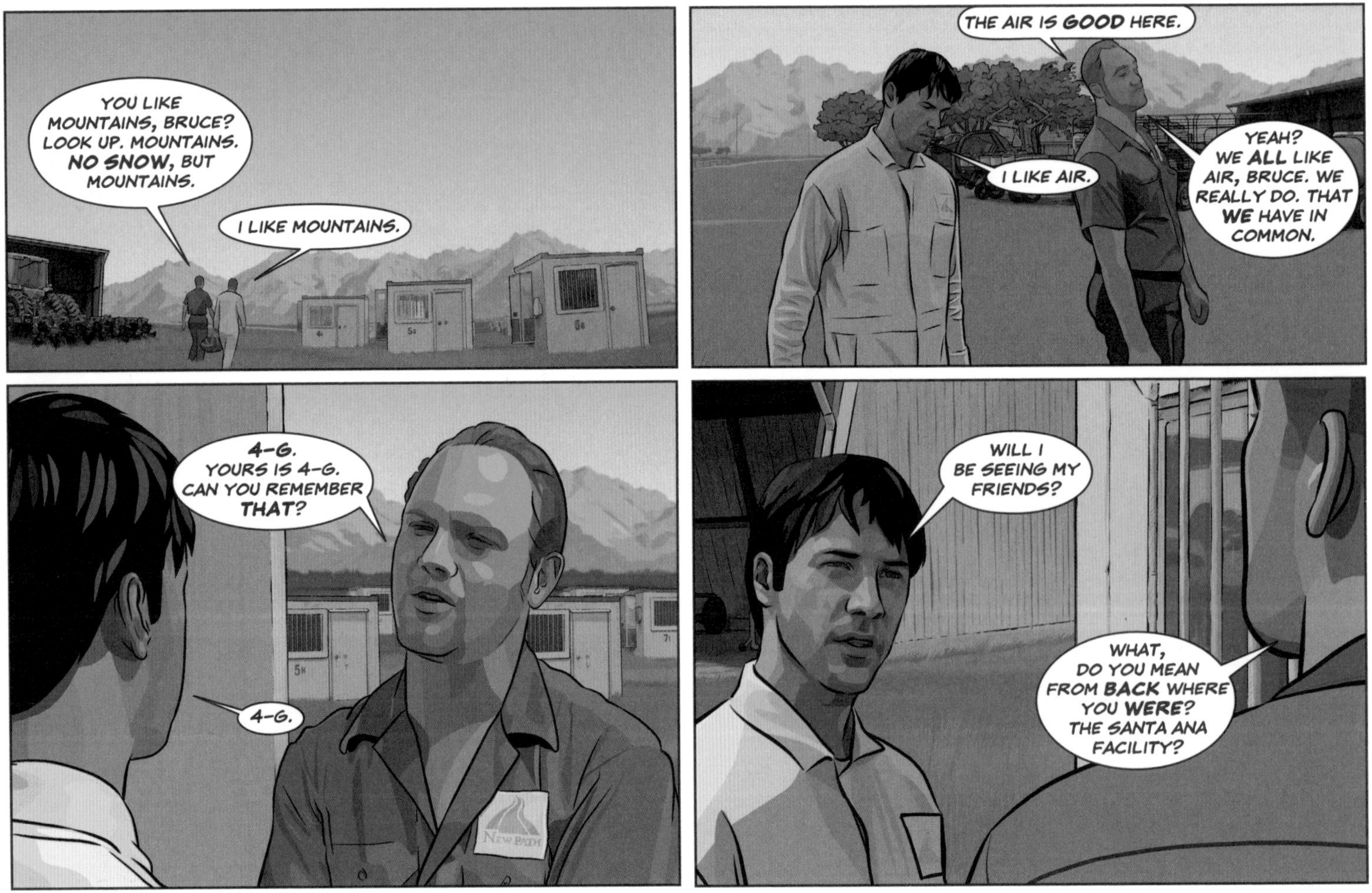
YOU LIKE MOUNTAINS, BRUCE? LOOK UP. MOUNTAINS. NO SNOW, BUT MOUNTAINS.
I LIKE MOUNTAINS.
THE AIR IS GOOD HERE.
I LIKE AIR.
YEAH? WE ALL LIKE AIR, BRUCE. WE REALLY DO. THAT WE HAVE IN COMMON.
4-G. YOURS IS 4-G. CAN YOU REMEMBER THAT?
4-G.
NEW PATH
WILL I BE SEEING MY FRIENDS?
WHAT, DO YOU MEAN FROM BACK WHERE YOU WERE? THE SANTA ANA FACILITY?

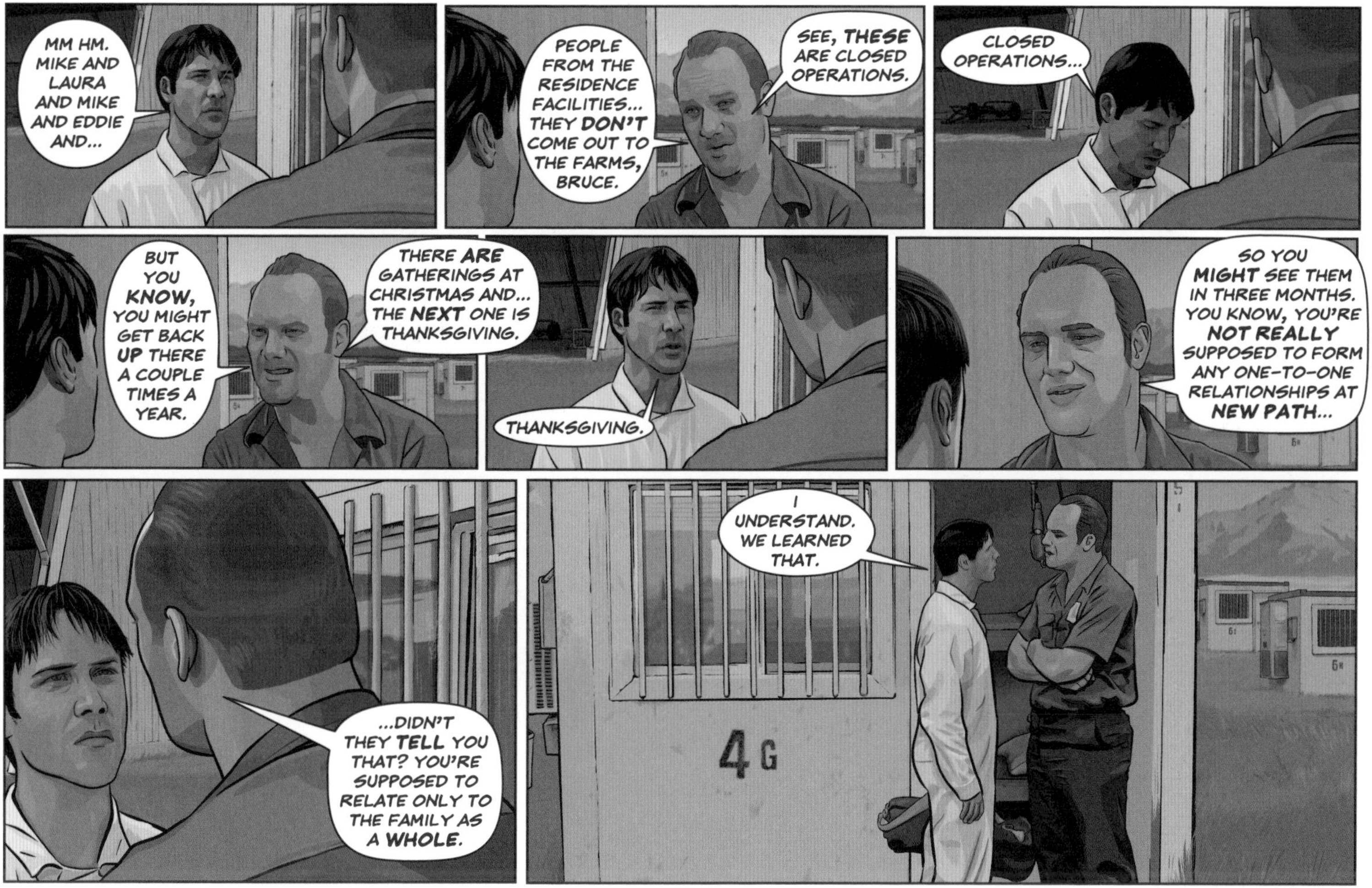
MM HM. MIKE AND LAURA AND MIKE AND EDDIE AND...
PEOPLE FROM THE RESIDENCE FACILITIES... THEY DON'T COME OUT TO THE FARMS, BRUCE.
SEE, THESE ARE CLOSED OPERATIONS.
CLOSED OPERATIONS...
BUT YOU KNOW, YOU MIGHT GET BACK UP THERE A COUPLE TIMES A YEAR.
THERE ARE GATHERINGS AT CHRISTMAS AND... THE NEXT ONE IS THANKSGIVING.
THANKSGIVING.
SO YOU MIGHT SEE THEM IN THREE MONTHS. YOU KNOW, YOU'RE NOT REALLY SUPPOSED TO FORM ANY ONE-TO-ONE RELATIONSHIPS AT NEW PATH...
...DIDN'T THEY TELL YOU THAT? YOU'RE SUPPOSED TO RELATE ONLY TO THE FAMILY AS A WHOLE.
I UNDERSTAND. WE LEARNED THAT.
4 G

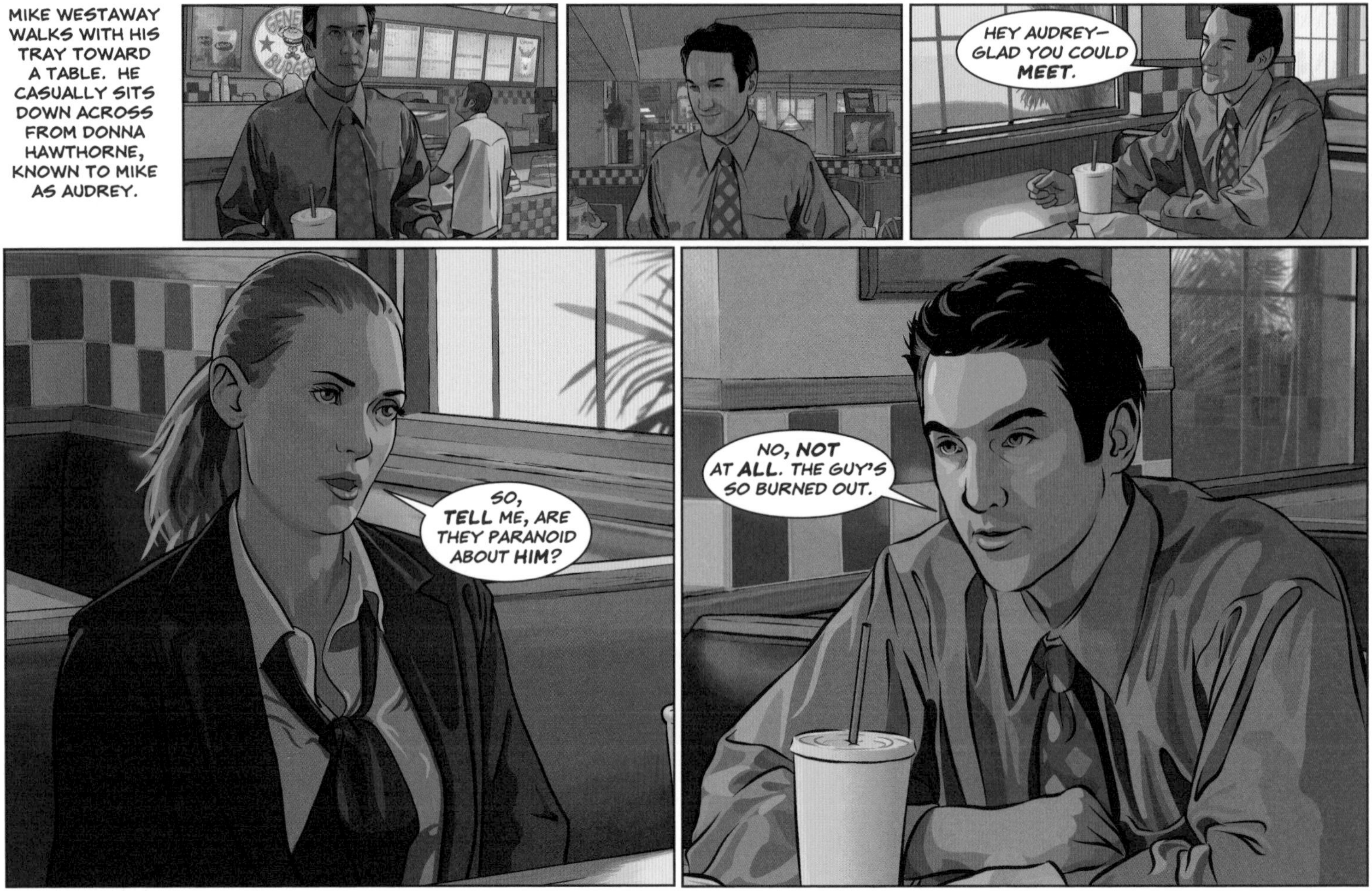
MIKE WESTAWAY WALKS WITH HIS TRAY TOWARD A TABLE. HE CASUALLY SITS DOWN ACROSS FROM DONNA HAWTHORNE, KNOWN TO MIKE AS AUDREY.
HEY AUDREY— GLAD YOU COULD MEET.
SO, TELL ME, ARE THEY PARANOID ABOUT HIM?
NO, NOT AT ALL. THE GUY'S SO BURNED OUT.

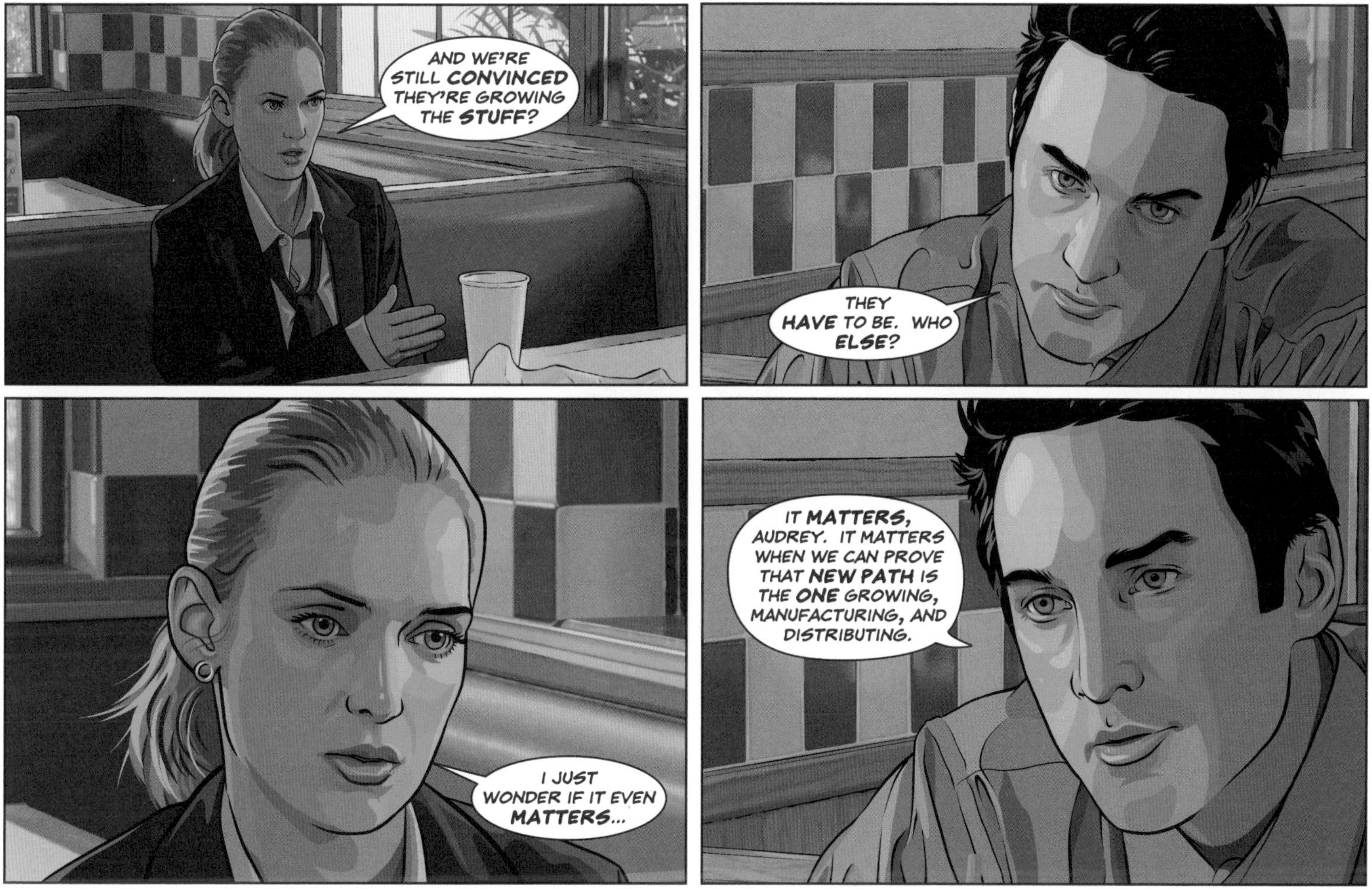
AND WE'RE STILL CONVINCED THEY'RE GROWING THE STUFF?
THEY HAVE TO BE. WHO ELSE?
I JUST WONDER IF IT EVEN MATTERS...
IT MATTERS, AUDREY. IT MATTERS WHEN WE CAN PROVE THAT NEW PATH IS THE ONE GROWING, MANUFACTURING, AND DISTRIBUTING.

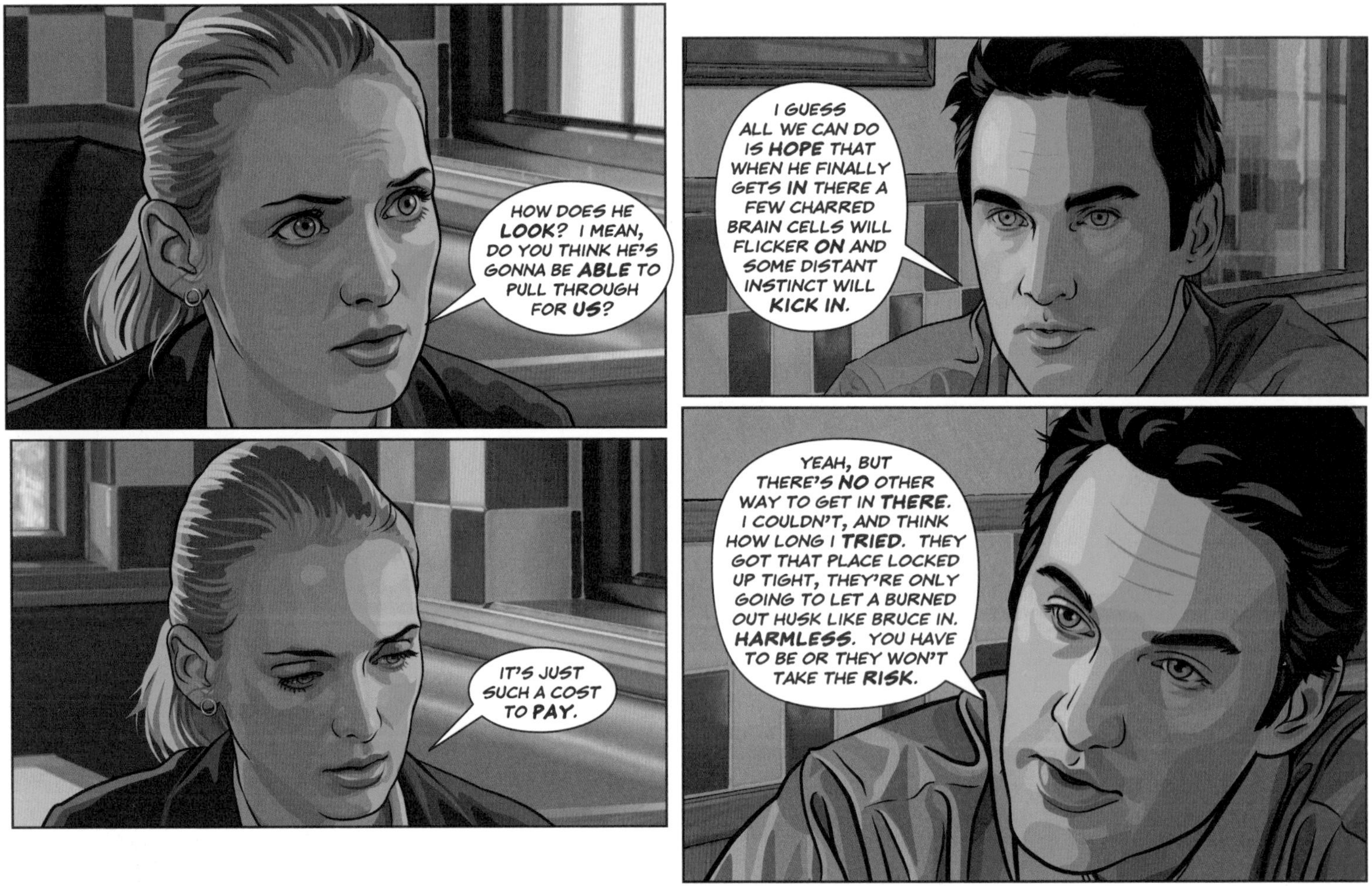
HOW DOES HE LOOK? I MEAN, DO YOU THINK HE'S GONNA BE ABLE TO PULL THROUGH FOR US?
IT'S JUST SUCH A COST TO PAY.
I GUESS ALL WE CAN DO IS HOPE THAT WHEN HE FINALLY GETS IN THERE A FEW CHARRED BRAIN CELLS WILL FLICKER ON AND SOME DISTANT INSTINCT WILL KICK IN.
YEAH, BUT THERE'S NO OTHER WAY TO GET IN THERE. I COULDN'T, AND THINK HOW LONG I TRIED. THEY GOT THAT PLACE LOCKED UP TIGHT, THEY'RE ONLY GOING TO LET A BURNED OUT HUSK LIKE BRUCE IN. HARMLESS. YOU HAVE TO BE OR THEY WON'T TAKE THE RISK.

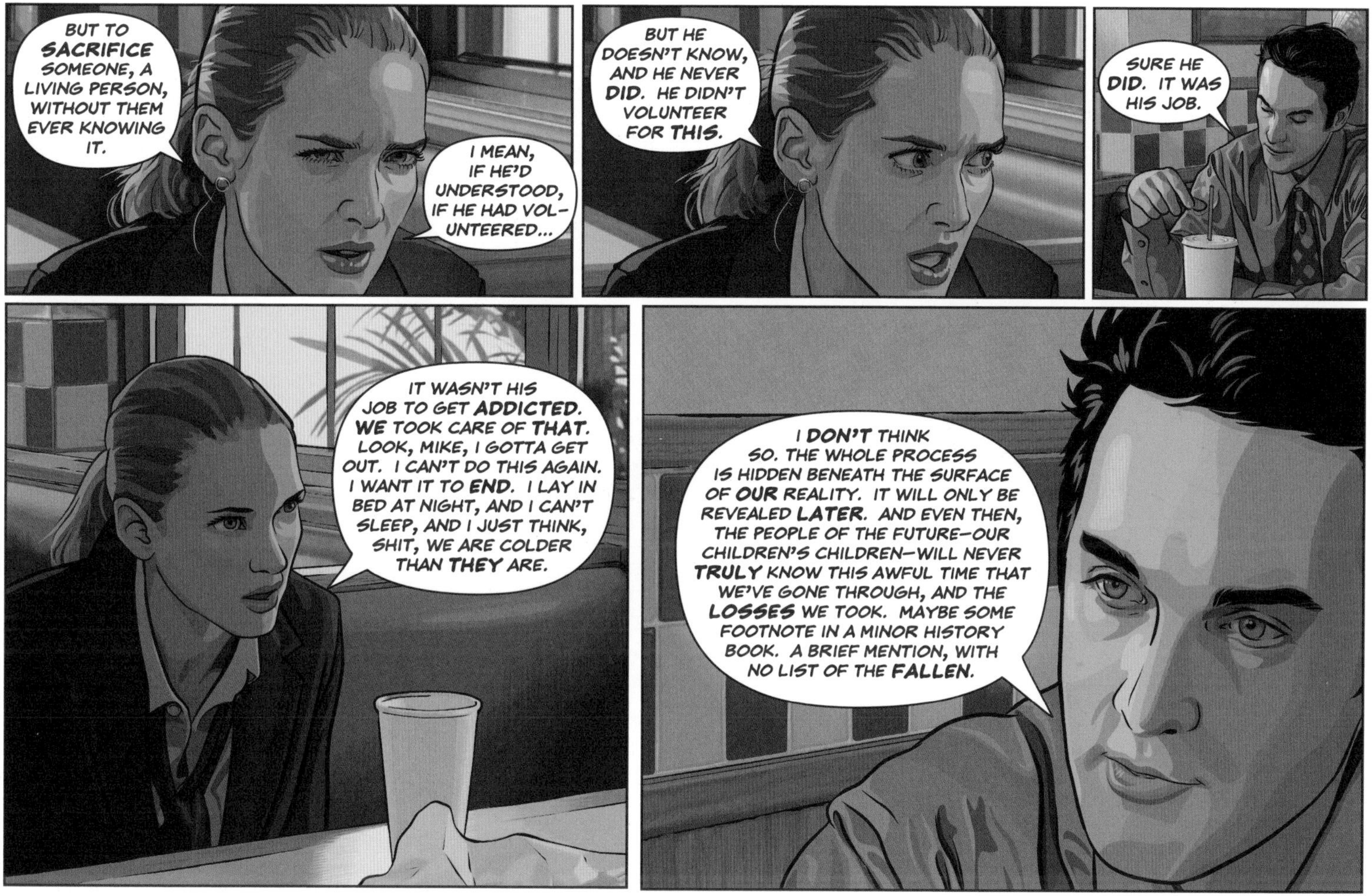
BUT TO SACRIFICE SOMEONE, A LIVING PERSON, WITHOUT THEM EVER KNOWING IT.
I MEAN, IF HE'D UNDERSTOOD, IF HE HAD VOL-UNTEERED...
BUT HE DOESN'T KNOW, AND HE NEVER DID. HE DIDN'T VOLUNTEER FOR THIS.
SURE HE DID. IT WAS HIS JOB.
IT WASN'T HIS JOB TO GET ADDICTED. WE TOOK CARE OF THAT. LOOK, MIKE, I GOTTA GET OUT. I CAN'T DO THIS AGAIN. I WANT IT TO END. I LAY IN BED AT NIGHT, AND I CAN'T SLEEP, AND I JUST THINK, SHIT, WE ARE COLDER THAN THEY ARE.
I DON'T THINK SO. THE WHOLE PROCESS IS HIDDEN BENEATH THE SURFACE OF OUR REALITY. IT WILL ONLY BE REVEALED LATER. AND EVEN THEN, THE PEOPLE OF THE FUTURE—OUR CHILDREN'S CHILDREN—WILL NEVER TRULY KNOW THIS AWFUL TIME THAT WE'VE GONE THROUGH, AND THE LOSSES WE TOOK. MAYBE SOME FOOTNOTE IN A MINOR HISTORY BOOK. A BRIEF MENTION, WITH NO LIST OF THE FALLEN.

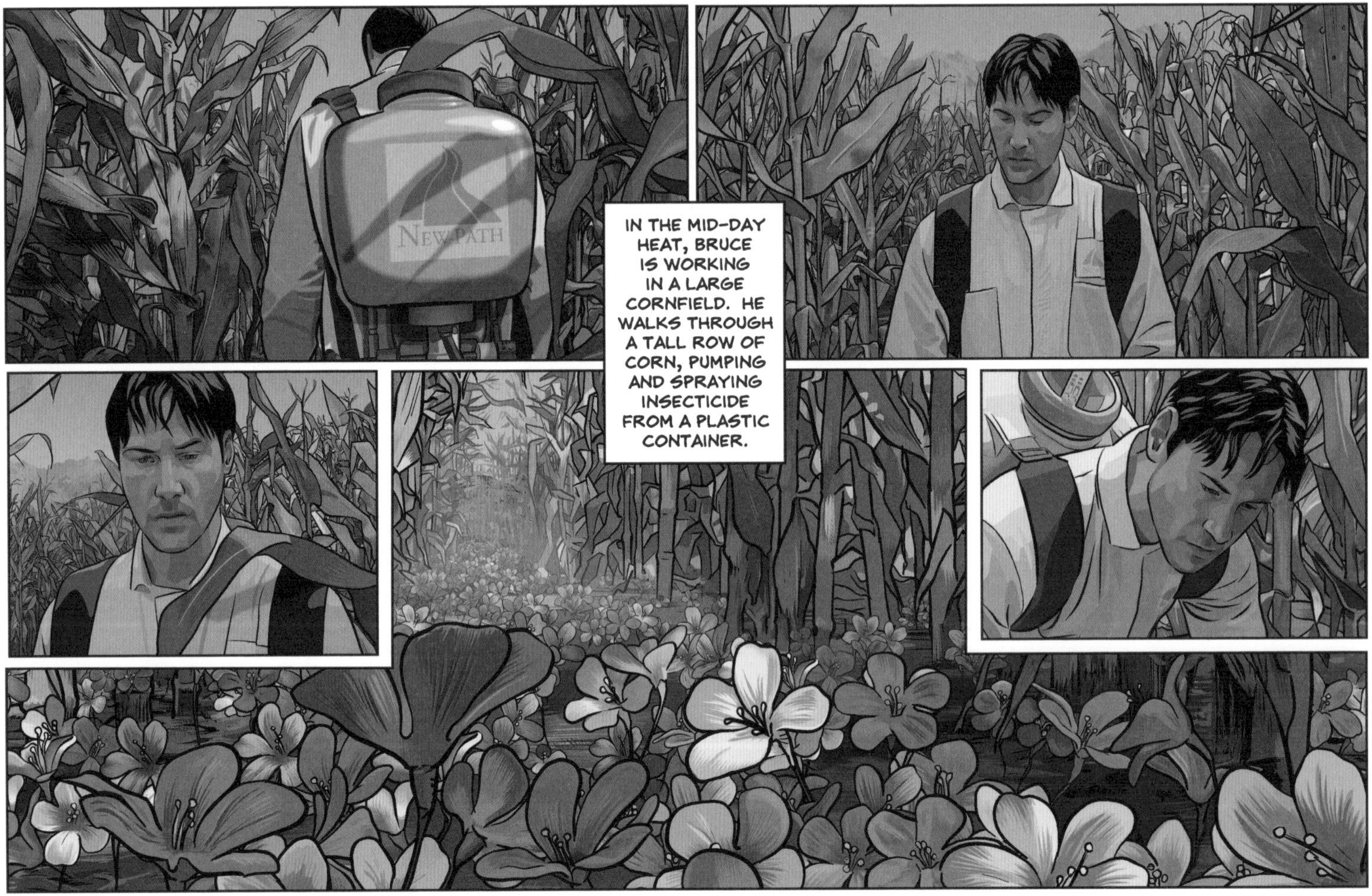
NEW PATH
IN THE MID-DAY HEAT, BRUCE IS WORKING IN A LARGE CORNFIELD. HE WALKS THROUGH A TALL ROW OF CORN, PUMPING AND SPRAYING INSECTICIDE FROM A PLASTIC CONTAINER.

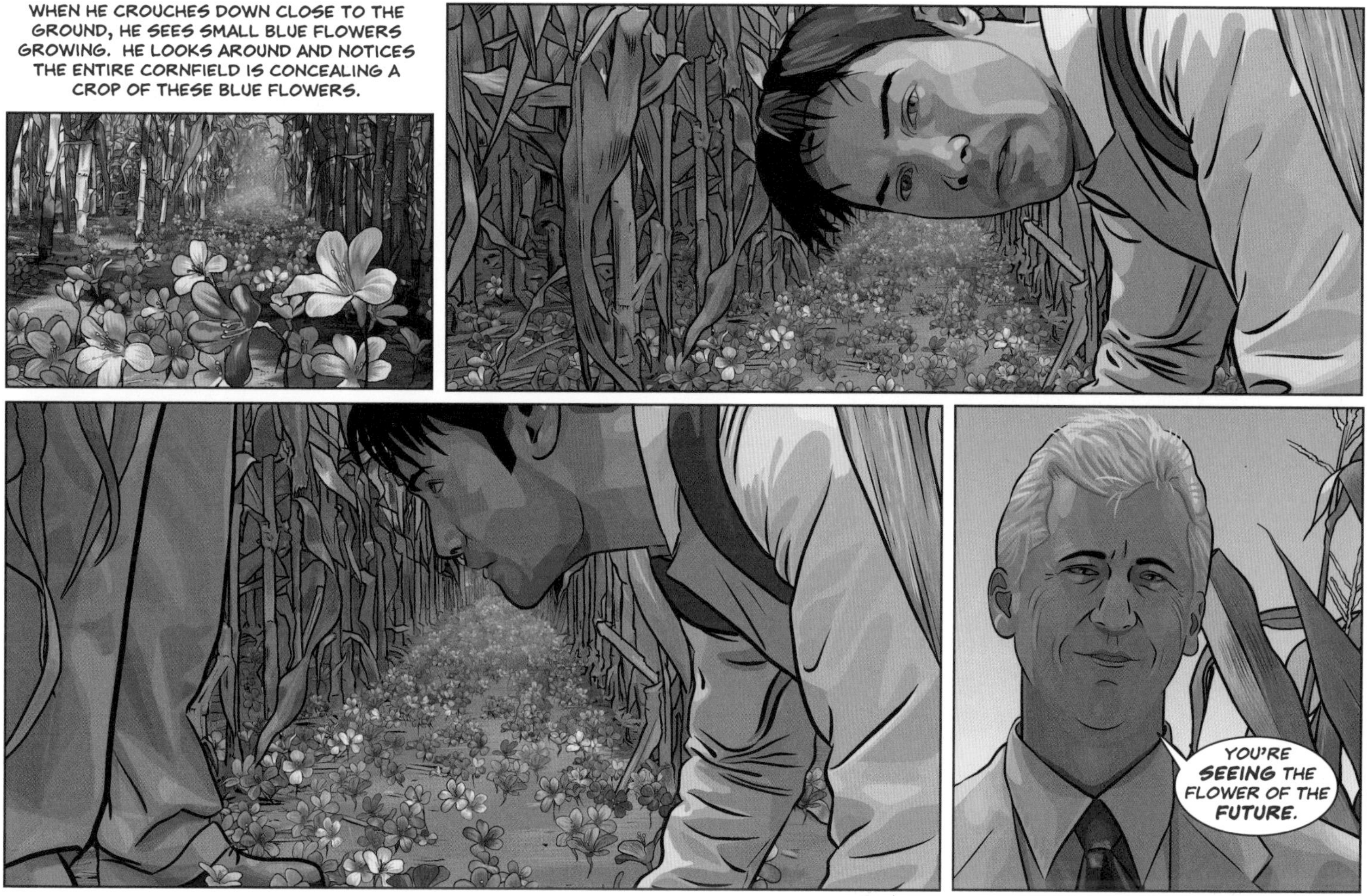
WHEN HE CROUCHES DOWN CLOSE TO THE GROUND, HE SEES SMALL BLUE FLOWERS GROWING. HE LOOKS AROUND AND NOTICES THE ENTIRE CORNFIELD IS CONCEALING A CROP OF THESE BLUE FLOWERS.
YOU'RE SEEING THE FLOWER OF THE FUTURE.

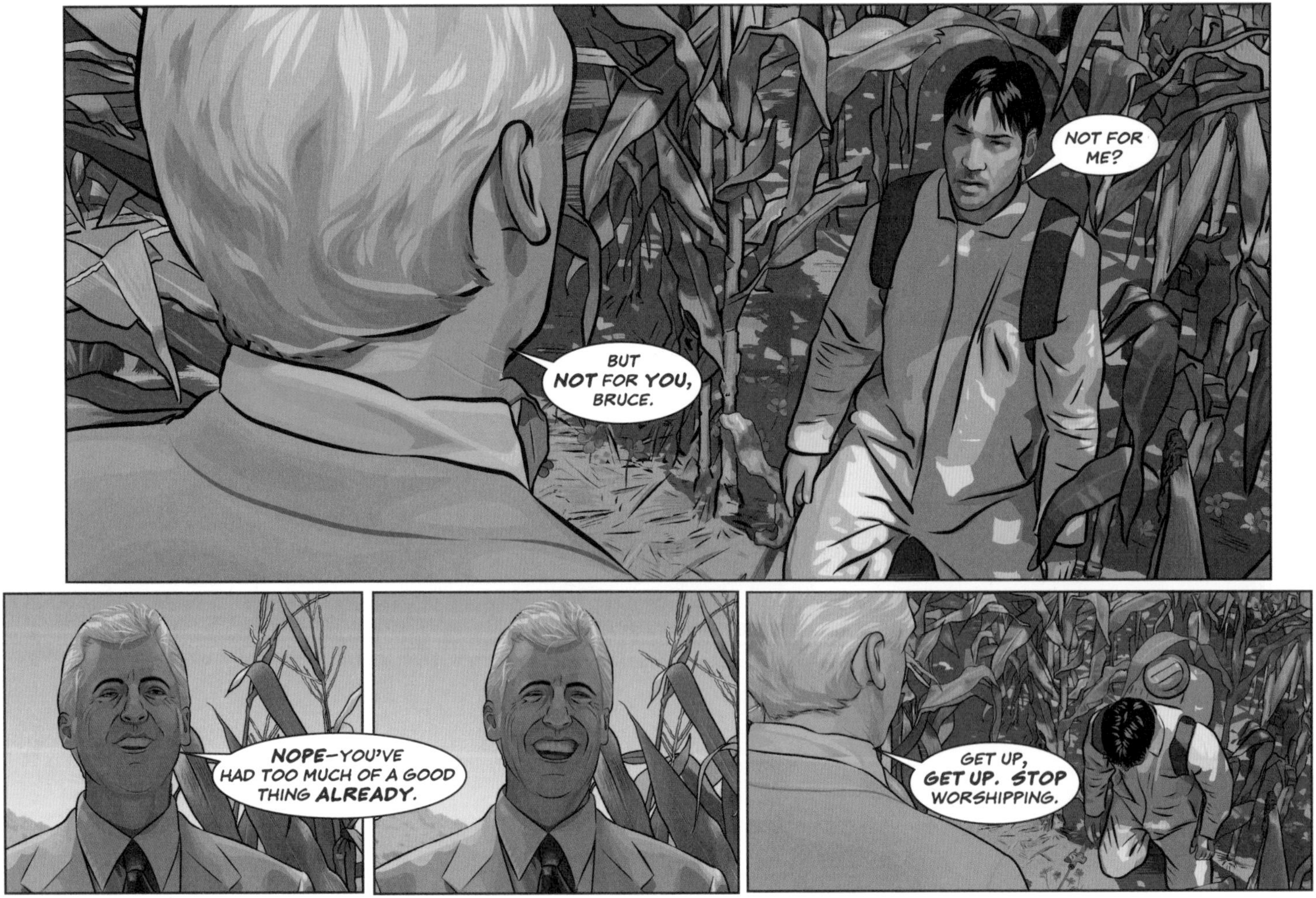
NOT FOR ME?
BUT NOT FOR YOU, BRUCE.
NOPE–YOU'VE HAD TOO MUCH OF A GOOD THING ALREADY.
GET UP, GET UP. STOP WORSHIPPING.

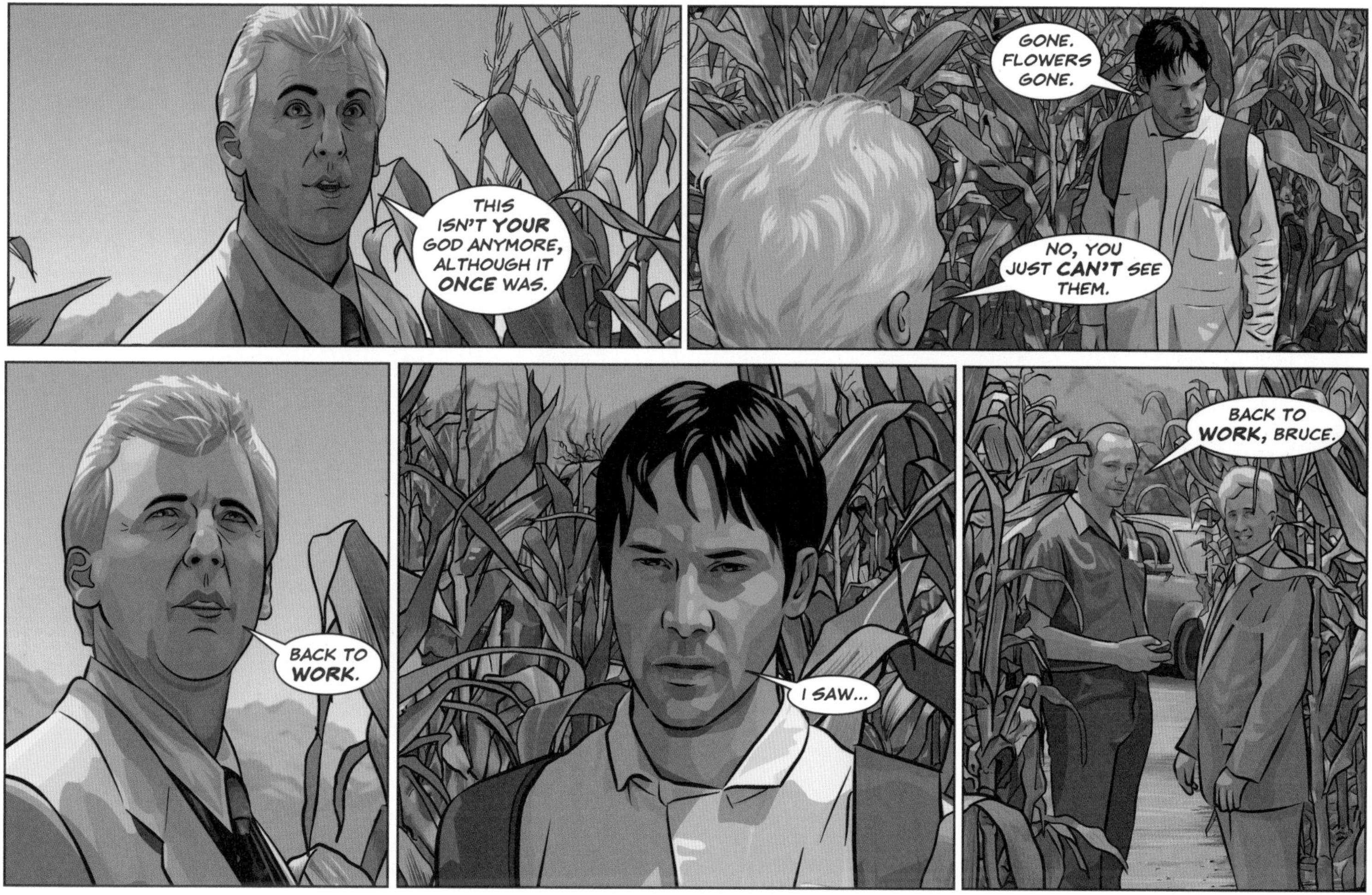
THIS ISN'T YOUR GOD ANYMORE, ALTHOUGH IT ONCE WAS.
GONE. FLOWERS GONE.
NO, YOU JUST CAN'T SEE THEM.
BACK TO WORK.
I SAW...
BACK TO WORK, BRUCE.

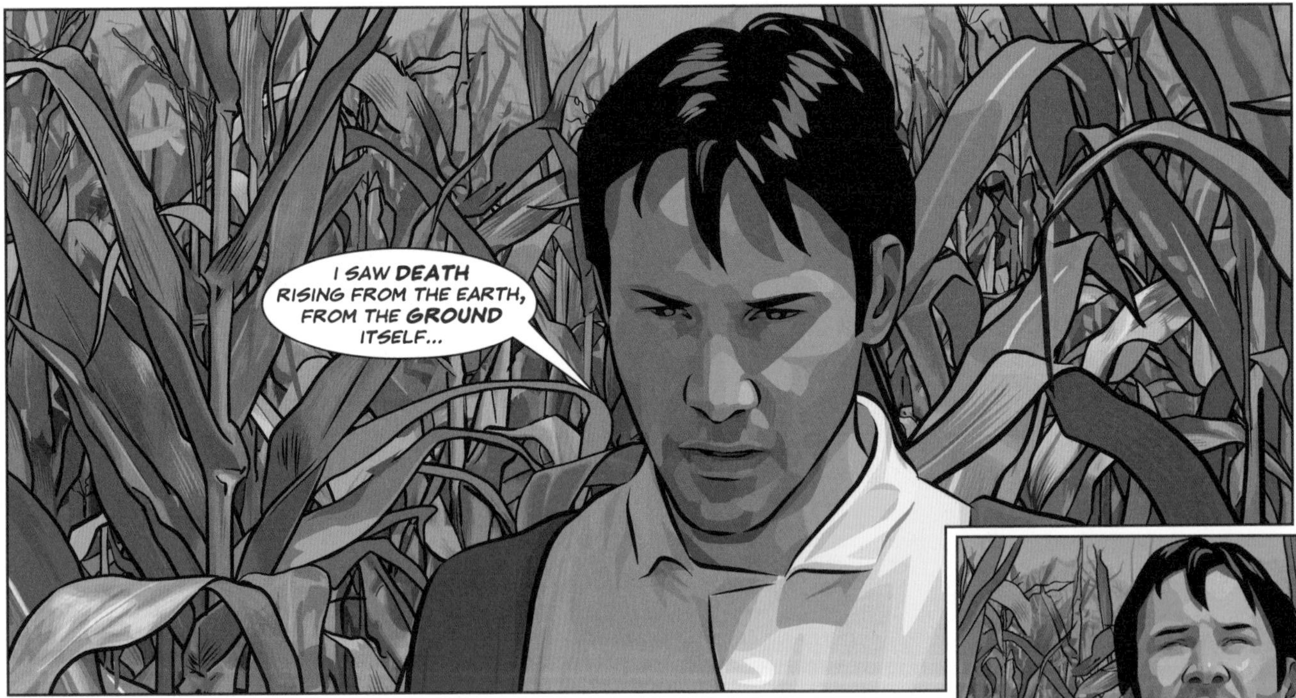
I SAW DEATH RISING FROM THE EARTH, FROM THE GROUND ITSELF...

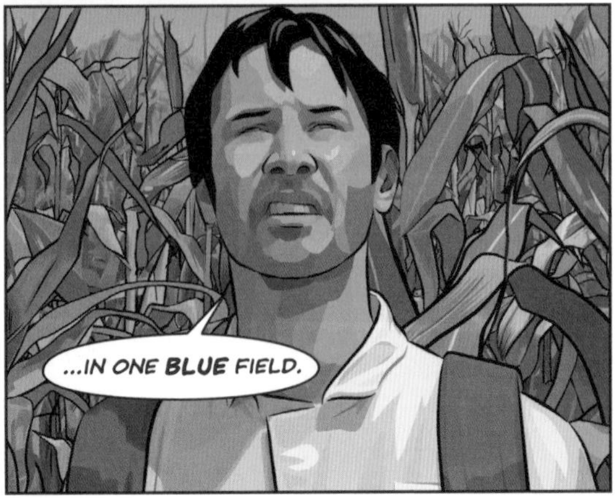
...IN ONE BLUE FIELD.

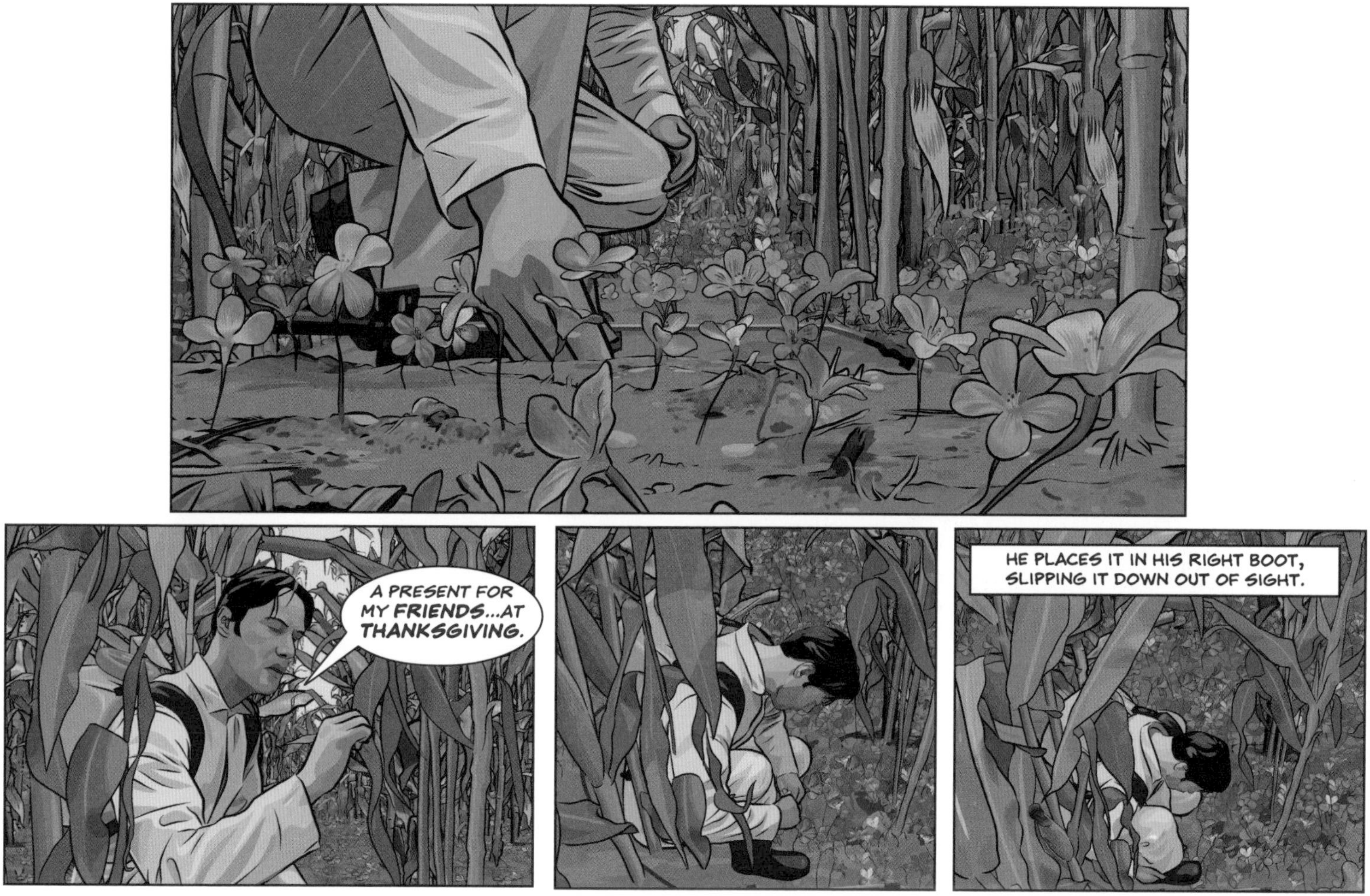
A PRESENT FOR MY FRIENDS...AT THANKSGIVING.
HE PLACES IT IN HIS RIGHT BOOT, SLIPPING IT DOWN OUT OF SIGHT.

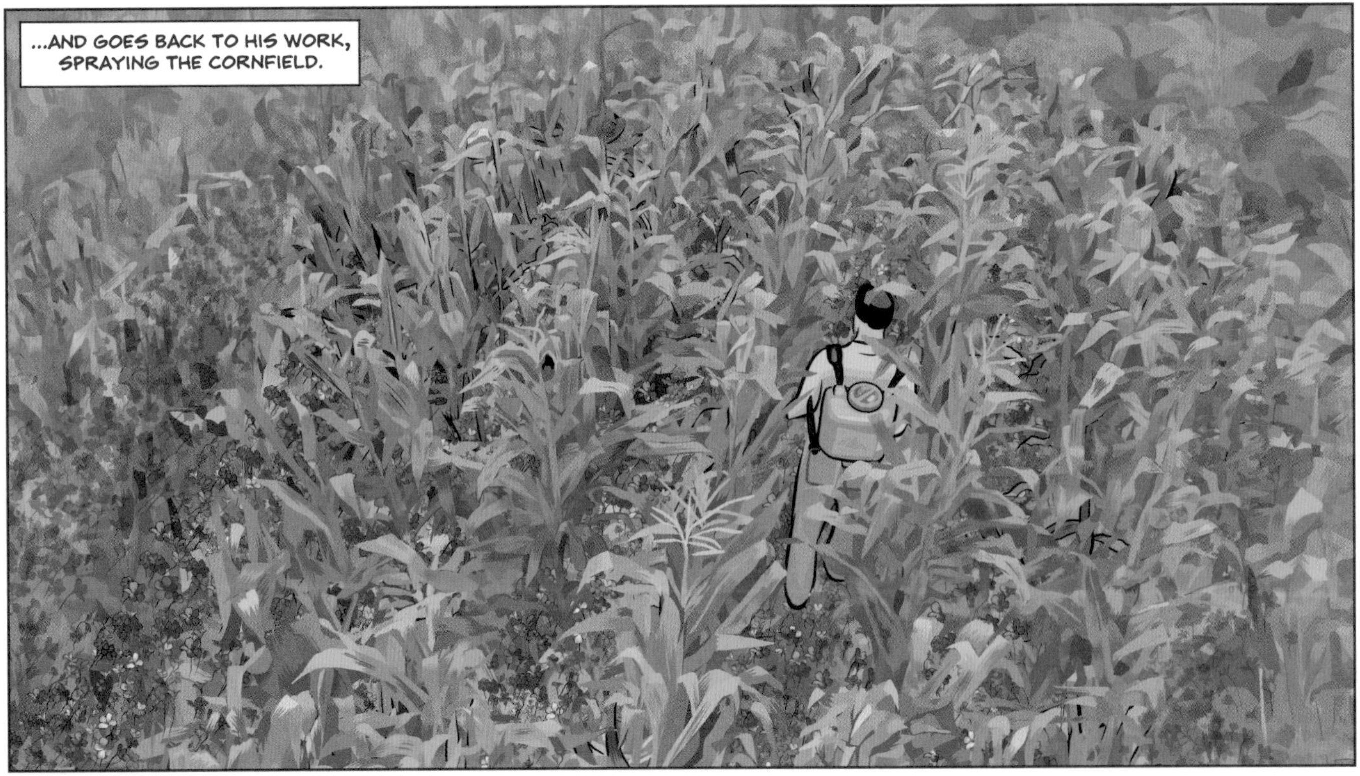
...AND GOES BACK TO HIS WORK, SPRAYING THE CORNFIELD.

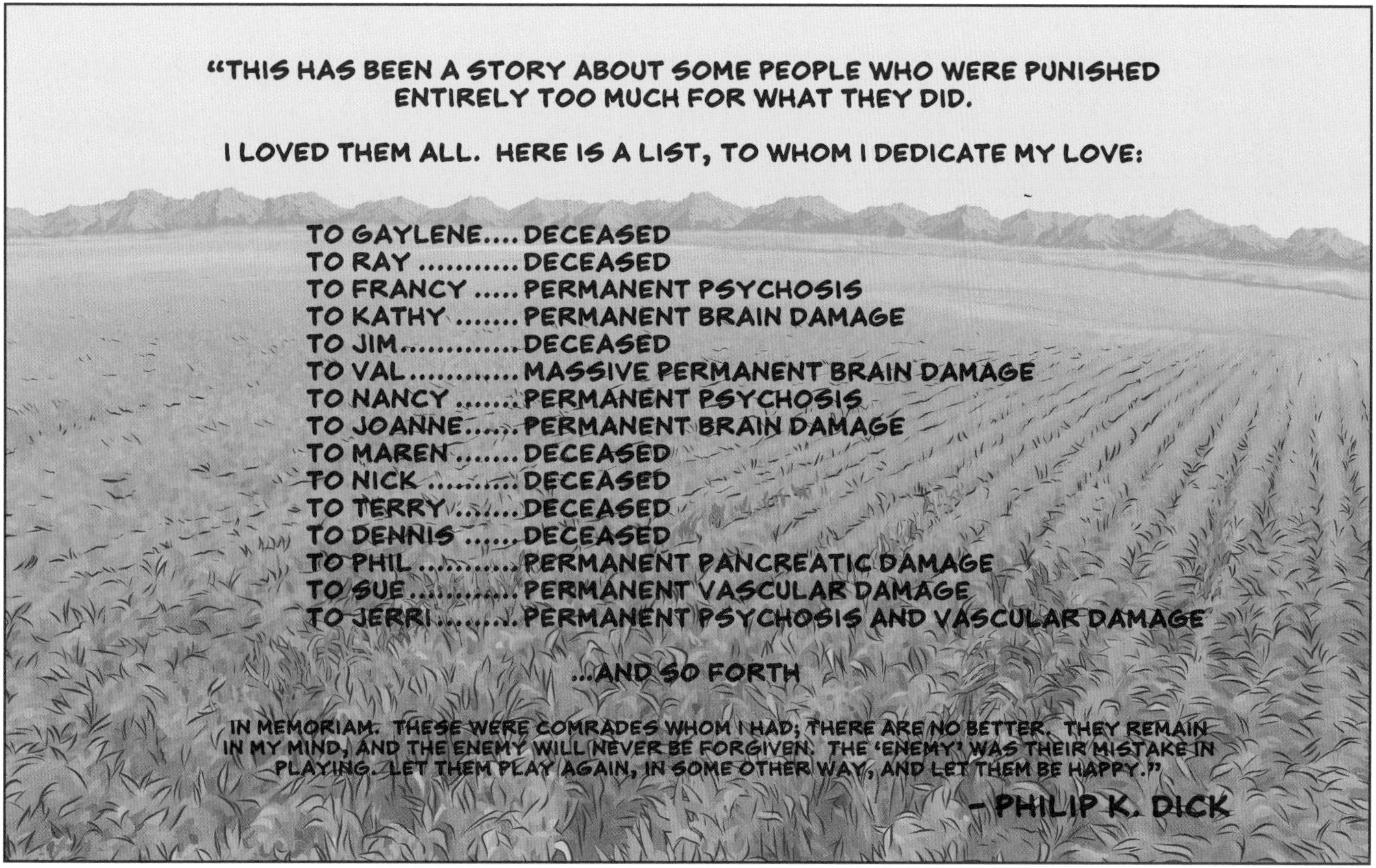
“THIS HAS BEEN A STORY ABOUT SOME PEOPLE WHO WERE PUNISHED ENTIRELY TOO MUCH FOR WHAT THEY DID.
I LOVED THEM ALL. HERE IS A LIST, TO WHOM I DEDICATE MY LOVE:
TO GAYLENE.... DECEASED
TO RAY .... DECEASED
TO FRANCY ..... PERMANENT PSYCHOSIS
TO KATHY .... PERMANENT BRAIN DAMAGE
TO JIM............. DECEASED
TO VAL............ MASSIVE PERMANENT BRAIN DAMAGE
TO NANCY .... PERMANENT PSYCHOSIS
TO JOANNE...... PERMANENT BRAIN DAMAGE
TO MAREN .... DECEASED
TO NICK .... DECEASED
TO TERRY .... DECEASED
TO DENNIS ...... DECEASED
TO PHIL .... PERMANENT PANCREATIC DAMAGE
TO SUE .... PERMANENT VASCULAR DAMAGE
TO JERRI .... PERMANENT PSYCHOSIS AND VASCULAR DAMAGE
...AND SO FORTH
IN MEMORIAM. THESE WERE COMRADES WHOM I HAD; THERE ARE NO BETTER. THEY REMAIN IN MY MIND, AND THE ENEMY WILL NEVER BE FORGIVEN. THE ‘ENEMY’ WAS THEIR MISTAKE IN PLAYING. LET THEM PLAY AGAIN, IN SOME OTHER WAY, AND LET THEM BE HAPPY.”
– PHILIP K. DICK